praise

10675443

"*String Bridge* is a rich exploration of desire, guilt, and the difficult balancing act of the modern woman. The writing is lyrical throughout, seamlessly integrating setting, character and plot in a musical structure that allows the reader to identify with Melody's growing insecurity as her world begins to unravel ... a powerful debut from a promising writer, full of music, metaphor, and just a hint of magic."
MAGDALENA BALL, AUTHOR OF *BLACK COW* AND *SLEEP BEFORE EVENING*

"This is one of those books that's so familiar, and filled with so much emotion, you'll be crawling for the door."
LEIGH TALBERT MOORE, AUTHOR OF *THE TRUTH ABOUT FAKING AND ROUGE*

"Jessica Bell wraps her story around you like a thick, fragrant Greek breeze you don't want to leave. From her vibrant descriptions to the plot twists that could make anyone gulp back tears, I fell in love with this book. Not only did this poignant story strike rich, beautiful chords within me, it made me look at myself and my own relationships in a way I won't forget easily."
MICHELLE DAVIDSON ARGYLE, AUTHOR OF *THE BREAKAWAY*

"It doesn't take much to make me reach for the tissue box, but you'd have to be heartless to not tear up while reading this book. It plays at your heartstrings, then it rips at them, then it tears them to pieces. You can't read this book and not be moved."
KAREN HOOPER, AUTHOR OF *TANGLED TIDES*

"Warning: Do not read *String Bridge*—unless you have plenty of spare time. Jessica Bell hooks the reader with a storyline so powerful it consumes you. A fantastic debut novel and I look forward to reading more from this author."
GLYNIS SMY, AUTHOR OF *RIPPER, MY LOVE* AND *MAGGIE'S CHILD*

"A rhythmic debut with metrical tones of heavied dark, fleeting prisms of light, and finally, a burst of joy—just as with any good song, my hopeful heartbeat kept tempo with Bell's narrative."
KATHRYN MAGENDIE, AUTHOR OF *SWEETIE, TENDER GRACES* AND *SECRET GRACES*

about the author

Jessica Bell is an Australian award-winning author and poet, writing and publishing coach, and graphic designer who lives in Athens, Greece. In addition to her novels and poetry collections, and her best-selling *Writing in a Nutshell* series, she has published a variety of works online and in literary journals, including *Writer's Digest*.

Jessica is also the Co-Founder and Publisher of *Vine Leaves Press & Literary Journal*, a singer/songwriter/guitarist, a voice-over actor, and a freelance editor and writer for English Language Teaching publishers worldwide such as Macmillan Education and Education First.

Before she started writing she was just a young woman with a "useless" Bachelor of Arts degree and a waitressing job.

Visit Jessica's website: *jessicabellauthor.com*

String Bridge
Copyright © 2016 Jessica Bell
All rights reserved.

Vine Leaves Press
Melbourne, Victoria, Australia

Third Edition
ISBN-13: 978-1-925417-44-9

First edition published by Lucky Press USA, 2011
Second edition published by Vine Leaves Press Canada, 2012

This is a work of fiction. Any similarity between the characters and situations within its pages and places or persons, living or dead, is unintentional and co-incidental.

Cover design by Jessica Bell
Interior design by Amie McCracken

National Library of Australia Cataloguing-in-Publication entry (pbk)
Creator: Bell, Jessica Carmen, author.
Title: String bridge / Jessica Bell.
Edition: 3rd edition
ISBN: 9781925417449 (paperback)
Subjects: Domestic relations--Greece--Fiction.
Husband and wife--Greece--Fiction.
Married women--Greece--Fiction.
Dewey Number: A823.4

string bridge

jessica bell

Vine Leaves Press
Melbourne, Vic, Australia

For Spilios

To receive the all-original soundtrack *Melody Hill: On the Other Side*, go to *jessicabellauthor.com/contact* and send Jessica your book purchase receipt.

The soundtrack is also available to purchase at iTunes and other online music retailers.

part one

If You Were Me

At times I wish I'd speak my mind
My thoughts are vile and you are blind
But what if I could house these thoughts
With wood and glue a hut of sorts

Chorus:
I'd lock them in
You wouldn't see
The things you'd say
If you were me
If you were me
If you were me

You'd never feel the sting of shame
Corrupted hope a need to blame
So let me hide away from light
Away from grace and out of sight

Chorus
I am not worth the effort, dear
Just solitude; no hate, no fear
This plastic smile is all I can give
Until the beat puts my heart back in

Chorus:
Don't lock me in
I need to feel
I need to sing again
Let me be me
Let me be me
Let me be me

preface

If music were wind, I would live in a hurricane. If it were a mother, I would sleep in her soothing womb. If I were music, I would simply be me, shrouding my existence in a monsoon. But I am not music, even though my name, Melody, suggests I could be. The closest I get to "being" music, is playing it, living it, embracing it as if it were the organ most vital to survival. I might say it was my heart. But no … I can't give it a name, because it's more like a sixth sense.

Music is the shadow of thought.

A muse for grief.

An unending moan.

A manic pandemonium that roams through rhyme and mimics my soul through mime. It masquerades selfish woes, masks my hollow lifestyle like warm, humming cellos. It's a blend of folly and secretive gen, acoustic vignettes—motionless, yet moving.

Music is not meek; it's neurotic, like me. An eternal vessel for pain that must be voiced and heard, but can't reach its desired destination because it is trapped in the skin of a four-minute tune. Because of this time limit, I reject the constant sorrow I feel for abandoning my guitar in a corner of my bedroom. If only a song could last my lifetime, then I wouldn't have to listen to that slice of silence, of domesticity, that makes me forget how much music means to me.

Now I'm a career woman—a mother, a wife, a "happy" homemaker—who lives a socially acceptable existence. Like a metronome. Tick. Tick. Tick. No dynamics, just monotonous responsibility. But between the octaves I play over and over in my mind every day, and the struggle to push my need to play guitar out of mind and get on with the life I chose to pursue, is the scent of reviving this need for music in my life; of understanding where this true love for music stems from and embracing the path I desire to follow. It's time to dust off my lonely guitar and press my fingertips into its strings so hard that they mould around them. It's time to live as *if I were music,* and if *music were wind.* It's time to live in a hurricane.

ONe

I gaze at myself in the full-length mirror that doesn't fit my head in. I suppose it's better that way, though, because I'm unable to see the ugly faces I make in reaction to my morning splendour. I focus on the haze of dust brought to life behind me in a beam of sunlight—my body becoming a blurry foreground image. Dust. One of the endless woes of living in Athens, Greece, and the root of my guitar's death.

"Alex?" I call for my husband, still gazing at myself, inspecting the wrinkles between my breasts that take forever to disappear now that age has left its mark on me. The hissing sound of gas seeps through the gap below the bedroom door. It means he's making his morning Greek coffee—a ritual that has become as important to him as being a good parent to our four-year-old daughter, Tessa.

"What, Mel?"

Alex's watered-down Greek accent is stifled by the filthy rugs we have yet to remove from the corridor for the approaching summer. His voice is smooth, deep, and gentle. Unlike mine, which will forever be polluted with a brutal Australian twang. Alex's voice was the first thing I was drawn to when we met five years ago at my debut solo performance in this city. It was just me, my voice and my guitar, battling the fear of laying my soul out for scrutiny, below the hot stage lights and in front of the quiet, unresponsive Greek crowd.

"Can you come and help me do up all these buttons on my dress?" I call, looking up at the ceiling, the crumbling paint, and the damp stains, wondering if I should bother trying to get it repaired or whether the old lady upstairs will forget she left the bath tap running again.

"I can't, I'm making coffee. I'll fuck it if I leave. You come in here."

There's that dreaded 'f' word again. Something that took me a long while to disregard. Alex, new to the English version, now uses it for every possible part of speech as if a nerd with a new gadget. I soon realized that swearing in a foreign language is like playing a game. The impact of the word is no greater than saying *flower*, or something to that effect. But when he swears in Greek, I hold my breath, waiting for the swing of his fist to finally cease toying with the idea of hitting me. Alex has *never* hit me. But I know he wants to sometimes. And I'm afraid that one day he will. I can see it in his face when it goes blank and pale. It means he's holding back rage. I've spent my whole life trying to escape this kind of rage. Will I ever?

I hobble down the corridor feeling the scratchy carpet fibres stick through my stocking. For some reason I forgot to put on my other shoe in my eagerness for Alex to help do up my dress. I'm in a hurry. Don't know why; I have plenty of time. Perhaps it's become a habit since my transition from musician to career-oriented, manic mother.

"Oh. Nice. You don't normally dress like this for work. What's going on?"

His soft fingers brush against my breast as he slowly buttons my dress with a smirk on his face. Is he silently mocking my enthusiasm to dress up? He hasn't even heard the reason why. The routine is, I wear the same black tailored pants (I own five pairs), and a drab gender-neutral mono-coloured shirt. But today is the start of a new beginning. One I should be proud of, unafraid to tell Alex about. But I am afraid. And in all honesty, I'm more anxious about succeeding than of my husband getting upset when he finds I've kept a secret for the past year. Hence the outfit. If I succeed today, will music remain a thing of the past?

I breathe in the sandalwood scent of Alex's shirt collar and absentmindedly watch his coffee as it overflows and smothers the flame.

"Oh shit!" Alex reaches for the paper towel and tears off more than is necessary. "Why didn't you say anything?"

"Sorry. I didn't realize till it was too late," I reply, not moving a single muscle to help him clean up the mess.

"You were staring right at it."

"Was I?" I ask, through gritted teeth.

Alex frowns, huffs, leans his weight on one foot and shakes his head. I look at the floor, wide-eyed, and bite my thumbnail. Why can't he simply clean up the mess and not make an issue out of every little thing that goes on in this household? It's coffee. Not a burst sewage pipe. Besides, it was his responsibility. He should have been watching it. I'm so tired of being the brunt of domestic mishaps no matter how large or small. Since when should a woman be responsible for her husband's incompetence?

My instinct is to argue, to tell my husband to stop blaming me for everything. Even though I'm not certain he is blaming me for anything at all. I feel rage too. All the time. The difference between my rage and Alex's rage is that I don't act on it. I bottle it up because it's not worth getting angry over ridiculous things like overflowing coffee. So, I take a deep breath. I remain calm. I keep the peace, just like I learnt to do when I was a child.

"I must still be sleeping," I continue, physically shaking off the unwanted wrath exploding within. "It doesn't matter. I'll make you another one. What time is it?" I take the coffee-covered paper towel from his hand and throw it in the bin. His hand rests on my lower back. He leans against the kitchen bench looking me up and down as if it's the first time he's seen me. He's putting on an act now—trying to be the good guy.

"Seven thirty. Have I ever told you how much I love you?" he asks, pulling me toward him.

He kisses my top lip with his mouth slightly open. I feel nothing. I don't even know if I love him anymore. I nuzzle my head into his neck, trying to convince myself that I do, that I haven't given up the last five years of my life for nothing, that I stopped playing gigs because Alex means more to me than music ever will. But I've carried around a larger resentment since giving birth to Tessa. Alex organizes music events for a living, so why did he insist I stop playing? And why did I *accept* that wish? Why didn't

I fight for my dreams? I never wanted to become a Greek housewife. And I married Alex because I thought he was different, and I would never have to. Clearly he isn't the man I thought he was.

If Alex were wind, would I like to live in a hurricane? No, I would not. If Alex were wind, I'd be forever trying to escape his debris.

"I need you to edit an email before you leave," he says as I pull away from him and begin fixing him another coffee. Has he totally forgotten about discovering why I'm wearing this dress? He's always been a bit self-centred, but I thought that would gradually disappear after the birth of our daughter. I was wrong. Men never change. They cling to habit like sap to a tree trunk.

"Your English is fine," I say, giving him a reassuring sideways glance as I put water into the biriki to make more coffee.

"Doesn't feel like it. Keep making the same mistakes. What was it you said? Prepositions?"

"Seriously, Alex. It's no big deal," I insist, burying a twinge of irritation with a fake smile.

"It must be the emails. British agents."

"Yeah. Must." A little voice in my head keeps prodding me to ask for a gig. Before I had Tessa, he used to offer me a thirty-minute slot on the stage to play whatever I wanted. Our daughter is growing up now. She doesn't need nursing twenty-four hours a day. And we can hire a babysitter if Alex wants to come and watch. I can juggle a full-time job and play music too. I *can*.

I touch Alex on his shoulder while he pours himself a bowl of Special K. I want to ask him to get me a gig so much that my neck constricts as if I've eaten a lemon. But I get distracted by flakes falling on the floor. He doesn't bother to pick them up, and hides them with his bare foot. They crunch. Like dry autumn leaves on a lawn. He looks at me as if he got away with something. The urge to call him out on it plagues my tongue like moss. *Don't worry about it. Leave it alone.*

"I love you, *vlaka*," I squeeze the back of his neck even though I know he hates it. Vlaka means 'stupid little person,' but this time, as I say it, I think, *What the hell happened to us?* Alex turns and kisses me gently on the forehead after rolling his eyes at my neck squeeze and sniffs my skin like one would a glass of vintage red wine. He's trying to be tender. Perhaps he's trying to save our marriage. Does he feel like I do? Is he scared to admit that it's really over?

"Where's Tessa?" I ask.

"In her room, I think."

"Before you go to your desk, can you get her dressed for preschool while I make your coffee?"

"Um, I ... all right. Clothes?"

"They're on the dresser. You'll see 'em." I almost lose balance on my one shoe. Ironic, really, as my literal lopsidedness mirrors my psychological state. A poignant reminder that all this emotional turmoil isn't just in my head. Life itself is offering me signs. I should listen to them, instead of flicking them away like a fly interrupting my concentration.

Alex runs down the corridor knocking on all the walls,

whisper-calling, "I'm coming for butterfly kisses! You better have them ready …"

I can hear Tessa giggling as a big bed-plonk reverberates through the apartment. He must have lifted her out of her sea of toys on the rug and thrown her up in the air. He doesn't do it very often. Only when he thinks our relationship is back on track. I should scold myself for making him believe so. Last night, when we finished arguing about the fact that we don't communicate properly anymore, I backtracked by insisting I was over-reacting and that everything was going to be all right. But it's *not* going to be all right because I couldn't muster the courage to be honest with the one person on earth who deserves the truth. Surely, if I had faith in this marriage, I would be able to tell him how I feel?

When Alex returns, he has a dressed Tessa on his shoulders. Her head misses the kitchen door frame by a centimetre as he walks in. Our daughter smiles at me with her incandescent green eyes, giggling as Alex sings and bounces her up and down to the tune of "Sugar Pie Honey Bunch." Her brown curls bob like rubber springs. She holds onto Alex's shaved head so tight that she almost pokes out one of his eyes. I take Alex's coffee off the heat and pour it into his cup. I look up at Tessa, squinting my eyes and pursing my lips for a good-morning kiss. Alex bends his knees so that Tessa and I are eye-level and she plants a big sloppy one on my cheek.

"Morning, Mummy," she says, still bobbing her head to the tune of the song.

"Morning, Blossom," I reply, stroking her silky pink cheek with the back of my hand.

"So what's the dress for?" Alex asks, taking Tessa by the waist and putting her on her feet.

"Er, yeah, let me put my other shoe on and I'll explain."

As I limp back down the corridor to get my shoe, I wonder how I can possibly bring up the idea of relocating to London in a way that makes it sound appealing. It wouldn't be a bad step to take, would it? There is greater opportunity in England than there is here in Greece for musicians. Perhaps I should use this promotion as a means of fulfilling my dreams. Think of it as a stepping stone, instead of an obstacle.

"We going, Mummy?" Tessa is standing in the doorway with her school bag that's covered in cartoon kittens.

"Soon, Blossom," I say, straightening my dress with splayed sweaty fingers, summoning the nerve to tell Alex what I'm up to once and for all. "Go and play with Doggy on the balcony and I'll come and get you."

The bells on the back of Tessa's sneakers jingle as she runs out to play with our black cocker spaniel. Her purple skirt is stuck inside her pink frilly knickers. Fury bubbles in my ears at Alex's oblivion to his daughter's appearance. I bring Alex his coffee, because he neglected to take it himself, and kiss him on the cheek with a 1950s-happy-couple phoniness you see in the movies, or in relationships like ours.

"Thanks," he says, staring at the computer screen, gripping his mouse like it might soon develop a mind of its own. I can't remember the last time he said "thank you" and looked me in the eye. How hard is it to look someone you're supposed to love in the eye? What I want to say in return is, "Are your arms broken? You couldn't take it to your office yourself?" But I don't.

I close my eyes for a moment, facing the window, pretending to look out at the overcast sky—at the clouds that make living in a high-rise building seem like living low in a valley, in the mountains, in the mist, in a place where self-doubt and fear have been erased from the dictionary, and self-belief and hope are not only feelings, but material objects that you can hold in your hands and confidently say you possess.

I am my own person. I have the right to make my own decisions. I do not need my husband's permission. What century am I living in? And I know I have always, and will always have Tessa's interests at heart. Following my dreams is not going to jeopardize bringing up my daughter. If anything, it is going to make her respect me and look up to me for doing something I believe in.

"Alex," I snap, shocked at the tone of my voice. I had not intended it to sound so aggressive. I clear my throat in my fist. Alex looks up as if I'm interrupting him. *Ignore* it. "I'm wearing this dress because I've got a very important presentation today—a presentation about a new English course. You know how I came up with the concept myself and have been working on it for the last year to produce the books? Well, the books have finally been printed and the first sample copies came in last week. So now I have to present the course and my bright ideas about how beneficial it will be for kids nowadays—which now I'm not quite sure of; they're not as bright as I thought—to the Greek Board of Education to try to get the course accepted into next year's curriculum. If it gets accepted into next year's curriculum, I'll know by next week and I'll have made the company a whole lot of money that I'll never see. But I could see some of it, possibly, because if it does get accepted into next year's curriculum, they'll want to make me chief editor of a collaborating publishing house—"

"Mel, that's fucking fantastic!" Alex interrupts. He gets out of his seat and approaches me with open arms, but I take his hands and push them to his sides. He frowns, shakes his head in question.

"Alex, the publishing house is in London. We would have to relocate."

I massage my left brow as if nursing a headache. Alex looks at me blankly. We stare at each other—his breath and my breath clash. His anger thickens the air around me like starch in water. His fists clench, but he keeps them by his side.

"London? Mel, I've just turned down a job in New York for you." Alex crosses his arms, making himself taller by straightening his back and broadening his shoulders. He hovers above me. *I will not let him intimidate me anymore. I will take no notice of this manipulation.*

"Last night, you said you were happy here," Alex continues. "My God, Mel. And you've known about this possibility for a year? And you're just telling me now?"

"Well, I could have told you back then—"

"Yes. Why didn't you?" he asks, his voice tight. "We're responsible adults. We can both decide what's best for our family, don't you think? And since when are you so gung-ho about your job? I thought you didn't like it."

"I don't. I'm not finished with what I want to say."

Alex squints. "Go on." He leans against the wall and flicks his chin up as if giving me permission to speak.

"I'm tired of this routine, Alex. I want to play gigs again. I want music back in it. No, you know what? I don't *just* want music back in my life. I want it to *be* my life. I want my dream; the dream you somehow convinced me I didn't need any more. So, if I get this promotion, and if you want to save our marriage, then we *will* relocate to London, where I will have the opportunity to follow my dream."

"No, Melody. We won't. *You* won't follow *any* dream. Forget it—we're not going anywhere." Alex sits back behind his desk.

"Excuse me?" I screech.

"You heard me. Just hope that your presentation *doesn't* go well, so that you don't have to regret turning the promotion down." Alex takes hold of his mouse again, clicks a couple of times, and pretends to read something.

"Alex. I ..."

I want to tell him that I'll just go without him. That I'll take Tessa and flee without even discussing it, but I lose my nerve. Am I being irrational? Selfish? Is it so bad to want something for yourself? Is it selfish not to accept living a life you didn't wish for?

"What?" Alex snaps. "Alex, *what*?" He glares at me. I

shake my head. "Go, to your stupid presentation. I have work to do."

Tears fill my eyes. My bottom lip shudders a little in the hope that what I want to express might find the words to do so. But I don't utter a word. I close my mouth, press my lips together and swallow my devastation. I have an important presentation to give. I must pull myself together. Tonight. I will continue this conversation tonight.

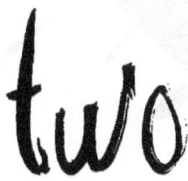

two

The sharp shrill of car horns and Tessa's wails prick my head from every direction like acupuncture needles, doing nothing to help lessen my grip on the steering wheel while I inch along in slow, gruelling traffic. It's so hot and congested that I feel as if I'm sitting in a box of melting forgotten chocolates. All we need now is an amateur string quartet to add some punch and a wince to this hyper-city soundtrack.

"It's stuck!" Tessa cries, dragging out the words in a teary and unnerved whimper. Her chewing gum is embedded high up her left nostril. She leans herself forward and her head back so that I can see via the rear-view mirror.

"Oh Tessa," I whine, furrowing my brow, trying to comprehend whether the jolt I just felt is from Tessa's legs flailing about, or from a car hitting my rear bumper bar. I wouldn't be surprised if it were the latter. My eyebrows remain together so long that the skin-crease tattoos itself between them. Another corporeal proof of exhaustion to add to my list.

I never asked for this career-driven life—to become another rodent in this stinking patriarchal and hypocritical nation, hanging from faulty strings of bureaucratic security. But this country is blessed with a persuasive charm that I still, to this day, cannot put my finger on. What drew me here? Was it really just my father's Greek roots? Was the need to keep returning to a land that oozes with unidentifiable mystique a habit merely instilled by ritual family visits? Or did the alluring Sirens' song succeed in tempting me here, in view of smashing me against their jagged cliffs? They didn't succeed with Odysseus. Perhaps I'm their next prey, knowing very well that song would undoubtedly cause me to stray from my anticipated path.

I bite my tongue, swallowing the urge to yell at Tessa's stupidity. But I will not get angry. *Yes, you're flustered and late. But you can't undo what is done. Just calm her down. Calm* yourself *down.* I take a deep breath and watch Tessa through the mirror, squinting with concern. She keeps trying to get the gum out, but seems to be pushing it up even farther in her eager effort to hook it with her pinky finger.

"Honey!" I snap, then immediately lower my volume at the shock of my frenzied voice. "Stop it. You're going to make it worse. When we stop the car, I'll help you get it out, okay? I can use my tweezers."

She sniffs outward, as if trying to dislodge it, and nods. A bubble escapes from her gum-free nostril. How could I possibly scold her? She's a child. Every child sticks things in holes, and are bound to make silly, experimental mistakes. I certainly did. Such as when I scratched my dad's gold Gibson electric guitar with my mother's box cutter. I was only four, sitting in the corner of a rehearsal studio, listening to my parents bash out their gothic guitar riffs, vocals, and synthesiser samples, in passionate determination, oblivious to the world around them. I decided to make memory cards out of a brown box I found abandoned in the corner, and I needed a table. So I found the next best thing—the back of Dad's guitar. Boy, did I pay for that. Not from Dad, from Mum. For blunting her knife. She whacked me on my backside several times with a rolled-up amplifier cable in front of all the rehearsal studio staff. Of course, she regretted it once her bipolar-induced rage died down and we got home. The rest of the night I was pampered with pizza, chocolate and ice cream, accompanied with her mascara-tinted tears and desperate pleas for forgiveness.

"What on earth inspired you to shove it up your nose, Tessa?" I ask, scrutinizing the dormant vehicles in front of me and wondering how much longer we're going to idle in this skanky heat.

"I was just smelling it, Mummy. But it's an alien. It's from Mars. It went inside to make babies!"

"What? What are you talking about?"

"Mummy, I want it out. It's hurting me!"

"We'll be there soon." I swivel around in my seat so that I can look her directly in the eye, riding the clutch so that the car doesn't stall as I inch forward with the traffic. "Look at me. How much does it hurt?"

"Lots?" she replies and shrugs her shoulders.

"How much lots? A lot-lots, or just a little-lots?"

Tessa hums a nasal "um" looking out the window. She rolls her eyes up in thought. "Medium-lots."

"Okay then. Medium-lots isn't *too* bad, right? Can you wait another ten minutes until we get you to preschool?" *If it is only ten bloody minutes.*

Tessa nods with a half-smile.

"Great," I reply, with a kiss in the air. "Soon. We'll be there soon."

Now the car behind me *does* nudge my bumper as the traffic moves forward at a more reasonable pace. I accelerate in haste, making it to the next set of traffic lights just in time for them to turn red. *I* can't *be late for this presentation. I* am *the presentation.*

I turn on the radio to distract myself from the anxiety bubbling in my throat like baking soda in vinegar. Rock FM—the only station I enjoy in this country. Patti Smith is on. What a legendary musician—an inspiration. A rock goddess, who in my opinion, puts every other female rock musician of her generation to shame. I would do anything to go to her concert tonight. Perhaps if I hadn't been such a social recluse lately, I would have heard about it sooner than yesterday and arranged to go.

The lights turn green, and we get moving onto a wider road where I can step on the gas. *Finally.* I take a fleeting look into the rear-view mirror again to check that Tessa hasn't continued to dig up her nose. She's bopping her head up and down to the music and twiddling her fingers around as if playing guitar. I sometimes wonder whether she's seen Alex do it, or whether she actually feels the rhythm and can't control herself. Unlike Alex, who does it consciously in fun, I catch myself playing air-guitar as if it were a common reflex.

To be honest, it can be quite embarrassing. My favourite colleague, Heather, once caught me at it by the coffee station in the office with my headphones on. I imagine it would have been a funny sight—a professional-looking thirty-year-old woman, who attempts to mask her post-baby stomach flab with bulky male shirts, strumming an invisible guitar with her tongue sticking out the side of her mouth. Yes, I stick my tongue out when I concentrate. A habit I have recently become self-conscious about since realizing I will soon have to concentrate in front of a large audience of strangers. I'll have to conquer this stage fright once and for all today.

Deep breaths. Do what Heather said. Pretend you are practicing on your own in your bedroom. Windows and doors closed. Free from interruptions.

Being a victim of stage fright is not easy, to say the least, for a woman with a passion for music sewn into her seams. In my world, the stage is a magnet. One side pulls me in, the other pushes me away, generating an involuntary psychological push-and-shove with no resolution in sight. Despite stage fright paralyzing me like a dose of tetrodotoxin, the overall thrill of performing survives the poison, and I wake up on the other side, ready to get back up on the stage and start all over again. I don't remember the angst; and the craving to perform again overpowers me like drug withdrawal. If Alex hadn't asked me to stop playing gigs would I be craving this now? Would I have become this tyrant of an editor who sports herself as a determined corporate ladder-climber? What if I followed this course in life because the stage fright had ultimately taken over? What if I subconsciously found an excuse to escape the fear? Should I really be putting the blame on Alex? Perhaps this is my fault. Perhaps it wasn't Alex's doing at all.

Before I met Alex I earned enough money to feed myself and pay the bills through random solo gigging. And that's not easy to do, especially in Greece where the mention of music generally sparks thoughts of bouzoukis and traditional dance in foustanela (male dress).

My first live gig in Athens was at a tiny venue that comfortably held eighty to a hundred people. That night there were a hundred and fifty ticket stubs collected at the door. And that's not counting the acquaintances of the promoter, venue owners or the press that slip in for free simply by having their names put on the list at the door.

During sound check I tuned my guitar at least ten times, because despite what the little orange light suggested, my guitar never sounded in tune. It was as if my anxiety was interfering with the frequency. The sound engineer's bloodshot eyes bore through my back, while a short petite man with a gray Mohawk fiddled with the stage lights—he seemed to like red. I hated red. Red lights make the frets on my guitar almost invisible. I kept trying to overcome my pride and tell him I was scared I would hit the wrong chords, but he spoke first. "Red lights are great, aren't they? They hide wrinkles." If I hadn't been so nervous, and perhaps could have injected myself with a shot of teenage aggression, I would have punched him in the nose for that comment. I clenched my teeth behind a polite smile and took a moment to compose myself while sitting on the edge of the stage with my eyes shut.

The light man winked and stepped outside onto the wet pavement. The foggy sound of the busy street crept through the large, heavy soundproofed metal door as he opened it. The deep thud of the door closing behind him remained with me for the rest of the night. A reminder that I was trapped inside myself—a victim of my own torture.

When the venue was full, I stepped onto the stage holding my breath. My footsteps vibrated through my body, as laughter turned to talking, talking turned to mumbling and mumbling turned to breathing. The first song on my set was *a capella*. I didn't introduce myself, or welcome the audience to the show. Looking down at my chunky black army boots, I let out a hot steady note that thrust the crowd into throbbing silence. Each hair on my bare arms rose one by one as the notes escaped me. But was the silence a sign of dislike or awe? Panic brittled my bones, and my limbs shook with immutable doubt. So much so that I feared the audience could see and were silently laughing at me.

I tamed my nerves little by little, doing invisible breathing exercises in between songs. But I continued my set with more original tunes without much reaction—bar the obligatory applause. They watched with steel eyes. Convinced they were just waiting me out to see the headlining band, disappointment pricked my skin like poison ivy. I thought, *I'm never doing this again. I just can't take it.*

But then I had an idea. I replaced my last song with a

cover. I had learnt it not long ago for a friend's party. I played "Wonderwall" by Oasis; despite believing it to be too commercial for my reputation, it had to be done. I had to do something to loosen up the crowd. As soon as the words, "Today, is gonna be the day ..." came out of my mouth, they recognized the song, and started cheering and singing along. Relief flushed through me like a sedative. The dissipating tension in the air cooled me down like sprinkler mist on a warm spring day. It was over. Finally over. And on a good note.

Performing to a live audience has always, and will always, create an explosion of dread and dignity within me like a balloon expanding in my stomach. I despise the feeling, but something about it—the release of steaming hot fear while playing the last song of every set— makes me want to do it all over again with the absence of such fear. Of course, this never happens. And I continue to go through the same torture again and again.

After the gig, I stood outside the venue in the rain with my guitar, waiting for a taxi to hail. I was praying one would appear out of nowhere and save me before the rain got any heavier, but a man with a shaved head and a long black leather coat appeared with an umbrella instead. He looked different than the typical Greek male, who commonly sported skin-tight jeans, open white shirts, and slick gelled hair. I was immediately intrigued.

"Hi, Melody, you were great tonight. I'm Alex," he said, holding out his hand, "head of Cat Events."

"Hi, thanks. Nice to meet you. Did you come to see The

Drovers?" I asked, wondering whether he was just trying to make friendly conversation.

A vague Greek accent laced his warm, humble laugh. His voice purred—a soft, deep, slow, mouth-watering purr from a big, fast wild cat, with the pitter-patter of drizzle in the background.

"Well, not really," Alex replied. "I came to make sure the whole event ran smoothly." Then I remembered the huge blue and black banner that read "Cat Events" behind me on the stage. *You idiot!*

"Oh, shit. I'm sorry!"

"Not a problem," Alex chortled. "It's refreshing to see a musician who's not concerned with kissing up. It shows you're sincere. I'm impressed."

"Oh. Well, in that case, thanks." As the left side of my lip stuck on my teeth, a crooked smile emerged. I dislodged it with my tongue, strangely captivated by the reflection of headlights passing over his dark blue-grey eyes. He put his hand on my upper back and guided me toward the entrance of the venue, which was under cover, and closed his umbrella.

"Listen," he said in a more serious tone. "I was thinking we could get together and talk about your music. I really like your stuff. I think we could make something of you here."

"Oh, wow, really? That'd be great." I turned my guitar case upright and rested it on my foot to move it around with ease. *Is this really happening? Am I seriously going to make an honourable musician of myself in the least likely country?* I pictured myself on a bigger stage. Fearless. Crowd roaring. Cameramen shooting the show from every angle. A huge line-up of professional musicians behind me, backing up my guitar and vocals with instrumental genius. I saw myself as Tori Amos with a guitar.

"How about we meet tomorrow for a coffee? Say about three p.m.?" asked Alex, wiping a few raindrops from his cheek.

"Okay. Where?" I was now as curious about Alex as the idea of pursuing my dream.

"See you at Thissio Station, three tomorrow." Alex held out his hand for me to shake again. But this time he pulled in closer and gave me a peck on the left cheek and then another on the right. He smelled like Chinese noodles. It gave me goose bumps. It gave me hope. I'd finally met a man who didn't drown himself in his mama's cooking.

"Er, okay, wonderful, great," I stammered. "See you then. And again, great to meet you."

I was about to step back out onto the street to find a taxi, but Alex offered me his gig runner to take me home. I accepted the offer, already feeling a little like a star.

The next day, we drank coffee in Thissio until the shop closed. He offered to be my manager. I accepted and we began exchanging emails. He requested promotional shots; I sent him promotional shots. He requested a written biography; I sent him a written biography. He requested a demo CD; I said I'd bring it the next time we met. I asked him if he knew of any worthwhile gigs to go to on Saturday night.

He said I should come to one that he'd organized, and that he would take me to a great little jazz bar afterward. So I went. But the night didn't turn out as I'd expected.

"So, what kind of music are you into?" I asked, letting this newfound confidence take reign as I perched myself on a bar stool and crossed my legs in my slinky knee-length black skirt. My long psychedelic beads collided, caressing my hardly-there and well-covered breasts. "You know, the stuff that *moves* you. The stuff you listen to at home," I continued after a few seconds of silence, wondering if I had asked a stupid question. The soft warm Frangelico glided down my throat, my voice sliding through my red lips like water over tanned, oiled skin. Alex's body heat travelled from his thighs to mine as he stood, leaning his elbows against the bar, slowly sipping his Vat 69. He squinted, and pouted his lips in thought toward the rows and rows of alcohol bottles behind the bartender—a very old, classy man who had worked there for thirty years and obsessively wiped the bar dry.

"The Kinks, Dead Kennedys, Elvis Costello. You?" Alex answered, turning to face me on the "you". He slid his body a little closer. My stomach tightened in anticipation. All I wanted to do was wrap my legs around his waist and savour his touch, the poignant tenderness I imagined he hid below his black leather tough-guy exterior.

"PJ Harvey, Nick Cave, Joni Mitchell," I replied, smiling so hard my lips stung.

"Nice." Alex nodded, took another sip of his drink, and turned to face the bar again.

"Get into a bit of trip hop now and then too. Night-mares on Wax. Stuff like that," I added, trying to get him to look at me again. His cool manner was so well executed I wondered whether it was even a manner at all. Perhaps that was just him. Naturally at ease. Sure of himself. And not afraid to flaunt it. *Perfect*, I thought. *This is the kind if man I want in my life. A man untainted with insecurity.*

"Trip hop, hey? Unusual," replied Alex, contorting his mouth into an intrigued frown.

"Why?" I put my drink down and reached for some nuts. "Why is that unusual?" As I put the nuts in my mouth, one escaped and dropped into my crotch. I pretended I hadn't noticed and slowly opened my legs to let it drop to the floor. Alex pretended not to notice, but I caught him take a fleeting look.

"Well, Greek girls don't usually mix tastes like that," said Alex, putting down his drink. He looked me right in the eye this time, as if trying to read my thoughts.

"Well, I'm Australian, so that's irrelevant, right?" Quirky innocence invaded the tone in my voice. I didn't want to be quirky and innocent. I wanted to be strange and myste-rious. I tried to wipe the grin off my face, to appear more in control of my feelings. But it was too late.

"Right," Alex replied, a semitone lower than usual, moving his face so close to mine I could feel his breath on my lips. I could taste his whiskey, smell his aftershave. My mouth grew moist as I imagined our tongues touching.

"I'm glad you're not Greek," he sighed. "I want ... not Greek. I want ... white skin ... green eyes ... long ... black

… hair." With each pause he inched closer to my lips. I couldn't move. As if my skin had been ·turned to stone. All I could hear was the gentle roar in his breath. As he reached the closest point before touching my lips he whispered, "Can I taste your lipstick?"

In the taxi home that night, the first song I heard on the radio was "I Want You" by Elvis Costello. And as it turned out, it was Alex's all-time-favourite song.

three

At Hilton Hotel. Biting nails. Reciting presentation in head with the notes of guitar scales. Standing by lecture hall door, fingers twisted behind back, toes clenched in black baby doll slip-ons. Changed shoes in the car. Watching freshly dry-cleaned suits, worn by impassive breathing corpses, walk by. Black pencil skirts and dusty patent leather high-heeled shoes on Stepford Wife splendour. Clop. Clop. Clopping. Past me like old slides. Bus boys with crisp white shirts and ugly yellow ties. Upper-class ladies in frilly blouses who eat with their mouths closed at all times, and wait for the thirty-second mouthful before swallowing, and pat their lips with expensive linen napkins.

A piece of nail gets lodged between my central incisors. I try to pry it out, exposing my teeth like a growling dog, but failing because I have no nails left to pry it out with. Middle-aged man in navy blue tailored trousers and pink shirt with collar opened three buttons down, grins at me in a ridiculing manner. His gold chain glistens amidst his thick dark chest hair as he passes below a chandelier. *Rich bastard. Trying to follow trends.* I bring my arms down to my sides and close my mouth, pushing the nail through my teeth with my tongue. Grimacing within, I smile back with my lips pressed together so tight I imagine them turning white.

I'm nauseous. Not because of presentation nerves, but because pink shirts make me want to vomit, for two reasons. One: they remind me of the time I was ten and put my white clothes in with the red bed sheets and mum pulled the heads off all my Barbie dolls as punishment. They also remind of when Alex got attacked by Greek rock venue mafia and was left bleeding with a few knife gashes to his chest. White shirt stained with blood. Nothing serious. But what if it *had* been? I tried to scrub out the blood from his shirt by hand in the white porcelain bathroom sink. I'll never forget that feeling of infirmity spread from my feet, through my body, to the tip of my tongue. I turned around and threw up in the toilet bowl. Then continued to scrub, and sung a stupid TV cheese jingle to distract myself from the overwhelming fear of what might happen next time.

It's time. I walk into the lecture hall and stand behind the podium. A bead of sweat tickles between my breasts. I want to scratch it. I grit my teeth trying to wane off the temptation, the air becoming a whirlwind of angst around my head. I cough into the microphone. Feedback. Feet shuffle. Voices murmur. Silence. A stray chuckle escapes from someone who was probably so preoccupied talking to the person next to them that they hadn't noticed I'd walked in.

Eyes focus on me as if I am an optometrist's letter chart. With shaking legs and a blank mind, I open my mouth to introduce myself, but words do not flee. Thank goodness for modern technology. I fiddle around with the projection screen with my back to the audience while I get my bearings, muttering silently to myself to focus on Heather's advice.

I begin my presentation. The audience pays considerate attention. They nod when I imagine they should. Laugh when I hope they would. Respond to questions when I think they could. And I'm relieved. *I'm making it through this. Try to smile a little, would ya?* But then the unthinkable happens. In the middle of my last slide, the button holding my dress secure around my bust bursts. I watch it fly in slow motion toward the eye of the Board of Education representative sitting closest to me in the front row. He's wearing a deep chocolate brown suit, and cream shirt. Full head of black hair, no tie, collar button undone, nicely built, but not so much that you really notice the muscle. One look at his perfectly angular, charming face, and I completely forget where I am. I stop mid-sentence. He looks right at me and lifts an eyebrow in an encouraging manner. *Is he rooting for me?* Then it happens. The button gets him in his right eye.

I turn toward the screen, and focus on the first bullet point. *What does it say? What am I meant to be saying about this?* My hands shake and I seek out my trouser pockets. *You're wearing a dress, you idiot!* I pretend to be smoothing my dress down on my thighs then fold my hands behind my back. I close the presentation like a robot. White noise fills my ears. I can't hear myself think or speak, or even comprehend what I'm saying. But the audience applauds.

It must be okay. Now they're standing. Getting up to leave. The BOE rep stands too. He holds out his hand. I shake it. He pushes my button into my clammy palm. I smile. *Am I smiling? Or do you just think you're smiling? Smile Goddamn it!*

"Mighty presentation, dear," says button boy in a British accent so smooth I can feel it on my tongue like crème caramel. "I'll make sure you get what you deserve." He winks. *Say thank you!* But before I utter a word he makes his way toward the exit. I watch his perfectly round and solid backside strut along the stained lilac carpet. He pauses at the door. Spins round on one foot. Catches me staring. I think I blush. My skin tingles like I've just opened an oven door to pull out a batch of macaroons, the only thing I ever learnt how to bake. I smile and nod, crossing my arms below my breasts, then immediately letting them loose just in case the gesture makes me seem nervous. He returns the gesture and brings his hand, shaped like a telephone, to his ear. I nod.

You nod? Oh my God. What the hell do you think you're doing?

When he disappears out of sight, I realize I am clenching my dress button in a tight fist. I loosen my grip, my fingers spreading like a blooming flower in fast forward. And with my button is a phone number, written on a tiny slither of newspaper, in handwriting so neat, one would think he'd prepared it earlier.

———

After the presentation I do some grocery shopping before going back to the office. I had planned on ordering take-out tonight, but I fear I've been neglecting Tessa. I may be busy and tired, but I do have a responsibility to feed her properly—so I bought pasta and canned tomatoes. *Don't beat yourself up over it. At least it's not souvlaki again.*

As I enter the artificially lit reception of UTD Publications, I sense a looming cross-examination on my way to my desk. My conscience is going to grill me until I start uttering my thoughts aloud again—another embarrassing habit I've acquired recently.

My heart beats with the fearful expectation I felt as a child when I had been disobedient—well, disobedient in my mother's opinion. *You just fantasized about a man other than Alex. What the flip has got into you?* Not once during our entire marriage has this happened to me. And to make matters worse, I can't bring myself to discard button boy's phone number. He *might* have given it to me to contact him for business. This is a logical and safe explanation. One I can rely on to tame my guilt. But of course, if that were the case, surely he would have given me his business card. *So stop kidding yourself!*

On the surface, this English Language Teaching world represents itself as the friendliest and most accessible in its field, yet drips with the pressure I imagine an interrogation room full of FBI agents would. Each department is separated. Not by glass, but by thick soundproofed walls, and for a strange tenuous reason, our boss expects us to avoid communicating with each other face-to-face. You would think that face-to-face communication between marketing and editorial would be vital for book sales, but in my boss's view, it distracts and causes superfluous chatter amongst us. So, email it is and remains to be, even though walking into the next room to discuss urgent issues would be easier and free us of impatience.

The editorial department is the largest room in this building that looks like a miniature White House. Bright and classy on the outside; dark and twisted within. It's painted dark grey from floor to ceiling, and consists of six pairs of desks, separated with two-meter high partitions covered in wood grain-patterned adhesive. I approach my desk and switch on my computer, dropping my handbag smack-dab in the middle of my scattered and incomprehensible presentation notes from the previous few days. Purple Post-its bombard my partition. Some have lost their stick and slipped through the crack between the partition and the back of my desk and fallen onto the floor. I stare at my bag's wrinkly, flaking, blue-vinyl exterior. It looks how I feel. Old. Poorly constructed. Depressed. Cheap.

I take a deep breath initiating yet another day of tedium, getting a good whiff of the sickening amalgamation of perfume and cleaning fluid. *Will any heads surface to ask me how my presentation went at least? Does* anyone *give a shit?* I look around the room, still standing. I put my hands on my hips and screw up my mouth to the left side of my face. Waiting. For. Some. Movement. You'd think my colleagues could fathom breaking their focus to ask me how my morning was. But no. Their disregard for my presence pisses me off like an unlocatable itch.

"Jesus Christ," I snap under my breath, as I sit in front of my computer. I hear quiet heads turn as the wheels of my seat roll me below the desk. One of the new editorial assistants giggles and clears her throat—probably nervous about causing a disruption. If I had the nerve, I'd speak up. Tell them what a bunch of inconsiderate fucks they are. But I suppose that would be "unprofessional" of me.

Heather walks in to fetch an empty coffee mug from her desk and spots me. She pauses and signals me to the coffee station with a flick of her head. Her straight shoulder-length, forty-year-old white-grey hair swings with grace. I grab my plastic container of onion soup out of my bag to heat in the microwave. My stomach is rumbling like a dog's low growl. Not from hunger. From nerves / guilt / anger.

"So? How did it go?" Heather asks in her bouncy London accent. She puts a teaspoon of decaffeinated Nescafé into her shiny black mug; her small, almond-shaped crystal blue eyes, thinly lined with silver-grey shadow, pop against her smooth alabaster skin as she stares at me, eyebrows raised, waiting for an answer.

I tell her about the presentation, and although quite reluctant to mention button boy, I do, knowing very well that if there is someone I can trust around here, it is Heather. When I finish talking, she empties her fresh mug of coffee into the sink.

"Whaddaya doing that for?" I ask, looking at the mug, then her face, then her mug again with my jaw agape.

Heather mouths the letters "PM" and starts making another coffee. PM stands for Project Manager. We have two, and they basically run the editorial department.

Sure enough in struts Dianne, one of the PMs, standing tall, shoulders spread, mousy brown hair styled as if hair sprayed in position since 1982. The three of us flash each other polite smiles as Dianne presses the elevator's up button. She must be on her way to see the boss. *Has she forgotten about my presentation too? Why are my actions so invisible? The day I never step foot in this wretched joint again couldn't come sooner.*

Standing there with her hands behind her back, Dianne swings backward and forward on the balls of her feet. She grins as though replaying a pleasant moment in her head. The elevator door pings open. My soup trickles into my hand and onto my dress.

"Damn it!" I exclaim, putting the container of soup in the sink and reaching for a sponge.

Dianne lets the elevator close without stepping in. "What type of container is it in?" she asks.

"Oh, I don't know," I say, scrubbing the stain from the only decent dress I own. Blue dye comes off on the sponge. "I bought it from my local supermarket." I throw the sponge in the sink with a heavy sigh and wipe my forehead with the back of my wet hand, eyes closed in frustration. Heather rips off a paper towel and hands it to me. I press it firmly on the wet patch to soak up the fluid.

"Well, it's perfectly understandable that your soup leaked into your bag with a container like that," Dianne replies, lifting her nose as though blessed with unique wisdom. She turns around to face us with swift enthusiasm, holding her Filofax in the air. She beams as revelation shines upon her face. "You should buy Tupperware. It's one hundred percent reliable, and they come in many shapes and sizes. You can even choose colours to match the décor of your kitchen!"

What is this? Are we in some sort of 1950s TV commercial?

"Er—" I try to stall my response. The last thing I want right now is to get into a conversation about plastic boxes. But my hesitation does no good.

"I absolutely *adore* Tupperware," Dianne continues, looking toward the ceiling with her head tilted. I imagine a cartoon thought bubble of her cradling a Tupperware container, like a baby, appearing above her head. "I have *every* shape and size for every purpose. I even put little labels on them so I don't have to spend time searching through the fridge or cupboards. They seal very w—Oh! And don't you just love the sound they make when you open the lid? Maybe it's just me, but it's *very* satisfying. Pshhhh. You really know that the container has done its job and kept your food fresh. Maybe you should invest in some *good* quality containers in order to avoid any such spillages in the future. Oh sorry, Melody, listen to me carry on like a *hen* being *chased* around a *barn*."

I don't know how long I stand there with my jaw open like a funfair clown, but Heather has to close it for me. Snap—shut like a compact mirror. I have never seen Dianne get *excited* over anything in the entire time I have worked here. The most words we've ever exchanged before now was during my interview three years ago. And even then the big boss did more of the talking, while she ogled him as if he were a member of the Royal Family. I'm amazed she didn't drown in her own drool.

"Oh, and Melody, as soon as I'm done upstairs, meet me in my office and we'll talk about your presentation." *Wow. Finally.* I force a nod of gratitude.

"And we *loved* the songs you wrote for the pre-junior course," she adds, holding the newly arrived elevator door open with her foot, "and it looks like we'll ask you to write them for the next level in the series too. Would you be interested?" *Next level? Does that mean I'm not being promoted?*

"Sure," I respond in a manner that shows more appreciation than I actually feel.

"Great. We'll speak again later this afternoon." Oozing with pretentiousness, Dianne nods goodbye and steps into the elevator.

Heather looks over her shoulder and then whispers with her hand to my ear, "You think she's having it off with the boss?"

"Don't be silly," I say, shaking my head. "She's just in awe of the man's superiority. Anyway, I can't really imagine her being the type."

"What type of person do you have to be in order to have a fling?" Heather retorts as she pours some milk into her second mug of coffee, now probably on the verge of being cold.

"Oh, I don't know. Not so—"

"Proper? Well, I wouldn't think of you as the type either, but you sure have the hots for button boy," interrupts Heather, raising the pitch of her last word with a little wink.

"I *do* not." I cup my face in my hands. Shame glazes my skin like hot steam in a sauna.

"*Yes*, you do. You should have seen the look on your face when you were talking about him." Heather takes a sip of her coffee, winces, and pours it down the drain again. She shakes her head, scrunching up her nose. "Don't worry, I don't think you'd *do* anything of the sort, but there's nothing wrong with a little fantasy, right? I mean, *honestly*, our husbands must do it all the time." Heather laughs, snorting a little.

"You think so?"

"Yeah. O'course."

"I can't imagine Alex even thinking about it. He doesn't seem—"

"The type?" Heather interrupts again. "Well, none of us do, really, do we?"

I can't help but wonder if I *am* the type. Not just to fantasize about someone else, but to actually *cheat* on my husband. The idea of a stranger's hands touching me used to seem as appealing as walking through a man-sized spider web. But now?

"Heather, we'd better get back to our desks before you start to make a third cup of coffee."

"Yeah, I suppose. Oh … Melody?"

"Yep?" I chirp, already halfway out the door.

"Are you okay?"

"What do you mean?"

"You look, er … blue."

"Nah, I'm fine," I say flicking my hand in the air and shaking my head.

"You sure? 'Cause your neck seems a different shade than your face."

"What?" I run to the washroom and look in the mirror. The colour of my dress has sweated off onto my skin. I grab some paper towel and try to scrub it off without much luck. Now I feel like a frump. An imbecile. A woman who has given up on her appearance. No purpose to make myself look, or even feel beautiful. Am I in danger of making a wrong turn? What if black is really white and white is really black? What if I am two shades of grey?

I return to my desk. Heather winks at me as I sit down. I think of button boy as I scan through icons on my desktop. They seem to change position every time I turn on my computer. I envision us on a first date. Button boy touching my cheek from across the dinner table—me blushing and shifting my eyes toward the food on my plate—button boy moving in closer to lightly kiss my upper lip. I get tingles in my toes at the thought. But then I replace button boy's face with Alex's. And the tingles turn to warmth. To the thought of his soft hand on my cheek—the touch I used to crave like water in desert heat.

The last thing I want is to have an affair.

All I want is to feel desired.

four

Argument with Alex. Chewing gum up Tessa's nose. Traffic jam. Stressful presentation. Flying dress button. Button boy fantasies. Held up at work. Late picking Tessa up from preschool. Bickered with preschool teacher—again. And now I'm faced with a broken elevator and eight flights of stairs to climb with bags of groceries.

I stare at the flashing red light by the elevator door. My glands thump and sync with the rhythm of the flash like a turn signal and windshield wiper creating their own symphony. My handbag drops from my shoulder to the plastic shopping bags I'm clutching onto with burning red-raw fingers. I clench my jaw, holding in the desperate scream pounding in my ears to let it out.

"Mummy, what's wrong?" Tessa asks sucking on a chunk of hair.

"It's stuck," I say, not looking down at her, tracing the frame of the elevator door with my eyes in a desperate attempt to find a way to make it work.

"Call Papa."

"Hmm?"

"Call Papa. He can come down and help us carry the

sopping." Tessa looks up at me and imitates my frown. I smile at her. She smiles back at me. I rest the bags on the ground and release my grip. My fingers ache and sting as I separate them from the sharp, stretched handles. She takes her school bag off her shoulders and puts it on the ground too. I can't help but laugh a little as she stretches her fingers as if she were the one carrying the shopping bags.

"Good idea," I nod, bending down to pull my mobile phone from my handbag. I dial home. It rings. And rings. And rings. *Surely he's not out?* "No answer," I say with a sigh and a shrug, clutching onto the phone so hard that I unfasten the battery cover by accident. I push back tears threatening to erupt like rainwater from a cracked drain pipe.

Tessa puts her school bag back on her shoulders. "Oh, well," she shrugs. "I'll help you carry the sopping." She picks up two bags full of serviettes, tea towels, kitchen roll and toilet paper and starts to walk up the stairs. I watch her in awe. At her casual acceptance. When did I become so tense? Why can't I handle frustration like that? How long do we go through life before the monotonous reality of our day starts to infringe on our psychological well-being? When *does* it all start to matter? And why? Why does it matter?

Tessa turns around and frowns at me. "Well, come on, Mummy. Spit spot!" she says nodding in determination with a taut mouth and wide eyes. Her Mary Poppins imitation sparks such a warm thrill within me that I burst into laughter. And with the laughter come tears of joy. They wet my cheeks like drizzle in a heat wave. If it weren't for Tessa, I wouldn't see the cracks in our walls as lodging for fairies and "plaster-people"; nor would I understand that the damp in our ceiling is "hydrating" their home. Another thing I wouldn't understand is that the constant frown displayed on Alex's face on his busy and stressful work days is just "Mr. Grumpy" coming out to parade in the "Let's Be Angry Festival" for fun.

Tessa shakes her head and sighs. I bend down and pick up the bags again, wincing a little at the cramps in my fingers and ache in my feet. But I follow Tessa up eight flights of stairs singing "Supercalifragilisticexpialidocious" so loud that one of our neighbours yells for us to "shut the fuck up" in Greek. Tessa giggles, knowing very well what the words mean, and continues to sing once we pass the autocrat's floor.

We reach our door. The second-to-last story. We put the bags down. I'm panting, but Tessa is still humming the Mary Poppins tune. I insert my key into the keyhole expecting the door to be locked. But it's not. Alex is home. *I can't believe he ignored my call!* Tessa looks at me as if she has a complete understanding of what is going through my head. She stops singing and looks at the wall. I take a deep breath and close my eyes, trying to control my temper— again. I reach for the door handle, my fingers brittle with rheumatoid-like tension. I grasp it. Lever it down. The click of it opening travels through my arm like an electrical current, seizing my heart with disappointment. *He ignored me.* The door swings open and Alex is at the end of the corridor, about to come greet us. I glare at him. His eyes glaze over with triumph. *He* knew *it was out of order. How am I supposed to take this? As some conniving attempt to punish me for wanting something out of my life? Or to simply piss me off out of spite? Can't he see he does that enough without trying?*

"Papa!" Tessa squeals, running inside, leaving me at the front door with the shopping bags. If only I knew where she got "Papa" from, I might be able to convince her to use "Daddy" instead. I feel like I'm in a scene from *Little House on the Prairie,* and I wince in conjugal torment every time she says it. I suppose it's better than *malaka* (wanker), though—a word I'm convinced Alex taught her how to say, but insists he didn't.

I look down the corridor at Tessa in Alex's arms, shopping bags surrounding my feet. My arms hang limp at my sides like banana skins. He lifts Tessa up. She wraps her legs around his waist and squashes his cheeks in her hands. She giggles as Alex's face warps like Play-Dough, exposing his teeth and gums. Alex moves his head side to side and kisses Tessa's palms. They smile at each other like the smile was just born into existence. The connection between Alex and Tessa is as rare and intriguing as a unique religion to a spiritually lost soul in search of something new to believe in. I'm jealous of it. I'm jealous that my daughter can turn Alex into the man I used to love and ache for, while I continue to sculpt him into a man I wish to hate with my irrational nit-picky behaviour, so that I can excuse myself for needing something other than him—than Tessa—than my family.

I kneel down to pick up a couple of bags to take into the kitchen, but as soon as my knees touch the ground, tears threaten to bleed through the walls of my mouth like a warning: *Don't become like your mother. Do not let your daughter become a target of your frustration.*

"Guess what? I was smelling my chewing gum this morning, Papa, and it, and it crawled up my nose. It was funny, Papa! It was really funny!" Tessa gasps for breaths between words as if her brain is working too fast for her lips to keep up. I stand, swallowing self-disgust, and take the shopping into the kitchen. I look at the floor as I walk past them, avoiding eye contact with Alex.

"Wow!" Alex exclaims, as I put the shopping bags on the kitchen table. "Did the gum tell you why it wanted to crawl up your nose?" he asks. I peek through the door and Alex has put Tessa on her feet and is kneeling down on his knees to speak to her face-to-face, stroking her hair. I pull out the can of tomatoes and packet of pasta. I leave them on the bench by the stove.

"Yep, yep! It said, it said it was on a business trip, Papa!" I walk back to ask one of them to give me a hand putting away the groceries. But Tessa's eyes are half-squinted. She does this when she thinks she is saying something really intelligent, and I wouldn't dream of interrupting her now.

I lean against the door frame, with my arms crossed, to watch and listen. Alex looks up at me. We smile at each other and catch a glimpse of something unsaid, but written in our eyes—something that reminds me of the early days, when small simple looks and smiles came from somewhere a lot deeper than our faces. I look at the floor, wondering what just happened, what it meant. A mutual glint of pride, perhaps? A brief moment where our daughter caused us to forget we are supposed to be angry with each other? Or was it real? Was it a taste of what we still have, and what we need to savour?

Alex focuses his attention back to Tessa. "A business trip?" he asks in a cartoon voice. "That's a funny place to have a business trip!" Alex says, squeezing Tessa's nose.

"No, it's not, Papa. It was from Mars, looking for a place to make babies." The end of her statement trails off a little, I think as she realizes the impossibility of what she is saying. As soon as it comes out of her mouth she puts her hands behind her back, tilts her head to the side, and looks at the floor with an impish smirk on her face. *Where does she come up with these things?*

"Babies?" Alex asks in his proper voice. "Babies from Mars, on a business trip, up your nose? Why?" Alex's voice is laced with amused confusion.

Tessa perks up again. Facing her nose toward the ceiling and pointing up her nostril, she calls out, "Because it's warm in there." I shake my head and go back into the kitchen, hoping Alex will follow and help me put everything away.

I can hear Alex's knees crack. "Come on, Tessa. Let's go and play with Doggy," he says.

And he leaves me.

Alone.

Once again.

To be the wife.

In the kitchen.
Where I belong.

I'm preparing pasta sauce when Tessa and Alex come skipping into the kitchen for some chocolate milk. Alex opens the fridge and lifts Tessa up to reach it for herself.

"Not before dinner," I snap.

"Why?" Tessa asks, looking to Alex for support. He winks at her and pats her on the head. I glare at him.

"Because you won't eat it."

"I will."

"You won't."

"I will!" Tessa screams stamping her feet in tempest fury. Her face goes red, and saliva splutters from her mouth.

Alex rolls his eyes at me and pulls the carton of chocolate milk out of the fridge anyway.

"What are you doing?" I'm cutting basil leaves. I grip the knife tighter. My nails turn white. That hidden scream isn't going to stay tame for much longer.

"Just giving her a *little* bit," Alex says, taking a glass out of the cupboard from above my head. His arm brushes against my shoulder. I have a sudden urge to elbow him in his side. I don't.

"How can you undermine me like that?" I ask, in a solid, low, civil tone, staring at the basil. I imagine picking up the chopping board and flinging it into Alex's face.

"What's 'undermine' mean?" he asks with a smirk.

I ignore the question and hand the half glass of chocolate milk to Tessa. She takes it and gulps it all down in one go.

"Finished, then?" I ask, holding out my hand to take the glass.

"Can I have a bit more?"

I shake my head. Tessa looks to Alex for support. I glare at Alex as he smirks back at me. Tessa turns her pleading eyes on me, but I dare not look at her for fear I'll give in. I narrow my glare on Alex. He finally shakes his head no. I reach for the glass, but she pulls it away.

"I want some more!" she yells, so high-pitched my ears buzz.

Alex rubs his hands over his face and makes a move to leave the kitchen. I grab his arm to stop him. "Don't you leave me to clean up your mess," I scowl.

"You *can't* have anymore, now give me the glass." I growl through gritted teeth. Tessa doesn't move. She just stares at me. I grab her arm and try to pry the glass from her hand. In a heavy struggle the glass somehow goes flying across the room and smashes against the wall.

"Oh for *Christ's* sake, Tessa, why can't you just *do* as you're *told*?" I scream. It's so loud, cavernous, and irate that my head vibrates and face stings. Tessa's bottom lip trembles as she involuntarily sucks in a tear mid-sob from her top lip.

"What did you do that for?" Alex sneers. "Melody, what's wrong with you?"

My first thought is to give Tessa a big cuddle and apologize. I'm angry at Alex, not Tessa. But I can't seem to move from the kitchen bench which I'm clutching behind my back in fear of breaking down into a blubbering mess. I'm dizzy and brimming with a rage that is still yet to escape since childhood. From all those years of keeping the peace around my mother. I don't think I've ever had the chance to let it loose. I have twenty years of pent up anger, and nothing to let it out on. I release my grip and look at my hands. They're red, dry and dented. Much like my heart.

"Nothing," I sigh with my eyes closed. "Nothing's wrong with me. Tessa, honey, go put your pyjamas on and brush your teeth." I smile at her apologetically. She doesn't move, tears streaming down her cheeks. "I bought you some of that purple sparkly toothpaste you wanted. I left it on your pillow." Tessa wipes her eyes in an instant and exclaims, "Cool!" and runs to her bedroom repeating it over and over.

Putting the chopped basil into the pot, I ask Alex to help Tessa get ready for bed, trying to ignore, or at least draw attention away from my outburst. He doesn't answer.

"At least help her with her pyjamas," I say, looking into the simmering sauce. "She always puts the zoo ones on inside out, for some odd reason." But just as I feel calm teasing the edges of my psyche, the nag in me rears its grievous head and pushes calm aside. "It's already Tessa's bedtime," I snap. "And she's up late because of you anyway. This could've all been avoided if you'd picked her up from preschool like I asked. I *told* you I had a busy day ahead of me, and all I asked from you was one day. Just *one* day to pick Tessa up from preschool. Just. ONE. Day. But no. You were *so* hung up about our conversation this morning that you just had to leave everything up to me again. Out of spite. Right?" I throw the wooden spoon into the pot and a bit of sauce splashes onto my hand. It burns. Stings.

But not as much as my impatience with Alex. All he does is *stare*. Arms folded in the doorway. Corner of his mouth hooked up in "he couldn't give a shit-ness".

"Can't you do *any*thing around here? I'm practically doing everything in my sleep. I'm. Tired," I hiss.

"I'm sorry, Mel, but you deserved it," Alex replies in a complacent tone.

"I what? How many times have you done things to hurt me? Huh? How many?"

"Should I have made a list?"

"That's not my point. My point is that I still sweep all your *crap* under the carpet and get on with things like a responsible adult. But what do *you* do? You play stupid manipulating games like a pubescent teenager. How dare you make me climb eight flights of stairs today with all those groceries. If I had done that to you I would never have heard the end of it."

"Sweep under the carpet? What's that mean?" Alex scoffs.

"Oh, for Christ's sake, Alex."

Alex snickers, then huffs "fuck you," and turns to exit the kitchen. But an unexpected wave of physical strength stimulates me like a shot of adrenaline and I hook my arm through Alex's and swing him around to face me.

"Why do you always *swear* at me? You *always* say that you won't do that anymore and the next day you do it again. No matter how many conversations we have about *anything*, they make absolutely no difference. What's the bloody point? What's your *fucking* problem?" I growl under my breath in the hope that Tessa won't be able to hear.

"You're my problem." He snatches his arm away.

"Yeah. *That* I know. You *always* say that. What I want to know is, what's your problem *with* me?"

"Everything."

"Argh! What are you? A broken record? Can't you act like an adult, just this once? We have problems. We. Need. To. Stop. This."

"And. You. Need. To. Fuck. Off."

After I put Tessa to bed I sit at the end of our three-seater couch clutching my knees to my chest. Through the open balcony door I can hear a man yelling at some driver for double-parking and blocking his car. I lean my head on the armrest. Still in my blue dress. Sticky. Stinky. Too lazy to take a shower. I stare at the TV, which is off. I look at my reflection in the screen. Quite warped in a pretty, yet indistinct kind of way. Like an eighteenth-century portrait of my soul on canvas, in a grey hue as if painted in darkness. Like the darkness I live in my head. If only I could remain in that reflection, as a painting, on a canvas—motionless, flushed with gothic candor, a lost spirit, a drifter, in a place where I will never be judged; a place where I can be hung in a gallery and be praised for my unconventional individuality.

I close my eyes and the image fades and moulds together like I had been staring at the sun. I'm just drifting off to sleep when I feel the other end of the couch move. I open my eyes. It's Alex. I watch him as he takes my feet and rubs them.

"I'm sorry," he whispers.

I don't move. But I do smile at him despite feeling too sad to do so.

"Mel," Alex says, lying down next to me and kissing my neck. "Let's get Tessa dressed."

"Pardon?" I ask, sitting up. Not quite sure if I heard right. "She just went to bed."

"Well, get her *out* of bed. We have tickets for Patti Smith."

five

Patti begins a Jimi Hendrix cover on clarinet. It murmurs a tragic mellow vibrato through Lykabettus Theatre like a wilting willow pleading to be left in solitude to wither and fade. Chatter hushes like ebbing rain as the guitarist's jazz scales move the clarinet's tune through waves. Rhythm guitar suspends the melody and the crowd roars. Patti puts the clarinet down, approaches the microphone and sings in her deep, gruff, aching voice,

> *If you can just*
> *get your*
> *mind together …*

The slow four/four beat of the guitar and Patti's voice thumps through the ground, through my legs, body, arms, tightening my throat. Synchronic drums, bass, and distorted guitar unite with the rhythm on the beat, creating an eruption of sundry emotion within me that startles the cold tears falling down my cheeks. I wipe them away with my smooth silk, silver shawl; I smile self-consciously at Alex. He's balancing Tessa on his shoulders so she can see above the crowd of bobbing heads. He winks and wipes a stray tear dangling from my jaw. I quiver from his touch, in shock at the tenderness, the warmth I feel through such a small gesture. *Has he realized what I'm craving? Does he understand?*

"You okay?" Alex screams into my ear, gripping onto Tessa's legs as he leans over. We are standing right next to a speaker twice the size of us, so I just smile, shake my head, and indicate that I have some dust in my eye by pretending to get it out. I give him a peck on the cheek, face the stage again and nod my head to the beat reverberating through the floor.

I didn't want Alex to see the tears. He says I cry too much. He also believes I use my tears to get what I want. But it's not so. He overheard my mother one day, whispering in my ear when she thought Alex wasn't listening: "There's nothing wrong with a few tears to give a little push in the right direction." The fact that Alex believes I'm capable of such a thing, alone, makes me want to cry. But if I was ever put on stage, or in front of a camera, and instructed to cry, it'd be like asking me to grow a penis. I can't stop my feelings but I can't fabricate them either.

Alex, on the other hand, doesn't cry. I've never seen him cry. I'm sure there's some psychological explanation for it, other than being an orphan and having to stay strong through the countless foster parents he's lived with in his lifetime, like our (long gone) marriage counselor proclaimed. Somewhere below his skin is Lake Eyre—only once every thirty-odd years does that dry salt lake in central Australia flood.

There may not be tears to show my husband's emotions, but I've seen how the melancholy turns his insuperable face pale with grief every time we talk about his deceased ex-wife, Angelica; a stunning, tall, olive-skinned Latina. My looks don't compare to hers one bit. I sometimes wonder whether Alex still loves her. After all, her loss was not his choice.

Patti's long gray hair hangs loose and scraggly over her eyes. She emanates an aura so potent that you have to look twice to realize she's dressed in an unflattering flannel shirt and jeans. *I want to be her, drenched in visible inner-beauty.*

As I look up at the stage I wonder if I ever knew her in a previous life. The atmosphere in this theatre and Patti's presence feel so familiar and accessible to me I could catch it in a jar, put it on my mantle like ashes in an urn, and take sips from it every now and then as if it were an elixir for life.

I gulp down the last of Alex's whiskey from his white plastic cup, crush it in my hand and squash it into his back jean pocket. I close my eyes; soaking up the melodious warmth travelling through my chest as one particular lyric Patti sings catches my attention. I open my eyes, watch her gifted thick lips move against her gaunt face; her jagged raw beauty weeping with roaring passion. She sings something about there being a wind over our land and that we live not to die but to be reborn. And right at this moment, relief flushes through me like holy water cleansing me of sin. Maybe not all is lost if I don't pursue my dream? Perhaps I'll have the chance to do so in my next life? Should I be patient, appreciate what I already have—take advantage of the good that already exists in my life?

If only I could remember this relief in the midst of a bout of my daily "what ifs". I signal to Alex to pass Tessa onto my shoulders for a while so that we can share a bit of dancing frenzy. I have a sudden urge to really just have some fun and to share it with my daughter. It would be better if she were a little older, but I suppose by the time she's old enough to appreciate having a bit of fun at a rock concert, she wouldn't want to be appreciating it with me— so I take the chance now.

But it doesn't last long enough. Tessa forgets whose shoulders she is on and swings her limbs around like a rag doll in a washing machine. I wince in silence as she accidentally whacks me in the face with her orange patent leather shoe. I tried really hard to get her to wear the black pair, but she'd insisted. I pass her back to Alex and we exchange head shakes. His meaning, "What's wrong?" Mine, meaning "Can't do it."

When we return home from the concert, Tessa is asleep, hanging over Alex's shoulder, her arms dangling down his back like thick rope. Our elevator is still out of order. We climb the eight flights of marble stairs listening to our breath and footsteps echo through the building. Exhausted, Alex puts Tessa to bed, and we both collapse on the couch in front of the TV. Alex has an absent smile on his face— one of those smiles we aren't often aware of, but that bloom like flowers triggered by sudden sunshine.

"Must have been nice going to a gig where you didn't have to run around networking," I say. Alex twitches his head in my direction as if I have disrupted his sleep.

"Sorry?" he asks, eyebrows raised, resting his elbow on the left arm rest, and chin on his hand. "Oh, yeah. It was cool."

A few moments of silence pass as I watch the blue TV light flash on his still smiling face. *I wonder what he's thinking.* I could ask. But I just sit there, a little drunk, staring at the wrinkles around his mouth; wondering if I'm capable of feeling anything other than this repellent emptiness; wondering whether the emptiness is normal, if I should see a therapist, if I should tell Alex that he has crow's feet and I don't, and that his stubble is flecked with gray; whether I should ask if he has got everything out of life he desired.

"Did you have a good time, babe?" Alex asks, seeming to realize I was trying to start a conversation. How long has it been now? Since we had a decent conversation? I can't remember. I can't remember.

"Um … yeah!" I chirp, false enthusiasm squirting from my mouth like poison. *I don't know how* to describe the time I had. Was it a good time? Moments of it were torture—a reminder of what I don't have. Other moments were sanctified with sheer joy—a reminder of how much music resuscitates my failing pulse. But most of it felt like trying to cross the ocean on a bridge made of fraying string—Will I? Won't I? Can I? Should I?

Alex rubs his eyes and mumbles, "Bed?" Looking at me with blind eyes, he slaps his hands on his knees in cue to stand.

"Er, not sure if I'm ready yet. I think I'll read a bit. Go if you want. Won't be long. I just need to get the buzz out of my head before I sleep."

Alex smiles with horizontal tight lips. "Okay. Try not to wake me. I'm fucking tired." *Try not to wake you?* I presumed he sympathized with me during the concert after the compassion he showed. I guess I presumed wrong. What *was* that? That moment when he wiped away my tear and I felt a hint of care?

Once Alex goes to bed, I close the corridor door so as not to wake him with my rattle. I shuffle into my office to grab a book to read, but switch on my computer instead. Perhaps I'll send a couple of emails back home to Australia. Tell my family my news—whatever that is. But to my surprise and relief my best and lifelong friend, Serena, is online.

MelodyHill(Billy?)
Heya! You busy?

Serena_Servais
G'day stranger! What u doin up?

MelodyHill(Billy?)
Went to see Patti Smith!

Serena_Servais
Really? Fab!

MelodyHill(Billy?)
Yeah was pretty fab! You at work?

Serena_Servais
Nope. Day off. Sittin with my mini laptop in the morning sun drinkin latte, eatin eggs Benedict in Fitzroy. On my own.

Lovin it. All peaches and cream, lovey!
How's you?

MelodyHill(Billy?)
I'm ok. Feelin bit low.

Serena_Servais
???

MelodyHill(Billy?)
You know me been to gig now feelin miserable story of my life

Serena_Servais
Sorry, egg yolk just went down my chin. On dress. Egg foam on latte. Reckon I could patent new egg latte? … C'mon Mel! Just speak to him. Alex wonderful man. Alex angel. Alex luv u, u luv Alex. What's problem? We both know he'll give u gig if u ask! Alex do anything u ask!

MelodyHill(Billy?)
I just feel so alone …

Serena_Servais
You're not alone Mel. You have beaut family. You have me too!

MelodyHill(Billy?)
But that's problem. He's really all I have. Not that I don't appreciate having

him, but it's hard sometimes. I can't
talk to him about some things like I
need to. Greek men have weird ways. Can't
talk without fear of maybe having fight
if blurt out thoughts wrong. He always
misunderstands my intentions. You live
on other side of world. My parents live
on island with weird ferry timetable. I
miss you. I miss Australia. Can I join
you for eggs Benedict? Order me latte,
full fat! I'll jump on plane now! ☺

Serena_Servais
LOL

MelodyHill(Billy?)
I wish.

Serena_Servais
Don't forget Tessa!

MelodyHill(Billy?)
Are you kidding? COURSE NOT! Tessa sometimes only saviour. Can escape in her
world. But not same. Nope. Can't tell her
I feel sad. I'll just make her cry and
psychologically damage her like my mum
did me.

Serena_Servais
LOL You'll be alright when u wake up in
morning. U always are.

MelodyHill(Billy?)
Yeah. Know. But can't live like this.
Need not to have these feelings. Need not
to go through neediness. I wonder if my
mum ever felt like this?

Serena_Servais
Like what?

MelodyHill(Billy?)
A yearning to play music.

Serena_Servais
Doubt it. She played gigs whenever she
liked, didn't she? Why would she yearn?

MelodyHill(Billy?)
I dunno. Depression?

Serena_Servais
She was sick, Mel. You're not sick.

MelodyHill(Billy?)
I'm not? LOL

Serena_Servais
No! Hon, let's chat again tomorrow. I'm
sorry, have to go. Please! You'll be ok!
Just think of Tessa. U told me yourself she's only 1 who makes u smile when
depressed. Luv u. xoxox

I turn off my computer, singing Joni Mitchell's "River" underneath my self-hating invisible sobs. *Oh I wish I had a river I could skate away on ...* I reach below my desk and pick up one of Tessa's teddy bears that she's left behind. It smells like her—Athens grime and Johnson & Johnson Baby Shampoo. Its fur is hard and stiff in places where Tessa has drooled on it in her sleep. I rub my cheek against its belly, remembering the first day Tessa and Teddy lay in the same cot together. That was the day Alex asked me to give up playing gigs. I was so high on being a mother that I didn't even care. I didn't even question it, fight it, or even try to understand it. *Did he take me to see Patti Smith to avoid continuing our discussion? Could he possibly be so cunning?*

I tiptoe into Tessa's room, to look at her, to try and remember the feeling that washed all my dreams away without a care in the world. Maybe I can find it again. To convince myself that motherhood is music. It used to be. When did that feeling cease? And why do I feel so guilty about it?

Tessa is curled up at the bottom of her bed—duvet and pillows and dolls and teddies all fallen onto the floor. I pick up the duvet and cover her petite body, being careful not to wake her. But all I want to do is take her in my arms and sing her a lullaby. All night. I want to sing to her for so long that she will wake up the next day and understand, deep down in her heart, why I need more, because she'll have realized that she needs it too.

It doesn't seem so long ago that I gave birth to Tessa. I

can still feel my legs in those stirrups—the sweaty doctor sucking the entire universe through my spasming black hole. Muscles being pulled from my spine, my thighs to my pelvis. What began as an insignificant seed, violently pushed itself like a fist through tearing fabric. The only thought preventing me from slipping into oblivion was that, for this miracle of life, there was light, not darkness, to launch her into this rutted world. Because in those days I was never two shades of grey. In those days I thought I would be a brilliant mother. Full of light. And happiness. Now I worry I'm going to neglect her like my mother neglected me.

I wake up a few hours later in a sweat.

I dreamt I was on my childhood front lawn in a cabaret dress with the snotty-nosed girl, Marlene, from across the road pointing her finger at me, looking very cross. Her nose was running as she sniffed, "My mum says that Winterberry Holly won't bloom in an Australian climate … My mum says that your dad doesn't know how to prune the rose bushes properly … My mum says that you have a bogan accent … My mum says your freckles look like someone threw dirt in your face and the wind suddenly changed." Then her voice grew deeper, and she turned into my mother. "I'm very disappointed in you, Melody. No more gigs for two months."

I lie back down. On my back. I monitor the adjusting darkness in the room and wish my days weren't full of so much nothingness. Days that resemble an ice cube in a glass of hot water. Days I psychologically slip in and out of in seconds because nothing of importance happens. I exist. I eat. I work. I sleep. And then I don't.

Do people realize the damage routine does to our psyche? *Routine* is a monotonous exhaustion; an annihilation of the desire to differ. It humiliates the soul, kills passion. It's a disease. I like to call it Routinitus. I've forgotten how to fight it, too. So lately I've been focusing my attention elsewhere. On mornings and nights. The times of day I can make it through without yearning pulling my mind every which way.

During the few short moments I lie in bed before I open my eyes at dawn, I soak up the silence—its precious freedom. I'm the only one who subsists in this cocoon of linen, soft on my body, from toe to chin, defending the intricacies of the flesh and spirit within; in a field of cotton, protected from the sun, the sea, the wind. There's no time to think, just to feel—near nothingness imprints peace onto my skin. Those few short moments of pleasant loneliness save me from sin. They save me from voicing my selfish woes, when I have everything anyone could need. They are my security blanket.

During the few short moments I lie in bed before I sleep at night, I like to introduce myself to the dreams that await me; to dreams I never recall when I awake; to dreams that take me so far from reality that clicking heels together will never return me home. I push my weightless body so distant into obscurity that I'm afraid to question where I am. But the fear isn't fear I experience on earth. It is a silent, hidden fear, which summons self-belief. For creed is cred-ible in dreams. And we don't need to make choices. They're already made. Sanctity prays for me instead of me for it.

But no matter how hard I try to hold onto these pleasant moments throughout the day, time races by, in slow motion. A truth I cannot outrun. I am tricked by moments. I once told my mother, "Live the moment." Advice offered to salvage her venture toward happiness. But then she retold it to me, as if wise in her old age, forgetting that it was *me* she'd heard it from. Forgetting it was *I* she once claimed gave her all the happiness she needed.

If time could stand still, if the moments are truly all that matter, then why can't we stop the clock when our children are born, when happiness is sewn into our seams? I can't live life just appreciating moments. I can't let time pass me by without anything to show for it. I don't want to reach that point in life when dreams become small and meaningless and unattainable, when small needs become embellished, and ardent passions no longer inspire a fleeting thought. I don't want to live my life and then realize I have nothing and can never attempt to get what I want again.

Alex starts to snore like a lawnmower's engine. I need to pull us out of this rut. Alex and I need to figure out what is going on between us—or finish it, so we can move on with our lives. We cannot keep going like this. But how do you heal something that isn't open to being healed? And how do you find the strength to keep trying to change something when your changes keep getting thrown back in your face?

Why can't relationships be like a job? Work is work.

Work is simple. When you have to get something done at work, you schedule a deadline and then you meet it. Object achieved. No ums and ahs, wondering how, when, why. You just do it.

I roll over and slip my arm around Alex's waist. I put my hand down the front of his boxers, in the hope that a little sexual contact might bring us closer together. But without moving an inch, Alex says, "Just because I took you to see Patti Smith, doesn't mean I forgive you."

Forgive me? For what? I pull my hand away, without a word. As I roll onto my back, the wrinkling sound of the duvet reverberates through the room. I close my eyes and focus on the bed linen caressing my body. But tonight it doesn't feel very soft.

SIX

As I open my mouth to yawn, my lips disengage like Velcro. The bedroom window is ajar. Our avocado-green cotton curtains flutter in a brief warm zephyr. I cock my head. I listen. If I were a cat, my ears would twitch as I interpret the time through the rhythm of traffic sounds below—a few swift travelling sighs, but no horns, or beeping garbage trucks yet.

It's quiet for a Saturday morning, so it must be early. My hand reaches for the mobile phone on the bedside table like an uncoordinated sea lion's flipper. It's only 7:30 and Alex has already gotten out of bed. I sometimes wonder whether he avoids waking me on purpose—to be alone. I've tried myself, but failed.

Saturdays for Alex are just as busy as every other day, if not more so—especially if he has an event planned for the evening. But as far as I can remember, he should be free tonight. Maybe Heather can look after Tessa so we can finish that conversation. Perhaps if we have the opportunity to vociferously disgrace each other like two squabbling Tasmanian Devils, we'll end up having a civilized chat. Right or wrong, it always works that way.

I prop pillows up behind me and lever my cumbersome and languid body backward against the head board. Pushing my knotted hair out of my face and rubbing sharp sleep from my eyes, I wonder what Tessa is up to. It's supposed to be my day off today from work and from care giving. Alex promised he'd entertain Tessa on his own so that I could have at least one day every other week with no responsibilities calling for my immediate attention. We did, however, organize this six days ago. I wouldn't be surprised if he has forgotten, because all I can hear is Alex's muffled aggressive Greek shouting and his thick heavy footsteps pacing back and forth.

"I've ridden *all* around Exarchia and I can't see even *one* fucking poster for The Incredible String Band … Where? *Where* have you stuck them? … Don't you fucking lie to me, you— What? That's bullshit!"

"Papa—"

"Not now sweetie, go play with your dolls."

Tessa's complying feet trot back to her bedroom. She mumbles something I can't make out and then something ricochets off her wall.

I get up and put on my white terrycloth robe. It smells like mould; week-old damp cloth. I thought Alex said he'd washed them. Or perhaps he just washed *his*.

I shuffle into my flip flops and make my way to the kitchen. But instead of heading straight for the percolator to make a coffee, I'm confronted with a Coco Pop tip. Along with Tessa's half-eaten Coco Pop, muesli and strawberry yoghurt concoction is a scattered mixture of cereal all over the table and floor. Again. He left Tessa to fend for herself—again.

I grab the brush and pan from under the sink. My head throbs from front to back like a pendulum as I bend over—a blatant reminder that my stress is not going to dwindle merely because it is the weekend. Weekend stress is like your airline losing your luggage on the way to a secluded holiday resort. When you arrive, you still want to enjoy yourself, to relax, but you can't. Want to take a swim? Well, sorry, you'll have to swim in your skanky underwear.

Once I clean up the mess, and prepare coffee, I walk by Tessa's bedroom to make sure she isn't sulking. Of course she's not sulking, she is cutting off her favourite doll's hair.

I contemplate trying to stop her, fearing a possible scissor hazard mostly, but then decide against it when I realize she's cutting away from herself like I taught her. An odd grin contorts her face as if she's been possessed by Chucky. Is she enjoying it? It's either that, or she's using it as a voodoo doll to exonerate her frustration toward Alex for dismissing her. *Hmm*. Like grandmother, like mother, like daughter.

I grab the morning paper Alex left on the small mahogany table in the hall and make my way into the lounge where Alex is texting on his phone, facing toward the balcony.

"Morning," I gurgle, rattling the paper about, trying to turn it inside out at the Holiday Packages section.

Alex raises his brow and hand in reply without making eye contact. Every time Alex ignores me I experience a brief moment of asphyxiation, as if I've poked my head into a room of smoke. Despite this, I say to myself, *Don't let it bother you. It's your day. And you're not going to let anyone ruin it for you. Sit back. Relax. Read a book. Treat yourself to a proper coffee from down the street. Take the dog for a walk in the park. Collect some pinecones. Make some decorations with Tessa. Remove your mind from this rotten routine.*

I sit on the couch, crossing my legs like a child on the floor at kindergarten, imaginary earplugs in place, and tongue in position to inadvertently slip out of the side of my mouth when I see something interesting while scanning the Holiday Packages section—a habit I haven't been able to kick since my mother's newfound career as a travel agent. I like to snoop. To see the prices of the packages she scores commission from. It gives me an idea of what kind of money she's making. And how much I'm not. *How did everything turn out so good for her? Whatever happened to karma?*

Alex puts his phone in the back pocket of his tailored black pants, spreads his legs apart like a bouncer, and crosses his arms in front of the Ramones logo on his T-shirt.

"Clothes on the line. Pasta on the stove. Do something about it. You know I hate things lying around when I've got business to do," he says in a tone so cold I can hardly recognize his voice. He turns his back to me and gazes out of the window. He pulls his phone from his pocket—again—and begins to type. Click, click, click on the keypad like boiled candy against teeth. *Who is he constantly messaging?*

I glare at the back of his head. If my eyes could emit an electric current I'm sure I'd render him unconscious. My nostrils flare as I clench down on the back of my jaw.

"Let me drink my coffee," I reply in an indifferent tone despite how I feel. "And then I'll do it." *If I have to control my temper any longer I'm gonna need to smash a window.* Maybe I am going to turn out like my mother, after all. Maybe I'll lose it, just like she did, like the day she hit herself over the head several times with a frying pan to make herself pass out—to escape reality—to "sleep through the shit."

"Hurry up and drink it then. I can't work with this mess around me. You know that."

I clear my throat. I want to ask how he can live with Coco Pops scattered liked confetti around the kitchen but not with the clothes hanging on the line where he can't even see them. But I won't. *Rise above, Melody, rise above.* "Er, sorry, but could you just put yourself in my shoes for a minute and try to realize that I need some time to chill out? Tessa is calmly playing on her own, the dog isn't whining and whacking the glass doors with her filthy paws, and it's Saturday—the day you promised I could have to myself. Remember?"

Alex exhales slowly from his nose, lips pressed together, and stomps out of the room and into the kitchen. I can hear him scrape the chairs on the floor as he pushes them under the table. He crashes crockery in the sink. The pantry squeaks as he swings it open and it slams shut with an elastic flick. He throws the pasta into the trash, then the pot in the sink. Something breaks. He yells, "Fuck!" I hang my head in my hands and wonder when the hell he is going to snap out of this. *What is going on? Is this some sort of mid-life crisis?*

"Mummy, Mummy!" Tessa wails as she runs into the lounge with tears streaming down her cheeks. "She's ugly! Look, Francis is ugly!"

"Oh honey." I look at the doll. It looks like David Bowie on a bad hair day. "Let me help Daddy clean up a bit and then we'll go and have a look for a new doll." I take her left hand and massage her palm with my thumb. "Okay?"

Seemingly satisfied with this answer, she skips back to her room, to probably mutilate Francis even more.

"What does she need a new doll for?" Alex yells above his racket from the kitchen. "She has plenty."

I get up and walk to the kitchen doorway, chanting in my head to stay calm. There must be *something* going on with Alex that he isn't telling me. Can this temperamental behaviour seriously stem from what happened yesterday morning? All I was doing was voicing what I want out of life. How is that a crime?

"She was giving it a makeover and now she doesn't like the way it looks," I say, picking at a fingernail, as if I'm having a casual conversation with Heather at a café.

"Don't. Buy. Her. A new doll. She should to *learn* to take *care* of her stuff. If you buy her a new one, she'll never value anything," Alex growls as he shakes a breakfast bowl in my face.

I lean backward and frown, looking for the gentle twinkle that is usually in his eyes no matter what mood he is in. But I can't see anything except my fishbowl reflection in their watery sheen. They're like double-glazed windows. You can see through them, but you can't hear what's happening on the other side.

"Sorry," he whispers, stepping back a little. He looks at the bowl in his hand, as if he has no idea how it got there, before putting it in the cupboard.

I move toward the sink to help him with the dishes, but he raises his hand like a policeman directing traffic.

"I'll do it. You have your, er, 'day off'."

I pull out a chair and sit at the kitchen table. I crush a runaway Coco Pop with my right index finger, and then lick it off. Alex is right about the doll. I know he's right. But I also remember how I felt when I destroyed my Barbie dolls as a kid—when I turned them into punk goddesses, with a pair of blunt nail scissors, green food dye, and a purple glitter pen.

"Alex, I did the same thing as a child. I know how it feels to regret experimenting with my toys and then realizing I liked them better the way they were. I'm sorry, but I'm not going to argue about it." I put my hands in the pockets of my robe, not knowing what to do with them on the table top.

"Fine. Do whatever you like. But if you're gonna buy bullshit, use your own money," he says, putting on the rubber dishwashing gloves.

"And why wouldn't I? And *why* is that even an *issue*?" I retort, craning my neck.

Alex doesn't respond.

"Alex. We need to talk about yesterday morning."

Alex tsks and shrugs. I glare at his back as he fills the kitchen sink with suds.

"Fine," I say. "Have it your way." I get up and walk down the corridor to get dressed.

"Take your keys," Alex calls, "I might not be here when you get back."

I pause, balancing myself with one hand against the corridor wall, staring at an oil stain on the carpet. "Where are you going?"

"Out."

"Where out?"

"Just out."

SEVEN

In a department store called Jumbo, the aroma of plastic purity reminds me of all the toys my parents could never afford to buy me as a child; when I would look over at the girl next to me in class, holding a "Li'l Miss Make-up" for show-and-tell, and I'd be there with the matchstick man my father helped me glue together over the weekend.

The scent of brand new calms me like a quaff of vodka as Tessa and I stroll down the aisle of stuffed toys. I drag my fingers over a row of toddler-sized zebras like a schoolboy bouncing his hand along a stranger's picket fence. The fluffy material used nowadays seems a lot softer than when I was a kid. My teddy bear felt like a heavy woollen sweater. But these feel like they're made from kitten fur.

"Mummy, I want *that* doll," Tessa says, standing on her tiptoes when we reach the shelf displaying a vast array of porcelain dolls. She points to the biggest, most frilly, and through my eyes, the most *breakable* doll on the shelf. My body stiffens when I see the price: *89 Euros!* Saliva spawns behind my molars like water through a squirt gun. Do I let myself make decisions based on my mood now? If I wasn't angry at Alex would I be averse to such a large purchase, or would I buy it with the enthusiasm Tessa craves?

"Honey, you, er, don't want that doll," I say, holding a closed fist to my lips as if about to cough.

"Yes, I doo-*o-o*!" Tessa replies jiggling about on the spot like wobbling jelly on speed.

"Of course you don't." I manage a tight-lipped smile and flick my head in some sort of attempt at a shake.

"I do!" Tessa puts her hands on her hips and looks at me as if she is saying, *Don't be ridiculous, Mummy. How would you know what I want and don't want?*

"I'll tell you why you don't want it. 'Cause our Doggy is going to like this doll too, and because it is too big to fit in your toy drawer, we'll have to keep it on the shelf. You know what that means don't you?"

"No." Tessa shakes her head, hands still on hips, and narrows her eyes like she's performing in a pantomime and addressing someone in the back row of the audience. An acute urge to put my foot down without any further discussion and say, "Too bad, take a small doll or no doll at all," sends needle-and-pin-like adrenaline through my limbs. I swallow and massage the bridge of my nose. *Please don't make this day harder than it already is.*

I kneel down to Tessa's eye level. "It means that Doggy will eat her. You don't want this poor doll to die, do you?" The image of my mother pulling the head off Lissy, my one and only life-sized baby doll, when I was five, flashes before me like a shorting lamppost in heavy rain.

"No," Tessa whispers, pouting her lips in thought.

"Okay, then. If you don't want this beautiful doll to die, you're going to have to leave her in the shop and choose another doll that will fit in your toy drawer, okay?"

Tessa frowns, then smiles like she has just caught onto the fact that I'm talking nonsense. She responds with another no and this time she sounds more sure of herself.

"No?" I ask, almost touching my chin to my chest and raising my brow.

"I'm not a silly duffer anymore, Mummy. I'm four. I'm big. Dolls can't die! That's silly." She snorts as if it's the most ridiculous thing she's ever heard. "If Doggy eats her, we can just come here again and get another one!"

I visualize Alex shaking his head and finger in my face. *I told you so.*

"Well, *noooo*. You can't just get a new one, honey," I say, trying to sound rational and in control. "Today is a special day. If this doll breaks, I will decide when you can get a new one … *if* you will get a new one. Deal?" *Did I just agree to buy the doll?*

Tessa scrunches up her nose, looks at the ceiling for a few seconds, puts her dainty right hand out to shake, and nods, "Deal."

When we arrive home, Tessa runs around the entire apartment looking for Alex to show off her new doll. But he's gone.

"Where's Papa?" she asks, with a hint of desperation in her voice.

"I think he's got some errands to run in town," I say, hoping it's a fact. I throw my handbag on the couch as if it reeks of garlic breath. "He'll be back later." I push paranoid thoughts to the side of my mind like Tessa pushes her vegetables to the side of her plate—at a psychologically tolerable distance from immediate view. Tessa replies with a little sigh and a forced pout.

"It's okay, Mummy," she nods. "I can go and play on my own."

I watch her, jaw agape, skip down the corridor and close her bedroom door a little *too* hard. The door handle falls off. It lands on the carpet with a thud. *Great. Another thing to fix.*

Rejection hits me like an unexpected fall. I flop onto the couch—listen to the distant dragging of Tessa's toy drawer—stare at an old cigarette burn in the armrest, reminding myself that Alex isn't really as selfish as he seems sometimes. I should cut him some slack. He quit smoking when I asked him to. He stopped inviting his cocaine-snorting best mate over to the house. He even promised to stop coming home drunk after his events. And he kept his word without a single complaint.

Silence endows the room with a lonesome hum and the echo of emptiness amplifies the quieter it gets. I need to make some noise; enough to bulldoze an exit into this dead-end alley, giving free reign to a new and undiscovered highway; to hear the bang of success fill a stadium like a thunderous bass drum beating the rhythm of risk.

What if I *am* offered the position in London? Would success really resonate as loud as I imagine it would? Can relocating to London really give me the opportunity to pursue everything I want?

It doesn't feel like it anymore. What if my outburst of

forged confidence yesterday morning really is the cause of Alex's behaviour today? And why won't he talk about it? Why can't we come to some sort of compromise?

As I walk past our bedroom to make myself a sandwich, I catch a glimpse of my black guitar case in the corner, collecting dust like wooden floorboards in a deserted weatherboard hut; abandoned like an old filing cabinet, storing years of written documentation I feel I ought to keep but will never need to refer to again. How could I have left it sitting there, untouched, for the last *four* years?

If I pick it up now, will regret reach a boiling point? Or will the vibrating strings stab me like an adrenaline shot in the heart, reviving the passion that once pumped blood through my veins? Will one pluck me from life as I know it, with no option to turn back?

There is a line that separates reality from reality lost, and when I'm alone, I can see the line as clear and straight and taut as the strings on my guitar. Do I take this opportunity to step over it? Or will that first step plunge me into some other desperate version of my life that I'll eventually want to escape? What if nothing will ever please me?

I walk into the bedroom and stare at my guitar case, propped up vertically against the wall. I run my forefinger along the top—the ridged black vinyl surface. A thick layer of dust renders my fingertip dark gray. I grab a pair of underwear from my drawer, dust the case off, and lay it flat on the bed. I unfasten the three chrome latches. They pop open, one by one. I lift the lid. I can see the reflection of my arm in its shiny jet-black body. Its stunning mother-of-pearl inlay still makes me giddy.

I used to admire my second-hand Maton acoustic as if it were a rare antique chair—contemplating its remarkable existence and all the generations of people who might have used it. And knowing that no matter how many times people might walk past the window it is displayed in, appreciating its beauty and its universal and durable function, it will one day be purchased again, find a new home, and will happily sacrifice its lull to forego another few more generations of use.

But this time I look at my guitar, and I'm afraid that if I don't pick it up soon, I will *never* pick it up again. I fear that *I'll* become a rare antique chair—but one that has been inaccurately valued and misguidedly put in the trash. But I'm also afraid to pick it up, because that will be the moment I rebuild my body around my soul—the moment when I know, there will be no turning back, and my life will never be the same. The beginning of a new beginning, or the beginning of the end?

I stare at it for a few moments longer, wishing I could get a handle on these feelings. If I were an outsider looking in, I'd probably want to slap myself in the face. Tell myself to *Get a grip*, that I'm being whiny, irrational, weak. "All words and no action." *My mother was right.*

I'm about to admit defeat and fling the guitar case shut—to close the lid on a world I once knew and try to forget it even existed, but when I hear Tessa singing, "Sugar pie, honey bunch …" I stop. It's our family song. Alex and I used to sing it to each other when Tessa was in my womb. I haven't joined in since …

I lift the guitar out of its case as if heavy handling might cause it to crumble. I bring it close to my face and breathe in the warm wholesome scent of Brazilian rosewood. I sit on my bed and press my fingers to the strings forming a C chord—the first note of "*Sugar Pie Honey Bunch*", and strum with my right thumb. Somehow the rest of the chords swim to my fingertips like fish to food.

Tessa runs into the bedroom with a huge smile on her face and starts jumping up and down and singing along. But her sweet bird-like voice summons such melancholy that a deep heavy moan comes out of my mouth instead of song. It starts in my chest, like I've just been winded, moves to my stomach, to my head, then throbs behind my face. I want to scream out the hurt, but when I open my mouth— nothing—like a silent film with a distressing script.

Tessa's singing trails off into short unknowing sobs. "Mummy?" she whispers, barely moving her lips. A small bubble of saliva escapes from the corner of her mouth. She blinks a few times as a frown taints her thick soft eyebrows. I put the guitar down and take a deep breath, clutching at my ribcage, trying to swallow the rotten air that spreads regret and misery through my body. Depression. Is it hereditary? I'd rather have dementia, at least then I would quickly forget this is happening. I thought I'd gotten through this as a teen. I thought I'd kicked it for good.

I do *not* want to experience how my mother felt. I do *not* want to breathe her pain. I do not want to live in a world full of irrational ups and downs that stem from barren seeds—from defective rationale. I need reasons for my feelings. I *can't* spend my life clutching at imaginary strings to get me through these debilitating mood swings, to sooth a pain with no source. *I can't. There has to be a way out of this grave.*

I curl up into a foetal position on the bed and pull a pillow over my face. I cry into it, sniffing in the scent of Alex's aftershave. I quiver as I try to breathe steadily through the ache.

Tessa rests her soft cold cheek on my shoulder blade, curling up with me, in silence, as if she understands. But how could she? How could she possibly understand?

Shame on you! Shame on you for letting your emotions run rampant in front of Tessa! How could I put her through the same torment I went through watching my mother break down all those times? I can't let her feel the pain I felt.

When I was a kid, I could sit and watch my mother yell and scream for hours, keep my mouth shut and my heart closed. But when she cried, it hurt me more than all those sharp slaps to my face. It hurt me more to see her in pain—the type of pain nobody could see—the type of pain nobody could understand except me.

I hated my mother for everything. I hated the fact that she even existed. But as I grew up—as I get older still—the memory of her expressing that invisible pain is what makes me die inside—little by little, day by day, an inch of me dies for every tear she shed—for every moment her pain crossed over to me like a cursed family heirloom.

I never wanted to subject Tessa to this. But I just did.

I roll over on my side and look Tessa in the eyes. Her

eyes search mine. For answers? For comfort? For a way she doesn't yet know to express how she feels? I wipe away my tears and run my fingers through her hair. She smiles as if forgiving me.

"Blossom, I'm going to have a shower," I gurgle, trying to control my fluctuating voice. I get up, get undressed, grab a towel out of the wardrobe and wrap it around myself, hoping I haven't flagged the beginning of Tessa's emotional demise.

"Do you want me to fix you some yoghurt, fruit and honey and pop a movie on?" I ask, in overstated mirth.

Tessa nods enthusiastically, but slows it down as though unsure if that kind of mood is allowed.

"Okay, up you get!" I chirp, and clap my hands. "Let's go and choose one together. I'll pop it on, and you can watch it while I make your yoghurt and have a shower, so you don't have to wait around, okay?" I turn to walk toward the lounge room, but Tessa tugs on my towel.

"Mummy?"

"Hmm?" I look down and realize she has tears in her eyes. I sit on the floor, cross my legs, and cup her face in my hands. "What's up, sugar pie? There's no need to be sad. Mummy's fine."

"I ... I wuv you, Mummy," she says and falls into my lap, wrapping her arms around my waist.

"I love you too, sweetheart," I whisper. "More than you know." *More than you'll ever understand.*

When Alex comes home later in the afternoon, Tessa and I are asleep, curled up together on the couch. The first thing I see when I open my eyes are Alex's feet in his heavy-duty black boots. Still. As if posing for a photograph. Or contemplating which way to turn. I don't look up when he moves closer. I don't even follow his feet when they exit my line of sight.

He sits next to us and strokes my hair. His breath is heavy. The elevator must still be broken. *He deserves it … No. He doesn't deserve it. That's … that's just spiteful.* Tessa squirms, but doesn't wake up.

Alex whispers, "You played guitar."

I nod. My hair crunches against my ear.

"Did I leave it on the bed?" I croak, still not making eye contact.

Alex takes my chin, moves my head around and looks into my eyes.

"What?" I mouth, twitching my head from his grasp. He bends down and kisses an escaping tear from my cheek. I want to smack his head away. Make his nose bleed. I want to tell him he's a selfish asshole and to leave me alone, that he can't just give me a kiss and expect everything to be all right again. Or, if he can't do that, to explain what the *hell* is going on in his life to cause his behaviour to fluctuate so much. I want to know why he seems to hate me. I want to know why I hate *him*. And how I can make it stop. I want know what happened to our happy marriage.

"We have to talk," I whisper, trying to sit up without waking Tessa. "We have to—"

Alex puts his fingers to my lips, nods his head, and kisses me between my eyes. He smells sweaty. His stubble scrapes my nose. I want to stick my tongue into his mouth. Fuck my anger away. Treat him like a one-night stand. Then throw a couple-hundred Euros on his bedside table and walk out without saying goodbye. Then I want to have a long hot shower. Scrub away the dirt, the pain, the frustration—my irrational despair. Then call him and ask him out on a date. To start again. Without a past.

"We'll talk. But later. For now, I've got cake." Alex holds a plastic bag up in the air. "You want?"

Right here. Right now. Another moment I have to bite my tongue. Tomorrow is Alex's birthday. The tenth of May. Now it's time for me to behave.

Tessa sits up. "Yes please, Papa!" She looks as fresh as ever. How do kids manage that?

"Hey, pumpkin, you have a nice sleep?" Alex asks.

"Yep! I made Mummy better, Papa. I made her watch a movie with me," Tessa says, swaying her head side-to-side in satisfaction.

"Yes, you did, pumpkin. Thank you. Mummy's much better now." Alex strokes Tessa's cheek and flashes me an inquisitive glance fringed with disapproval. My gut sinks at the thought of Tessa seeing that ridiculous display of emotion earlier. *Don't worry, Alex. I disapprove too. I'm working on it.*

The phone rings.

"You want me to get it?" Alex asks.

"No, I'll get it," I say, pushing my hair behind my ears.

Alex leads Tessa into the kitchen to slice the cake, while I head for the phone. I feel a little dizzy, and trip over a raised corner of the red-and-black striped rug. I regain my balance by catching my fall against the bookshelf. I pick up the phone.

"So where are we going to celebrate?" my mother, Betty, asks before I've pressed the receiver to my ear.

"How about, 'Hello, Melody, it's Mum,' first?" I reply with a scoff. My head starting to throb.

"Hello, Melody, it's Mum first. So where are we going to celebrate? Should we go out to that great Oriental restaurant you took me to last time I was in Athens? James and I can catch the last ferry over and then perhaps stay the night. Just make sure your spare room isn't full of dog hair like the last time. I didn't stop sneezing for over a week."

"Mum. It's Alex's turn to celebrate. We aren't celebrating together. Remember? We're going to celebrate alone."

"Alone? You have to invite us. It's my birthday too."

"We had an agreement, Mum."

"Yes, but that was on the condition that we all celebrated together."

"We never agreed to anything like that. Anyway, if that were the condition, then what was the point in agreeing to alternate celebrating years?"

"The point was that the other person shouldn't expect a gift or the birthday wishes. I thought I made that clear."

"I still don't understand how that's a reason to make such an agreement, Mum. It's easy for me to give you a gift and wish you happy birthday. That I do, regardless of whose turn it is. The point was to be able to choose how you want to celebrate it without feeling obligated to involve the other party."

"Yes, but when it's my turn, I always invite you."

"Yeah, but that's your choice."

"Melody, of course I'd invite you. You're my *family*."

"Yes, I know I'm your family, but Alex has family too, you know."

"No he doesn't. He's a bloody orphan."

I grit my teeth, praying I don't spurt out something I might regret and set her off on a verbal rampage.

"Me and *Tessa* are his family, Mum." My lips pop from pressing them together too hard.

"So why can't you *tell* him to invite James and me?"

"Because it's against the agreement!"

"How can you be so ungrateful?"

"Ungrateful? For what? Alex only celebrates his birthday every two years. *You* should be grateful. Alex gives up his birthday every other year for *you* to celebrate with *me*. And I don't even want to most of the time. But Alex *makes* me do it. For *you*." *Shit. Melody, stop!*

"Oh, you un*grate*ful, *self*ish little bitch. How *dare* you? Wish *Alex* a *happy* birthday. And clean the spare room for next weekend. We're staying over."

And with that she hangs up. I put the phone down, lean against the wall and close my eyes. My limbs melt into the floor.

Selfish little bitch.
Selfish little bitch.
Selfish little bitch …

A potent tangy chocolate orange scent wafts by my nose.

"Cake?"

Startled by Tessa's voice, I flick my eyes open. She's holding a slice of cake in front of my face with a purple party napkin. She sits down next to me on the rug and crosses her legs.

"Cool. Picnic." She breaks a chunk of cake off the slice and holds it to my mouth. "Here. I'll feed you." She giggles, wriggling with joy, the chocolate orange goo squishing between her tiny pink fingertips. I smile, and open my mouth. Tessa feeds me the cake and scrapes her fingers on my bottom teeth to make sure it all goes in.

The cake is soft like hot fudge on my tongue. The walls of my mouth grow moist. I take a deep breath as I chew, the flavour soothing me like eucalyptus to a congested nose.

Simple pleasures. You keep forgetting the simple pleasures. And that life is so much better than it used to be.

eight

Three pieces of cake later, I am numbed into submission. With every piece, my thoughts became clearer and clearer, as if I was participating in a new wave three-step program to sanity.

Cake one: *Do something about this marriage. You didn't fall in love with Alex without reason. Find out what it is again. I know that right now you love Alex like a limp, burnt, and grey slither of cigarette ash. So what? With the right attitude, there is someone inside you, who might be able to take the ash, use it to give your relationship a polish, and make it shine like antique silver cutlery. So tell Alex to pitch in with sprucing up the silver of your marriage or it's over.*

Cake two: *Ask him to get you a gig. Serena is right. Stop clutching onto regret like it's a security blanket. Because, that's what this marriage has become, hasn't it, Melody? A security blanket? And as long as you clutch onto it, you give yourself the excuse to behave like a mental patient and wallow in unjustified sorrow. Stop it. No more.*

Cake three: *Talk to him about the promotion and don't let him walk all over you. Discuss it like responsible adults, and make Alex realize that it's not the promotion that's the problem, but rather the fact that you didn't say anything about it for a whole year, and now he's angry because you just expect him to jump. But don't forget to emphasize the fact that you jump when he says "jump." So of course you expect him to jump. It could very well save you. Insist that he stop intimidating you with his temper and he help you crawl out of this miserable rut—support your needs—then yes—your marriage may very well be saved.*

Alex suggests we go out to dinner tonight. If not to celebrate his birthday, then to do something nice together, as a family, before we talk. Excellent. I get to live like Alex—sit, get served, eat, get waited on, drink, watch the mess magically disappear from the table—even if it is just for a couple of hours, it's a blessing I do not take for granted. So yes, I'd *love* to go out to eat, even if it is a means to manipulate me.

We arrive at our favourite restaurant, which is around the corner from our apartment. It's a jazzed-up version of a traditional Greek tavern, surrounded in bottle-green plastic grapevines and decorated with miniature, moulded, melted, morphed cutlery in wooden frames, which seems to be an art form the Greeks have recently discovered and think is trendy. But I remember, twenty-odd years ago, when people were hanging bent cutlery mobiles in their back yards—and they'd chime in the breeze. I'd sing harmonies to them. My mother said I sounded like a stoned hippy bluffing a Buddhist chant.

Bill, our faithful waiter, seats the three of us by the window looking into the beer garden. I feel at ease here—a place where the waiters don't judge our parenting abilities if Tessa decides to spit out her food and throw a tantrum. This, on many occasions, has happened if her food isn't 99% sugar.

Bill walks by with a tray of someone else's meal—meatballs in rich tomato sauce and red wine. I breathe it in as if standing all alone in a field of tomatoes. The aroma reminds me of the night I introduced Alex to my parents. My mother cooked, a rare occurrence. But when she does, you'd think she's been a chef all her life. Another item on her long list of skills she boasts about.

James, my father, turned into a schoolboy discussing common favourite 1970s psychedelic rock bands with Alex. It was the first time in years I'd seen him move his hands so much. They are usually squashed between his crossed legs in silent languor masked by a lacking yet compelling smile.

My mother could hardly get a word in all night. Tight-lipped, she watched my father and Alex chatter away as if she didn't even exist. She slipped in a few comments about the music she'd been working on now and again. But my father's eyes glazed over as if blocking her voice out entirely when Alex humoured her for a few moments before continuing their conversation. Then she glanced over at me, as if I could somehow steer the conversation towards her again. But I didn't even try. I was silently thrilled. I'd finally found a man that didn't let her steal the limelight. I was proud to be with him. *When did that fade?*

"New mee-alls," sings Alex in faltering English, looking at the menu and moving his eyebrows up and down as if a mystery were unfolding. "You see anything interesting?"

I smile as if rehearsing a scene for a movie—a frame of mind I often adopt in situations where I need to be sociable, happy, on good behaviour—when life needs to be a 2D picture; a view of what only rises to the surface of the polluted pond.

Tessa looks up at me as if preparing to laugh, to join in on the joke, without really understanding why.

"Should I order the 'Lamp In Lemon Sauce'?" I reply in an aristocratic British accent, as if reading from a script.

"Yeah, that'll be *loight*," replies Alex in his best attempt at my Australian twang.

I exhale a one-way scoff as Alex shakes up and down with forced silent laughter. He must have prepared the response when he saw it on the menu. He tickles Tessa's neck and she brings her shoulder to her ear as she chuckles.

I appreciate him trying to smooth out the tension, and I know that he had a fun afternoon taking care of Tessa, while I sat in the bathtub surrounded by scented candles, listening to Joni Mitchell.

Does he really think it's that easy? Does he really think clowning around is going to make everything all right?

"What about the 'Beef with Wine and Beetroot Compost'," Alex asks. His mischievous stare burns through my forehead like sun rays shining through a magnifying glass.

"Er … not the 'Rubbit With Onions'?" I ask, not at all amused by the mistake. How can I be? I edit when I eat, sleep, clean, drive, anywhere my eyes pass by text of any kind. I can't even read the ingredients on a juice box without finding mistakes. I see mistakes on street signs, on junk mail, even on TV commercials. I'm over it. They're not funny anymore. All it does is remind me of how disorganized and incompetent the majority of the Greek corporate population is. For instance, if you want to hire an architect to design your dream home, don't expect the house to remain upright through its first heavy storm unless *you've* learnt how to do the architect's job and guided him through the process yourself.

Alex breathes inward through his teeth as if a football has hit him in the groin and his face twists like someone stuck a straw too far up his nostril. I raise my eyebrows, thinking I might laugh, but no … the sensation doesn't move beyond the slight clench in my throat.

"Find any other good ones?"

"Nope," I pop. "Only a crappy grammatical error."

Alex grins from behind his menu like a bald middle-aged pixie. All I can see are his puffy cheeks and how much deeper the wrinkles around his eyes look. Tessa gazes at him in awe—her eyes glowing like marbles in sunbeams. Alex is her king. And he knows it. I sometimes wonder whether he uses it to his advantage.

"Mummy, what's crappy grammatical err-ah mean?" Tessa kicks the leg of the table in two/two rhythm, making the cutlery rattle and wet rings form around the bases of our glasses.

"Tessa, *please* sit still. We're in public. We need to behave a little better than we do at home, okay?" I say, rubbing and squeezing her knee.

The old lady, in black widow's attire, sitting at the table next to us offers a kind, shaky smile.

"Why?" Tessa asks as if this is the first time she's heard me say such a thing. The kicking comes to a halt as she crosses her arms so high on her chest they are almost touching her chin.

I roll my eyes, unfold my napkin, lay it on my lap, and straighten the crooked cutlery around my plate with flared nostrils and a huff. I feel like I'm miming a whinnying horse.

"We've spoken about this before, remember?" I say.

The old lady opens her napkin and lays it in her lap too. She winks at Tessa and gestures for her to do the same thing. Tessa smiles and copies her.

"Anyway, grammatical error just means mistake," I add, "with words."

"And crappy?" Tessa asks still staring at the old lady who has now diverted her attention toward the other people at her table.

"Um, it means bad." I take Tessa's chin and turn her head to face me. "But, please don't use it. It's a bad word."

"It's a *crappy* word." An audacious grin emerges from ear to ear as Tessa slaps her hands on her knees, just like Alex often does.

"Yes, but *please* don't use it. It's not nice. *I* shouldn't have used it." I hold out my hand. "Come on, give me a little smack and say, 'naughty Mummy'."

Before tapping me lightly on my fingers, she looks to Alex for what seems to be approval. He nods, she giggles.

My stomach sinks. I look into my lap—my face burns from the pressure of ... *jealousy? You're winning her away from me.*

Bill approaches our table to take our order.

"Sorry, Bill, could you giv'us another coupla minutes?"

"Of course, Mrs. Me-low-dy," replies Bill with a courteous torso nod and a step backward.

We asked him to call us by our first names when we started to regularly dine here, but I guess he thinks it's disrespectful, and so compromised.

As Bill turns to leave, Alex interjects, "*Den chriazete,*" nodding upward and raising his eyebrows toward the ceiling—a typical, abrupt and insipid Greek gesture for no. "*Ferte mas ta synithizmena.*"

Bill glances at me in question. I snap my menu closed and nod in defeated affirmation.

"What's the problem?" I whisper when Bill leaves. "I don't feel like eating the *usual* stuff we order. I wanted something from the specials board."

A melee of Alex's past offenses flood my mind. I'm on the brink of reeling them off like verbal inventory, but then realize I'm overreacting. Again.

"Sorry! I didn't realize. You didn't seem bothered. Just thought I'd save Bill the trouble. I'll go change the order. What did you want?"

I don't know. I don't particularly like what's on the specials board now that I think about it. "Don't worry," I sigh, flicking my hand in front of me. "Next time."

"You sure?" Alex asks.

"Yeah. Don't worry about it."

I reach for my glass of water, but Alex takes my hand mid-air. It's warm, gentle, reverent. He lowers our joined hands to the table and holds my stare. An ambivalent sadness imbues his gaze. Melancholy, nostalgia—disappointment? Everything. *Hope*.

"We'll make this work," Alex whispers, certifying the compromise with a blink. The corner of his mouth twitches as if he were about to smile, but changed his mind.

"I need to go pee-pee," Tessa says, pushing her skirt between her legs.

"I'll take her." Alex lets go of my hand and jumps out of his seat.

"No, it's okay. I'll go."

"Don't be stupid. Sit. Relax." Alex is already out of his seat and helping Tessa out of hers. As they walk to the washroom hand in hand, Tessa jumps up and down, tugging and bouncing his arm around like a skipping rope.

As they disappear from view, I begin to map out my speech in my head. Tonight we'll talk. *I'll* talk. Tonight I will say what I should have said a *long* long time ago.

N1Ne

"Sweet dreams say the jelly beans, it's time to sleep, that means," sings Tessa wriggling her feet beneath her duvet.

"Nighty-night says the little mite, then switches off the light." I tuck Tessa in, hooking her new doll under her arm. The purple nightlight illuminates the left side of her face as if impregnating her with knowledge. A lorry rumbles below. Binweed, the homeless fairy Tessa claims to have found refuge inside her bed frame, was sure to feel the vibrations.

"Lights off at freckle o'clock, okay?" I tap my wrist. Tessa nods and kisses her doll on its head as I walk out of her room. I leave the door open a crack.

Alex suggests we retire early to watch a movie in bed. Another thing we haven't done in a while, which I love to do. He's making an effort. So why are you wishing he wasn't? *So you can stay angry with him for neglecting you and break free from this dire world of domesticity? Maybe you should just let him be nice? You might actually remember why you fell in love with him in the first place.*

In bed, Alex lies flat on his back and presses play on the remote control. Deep bass and fast-paced electronic intro music fills the room like a mortal roaring gust of wind. *Great. Action Adventure. Ugh.* I cuddle up to Alex on my side, and nuzzle my head into his neck. *Why do you keep using Tessa's shampoo? You have no hair.* I lift my head to kiss his cheek out of habit. The grey shade of stubble contrasts against his pale, olive-tinged skin—the result of spending half his life in dark, soundproofed, underground rock venues, and the other half in front of his laptop.

Through a medium-thick coat of curly greying chest hair, I focus on a film of dust settling on our jet black cotton sheets. In an instant, I imagine creepy-crawlies making a snug home under my skin and shudder at the thought. I *hate* black sheets. You can see *everything.* When I get into bed I feel like I'm wrapping myself up in a used vacuum cleaner bag. But they were the only clean set this week, so they had to do.

"Can I turn the light off?" I ask. *If I can't see the dust, maybe I can relax and pretend it's not there.*

Alex nods, switches off the orange-tinted light by the bed, kisses my head, and increases the TV volume.

I listen to the opening dialogue as if it were background noise. I press my eyes together. Tight. Trying to picture myself on stage. Willing myself to speak up. Now. Before the movie starts properly. Psychedelic colours form beneath my eyelids—a cocktail of animals and Jesus. I smile—an involuntary reaction. My face flushes with brief content-ment lying in Alex's arms, breathing out and in to the rhythm of the soundtrack. *I love you. I hate you. I love to hate you. I hate to love you. I'm scared.*

"You sleeping?" Alex murmurs.

I open my eyes. My lashes brush against his jaw. "Nope. Just relaxing."

"What about the film?"

"You know I don't like action stuff."

"Why are we watching it then?"

"Because you wanted to watch it."

"Why didn't you say you didn't want to watch it?"

"Didn't bother me. I just like lying here."

Alex sniffs outward and rubs my back. *It's now or never, Melody. Do it while you've got the nerve.* I slide the remote control from Alex's grasp and press Pause.

"What's up?"

"Before we get sucked into this movie, we should really have this talk."

"Now?" he whines. "But I made it clear we'd work it out. Let's talk about details tomorrow. Can't we just enjoy this quiet time together?" We both sit up. Alex strokes my cheek and leans in for a kiss. I put my hand on his chest. His chest hair spreads between my fingers; his heart beat warms my nerves.

"You'd *said* we'd talk later. *Now* is *later*."

Alex grunts, pushes his back against the headboard and runs his hands over his face as if brushing off a cobweb. He takes a deep breath through pouted lips and gritted teeth. Perhaps he's trying to control his aversion to the words I've practiced in my head. I wait for him to stop making noises before continuing to speak. My heart beats like a cog train increasing in speed.

"First, I'm sorry for not telling you about the promotion earlier, but—"

"We'll discuss *that* at the appropriate time. When you know for sure what's going on. Don't worry."

"May I finish?"

"Yeah," Alex huffs, puffing the duvet up around his legs.

"It's just that *some*times I'm …" I close my eyes in quiet meditation, willing my pulse to slow down.

"You're *what*, Melody?"

"I'm … *scared* of you sometimes." False calm squeezes me like a boa constrictor. I hold my breath.

Alex turns the main light on using the switch behind his head on the wall. He scoffs.

"You're kidding me, right?"

I exhale. "No." I bite a dry piece of skin off my lip and spit it out between two fingers. I wipe my hand on the sheet by my thigh. "And sometimes I'm afraid to say things because I'm scared that you'll yell. And your yelling is irrational and … terrifying."

Alex stares—blank-faced. I scratch a non-existent itch under my arm. "You yell before you even know what you're yelling about. And you know I *hate* it when you get aggressive. You remind me of my—"

"Mother." Alex rubs his eyes. He sighs and looks at the wall.

"Yeah. And I *really* hate it. I need you to *stop*," I say, nodding assertion and weight into each word. Alex's eyes flick erratically over the wall as if searching for cracks in the paint.

"Alex! I really *need* you to stop. Please look at me!"

Alex meets my gaze and nods clenching his jaw. I lower my tone. My hands shake. Fear re-emerges like aggressive bacteria. "Otherwise I can't feel confident about telling you things I think you might get upset about, or trust you won't jump to conclusions before you've heard everything I have to say. And I don't want to be afraid to tell you—"

Alex narrows his eyes.

"… that I really want—"

"Me to get you a gig." Alex pushes the duvet down to his knees and laughs as if he's been expecting this request all along. *So why didn't you just offer instead of make me suffer through this unspoken torment?*

"This is ludicrous," Alex continues, getting out of bed and towering above me.

"What is?" My shoulders recline. My voice turns to kitten squeak. "That I want you to get me a gig?"

"No!" Alex tosses his arms in the air, his fingers outstretched; the lines inside his hands redden. "That you think I'm like your mother!"

"But you *are*," I say, wishing I could control myself. But I can't. Unspoken ache drives the volume of my voice to a level I've never heard before. It's not very loud, but the pain in it is—like a mute trying to express grief. "I mean, it's how *I feel.*" I clench my fists and bang them on my chest, knocking the last breath of confidence out of me. My palms burn as I press my fingers into them. *This is what I have needed to say—all along. How could I not have realized this?* "Can't you see that that's how you *make* me *feel*? I'm afraid to speak about everything to you in case you blow up. And I *know* you've thought about hitting me. I *know* it. It's just a matter of time, Alex. I can see it in your eyes every time you—"

"Mel!" Alex bangs his fist on the wall. "I have never hit you. How can you—"

"Stop! See what I mean? Look at you! Look at that fist, that anger. You could snap me in half with one swipe. And for what? What have I done to you?"

Alex loosens his fist and sighs as he crouches down. He looks at his feet through his parted knees and balances himself on the edge of the bed, rocking himself backward and forward.

"Stop being so defensive for *just* a second and try to look at this from my perspective, huh? Look deep into your own heart and tell me, do you seriously have *no* idea what I'm talking about here? If you can honestly say you don't then … I guess, so be it. You can't see it." I shrug. "But can you at least *try* to understand my problem here?"

His eyes become watery, and his intimidating demeanour ebbs as if he's been injected with a tranquilizer.

"I love you. You know that right?" he whispers looking up at me like a lost child.

"Yes. I do." *I do. He loves me. Otherwise what would be keeping him here? Right?*

"Okay. Do *you* love *me*?"

"Yes." *I think so.*

"Okay. I'll, um, watch my temper. And if I lose sight of it, if … if I forget, just, I dunno, yell at me or something. I *promise* I won't hit you. How could I *ever* hit you? You're my ... Melody, you're my music. I'm sorry. I've been so wrapped up in my business that I forget you're not as strong as you show on the outside. I'm sorry."

Alex steps back into bed and wraps his arms around me. He rubs my back and shoulders up and down as if I need warming up. I always thought an apology would seem empty after the way I've been feeling lately. But, surprisingly, it has given me hope. I feel *hope*. And it's exactly what I need to replenish what we had. Because what we had was precious.

About a year or so after Tessa was born, we used to set our alarms for an outrageous hour of the morning, to make sure we were awake before her. Sometimes we didn't even speak. We would just lie there, touch each other's skin, stroke each other's cheeks, our hair, or warm our hands between each other's thighs. We didn't make love. We didn't have to. Being awake in each other's presence was enough—to remind ourselves that we existed. Even if we drowned in chaos in the outside world, we knew that in here, in our tiny cocoon of 'us time' at the crack of dawn, we were together, and that was all that mattered. It represented love in its most simplest form—Me. Him. Us. *I want that back. We can get that back ...*

"Mel?"

I look up and touch my nose to Alex's chin. "Hmm?"

"How soon would you like that gig?"

part two

Please Don't Break Me

A puncture wound, will never heal
its hole forever hollow
Can't fill the void or roll the wheel
or flee its crushing sorrow

Chorus:
You might wanna mask it, patch it
get it stitched up and cleaned
You might wanna fill it, peel it
or sew it up into seams

Pretty girls with bouncy curls
They trigger long lost dreams
Oh oh. Oh oh.
No sticks or stones, or brittle bones
Don't aim to crack my knees
No, oh, oh, oh.

Chorus

Soothing words aren't set in stone
Should I believe in you?
Should I believe?
Or will it end with me in bed
Feeling torn and bruised?
Please don't break me.

Chorus

ten

Selflessness. An animal instinct; an innocent whim, present only in a child. An unconditional inclination to assist without personal gain. For an ape, that's life. But for us, as we grow old, our naive allure toward altruism; our aspirations to aid anyone in need, abates. We keep tabs on each other's behaviour, and feel proud about what we give only when the favour is returned. Always anticipating the arrival of "the one" to accept us for who we are; all future action expectation-free.

Yes.

Expectation-free.

As certain as the fact that a guitar needs strings to make sound; as pleasant as the muffled silence after screeching amplifier feedback.

I stare at Alex until he opens his eyes—hoping his enthusiastic offer to secure me a gig is void of agenda. My instinct tells me he either wants something or is hiding something. The latter being the strongest jackhammer in my gut. It's been drilling so many holes in me lately that I'll soon need a colostomy bag.

When did I start thinking nice gestures must be spiked with impure intentions?

"Happy birthday," I whisper as if a 'sweet nothing' and nibble his earlobe. The bed linen crumples. A spring pings: a faerie soul puncture stifled in cotton wool. If Tessa had the vocabulary, that's what she'd say the noise is.

With a groan, Alex stretches his arms; his walnut shell elbows blending in with his pale bed-sheet wrinkled skin. "Mmm, thanks, babe. I'm forty fucking years old." He kisses my cheek—lips so coarse they could sand away the cracks in the ceiling. *He should drink more water. He should look after himself better.*

"So? You don't look a day over thirty-five … and once you wake up a little and the pillow imprints have disappeared from the side of your face, you'll probably look thirty-two," I say with a wink, thinking he looks more like *forty*-five.

It was only a year ago that I thought he could still pass as thirty. How did he age so quickly? Is life beginning to burden him? Am I? Am I now the extra pinch of salt that causes the heart attack?

And what happened to the wife who would give him a foot massage first thing on a Sunday morning before offering to cook him French toast? Or the wife who used to wake up singing the song she'd just written the day before? The woman who would gladly forfeit music time for quality Alex time, because she … because I … knew how to keep a balance?

Who am I now?

I'm no silicone spatula, that's for sure. I'm the wooden spoon with the snapped handle.

"Ha-ha. Thanks." He yawns, opening his mouth as wide

as a cookie cutter; his breath like off milk—the smog of bodily fluids.

For the last five years I've been speaking like a ventriloquist in the mornings until I brush my teeth in fear that mine might smell the same. Our breaths never smelled bad before we got married. What's with that? There must have been something in the ceremonial wine. An eternal curse of discomfort. Once married, always harried. It should have been in our vows. Warnings are always better than surprises.

"So, seriously now, you're bringing Alana Miles?" I twist my hair into a bun and lean my head against the wall to momentarily secure it.

Alex nods, his stubble brushing against the duvet below his chin. The sound of tires passing over a wet patch of road.

"Isn't she like, fifty, now?" I ask, screwing up my nose, wondering why I would even consider it an issue. *It's not an issue. At all. What's with you?*

Alex laughs through his nose, rubbing behind his ear. Looks as if he's been bitten. *Do dust mites bite?* I envision dust mites burrowing under my skin; a giant cockroach dropping me into a greenhouse swarming with flying ants. I squeeze my eyes shut to shake the thought.

"So when are you bringing her?"

"Gig's not definite yet, we're negotiating a fee."

"So when are you thinking, then?"

"In about three months." Alex sits up and scratches a dry flake of skin from his cheek. "You can get your shit together by then, right?"

"Of course!" *Better start practicing.*

Alex's cell phone rings. He looks at the caller ID, swallows and flares his nostrils.

"Sorry. Have to get this." He jumps out of bed, ties his robe around his firm yet slightly protruding stomach, letting it ring and ring.

It stops.

Offering a tight-lipped smile in apology, he puts an ear bud into his left ear, presses a couple of keys, and walks out onto the balcony.

Ten seconds later he returns.

"That was a quick conversation. Mustn't have been too important." I sit up in bed, pulling the duvet up far enough to cover my breasts.

"Um, no. It was just my accountant. Problem with some invoices. Want some coffee?"

I nod, force a smile of gratitude to tame resurfacing suspicion. I watch him walk out of the bedroom with his cell phone clenched in his hand.

Ever since Tessa and I visited my parents on the island last weekend, and Alex stayed home, suspicion has been beleaguering me on and off like the transitory sting of an injection. In fact, last weekend was the catalyst of many things—including my current emotional state.

The catalyst of cataclysm?

When I was about six years old, arriving to the island was like stepping foot into an enchanted pop-up fairytale book. At dawn, especially, it was a Neverland of lush luminescent green mountain, deep purple sea, sherbet orange sky and sharp-toothed cliffs so high you could literally walk on clouds—a much needed change from falling asleep on a vibrating carpeted floor that reeked of old amplifier wheel grease and waking up to cigarette smoke wafting through ducted heating vents.

The island's windy mountainous roads are framed with olive groves and air so crisp you could snap it like celery. The houses are stained with whitewash and embedded with old-style wooden shutters, tailored by the locals to keep the summer swelter out. They are painted blue, red, or green, but occasionally you may come across the odd pink or orange shutters, which are more often than not inhabited by the eccentric barmy type who are colour-blind, or the young and loaded foreigner who believes an island revolution should be in order.

Goats meander about the streets, butting each other's heads senselessly as they try to escape oncoming cars and motorcycles. The roosters, chickens, and geese fire up the locals at the first sign of sunrise. Birds chirp, cicadas "jijiga" in the olive trees, and dogs bark as the bread truck, a red beat-up Ute, delivers fresh hot loaves to each residence and slips the required amount of bread into handmade cloth bags hanging from wire fencing.

Summer on this island engraves your skin with a longing to spend sunrise to sunset lying on a small, empty, white-pebbled beach in a secluded cove at the end of a private dirt walking track. At midday, it gets so hot you need to wade through heat waves rising from the unevenly tarred road like kindred spirits before you can wade in the Ionian to cool off—a flat, motionless oil bath which glows with an infinite turquoise glint. It may seem you are stepping into velvet, however, you emerge covered in a thin salty crust you can brush off like sand when it dries.

Most folks have a siesta between two and five in the afternoon, so there isn't much to do except wander the streets and explore. By about six the sun still reads midday, and the waterfront cafés fill with shouting teenagers drinking frappé. They stay until it's time to return home, quickly scarf down some homemade *mousaka*, and get dressed to party until seven the next morning.

By about ten at night the sun hides behind a mountain of shrubby arid terrain, and the cool edge to the air is relieving. At the mountain's topmost peak, a silhouette of an Orthodox church can be seen, accompanied by a soundtrack of owls and crickets. At this time of day mosquitoes congregate for their evening feasts. Shepherds' voices echo through the valley while their goats' bells jingle as they steer along the hot dusty trails home.

In the morning, when glittering sunlight made patterns on my wall through the thin slats of my bedroom shutters, my mother would make me Vegemite toast. I'd eat on the veranda, without a plate, propped up on a whitewashed ledge full of tacky red plastic buckets, where my Yiayia would hand-wash our laundry. Dad would play guitar in the garden, and Mum would sing along as if she were the happiest person alive. Papou would tend to his veggie patch, and as soon as I'd finish my toast, I'd probe the olive trees for camouflaged cicadas.

At night I would ask Papou to play cards with me on the wobbly kitchen table covered in clay-brown, chequered laminate which matched the wrinkly brown-orange lino floor. We'd sit by the wood-fire oven to use it as a side-table for our flat orangeades.

The flicking neon light of the mosquito zapper would accentuate Yiayia's oily fingerprints all over the once-white cupboards and plastic yellow-stained handles. The sink, which was used as a place to hold the bucket of water collected from the well to do the dishes, stunk like stale grease. Yiayia would use the same water several times before transferring the bucket to the outhouse to flush the toilet. As a result, all cutlery and glassware had a slight fatty glaze to them and would sustain the exact pattern of one's fingerprint.

Papou would show me his clever shuffling tricks with his sun-spotted trembling hands—one of which had a thumb missing—and I would smile and nod at his mumbling despite hardly ever understanding what he said. My father later said he often told stories about the earthquake that initiated the mass migration to Melbourne in 1953.

However, I do recall *one* instant when I'd understood. It was one afternoon before going for siesta that Papou and I sat together in the lounge room for a while. I was flipping through old photo albums as he picked up the newspaper and sat in his faded maroon armchair facing the window. I glanced up for a second to see him looking from side to side and then patting his shirt pockets.

"They're on your head," I said.

His eyes lit up as he removed his reading glasses from his balding and scratched head (from consistently knocking it against the wine cellar entrance), put them on his nose, and said as if he had been touched by an angel, "How you know? How you know what I look for? My God, my God, you have *gift*!"

At six years old, of course, I believed him, until my mother explained I had just used common sense. At least she'd made me feel intelligent instead of crushing the novelty of possibly being psychic.

In the evenings, Yiayia would fix herself a plate of bread, feta cheese, tomato, olive oil, and oregano. She would eat it with her fingers without having much control over the oil dripping down her chin and wrists—then she'd pinch my cheeks.

"*Ella tho* Melody, *ella na fas* some bread tzeez 'n' domata, is goud for yoo, ya knah! No *kreas* today, *eenai poli* tough today ya knah," Yiayia would squeal in her high-pitched half Greek–half Australian accent.

She'd fumble around the kitchen with a ripped straw hat, that was maybe as old as I was at the time, greasy 'eighties-style sunglasses (even at night), a faded floral dress, and an overused apron for pre-cooking the following day's meals. When the food was ready to "look a'er itself," she would sit out on the rear balcony in the moonlight, drinking "mountain tea" and dipping in teddy bear biscuits she'd had sent over from Australia.

Yiayia was eccentric to say the least. I'll never forget the day my father returned from spear-fishing one morning and had brought home a massive live sea creature as big as his head, thinking it was just an empty shell.

We all gathered on the veranda to take a closer look at the twenty-centimetre thick monster that slowly emerged from its shell like a slimy skinless muscular arm. It was bright red with purple veins and a slippery transparent membrane. But Yiayia suspected it was a local delicacy and promptly prepared it for the grill. She put it in the washing machine. To tenderize. The whole house stank of dead fish for weeks, and thank God the washing machine was never used for its intended purpose. Most of the time it just sat, unplugged, by the toilet as an "asset."

The shell still sits on Mum's mantelpiece—as rare and precious as ammolite. Although multicoloured on the outside—brown, yellow, green, blue, and red—the inside is lined with what looks like jet black glass. Any local that visits and sees the shell asks about it in astonishment and with great interest. It turns out the creature was deadly. If its poison hadn't been sucked out during its two-hour cycle in the washing machine, Papou and Yiayia would have been poisoned to death!

The first thing you see as you walk through my parents' front door, except for the magnificent shell, is my mother's grand piano.

It shines like a freshly glazed tart. And whispers haunting melodies to me as if it were once a living soul; the mother of musically-triggered melancholy.

Last weekend, the resonance of my entering sandaled feet

had hardly bounced off the walls when Mum said, "Why don't you sit down and see if you can remember to play it?" Her eyes blazed with a need to swank her own musical skills and show me up. I tamed an irrational urge to scratch its glossy dark chocolate body with my wedding ring by shaking my dusty cardigan too close to the keys instead. Mum whipped out a duster from inside the piano stool and brushed it away—seething clenched teeth hidden by a civil smile.

My father, James, took our bags and challenged Tessa to a race in the nearby field of goats. Their bells jingled like wind chimes weighed down with anchors in muddy water. One second the house was full of shrieks of joy and the next Tessa disappeared behind a slammed front door.

"Don't slam the door!" Mum banged on the window, creating an echo highlighted by an abundance of country air. Dad, immersed in oblivious child-imitation giggles, ran after Tessa, shrivelling up his body as if trying to shrink to her size.

"Well?" Mum nudged me toward the stool and tapped her left foot. The sound wavered between an annoying dripping tap and approaching suspenseful footsteps.

"Um …" My voice dithered like vocal heat waves, reluctant to make a fool of myself. "Maybe a bit later? Have you got any warm water? I feel really dehydrated." I nursed my head and limped to the couch, legs heavy with unbalanced fatigue.

You can't drink the water on the island, so everybody stocks up on plastic bottled 'consumerist crap' (in my opinion) labelled with try-hard environmental campaigns that Greek society generally ignores. I don't blame them. If they can think of a way to make recycled paper bottles, I'm all in to support their efforts.

Mum usually remembers that I don't like my water cold and leaves a few bottles out of the fridge for me, but it seems Dad saw them lying around and put them back in, probably thinking he was doing the right thing, and hoping to avoid being blamed. So I forgive him. I understand.

"Jesus! Bloody James put them in the fridge. I can't count on him to do *any*thing." Mum felt every bottle of water, wrapping her long soft and petite piano-playing fingers around the crisp crackling plastic bottles of false environment-saving hope to see which one was the least cold.

"It's okay, Mum, don't worry, just run it under the hot tap a bit," I said, lifting my feet up onto the hospital-white couch and puffing a crimson no-frills cushion behind my head.

"Got any good pirated movies from the black dudes lately?" I asked, grabbing the pile of movies from the edge of the locally made and too-high coffee table. I sifted through them on my stomach, the sharp plastic corners of the covers digging into my flabby pale skin.

"No, not really," she said, throwing me the bottle of water, and then wiping away the splashes around the sink with her beloved orange microfiber cloth. "They're not coming round this end of the island much anymore."

Thank goodness for the remnants of high-school tennis reflexes, otherwise I'd have spent the entire weekend nursing a bruised forehead.

"They probably got sick of everybody turning them down. Everybody treats 'em like shit." The microfiber cloth made a thud, like a bare foot stamping on flat soil, as Mum threw it into the sink on "shit". "Except for James—he spends at *least* an hour looking through bundles and bundles of the bloody things, and then gives 'em about *fifty* Euros for *twenty* Euros' worth of movies."

Mum shuffled a few things around on the kitchen counter, opened and closed a few cupboards, muttered "Jesus Christ" under her breath, opened and closed a few more cupboards, then finally pulled out a packet of cherry liquors. "I keep forgetting James is a saint—or so everybody keeps telling me. I wish I could *see* the *saint*," she continued, shuffling to my side, then flicked her head left, right, over her shoulder, and up at the ceiling. "Nope. *No* saint in my house—unless I'm mistaken, and a saint is someone who never puts things back where they belong, requires someone to pick up their shitty toilet papers off the bathroom floor because he always misses the bin, and who needs to be told to breathe in and out just in case they forget. Then yes, I *do* have a saint in my house."

With an acerbic smile she ripped open the packet of chocolates like a scavenging monkey and offered me one with a sigh, holding the open packet toward me like a bag of potato chips.

"Mind if I have a sleep?" I asked, taking a chocolate from the bag.

"Already? You just got here." Mum puffed up the cushions around me on the couch.

"I'm really tired, Mum. You know what it's like travelling with Tessa. She wants me to tour her around the ferry until she's seen every nook and cranny a kazillion times."

"How about I make you a coffee?" she asked, lifting my legs and sitting on the couch to rub my feet.

"Agwgh," I groaned, letting my head drop backwards like a wet towel. I closed my eyes and began to drift off, completely aware of Mum's manipulation, yet totally ignoring it. We could talk about holiday packages and how the island is full of small-town patriarchal pompous hypocrites, or in other words, Man, after a refreshing nap.

I let my body sink into the couch like a hollow branch in quicksand.

But I was startled awake about half an hour later when Dad and Tessa came storming in from habituating with the goats.

"Last one to the music room loses!" Dad cried, almost bursting a blood vessel in his face. He ran on the spot, the way they do in cartoons when they're trying to run but can't seem to get anywhere. Tessa passed and made it to the music room first.

"You lostht! You lostht!" I glared at her for making fun of her grandpa's lisp. But she just shrugged at me as if to say, *It was harmless.*

"Grandpa lost! Grandpa lost, Mummy!" Tessa pounced at me, and started to jump up and down on the couch as if it were a trampoline. I half expected Mum to bring out the 'Betty Boo Hoo' (Alex's phrase), but to my surprise, instead of getting upset, she grabbed her camera and snapped a few shots.

"Okay, okay, come on, enough, someone's going to break my ribs." I coughed, bringing my knees to my chest to protect myself.

"Right! Who's up for some mushroom and *spinahchi* lasagne?" Mum blurted out lieutenant-style, as if we had to fit a week's worth of events into the time frame of a single evening. She put her camera into a small chest decorated with metallic elephants (more street-seller's paraphernalia), by the TV.

"You cooked?" I asked, furrowing my brow; the taste of the unpredictable stung my tongue like the end of a magnet.

"Yeah. You know I *can*. I'm just usually *really* busy every time you come over. But this weekend I'm all yours. No tuna pasta this time. Ya hungry?" She rubbed Tessa's belly with a wink.

We all cried out "yeah," even Dad, who apparently had no idea Mum had cooked either by the look of his deracinated smile. Nor did I blame him. Something wasn't quite right.

"James, set the table," Mum ordered, her tone switching from bouncy biscuit baker to authoritarian chef.

"Okay," he said, as if someone had shoved a whisk down his throat and got it caught in his vocal cords. He reached for a set of placemats in a drawer, eyebrows raised, lips pursed, and something like a fleck of tissue hanging from his nose hair.

"No! Not those ones, you *idiot*. We never use those! The *real* ones!" Mum barked as she cut up the lasagne and then burnt her wrist on the edge of the tray. "Ouch! Shit! Fuck!" *Bang* went the spatula in the sink after it's quick two-meter journey through the air.

Dad looked at me as if I should *know* where the "real" placemats were and could signal him in the right direction. But I had no idea and shook my head in silence. I stroked Tessa's hair as she watched with amused intrigue.

Mum caught sight of the fleck of tissue hanging from Dad's nose and squeezed her own nose with a "tsk" as cue for him to brush it off. Dad, seeming to take his unco-ordinated tendencies into account, cupped his knobbly-knuckled hand, speckled with tiny tufts of wiry sprouting black hair, over his whole face, and loosened the fleck of tissue with one swift downward swipe.

"They're in *there*! Next to the … the *things*!" Mum pointed in the general direction of the drawers with such a hard flick I was amazed she didn't dislocate her elbow.

"Where? We have fifteen drawers."

"Oh look, you've learnt how to count," Mum snapped putting her hands on her hips. "They're in *this* drawer." She pointed again, without actually indicating *the* drawer the *real* placemats were in or what things they were next to. Dad opened and closed all the drawers and inspected their contents, but to no avail. Tessa giggled. She loves her grandparents' bickering. Especially the way Dad makes faces every time Mum talks. Tessa started imitating him one day, in reaction to one of Mum's obsessive fits. Mum then scolded Dad for subjecting their granddaughter to bad habits. She'd hit him with a wooden spoon.

"Oh, for God's sake," Mum muttered and accidentally dropped her oven mitt on the floor. Dad picked it up and looked at her as if to say, *see I'm not the only one who drops things*, and Mum snapped back, "They're in this drawer, you dipshit. They were staring you right in the bloody face. An' I drop things by *accident*—you drop things because you can't coordinate using two hands at once. For Christ's sa—"

"Since when do you guys set the table?" I asked, wondering why I was putting myself in the middle of an argument. If there's anyone in this world who knows why *not* to, it's me. But my mouth overpowered my mind for a second too long. "I don't think I've *ever* seen you set the table. How would Dad know where the placemats are if you never set the table?"

Mum spun round on her Birkenstock heel and glared. Her jaw clenched as she flashed a disapproving glance toward Dad, who was grinning in triumph by default. She sighed and said through gritted teeth, "We. Invite. Colleagues. For. Dinner."

I mouthed the word *oh*, removing a strand of hair from the corner of my mouth and gave Tessa a little wink. She wriggled in her chair, straightened her skirt, took a napkin from the table, and hooked it into her collar like a bib.

What? Was my daughter having an identity crisis? Most of the time, it takes Tessa throwing a five-minute tantrum and a succession of threats to get her to do that at home.

Thankfully, as Mum served the food, Serena, my best friend from Australia, called. I grabbed my cell phone out of my bag by the couch, silently thanking my piano spirit for saving me from Betty Boo Hoo. But what saved me from one psychological torment sent me full-throttle into another.

"Hey hunk 'a' spunk. Where you at? Been calling your house for ages."

"Hey. I'm on the island. Just a sec and let me go outside where there's better reception." As I approached the front door, Mum gave me her hurry-up look—the one that makes her look like a confused ferret.

"What a surprise! What's going on?"

"Just checkin' to see how you are, hon."

"I'm good. I'm in the middle of dinner with my folks, and my mum's getting … well I'm sure you can guess. So, how are you?"

"I'm fine, but my grandfather died," Serena said in a flippant tone.

"Oh? I'm sorry. When?"

"This morning."

"Are you okay?"

"I don't know. I haven't seen him for years. But apparently he's left me something. I have to go and claim it at some point. Feel a bit weird taking something of his. We hardly knew each other."

"Didn't he always send you birthday cards? Full of money?"

"Yeah. And I always called to say thank you, too. But otherwise, we never spoke."

I could hear the faint calling of my mother for me to

come back inside like grilled greasy whinnies from tavern kitchen chimneys. *Yoo-hoo! Melody! Come back inside before I sear your father's cheek with my scorching hot spatula.*

"Serena, I'm really sorry, but I have to go … oh, wait, you said you were calling my house for *ages*?"

"Yeah, why?"

"And there was no answer?"

"No. Why? What's wrong?"

"Alex should be there."

"Oh? He's not there with you?"

"Alex? With me? On the island? You kidding?"

"Well, I just assumed … "

"Yeah, well … . Maybe he's just gone out with his mates."

"Probably," replied Serena, clearly trying to not make me worry.

"Okay. I'll call when I'm back in Athens."

"Okay. Ciao, Bella!"

As soon as I hung up, I called home and there was *still* no answer. Then I called Alex's cell and it was switched off. My stomach imploded like sinking pavlova. A common reaction of mine when Alex and I are apart. *I'm making irrational assumptions,* I thought. *Do not get sucked into your mother's absurd psychological framework.* Such as: getting angry over an overflowing bath, and screaming about a piece of burnt toast that pissed her off two years earlier.

The moment I got back to the dinner table, my mother said, "Now, Melody, I know it's a lot of money, so I'll give it to you if you can promise me that you won't waste it on investing in one of Alex's stupid business ideas."

What? Did I miss her first sentence, or did I phase out?

She took hold of my hands above the salad bowl and looked at me as if we had just been informed I had two months to live, stroking my knuckles with her silky smooth thumbs. I sucked my tongue till it stuck to the roof of my mouth, then twisted it upside down, which resulted in me puckering my lips. Mum smiled—showed her teeth. Dad and Tessa stopped fidgeting with their cutlery, and looked at their plates. A spiny silence ensued. Like a paper cut. You don't notice it's there until it *really* stings.

"Um, what are you talking about?" I asked, glancing at my father for some sign of moral support. But he didn't look me in the eye. He knew what was coming and he knew how I would react. Any time my mother jumps straight into a conversation without any lead-in, she has an ulterior motive. I've learnt to recognize the signs.

"The twenty thousand Euros I'm giving you."

"What? Are you kidding me?"

"Not at all," she said.

"You want to give me a *gift* with *conditions*?" I screeched, snatching my hands away and shaking my head. "I'm sorry, Mum, but I don't want a gift like that."

Dad and Tessa rolled their eyes at each other.

"Come on, Tessa," Dad said, "let's take a walk to the village and get some yummy cake."

"Yeah!" Tessa jumped into Dad's arms as he stood and scraped his chair backward.

Mum winced. "Melody, can you not jump to conclusions and just hear me out? You see, it would be *great*, because you'd be able to quit your job and maybe invest it in a property and collect some rent."

"Mum." I laughed, trying to trick myself into gaining composure. "First, if I quit my job, how would I support Tessa when the money runs out and I can't find another? Second, twenty thousand Euros is nowhere near enough to buy a property. And third, I paid your rent for a *whole* year when you were going through that financial crisis, so, *sorry* if I expect a gift like that to come with no strings attached."

With each sentence my voice grew louder. I almost regretted it, but knowing that it was high time I stopped holding back, I just let myself go. Perhaps I was overreacting. Perhaps I should have been less defensive, but being so hardened to my mum's usual manipulative behaviour, I suppose I just couldn't perceive the offer as a gesture with no strings attached. All I saw was her attempt to control me. And all I could foresee was her forgetting about me when she got what she wanted. Such as the time she forced me to take a waitressing job to pay board when I was a teenager, and then wouldn't let me make any choices about what food to buy, and I did the cooking!

Alex and I had been tossing around the idea of opening a live music venue/bar together and I had mentioned it to Mum. She didn't like the idea and thought it would ruin my life, and brain bashed me with all the horrible things that could go wrong. It worked—we never did it. Another effort of Alex's to bring us closer together flushed down the proverbial toilet of fabricated doom.

So. I *had* to turn the money down—out of principle. If I

was going to have a spare twenty thousand to play with, I'd like to be able to do with it what I please.

"Melody, don't be silly, I really want you to have it. I want the best for you and Tessa."

"And what about Alex? Why the best for me and Tessa, and not Alex?" I narrowed my eyes, focusing on the hairline wrinkles bordering Mum's dark brown pencilled lips.

"Well, Alex too … of course, Alex too. It's just … he makes a lot of decisions on the spur of the moment without thinking them through, and he doesn't really know what he's doing, does he? I just don't want you to risk losing *my* money over something that is going to make you work too hard—"

"Pardon?" I craned my neck forward, "my money" echoing in the rear of my sinus cavity.

Mum extended her hand, palm up, toward me.

"I want to give *you* a gift—that means …" Mum sniffed, shaking her head as if she'd just snorted stinging cocaine, "it should give you the chance to work less, not more." She scraped the leftovers into my empty plate, avoiding eye contact.

"Mum, twenty grand isn't going to help me work less. What you're suggesting will make me unemployed and then broke when I can't find another job when the money runs out. And what are you basing your opinion on anyway? One, just one, failed venture on Alex's part? Come on, you can give him a little more credit than that, can't you?"

"I don't mean it like that. I don't mean to put Alex down—"

"Yes, you *do*. You've *never* liked Alex. You've never *said* it, but I can tell. You *pretend* when you're around him. Who are you trying to protect here? You usually just tell me how you feel straight out. But ever since I met Alex you've stopped. It's like you're pretending he doesn't even exist."

"Excuse me?" Mum yelled, slamming a fist into a cupboard by her head. "And that is bad? How is that bad? I'm just trying not to create any friction between you two. You look happy with Alex. I didn't want to stick my nose in like I did with all your other boyfriends."

"Well, thanks, thanks a lot. Thanks for saving my marriage."

I stood, removed the chair from behind me with an aimless flick. It wobbled, threatened to topple over, but regained balance, proving I maintained restraint. I walked over to a window by the couch and stared at the mountains—the real mountains, the real place where insecurities seem to melt like caramelizing sugar.

"Oh, get off your high horse, Melody. I'm trying to do something *nice* for you here! And this is the thanks I get? You're such a—" Mum screamed, smashing a plate in the sink by accident. *Was it by accident?*

I turned around to glare at her. "Such a *what*? Such a selfish little *bitch*? Jesus, when have I heard that before?"

"You're such … AN AWFUL PERSON!"

Mum groaned and belted her microfiber cloth against the sink over and over as if tenderizing an octopus. With squinted eyes her face flushed. If there was anyone on Earth who could convincingly emit smoke from their ears I'd have to say it would be my mother.

I watched, blank-faced, wondering when we could ever be in the same room without having an argument. She went over to the piano and sat, poised, facing straight-ahead and closed her eyes. Her fingers rose through her inward sigh, hovered above the keys, searched them for the correct notes like Braille. She began to play Joni Mitchell's "Blue." A song I've always wanted to learn; one I've asked her to teach to me on so many occasions I've lost count. But she never did teach it to me; she rolled my requests into tiny little balls of dough, put them in the oven and forgot to set the timer—burnt them to a crisp. My desire to love Joni was charcoal to her—brittle, lightweight, void of oxygen. Could I not share the love? And it wasn't just the song I wanted to know how to play; I wanted to be *taught, by my mother*. I wanted to see music through her eyes, too; for her to take me under her wing, and say "See, this is how I *feel*. Understand this, then you'll understand me."

I approached Mum from behind, hugged her shoulders, and held my cheek to hers. She kept playing, but moved her face like a delicate brush stroke against mine.

"I'm sorry," I whispered and sat beside her. "I really can't afford to lose my job. Twenty thousand Euros is a very nice gesture, but I'm afraid I can't do what you want me to do. I have Tessa to think about. I can't risk the possibility of not finding another job once the year off is over with."

Mum stopped playing and held my face in her hands.

"I know. I just wanted you to know what it's like to not feel *burdened*."

Money issues don't burden me, I thought. *You burden me.*

We both stared at indistinct areas of each other's faces. My lips buzzed with letters aching to be strung together in words, sentences, pleas, confessions of dissatisfaction. I wanted to tell her how she has ruined my life. That I can't live a single moment without wondering how it might be different if she had been "normal."

"I still want you to have it," she said closing the lid over the keys.

"Mum—"

"No, no, no. You can put it toward your *music*."

"Oh?"

"Yeah. Twenty grand should be plenty to cover the expenses of recording an album. Shouldn't it?"

eleven

It's just another manic Monday, Oh oh oh, I wish it was Sunday, 'cause that's my funday, my I-don't-have-to-run day … I reach my desk at UTD, humming The Bangles. As much as I don't like to admit it, 1980s pop-culture lines my veins like milk to an acidic stomach. The buzz of future possibility is sweating through fear and materializing into song. And I'm so preoccupied with what lies ahead, that I don't realize what is directly ahead—my swivelling chair. I spill coffee all over my keyboard.

"Damn it!"

The girls' heads turn. They stare. I stare. The coffee stares. Then, as if blessed with the momentum of freedom, its mercury-like globule separates, and cascades down the side of my desk.

Sonia's pending smile is threatening to emerge at my expense, her too-long shaggy ash-brown hair covering her eyes. *I wonder if she's related to* The Addams Family*'s Cousin It.*

Lucy, another assistant, is kind enough to offer me help, but can't seem to find a way to help and just stands behind me, watching, pushing her bifocals up her nose, as I shake the keyboard upside down and spread used tissues from my handbag all over my desk.

Jodie, the other Project Manager, pokes her head out of her office, and I can see Dianne through the slightly open door.

"Melody?" Jodie asks in her ornate Scottish flair. "Could ye come in here for a wee moment?"

I gulp down what's left in my *Without Music Life Would B-flat* mug, and buoyantly gurgle, "Sure! Just a sec!" managing to suck escaping coffee in from the corner of my mouth. I shuffle into Jodie's office. Everybody stares at my flip-flops as if willing me to trip over.

"Good morning, did you both a have a nice weekend?" I ask in a jovial editorial tone—a voice I save for meetings in the PMs' office.

"Luvley, thanks, Melody," Jodie says, mirroring my merriness. She creates some space on her desk to rest her folded hands.

"Fine, thanks," Dianne says, nodding her head, careful not to let her hair-sprayed fringe fall in her face. *Ugh.*

I take a seat, watching Dianne flip through some papers on her lap, biting the end of her pen, screwing up her nose, and then flipping some more. Jodie is watching her too, with pursed lips and one raised eyebrow. She pinches the concave between her bottom lip and oily chin as if trying to burst a pimple, or pluck a menopausal hair.

"Right, are we ready then?" Jodie directs the question to Dianne, and winks at me, crossing her stocky bare legs and hitting her knee under the table. She winces. "D'ye want to get ye coffee before we start?"

"No, it's okay." I smile, clicking the sole of my right flip-flop on my heel. "I accidentally spilt it. I'll make another one when we're done." My dry lips stick to my teeth as I try to compose myself. *Should I be worried about this sudden meeting?*

"Okay, then. Erm, well, I, well, *we*, asked ye in here to tell ye … Dianne? D'ye mind if ye put those down for a wee moment?" Jodie glares at Dianne's noisy paper-stacking hands. Dianne looks up. Face as stiff as dried putty.

"Right, yes, Melody, ye presentation. Congratulations! Ye got the job in London!"

My breath comes to a halt on the inhale.

"Yes, congratulations, Melody," Dianne reiterates, her spurious smile lingering on the cliff of professionalism. "We were informed first thing this morning, by Mr. Richard Viadro, the academic director of UTD Publications in London. He said you gave an extraordinary presentation and that it would be an honour to have you as a part of their team."

Academic director? At the presentation? I thought they were just Board of Education representatives!

"Melody? Aren't ye excited? Ye got the job. The job ye've been working towards for over a year!" Jodie leans forward above her desk—her cheeks filled with rosy expectation.

I don't know what to say. I should be excited, shouldn't I? But I feel trapped inside a cocoon of mixed emotion.

"Um …" An outward sniff moves a strand of hair from my face like a breeze to a flag. "Thank you. No, I'm excited, I'm just … in shock, I mean, I wasn't expecting the decision to be made so fast. Wow! Um … so … what now?"

I feel foolish. Unprofessional. I was just coming to the conclusion last night that I'd turn this down, focus on music, use the money my mother gave me to finally do something for myself, but now I feel like I shouldn't. It would be irresponsible, right?

"Well," Jodie begins, "It'll be a wee bit different than the work ye do here. The books ye'll be producing won't be for ELT—they'll be college and university textbooks about English literature and history—"

"—so you might want to do some Internet research and get familiar with the materials you'll be working with," Dianne adds, twitching her nose like an irritated rabbit.

This could be good for my future. Maybe I should put the music off for a little while longer. No! Oh, Melody, what are you doing? I shift in my seat; it creaks as if I've just farted. The PMs flash a glance toward my chair.

"Hold on a minute, Dianne, we haven't even asked Melody if she's going to accept the position. It's a big decision to make. Shouldn't we give her a wee bit of time?" Jodie gets out of her seat and sits on top of her desk. She pulls her stapler out from under her bum as casually as one would scratch one's head.

"Well, I'm afraid we're going to need an answer soon. There's not much time for her to twiddle her thumbs in thought," Dianne replies with a stringent waver.

How soon? Holy shit! How soon? My face burns.

"Um, sorry to interrupt," I croak, trying to swallow an imaginary lump the size of an apricot, "but could you tell me how soon?"

"I'm afraid they need a decision by the end of the week in order for the appropriate arrangements to be made," Dianne says. "And if you decide you'd like to take the position, you'll be required to start work two weeks from today."

I can't leave Athens in just two weeks!

Jodie kneels down beside me and touches my knee with such maternal kindness I have an intense urge to hum and rock back and forth in her arms.

"Melody, dear, I know this is a wee bit quick, but we *have* been anticipating this for a year. Ye do want this, don't ye?"

I nod, straightening my back, in the hope that I can regain some form of power and courage. Dianne looks at us with distaste. Right now I wish I could say something about her Tupperware fetish, tip her off her icicle.

"Listen, if ye do decide to take the job, ye'll have next week off, fully paid, to organize yerself, okay? So ye won't be too rushed off ye feet, hmm?" Jodie adds.

"Okay," I sigh, trying to reassemble my mental list of priorities. I stand and smooth my shirt over my stomach. Buttons ping on my wedding ring. "I have some serious thinking to do then. Thanks for this. Thanks for everything, Jodie ... Dianne."

"Well done," Dianne nods with pursed lips and lowered eyelids as she gets up to leave Jodie's office. Just as I open the door to exit, Jodie half-whispers with a satisfied grin and a wink, "Oh, and before I forget, ye annual income will be forty thousand pounds—if you accept, that is."

My scalp seethes like a tormented pressure-cooker. *Damn. It. I have to take the job now, don't I? But I don't know if I really want to take the job at all. I don't need to get away from Alex, or this dire domestic drudgery, anymore. I have my husband's support to play music, and that's all I really wanted, right? I don't need this flash-hot job to mimic a socially accept-able existence. I'm allowed to be what I want to be now. Oh my God. What do I do?*

As I turn to go back to my desk, dizziness creeps up on me like a hot flush and I whack the right side of my head on the edge of Jodie's door in a blurry daze. The entire editorial department cries, "Oh!" I'm too stunned to feel any pain or care who is watching me walk back to my desk with my hand over my right eye. Perhaps they think I've been fired. But who cares. I don't. Should I? I've got more important things to think about.

At lunch time Heather and I sit on the meticulously cut lawn outside our office during break, and the smell of sun—the perfume of happy childhood memories and growing pains—reminds me of the island. *Would I really be happy in a place like London, where the sun doesn't smell?*

We're not really supposed to be out here, traipsing on the ornamental grass, but hey, no one's told us not to—today. So bugger it.

I look at the lawn and wonder who in their right mind would put so much energy, care and pride into maintaining a corporate garden. And what for? It's fenced off. The public can't see it, and we're stuck at our desks, trapped indoors for the majority of the day. What's the point? *Pathetic.*

"Why did the gardener mow the sodding lawn? Didn't

he do it two days ago?" Heather asks. She squints, takes her lunch from a brown paper bag. I laugh at the coincidence. "What's so funny?" The crunching paper accents her catechizing look which seeks answers she doesn't ask for.

"I was just wondering about the same thing, that's all. What's in your sandwich?" I add without taking a breath between sentences—staving off a twitch fuelled with equivocation.

"Fish paste," she replies, holding it out in front of her like a limp vegetable. I contort my face to summon more information.

"I made the kids their sandwiches this morning and didn't leave anything bleedin' decent for myself. We're due for a trip to the super."

"Oh," I reply, a little disappointed. I was hoping for an answer a little more exciting. Something to get my mind off things—to spark a conversation about something passionate, teenage angst, marital problems? I could contribute to that conversation.

"And Chris took the last can of tuna, and I couldn't find anything else that went with mayonnaise."

"Yuk." I gag. "Fish paste and mayonnaise? You can't be serious?"

"No. There was no mayo left either. All I had left worth putting in a sandwich was a wrinkly old cucumber, but fish paste and cucumber didn't really take my fancy, nor did just cucumber, 'cause it would taste too dry, so I just put fish paste in."

"I see." My voice teeters off with a retracted giggle. "What bores are we? Huh? What kind of conversation is this?" I laugh, cupping my hands over my ears as if I might mute my own thoughts.

"I'm talking shit again, aren't I?" Heather sighs, nods at her knees as if they're the ones to blame for her tendency towards hogwash.

They say men think with their dicks. Well, I say women think with their knees. You see, there are two, perfect for multitasking. They're separated, as opposed to a penis which is one solid area. In the female mind there is never one solid thought in one solid place at any one time. And this 'jumping' from knee to knee can cause us to talk gibberish on occasion. But the knees are also our source of balance and they are the first point that leads to our source of power, our core, our centre.

We stare at the lawn, listening to each other chew, when I smell something a bit off and sniff the air like a detector dog.

"What's that?" I ask, nose towards the sky.

"What's what?" Heather turns to face me, chewing with her mouth open like an untrained child, pushing food through her teeth with her tongue.

"Oh, it's you," I hold my nose and hang my head between my knees.

"Whatcha mean?" Heather asks, nudging my shoulder and almost toppling me over.

"The fish paste! That's got a whopper of an odour!" I stand, trying to catch a breeze.

Heather cackles and it sounds like a dozen people

popping plastic bubble wrap—and runs after me with her mouth open. We end up on the flower bed outside the PM's offices, giggling like little girls about to play a prank on the school principle.

Jodie and Dianne peer through their windows like timed machinery, countenance identical—which is pretty amusing because they can't see each other—and gesture for us to get off the flowers with the same flick of their hands and stretched lip movements. We do so in haste, still laughing and mouthing the word *sorry* over and over, trying to resurrect the flowers we trod on.

Heather and I return to our desks as soon as the rest of the editorial team has traipsed upstairs to eat around the kitchen table like civil well-behaved employees. I tell Heather about the big career decision I have to make, Alex's pledge to get me gigs, and of course, our domestic disabilities. She doesn't say much except "shit," while poking a fingernail into her dessert—one Rusk with honey. I really appreciate her support. She (s)hit the nail on the head.

"Hey, Melody. Let's go out tonight. Might make you feel better."

"Yeah," I nod, trying to mentally grasp what 'go out' means to people other than Alex and me. "Okay. Where would you like to eat?"

"Um, well, I was sort of thinking of doing something a bit out of the ordinary," she replies, valour intensifying her cheek bones.

"Oh, yeah, like what?"

"Let's go clubbing!"

"Clubbing? You? *Clubbing?*" I roll my chair backward so I can see her properly. "I never thought of you as—"

"The type? I'm not the type. Hence the phrase *out of the ordinary.* You're not the type either. Can't imagine seeing you out of your comfort clothes." Heather waves her hand indistinctly. "That being said, what's with the flip-flops?"

"Uh ... my thongs?"

"Yeah. Sorry, *thongs,*" Heather repeats, attacking the Australian twang.

"Pure and simple laziness. They were beside my bed this morning."

"Well, don't wear them tonight; you'll get your toes squashed. So, whatcha think? You in?"

"Um, okay. Let's do it. Oh, wait ... what about work tomorrow?"

"It's Tuesday. Annual Book Exhibition, remember? *Of*-fice is *clos*-ed," Heather sings, wriggling in her seat with ebullient moxie.

"Oh, yeah. Forgot." The prospect of reliving a little teen spirit brings to mind a pink bear and my sixteen-year-old exploratory lesbian relationship with a classmate who painted her eyebrows with magenta glitter and ended every sentence with a whine—and Nirvana—the grunge band which made dressing like a construction worker in flannel shirts and Blundstone boots a fashion statement.

"Dress up," Heather whispers as the girls wander back to their desks, dragging their feet like sloths on speed. "I wanna see a completely different person when *Oi* see you *git* on that *trollee.*"

Different person. I think I already am one.

twelve

The vehement whoosh of the stove fan and bubbling chicken soup puts me into a trance. I stare at steam being sucked away into noise, a truck swimming through a giant whirlpool. A school of singing plankton amplified to human frequency. What am I going to wear?

Ring ring … ring ring … ring ring …

Alex brings me the phone. Taps it on my upper-back, looking at the floor. I take it. My wedding ring clicks on the plastic like acrylic nails to a table top. I hold the phone to my left breast. It vibrates against my nipple. Alex walks out of the kitchen, hitching up his quarter-length shorts. *Has he lost weight? Am I turned on? I have to tell him about the job.*

"Hello?"

"Oh, hi! I'm so glad you answered, I was beginning to get worried," Mum says with a sigh.

"I'm in the middle of cooking. I couldn't hear the phone over the fan. Is everything okay?" I hold the handset to my ear with my shoulder, so I can stir.

"Oh, yeah, but I think I'm going downhill again. Head-aches—nerve pains down my arms. You know, I fell onto a rock yesterday while trying to take some photos and really hurt myself. Bloody James just gazes into the sky pretending that he can't hear me while I ask him to help me get up."

"Er—"

"Do you think he has a problem? You think he's becoming senile?"

"Mum—"

"No. No, that can't be it. He's always been like this. He's just plain selfish."

"Um ... so have you sold any more packages this month?"

"Yeah. I have to attend some board meeting Friday before we get on the ferry. The company wanted to hold it on the weekend but I kicked up a stink. Why does everyone want to book my time when I'm not here?"

"Oh? Where you off to?"

"*Don't* tell me you for*got*. I asked you to book a *hotel* room!"

The wooden spoon slips from my hand and clatters on the floor. As I bend down to pick it up, Doggy wanders in, licks up the splattered broth, and I hit my head on the edge of the stove.

"Ouch! Mum, I have to go. I'll call you back later."

Alex shuffles in on his slippers as if they're skis, shorts hanging halfway down his bum. He takes the phone out of my hand as I obliviously hover it above the pot.

"What's up? You okay?" He winks, massages my neck—talks in cartoon.

"Yeah, just whacked my head on the damn—"

"Who was it?" He jiggles the phone.

"Hmm?"

"On the phone."

"Oh. Just Betty the bloody Banter-ress." I hold my breath, cheeks puffed, as I turn the heat down on the hot plate. I put the lid on the pot, leaving a small gap for it to simmer down a little, and then gesture for Alex to turn around. "Um ... have you lost weight? Your shorts are ... kinda loose."

"Don't think so." He pulls them back up above his hips with a frown.

"You have. You've lost weight. Have you been ... exercising?"

"Of course not," he snaps, looking blank-faced at the stove. "What are you cooking?"

"You know exactly what I'm cooking."

Alex nods at the floor and turns to leave.

"Hey. Wait."

"What?"

"Where are you going?" I ask, in the most non-threatening voice I can possibly muster. I look him up and down, pause on the patch of bald smooth skin on his right calf, where he pulls his hair out whenever watching TV, rolls it and flicks it like snot. Fur balls. But no cat in the house.

"Back to my desk. Why?"

"No reason." I stare, trying to smile.

Alex's eyes shift toward the greasy cupboard handle, to the floor, to my knees.

"I'm just wondering what's going on with you," I add.

"Nothing's going on!" The tone of his voice shifts into

defensive mode and he throws his arms in the air and storms out. I want to grab him by the ear and drag him back in; threaten to cane him if he doesn't speak up.

"Okay. Whatever." I shake my head.

I squeeze lemon-scented detergent into the sink and run the hot tap. It reminds me of the time my mother filled an old foundation bottle of hers with no-frills washing up liquid, made a wand from a wire coat hanger and blew bubbles with me in the driveway until the mixture ran out.

She didn't care about tidiness then. She didn't cry or scream, insult my father, or threaten to kill herself. She even baked me cookies once in a while. I must have been about three or four years old. Before bipolar took her away to a place I never want to revisit.

I wish I could recall the memories my mother cherishes so much; like when she would throw me in the air and catch my limp, trusting body seconds before I would have hit the ground. I'd do anything to remember flying for those few fantastical seconds—being greeted back to Earth with ardent tickles, on the green lawn of our suburban Aussie backyard. I want to remember her lifting me to reach the Vegemite on the top shelf, and giving me butterfly kisses until putting me back on my feet. I want to remember being carried for hours around The Queen Victoria Market, snuggled in my mother's arms, with my face nuzzled in her warm, Estee Lauder-scented neck. But I don't remember these things—my mother does. All I have are photographs and my mother's word.

But if I roll them up—Mum's words—into a tight sacred

ball in my palm, I can *almost* feel the innocence we once shared; I can *almost* taste our love and her memories as if my own. Until she makes that call. *Selfish little bitch. Selfish little bitch.* And I begin to wonder: Why do I only remember bad things?

I'm rinsing the last of the dishes when Alex comes back in. I dry my hands on an overused tea towel which smells of garlic, onion, off yoghurt. Embedded in this stench is something warm and wet. And white. Cappuccino froth.

"For Christ's sake, Alex, can't you use the paper towel to wipe up your—"

"I lied." Alex leans against the door frame, hanging his head.

"And you don't know why."

Alex smiles, sniffs, pushes nose hair up a nostril. "Sorry," he says, stepping forward. He kisses me on the forehead.

"So, what's the truth? Why you acting so out of character? And *how* did you lose all that weight?" I stretch my arms around his waist and lay my head on his chest. *Please don't lie. Please.*

"I've been feeling, er … unattractive?" he whispers, as if seeking approval for his response. He rocks me back and forth, lips planted on my temple like a statuesque kiss.

"And you've been exercising?"

"Yeah. I thought it might, you know, make you more attracted to me."

"You worry I'm not attracted to you anymore?" I ask, looking up, the tip of my nose touching the dimple in his chin.

"Yeah."

"Me too." *Is this for real?*

"You do?" He rubs my upper back as if burping a baby.

I nod, grinning as wide as Tessa draws smiles. I want to believe him. No. I *do* believe him, but the blister isn't bursting. There's no 'pop'. No instinctual psychological reflex to relieve my suspicion. There should be. If there's anything my mother is right about, she's right about a woman's instinct. But, I'll let it slide. I let it slide because the desire to believe Alex right now is as strong as my umbilical cord to Tessa. And, he did admit he lied. So that's good. That's one foot in the right direction.

"I should get dressed. Wanna help me choose some clothes? Maybe, you know, you can *dress* me?" I wink, pulling away from his embrace, so I can see his face.

"Er, not *really*." He scoffs. "Got a few emails to write. Sorry. Might have closed a deal with Samantha Fox, though. Wanna be her support act?"

"Um …" *I can't make this decision now. I can't. What if we have to move to London?* "If you book her, let me know when it is and we'll talk about it."

"You seemed more enthusiastic last night. What happened?"

"Um, nothing, nothing at all." My cheeks tingle like aftershave on open pores. "It's just that book exhibitions are coming up soon and I have to be there this year. Just want to make sure they don't collide. I'll just be too exhausted after standing on my feet all day." *Phew. Nice save, Melody. He doesn't know that they're tomorrow. Does he? Oh God, if I told him, I'm—*

"Okay, cool. I'll let you know."

Tessa's sitting cross-legged on the balcony, trying to accessorize Doggy with purple sunglasses with star-shaped frames, but Doggy keeps shaking them off. Totally void of frustration, Tessa chuckles and licks Doggy's nose.

"Tessa! What are you doing?" I walk out and lift her off the ground. The shoulder of her white T-shirt is drenched with drool, her sandals are on the wrong feet, and she has a smudge of dirt above one eyebrow in the shape of an adult thumb.

"What?" Tessa squeaks in chaste, cocking her head to the side, just like Doggy does when I give her an order she pretends not to understand.

"Don't *lick* Doggy's *nose*." I put her back on her feet. "You might get sick."

"Why? She licked *me*. Will she get sick?" Tessa frowns.

"If she jumped off the balcony, would you follow?"

"Don't be silly, Mummy."

"Yes, you're right. I'm a silly mummy." I hold out my hand. "Come on. Come help me pick a dress to wear."

In my bedroom, we stand staring at my open wardrobe, hands on hips, as Tessa tends to enjoy the stance, inspecting its contents—an array of wrinkled black, gray, and olive green. Remind me—do we even *own* an iron?

I pull out a short black taffeta body-fitted dress that is pancaked to the far right side of my wardrobe with short sleeves and a high neck line. I hold it up against my body, my floppy man's clothes, and look in the mirror. The coat hanger hook is almost digging into my neck. I envision thrusting it into my skin and piercing my carotid artery. Gushing blood. Nice. Quick. Death. I blink. *Jesus!*

"Put it on," Tessa says, shaking her head like a disapproving sales assistant. "It looks silly like that."

I nod, stripping myself bare. Tessa's face goes pale.

"What's wrong?" I ask, stepping into the dress.

"Your legs have got … lots of holes," she whispers, protruding her bottom lip as if she has just understood what's in store.

"It's called cellulite. That's what happens when you sit at a desk all day and don't do enough exercise."

"Will I have to sit at a desk all day when I'm all grown up?"

I laugh, bend down and kiss her cheek. "No, Blossom, you won't."

Tessa smiles and smacks her lips together.

"Zip me," I say. Tessa holds the zip and I lower my body to the floor so she can reach up to my neck. *It fits!*

I turn to the mirror with my eyes closed. It's been so long since I've worn a body-fitted dress that I'm afraid seeing myself will just dampen my self-esteem to a point where I'll never want to step foot out of the house again.

I open one eye.

Okay. Disgust is not spreading through me like tear gas. That's good.

I open my other eye. *Hey, I don't look too bad.*

I slide my hands down my thighs, smoothing out the edges of the dress, semi-consciously checking for unflattering bumps. *Maybe I'll snazzy it up with those psychedelic beads I used to wear. Yeah.*

I straighten my back, suck in my stomach and turn to inspect my profile. *Big ass. Ugh.*

"Whatcha think, Blossom? You like?"

"Mmm …" Tessa scrunches her nose. "Nup."

"Why? What's wrong with it?" I ask, looking myself up and down, as if Tessa's opinion means life or death.

"Put the pink one on." She points to some purple-pink fabric sticking out of a plastic bag behind my shoes. How she even knows it's a dress is beyond me.

I pull it out, and hold it up. Yep, it's a dress—a jersey dress, wrinkle free—off-the-shoulder sleeves and a low-cut neckline. I can't even remember owning it. Was it Serena's? God! What would Alex say?

"Honey, I can't wear this." *Of course, you can. Why do you need Alex's approval?*

"Why not?"

Why not? Well. Trash, trash, trash. Or sexy? Can't wear a bra with this thing either. My boobs will look like saggy bread dough. How do you explain trashy to a four-year-old girl? How do you explain the woes of Earth's gravitational pull?

"Because … Look, I'll *try* it on, but that's all okay?"

Tessa nods, runs on the spot and jumps onto my bed giggling. Usually I'd tell her to get off, but I didn't make the bed this morning, so there doesn't seem to be any point.

I put the dress on.

My boobs are *a little lower than they should be, but that can be fixed, I think, with Alex's two-inch wide sticky tape. I could pass for a twenty-five-year-old, I suppose, with a little make-up, not too much, I don't want to look like a prostitute, and a little straightening of my hair … Do I still have that thing? Hmm, maybe …*

I look at Tessa, who is staring at me the way she stares at her Barbie dolls.

"You don't want to hack my hair off do you?" I ask.

"What?" Tessa asks, looking at me as if I've totally lost it.

"Never mind. You win. I'll wear it," I say expecting some sort of vocal parade.

"Cool." Tessa nods and jumps off the bed, landing a little too hard. She hurts her ankle, but tries to hide it, stands up, brushes off her hands and says, "My job is done."

She walks out of the room, wagging her bottom like "the stick ladies on TV."

In the bathroom I find the hair-straightener in the towel drawer—*under* the towels—and complete the picture of Melody/ teenage clubber. I feel absurd—eyes embossed with black liquid liner, eyelashes curled, eyebrows darkened with a layer of brown lip pencil, lips glossed in shimmering pale pink. *Who are you?*

I take one last look at myself in the full-length mirror, wondering how I should present myself to Alex.

Sexy, yet demure?

Shy and insecure?

No.

Better not hesitate. No signs of weakness.

"Vogue! Vogue!" I leap in front of Alex's desk, striking a pose, "let your body *mooove* to the *muuuusic*. Hey, hey, hey!" I move my hips to the rhythm, roll out his chair and sit on his lap, all the while thinking: *Please let that interrupted frown turn into an impressed smile.*

"Wow." Alex scratches his head. His penis twitches on my thigh.

"Stand up for me. Spin around," he laughs, waving his finger in a circular motion. I spin around, curtsy, wink.

"Will you be home in time for me to have a piece of you?" Alex asks, biting his bottom lip.

"If that's what you'd like … " I whisper all feathery-voiced. I bite his earlobe, breathe softly into his neck, massage his groin, taking my role to an entirely different level—a level I would ordinarily cringe at if I observed another woman doing it. Sexual manipulation. Others might call this foreplay. Why do I see it as something negative—cheap? What has happened to my femininity? Has motherhood sucked it dry? Marriage? Lack of aspiration? Libido detached, cloudy, like a used condom.

He moves in for a kiss, slides the tip of his tongue between my lips. But no goose-bumps. No heat between my thighs. I remember when the mere caress of his gentle fingers on the inside of my wrists made me shiver—made me want to slam him against a wall and fuck him until I could fuck no more—until it hurt to walk.

"YUK!" Tessa screams, and runs down the corridor yodelling like a turkey.

Beep beep. Beep beep.

I get up off Alex's lap as he reaches for his cell. He opens the message and almost instantly presses delete.

"Who was that?" I snap, with my arm already in one sleeve of my light blue denim jacket, ready to pounce, to reveal all, find an excuse to get meticulously inebriated.

"Oh. No-one. Just my father."

"Is he okay?"

"Hmm-hm."

"Why'd you delete it?"

Alex looks me right in the eye, not a flinch, not an ounce of hesitation.

"Trying to keep my inbox clean. That's all."

The lights in this underground club are kaleidoscopic enough to bring on an epileptic fit, and the music is so loud that Heather and I have had to revert to lip reading. My face sets in concrete; my body stuck, numb against the prickly walls of a theme park Graviton. I lean against the bar, trying to avoid eye-contact with the sleaze in the unbuttoned luminous shirt.

"Loosen up, Mel. Just pretend you're eighteen again. You look hot!" Heather screams, looking me up and down, a treble shrill sharpening her voice.

"And how do you suggest I do that?" I scream back into her ear.

Heather reaches for a glass of something that looks like toxic waste and hands it to me. "Here. Slam this down."

"Jeez. How? What is that?"

"Can't remember what it's called. Just made a fool of myself asking for it. Typical—the *gorg* bartender had to take my order, didn't he?" she screams into my neck.

"What did you ask for?" I question with a flick of my hand.

Heather leans in. I can hear the indulgent squint in her

eyes through her hot, moist, rebellious breath. "I said, 'You know that beer drink with the shot glass inside? Can't really remember what kinda alcohol is in that shot glass, but it made me drunk. Can you give me one of those?' Ha!"

I tsk, hang my head in my hands, wonder what I have got myself into. But there is also a twinge of hunger for a reckless, thoughtless eventide of poppycock. Heather's right. I *should* loosen up. Swallow this bomb in a glass—sooth my pharynx.

"Yeah, well, you know Heather," she winks. "She don't make small talk 'bout weather! Ha-ha!"

We clink glasses and imbibe our juicy backbones. Heather asks for two more, winks at the bartender and almost falls off her stool. Her chortle pacifies the compressed punch of retro beats. Non-music to my electronically fused ears.

Three more bombs later and we're slow-dancing to disco beats. Heather proclaims to be the man in this relationship because she's taller. This triggers a flurry of slurred feminist opinions on my part. I'm drunken and disorderly and as soon as my anti-sexism theories have exploded like verbal shrapnel, I sob and slobber on Heather's shoulder.

"Alex doesn't love me anymore," I whimper.

"Of course he loves you, Smel. You're just goings through rough time." Heather tries to sooth, slurring in my ear, on the verge of licking it like a lollipop.

"Nope. He doesn't love me. I know it. Something's going on. He's hiding something from me. I know it."

"Smelody. He loves you. It takes two to make a relationship work and it takes two to break one up. If you really want your marriage to last, the two of you will work something out eventually. Believe me. I've been there before. Anyway, what are you doing sobbing on my chest when you should be having fun? I feel like I'm leaking breast milk."

Heather's words, though uttered at the rate of a tortoise's saunter, race through my head in search for some sort of validity—a sign, memory, something to deem her words true, when I actually get one. A dance version of "Sugar Pie Honey Bunch" comes on and we both burst out in song, our heads wobbling on our shoulders like dashboard bobble head dolls.

Wanna tell you I don't love you, Tell you that we're through, And I try, But ev'ry time I see your face, I get all choked up inside, When I call your name, ALEX, it starts to flame, Burning in my heart, Tearing it all apart. No matter how I try, My love I cannot hide …

It's been a long time since I've been out like this. I mean, *properly* out, doing girly claptrap, rather than eating a respectable meal in a reputable restaurant. The last time I spent a night getting sloshed at a club was a few months before moving to Greece. Life was one big experiment then. I'd go through phases of Goth, punk, intellectual, muso, introvert, extrovert, comedian, poet, and sometimes bitch just to see how people would react to me. A subconscious effort to fit in with my mother's mentality? Who knows.

"Heather!" I grab her arm and point toward a man standing at the end of the bar with a young, tall redhead. "Who's that? Does he look familiar to you?" The red/blue lighting effects distort my view. I hold my hand over my eyes as if protecting them from the sun.

"Er, nope. But don't think anyone would look very familiar to me right now … oops … where's my shoe? You seen my shoe? Oh, there it is … is … is my shoe … stay here, I'll just fetch my shoe …."

Heather stumbles to the middle of the dance floor, almost colliding with the open-shirted man doing the limbo.

The guy at the end of the bar catches my eye, whispers something into the redhead's ear. She nods, walks away. He heads toward me. *Me? I wasn't eyeing him off. Does he think I'm flirting?*

"Hi, Melody, you never called," the guy says, imitating a sob.

"Right," says Heather, leaning heavily into my shoulder. "Found my shoe … er, hi, pleased to make your acquaintance, sir, and you might be?" Heather slurs, hopping on one foot in an attempt to put the missing shoe on at the same time. I point to the button on my shoulder of my jacket, pretending to scratch it, and raise my eyebrows.

"Oh! *Button* boy! I've heard—"

"Heather!" I cry, putting my hand over her mouth. "I'm terribly sorry, Mr—"

"Richard. Call me Richard."

"I'm terribly sorry, Richard, for my friend's behaviour here, I-I—"

"No problem at all, Melody," Richard touches my hand. "Just nice to know you actually didn't forget about me."

"How could I forget? My button bull's-eyed you!"

What am I saying? You idiot! Melody, YOU IDIOT!

"Oh, you noticed that? You seemed so calm and collected I thought you hadn't realized." Richard laughs.

"Yeah, well, my career was on the line." I scratch my brow despite not feeling any itch.

"Yes. Indeed. Well, now that your friend, um … "

"My name's Heather, luv."

Oh, Heather. Could you embarrass me more? Luv? You've gone into hick mode.

"Heather here," Richard interrupts, gesturing apologetically with his hands on Heather's shoulder, "has implied that you spoke to her about the incident. May I ask why you didn't call? I assume you have been told you have the position in London? Correct?"

"Yes. How embarrassing. For a second, here, I thought you were trying to pick me up."

"I was."

"Oh."

Queasy. Knots. Stretching. Fraying. Lubricating. Draining. Fraying. Breaking. Don't pull. Stop!

Wait.

Richard?

His name's Richard?

Richard Viadro, academic director in London? Is this man my potential boss?

thirteen

Television light creeps beneath our bedroom door, igniting the corridor with liquid sleep waves. I tiptoe to my office to get undressed.

As I fumble for the light switch, Doggy appears between my legs and trips me. My handbag flings toward my desk, knocks off an empty water glass, and smashes on the floor. Tiny glittering shards of clumsiness float around my feet, threatening to spike me with lament.

Alex calls, "Eh!" I freeze, cold with guilt for not putting the glass in the sink before I left. I examine my blurry surroundings, making sure there's nothing else I might hit, before I attempt to switch the light on again.

It's only Monday night and I feel like this relationship/ career/dream—and now fatal Richard-attraction-dilemma—has been brewing since yesteryear.

Time drags on and on, and on … (One more! Clap your hands!) and on, but there is still not enough time to make rational decisions anymore. Life is just one big rush. There is never enough time for anything anymore. I don't make any *sense* to myself anymore. I don't understand what I'm *thinking* anymore. I don't understand why I'm having so much trouble making this *decision*. Anymore?

Why can't I just be mature about the whole thing and do what's right? But what *is* right? And I *am* being mature about it, right? Write. I should write all of this down. Keep a journal. Maybe it'll free my mind of all this ... stuff. I've slipped off the beaten track. Yes. I should keep track of my thoughts. Then maybe at the end of the week I can back-track and come to some sort of logical solution. Have I been brainwashed with Dad's philosophical ramble?

I nudge Doggy onto the balcony despite her resistance, sweep the glass to the wall with a magazine, and pick up the cordless phone. For a moment I think it's sticky with Heather's vomit. But no, that was in her house. Not here. *How did I get her home? I don't remember the cab ride at all.*

Dad. Speak to Dad.

It's two o'clock in the morning, but I know he'll be awake. My parents have a tendency to record music on their computers till the sun rises and burns their eyes out. Especially my father—Frank Zappa's zombie turned *Radiohead* in *Weird Science*.

My mother answers the phone.

"Hi, it's me," I say, trying to balance the waver in my voice.

"Hi, Melody. Right. Where were we?" She coughs. I realize she assumes this will be a continuation of the conversation we'd started earlier in the evening.

"I was actually wondering if I could speak to *Dad*."

"He's fine. The usual. Not listening to a word I say," she says, clearing her throat again.

"You didn't hear what I said. I said, I want to *speak* to

him. I didn't ask how he was." I walk to the kitchen table, pull out a chair, careful not to scrape it. It doesn't, but the sound of metal legs landing on spotted marble is nothing short of an echoing pop. I wince at the thought of waking Alex. Why? Habit.

"Oh."

Kitchen appliances sway around my head like tornado debris.

"Hold on a sec. I'll get him. You know him. Glued to his computer with the headphones on." Her hand muffles the receiver.

"James! Phone!"

A dampened stampede through her house ensues—the thunder of a tent being blown in the wind. *Does she really think I won't hear anything?*

Dad yelps. *Thump!*

Did she just hit him over the head with the phone?

"Stop fucking around for a minute," she demands. "Melody's on the phone."

"Oh. Sorry. I'll turn the music down," Dad says. I flinch, suspecting what might follow.

"No*oooo!* You're wearing *headphones* you fucking *idiot*. She wants to *speak* to *you*."

"Me? Oh." He sounds pleasantly surprised and not at all troubled by Mum's behaviour. I hear the phone slide from one hand to the other.

"Hi, Melody." His voice gurgles like a fourteen-year-old pubescent boy.

"Hi, Dad. How's things?"

"Good."

"Whatcha up to?"

"You know me. Fucking around on the computer."

"Is Mum still there?" I imagine her standing in the doorway, watching him speak and nod with a smile that acts like a mask for resentment.

"Yep."

"She watching you?"

"Yep."

"Is there any way you can stop it?"

"Nup."

"So we need to talk about meaningless things until she gets bored and goes back to her own computer?"

"Yep."

Mum grabs the phone from Dad and says, "Sounds like a nice intellectual conversation. I'll leave you two to it. When you're done, remind him to pass the phone to me before hanging up 'cause he won't remember to do it himself, okay?"

"Givvim a break, Mum," I plead, trying to save Dad the torture.

"I'm not joking."

"All right, don't worry. I'll tell him to pass the phone back to you." I suddenly feel quite sober.

"Why do you want to speak to him anyway?"

"I just realized I haven't had a proper conversation with him for about ten years, that's all," I say flippantly, realizing how not "that's all" it is.

"Pfft. Okay then, don't come back to me brain dead."

I hang my head wondering when she'll ever stop being so mean; whether it's intentional, facetious, an irrational fear of losing control, or even just habit.

I tell Dad everything. About music, Alex, and my potentially lucrative career opportunity. I even talk about my guilty button boy fantasies. But also, how when the man was standing right in front of me, I felt so sick and afraid, that vomit rose up into my throat. I tell him how confused I am—how *depressed* I feel. That I've been having the most horrible thoughts. Thoughts I prefer to deny thinking.

But, do I ask Dad whether it's the right thing to uproot my family, move to another country, and expect Alex to commute from London to Athens whenever he has to attend an event? Do I ask him whether he thinks Tessa will adapt to her new environment easily? No, I ask him how I'm supposed to work in the same office as button boy and not be tempted to have an affair. When did I become so selfish? *Why* am I so selfish? Why do I feel like I'm constantly scraping off old mouldy wallpaper in search of the clean white wall?

Dad just listens and nods against the receiver. He doesn't try to tell me what to do or how to solve any of these issues. He doesn't even scold me for being so self-centred.

I like his nodding. And I know he knows all I *need* is nodding; that all I *need* is to get things off my chest. Because it's something he can't ever seem to do himself.

I don't ask him to pass the phone to Mum; and he doesn't remember.

When I hang up, I drift off to sleep. Who knows how long I've been drooling the six toxic bombs I consumed all over the kitchen table, when I am woken by a light touch on my knuckles. I travel, momentarily, back to Heather's house, where a crisp clean powder-like smell of porcelain dolls overpowers her puke when she trips over her welcome mat.

I lift my head—squeaky like polystyrene; dense as a bowling ball.

Tessa takes me by the hand, walks me to my bedroom, and tucks me in. She whispers, "Sweet dreams, say the jelly beans; it's time to sleep, that means." As she strokes my forehead, like I do hers, I remember. My mother's unadulterated smile as she used to put me to bed. A *real* memory—and my *own*.

My alarm rings, it shouldn't have, and I prematurely awake in the sediment of alcoholic self-mutilation. After thirty minutes of nagging an answer out of Alex, he admits he changed it for himself. He didn't think it would matter, seeing as I was sleeping on the kitchen table—I wouldn't have heard it from there. Apparently.

"How could you just leave me there?"

"You made it to bed eventually."

I look out the window, trying to recall how I got here.

"Tessa brought me to bed," I croak after a moment of silence.

I rub some sleep out of my eyes and rehydrate the inside of my mouth with the dregs of bottled water on the floor.

"Why were you home so late? I thought you said you would come home for me," Alex says, sitting up.

"I was having fun. Is it a crime?"

Alex exhales a sarcastic grunt. "Tessa spilt milk all over the floor again. I cleaned it up."

"That'd be a first," I whisper to myself. "It'd be nice if you didn't complain so much, you know. I don't go out very often."

"Don't be ridiculous; I've cleaned up Tessa's spilt milk before." Alex puts on a T-shirt in haste, getting himself tangled in its elasticity—his elbows poke into the fabric like an ostrich trying to break free from its pliable egg.

I tsk between gritted teeth as Alex searches the floor for clean-ish socks.

"It'd also be nice if you cared more. If you really wanted to see me when I got home, why didn't you get out of bed and try to seduce me?"

"I didn't want to wake you. Doesn't that show that I care?"

"I wasn't asleep when I walked in the door, Alex." I throw a pillow at him. He catches it with one hand without even looking and drops it to the floor.

Alex lies down again, fully clothed above the duvet, stares at the ceiling, and plays with the hem of his T-shirt. He opens his mouth to speak. Three times. He doesn't say a word.

With a gag-infused sigh, I get up and start to dress. Gray nausea tints my vision like textured windows.

"I was worried about this," Alex snaps, still staring at the ceiling.

"Huh?" I pull on a pair of tracksuit pants without putting

any underwear on first. My stomach screams mercy as I lift my body upright. I pause mid way, willing my bile to remain where it belongs.

"You acting like you're single after me agreeing to get you a gig."

"What?" A flash of smooth button boy charm turns the corner of my mouth up. Ignominy pans from my left ear to my right as if I'm listening to it through headphones.

"You know what I'm talking about."

I can't manage more than a confused and defeated stare. Does he know?

"Don't look at me like that," he says, scratching under his chin.

I stand there with my pants halfway up my legs and watch him storm out of the bedroom with a huff. *A huff. Not by the hair of my chinny chin chin.*

My warm calves ground me. My cold thighs will me to go after him to soothe my angst. My stomach says: just die now before I explode all over your dusty carpet.

Paranoia. An intense unfounded fear or suspicion.
Paranoia is a symptom of bipolar disorder.
Paranoid. Exhibiting unwarranted suspicion or fear of persecution.
I'm paranoid I might have bipolar disorder and that Alex knows I've mentally cheated on him.
Paranormal. Beyond ordinary expectation.
Alex's paranormal instinctive qualities make me paranoid that I suffer from severe paranoia and might have bipolar disorder.

I crawl out of bed, make myself a honeyed green tea and shuffle my way to Alex's office. I sit opposite him at his desk. I breathe in the comforting steam and a sigh of limited relief.

"Where's Tessa?" I ask.

"On the balcony."

"What's she doing?"

"Making mud pies."

"With *what*?"

"The pot plant she tipped upside down."

"What pot plant?"

"Rosemary."

"I just planted that."

"I know. Sorry. Can't make time move backwards, unfortunately."

Alex taps at his keyboard, squints at his screen. The morning sunlight casts a shadow on his face. A compass. An Arrow. Pointing to his forehead. To his *brain*. It occurs to me that I haven't asked him how *he* feels. I've spent the last two weeks burdening him with my feelings, *my* woes, that I haven't even *considered* he might be having a hard time too—or that these suspicious messages might be the result of ... *Oh. My. God. His business! Why didn't I think of that before?*

"Alex, are you okay? Have I, um, stopped being nice to you?"

"Nice?" He scoffs—body shaking like a shiver from the cold. "No, you've been 'nice'. But you haven't been *thought*ful."

I nod, looking into my mug, at the murky yellowish

brown that is supposed to be green. I hold it below my chin to feel the warmth of steam on my face. Despite the moderate weather, there seems to be a chill hanging over my shoulders.

"I'd like to change that."

"I'd like that." Alex looks at me with his head tilted.

"Let's take Tessa to be babysat tonight," I suggest, hoping that if I relax him enough, he'll be willing talk about what's bothering him. Stress-free Alex equals rubber Alex—flexible and keen to erase mistakes.

Alex smiles, stands up and walks to my side. His knees crack as he kneels to my level, and massages my upper arms.

"Sorry about before," he says, lifting my chin. "Guess I was, er, a bit jealous?"

I cup my cold hands to Alex's unshaven cheeks, each grain of stubble injecting me with relief. *He's just jealous.*

I take a deep breath and hold it. "I've been offered the job in London."

Alex's arms go limp. He looks at my feet, stands, shrugs his hands into his pockets.

"Well, I suppose we'll just have to—"

"I've decided I'm not gonna take it."

fourteen

Love should stop the world from spinning, on demand, and obsession should be the need *to* spin it, rather than anger, regret and yearning lodging themselves below our nails. Love and obsession, together, should make the heart heave in anticipation to experience the most desired intimate act, before, during, and after the words "I love you" become routine. They should thrive through touch, through body—a vessel to help combine our souls and minds.

I dissolve into this thought, this heat, this wave, letting my arms fall to my sides, as Alex's saccharine mauve taste plunges me into a place I have yearned to rekindle since I turned thirty this year. A place where love is not an expression of lust, or ink, or the familiar yet distant voice I remember now and then; it is a place where love is tangible, and lush, like fruit hanging from a grapevine in the rain. Ripe. Wet. Waiting to be devoured. Hanging. Expecting. Anticipating my need to bite the apple. Except this time, breaking the rules will make everything right again. I know it will.

I look toward the sun setting behind the mountains and eat another grape. Its crisp mauve skin breaks between my tongue and the roof of my mouth. Juice squirts into the back of my throat. It's hot, cold—acidic sweet. I wash it down with a slice of brie and a generous sip of red wine. After an intimate evening watching romantic movies and eating sushi, I put on Enigma's *Le Roi Est Mort, Vive Le Roi!* album, and skip to my favourite track, *"Almost Full Moon"*. Instrumental, spiritual. Bringing forth a smooth connection with Mother Nature, and the calming silkiness of my jet-black full-length nightdress against my skin. I breathe in an imagined scent of the ocean as low ethnic drums beat along-side photoelectric chimes.

I sit back down on the couch, and whisper close to Alex's ear, "Do you really still love me?"

"Melody, I love you so *so* much. I love you *so* much that I can't *breathe* anymore," he whispers in return, stroking my hair, kissing my forehead.

I realize that I've been looking at our relationship through the rear view mirror instead of the windshield. And I've been putting the blame on Alex for destroying my dreams, when the fact of the matter is, I can't blame anyone but myself. I made these choices. But the biggest realization here is, I don't need to go back in time to fulfil my passion. And from today, I will look forward—we will look through the windshield—no matter how depressed or sorry for myself I feel.

I swivel around and wrap my legs around Alex's waist, kiss him softly on his lips. Right here, right now, I don't feel cheap. I feel free, hopeful, and grateful Alex and I are finally on the road to seeing eye-to-eye. Love doesn't ever die. We die. And it is up to us to keep ourselves alive.

"So glad you're turning the job down. Don't know what I'd do without you," Alex says, running his fingers through my hair.

"What do you mean, 'without you'? What … you wouldn't have come?" I ask, struggling not to jump to any conclusions.

"Of *course* I'd come."

I release my breath.

"I'd just have to take care of a lot of business *malakies* if we moved. It would be a lot of work, and we'd have to spend time apart. I'd be travelling back and forth for months before being able to base myself in London. Trying to figure it all out has been stressing me out to no end. Especially since—well, doesn't matter now, does it? You're staying. My worries are over."

I don't want to ask. *Especially since what?* He'll tell me. He'll tell me in his own time. I close my eyes, trying to swallow myself back into the moment, focusing on the rhythm of Enigma—heartbreaking, yet consoling, soft screams from darkened souls hovering with humming harps, contorted wind instruments, canorous guitars, and cathodic waves.

Hot tears nestle in the corner of my eyes. Alex licks one as it escapes down my cheek. I've been so selfish. I'm going to change. I move in for another kiss, but he catches my tongue between his lips and sucks it into his mouth. He pulls me closer, wraps my left arm around his neck and puts my right hand down the front of his unbuttoned linen pants; I push my tongue in deeper. We groan in unison.

My head spins. Heat from Alex's abdomen radiates through my inner thighs.

We rip each other's clothes off in front of the sliding double glass doors that lead out onto the balcony, oblivious to possible onlookers across the road, and fumble into the bedroom. Alex pushes me against the wall, pulling my thin black lingerie straps off my shoulders, down around my waist. He rotates his tongue around my left nipple, sending orgasmic currents through my fingers and toes. Our breaths heavy, I pull his face close to mine, and bite his ear while forcing his pants down with my right foot. Just as he lifts me up, hooks me around his waist to enter me, he stumbles on one of Tessa's toys and kicks it backward under the bed. Panting, I look down between our naked bodies. And right there, sticking out from under Alex's big toe is … a used condom.

I lower my legs—stare at it.

"How long has that been there?" I gasp, my breath dry against the back of my throat.

Alex hesitates, "Must be weeks," and tries to lift my legs back up around his waist.

I feel sick. My head grows hot as I bend down to pick up the condom—take a closer look.

"Alex, this condom is … glittery. Alex! This *connnndom* is *glittereeeee*!"

I push him backward and he falls on the bed. My breath is thick, like an invisible hand is pushing me under water and I'm struggling to reach the surface for air.

"Oh my God," I whisper, holding onto the bedpost as I

lower myself to the floor. "Oh. My. God. I was *right*. I was right *all* along!" I howl into my hands. I lean my naked body against the wall and bring my knees to my chest. "What have you *done*, Alex? What *have* you *done*?" I kick the wardrobe door closed that is slightly ajar. It bangs so loud—I think I hear wood crack.

Alex sits on the bed. Stares at the wall. Doesn't speak.

Do I cry now? Am I crying already? I shiver. Blink the throes of betrayal from my eyes, my head, my face, that sting and pound in my throat, my glands: a waterfall of drained hope. I remain. Naked against the wall. I should just stretch my arms out to my sides. Nail them to the wall.

Somebody just crucify me. I can't do this anymore.

I pace the house, wiping away dust with my night-dress. I can't bear to walk back into the bedroom and put it in the laundry basket, so I throw it in the rubbish bin. The tainted in the trash.

Ire stings like a metallic taste—a battery on my tongue—waiting for approval to charge—a bull to a red cape in a confined space.

"Mel, can you please come back in so we can talk about this?"

Alex's voice hangs in the air.

I don't want to. I want to grab a kitchen knife and *stab*—at anything—a cushion, a watermelon—Alex's head. I take a steak knife out of the drawer. The serrated blade shimmers in the moonlight. Glistens with revenge. I blink. Shake my head. Throw it in the sink. It clangs with iniquity.

I force myself to return to the bedroom. Each footstep a spasm of ache. Alex is still sitting on the bed, naked, staring at the wall. I stand by the door. He doesn't look my way.

Red eyes weep without a sound. Disjointed from his face, hanging somewhere around his feet. His wrinkles are embedded with grit. The grit of lies. I hope they burn. I hope they get deeper. Cause him pain. I want him to hurt.

Alex looks at his feet. I put my dressing gown on, focus on its texture, its frayed appearance.

"It'd probably be better for both of us if … you slept in your office."

I narrow my eyes.

Alex lifts his hand as if directing me to stop in traffic. "Just … just for tonight. It's late. Get some rest, and we can talk tomorrow."

I step forward. I slap him. He looks through me, eyes glazed with tears, as if I might offer pity. I slap him again. He holds his head and neck stiff, creating a stronger impact. My wedding ring hits his cheekbone. He flinches, face contorts in pain. Tears unite behind my teeth. I clench my jaw. Headache. My head aches with contaminated, faulty, frail ardour. I want him. I finally want him back and now I want him gone. I *hate* him. I … *love* him.

Again, he looks down.

I jump on top of him, punching, kicking, screaming, crying, "You fucking lying bastard! You fucking lying bastard!" over and over. When I stop, I can hardly breathe—panting on all fours, on the bed, above him.

"You fucking mother*fucker*," I scream again, hot tears

streaming down my cheeks. "You love me so much that you can't breathe? What the *fuck* was *that*?" I move so close to his face that our noses touch. "What the *fuck* does that mean *now*?"

"I'm … I'm sorry." He protects his face with a bent arm. I sit up, panting, crying, he tries to get me to lie down.

"No way! No. *Fucking*. Way!" I lean backward against the foot of the bed; try to catch my breath, and put my head between my knees. I feel like I'm rocking backward and forward in this dizzy fury. I focus on my breath, the way my father taught me when I started getting migraines. Meditation. Healing. Summoning the right energy.

"When … did this …?"

"I— "

"Who?"

"Baby—"

"How?"

"I just—"

"You *just what*?

Alex stretches his neck, looks at the ceiling. His eyes flicker back and forth as if trying to decode a computer encryption.

"When?" I ask.

"About a week ago." He blows his nose into a eucalyptus tissue from the bedside table. He shakes his head in what seems to be disbelief.

"About a week ago," I nod, biting my bottom lip so hard I have to consciously stop myself before I make it bleed.

"In this bed? In *our* bed?" The thought sends convoluted

images through my mind so fast I feel the need to look away. "Alex?" I swallow.

Alex nods, hangs his head in his hands. I try to lick my dry lips, but my tongue is stuck to the roof of my mouth from holding it together with suction force.

"Alex … who was it?" I ask, my hands beginning to tremble.

"Just … just some …"

A pang of cold impatience releases as a roar. "Oh, for Christ's sake, Alex, just answer the fucking question!"

"Melody, I was *really* drunk, I wasn't able to drive. She drove me home. It wasn't meant to happen, Melody. I'm so sorry! I am!" Alex takes my hands and brings them to his cheeks. I pull away.

"And where was I? On the island?"

Alex looks me in the eyes, all colour draining from his face. "Yes."

With poise, I stand, wipe my eyes with the bottom of my palms. Pull a few clothes out of the wardrobe, take a deep breath and close my eyes. I can sense Alex staring at me— willing me to forgive him.

"I'm going to sleep in my office," I say, nodding as if the action will convince me it's the right thing to do. "I don't want to hear or *see* you. Just stay *out* of my *fucking* way."

At three o'clock in the morning I'm still awake, shivering from the unusually cold night. I turn on my computer and log onto Facebook, do a few quizzes, play online backgammon.

Charlie.

I search for him—friend him. My ex-boyfriend, from Australia. Serena had suggested his friendship to me a long time ago, but I never sent a request, fearing that it'd be betraying Alex. *Betraying Alex. Ridiculous.* I leave Charlie a message, half crying, half laughing—reciting as I type like a lunatic.

"You still playing music? Can I play too?"

part three

Selfish Heartbreak

I used to thrive on hate
until I learnt to love
you.
I used to bite my tongue
until betrayal scarred
virtue.
I used to feel selfish
til you proved it weren't
true.
Look at this.
Look at this selfish heartbreak.
Look at this.
Look at this selfish heart break.
You destroyed what I learnt to value most
the reason behind my
tattoo.

fifteen

Doggy scratches at my door. It's five in the morning. Can't sleep. I let her in. She throws up at my feet. Squirts a whopping puddle of missile diarrhoea not only between my toes, but in a trail toward the front door when she realizes she should be doing it outside. Of course she steps in it. And spreads it through the entire apartment. I grab the mop, but she chases it—something I'm really not in the mood to be dealing with right now. Normally, I'd play along, but I don't want to wake Alex. Seeing him now might make me throw Doggy's shit in his face. I feel more disgusted of Alex than I do of dog diarrhoea on my hands. Perhaps I could do a bit of finger painting with it. All over his desk. And computer. And mouse. And … Screw it. Why not just bathe him in the shit?

I throw on a dark gray tracksuit to take Doggy out for a walk through Lykabettus national park. My face is numb to the chilly morning air. My fingers numb to the plastic handle on Doggy's lead. My eyes numb to the dim pre-morning light. My bare feet numb to the pebbly black asphalt of the road and the damp scattered grass as I step foot into the park. My nose numb to the scent of pine. My rationale numb to the possibility of stepping on a syringe. *I should have put some shoes on.*

My senses are blurred in a place I usually soak up like fragrant moisturizer. The tall trees, the scattered pine cones, the narrow pebbled paths, the *quiet.* A serene inner-city haven that blocks out traffic noise like double-glazed glass—where my brain is free to stop. And I let it stop. Here. Usually.

I sit on *my* park bench—the only old and tattered one left standing that's missing a plank and has psychologically moulded into the shape of my behind. I remove Doggy's lead, and inch my toes into the dirt until my feet look like stumps. It's cool and smooth on my skin—feels wet, but it's not. I wish I could lie in it, bury myself with it like sand—deep pressure touch to calm my nerves. Doggy digs her front paws into the same place and scratches my toes. I give her a light nudge. She glares at me—cocks her head. She stops digging, sits with one hind leg tucked under her bum, pushes her body against my right calf and rests her head on my knee with a grumbly sigh. *Is she trying to listen to my thoughts?* I run my thumb between her sad eyes.

"Don't worry. I won't abandon you," I whisper.

My phone beeps. *If it's Alex, I'll smash the phone into a tree trunk. I pull it out of my pocket,* turning my pocket inside out. It flops against my thigh like a cocker spaniel's ear.

Yep. Still playin music, mate. How r ya? U still draggin out de ol gee-tar?

It's Charlie.

Ashamed to tell the truth, I answer:

Yes. Nice 2 hear from u. Where did u find my no.?

I stare at my phone. Waiting for an answer—as still as a pencil on an old-fashioned school desk until the gifted student moves it with his eyes. A quick breeze blows through the trees, soothingly brushing against the back of my neck. As much as I wish the leaves were whispering secret messages, I think I'll leave that illusion to blockbuster television series' and clichéd song lyrics. Instead, I breathe in the air, and try to reignite my sense of smell—and the simple pleasure it used to give me.

Still hit da pub 4 a beer w/ Ser now & then. We both saw yr msg on fb. Ser wants 2 say hi. Ser goin 2 call in a couple hrs. I want 2 chat w/ u about sth.

Chat? With me? About something?

"Don't forget to pick up Tessa," I snap as I put Doggy out on the balcony. I can hear Alex rummaging in the kitchen. Most likely seeking out his coffee cup under a mountain of dry dishes that he will neglect to put away.

"I … I can't, I … I have an appointment in town," Alex follows my every move through the kitchen door. I refuse to make eye contact. I don't even want to remember—anything.

Is there any way I can just completely ignore this? Pretend that I haven't been shoved into a well and left there to rot? Pretend that the disappointment in myself for believing in our marriage and having the wool pulled over my eyes isn't bigger than my disappointment in Alex's infidelity? How did I let our marriage come to this? Why didn't I do anything about it earlier? Can I trust my own instincts anymore? Has everything I have ever known about Alex been a lie? How do I know there aren't more lies?

"Right," I reply. Sarcasm lines my tone like poison around the rim of a crystal glass. I fill Doggy's bowl with water from the outside tap, then glide toward the kitchen to make myself some breakfast with my head held high—feeling nothing short of helpless. My head has morphed into a giant bowling ball. It weighs my shoulders down like wet wool. Any minute now I could buckle under this weight and surrender to the force that will jackhammer me into the ground. Cry. Forgive. Make Alex promise that he will never do it again. But I won't. My determination to mask this vulnerability will not cease.

I *will* get through this with dignity.

I *will* assume the power.

I *won't* let him manipulate me.

I *won't* give in to my emotions.

Enough is enough.

"Listen, Melody, it only happened once— "

"That's what you all say, isn't it?" I open the fridge and scan its contents for the tub of strawberries, wishing I had something smarter to say, something more articulate, something he'd have trouble understanding. "It only happened once. It will never happen again. She didn't mean anything to me. You're the one I love. Blah blah blah. What is it with all you Greek men? Do you all get together one day and work out what to say when your wife catches you out? Is there some sort of club I should start boycotting?"

Alex holds the fridge door open, clutching onto the edge so hard his nails form a rosy rim. "Mel, *please*. I know I have no defence against this. And I lay myself open to … to whatever you want to … to say to me. I … I was wrong. If I could take it back … I truly, truly am so so sorry, and I *love* you; I love you and *only* you. And I promise you it'll never … never, *ever* happen again."

I grab a tub of yoghurt with one hand and a tub of strawberries with the other. I close the fridge door with a little too much force—its contents rattle. Alex moves to stroke my hair while I wash the strawberries under chlorine infested water, but I flick my head out of the way before he manages it. I grab a bowl out of the cupboard and slam it on the kitchen bench. Any harder it would have shattered.

"So you expect me to just forgive you?" I laugh. "After all the beautiful words we exchanged last night? How could I resist, right?"

I spoon the yoghurt into my bowl, flinging it off the spoon so hard that specks splatter in my face. I scrape the remaining contents of the yoghurt out of the tub and drop the spoon into my bowl with a clang.

"Mel, please." The sides of Alex's mouth curl up a little. "Let's just work it out—I know we can. And if not for us, for Tessa." Alex wipes the yoghurt freckles off my face with the tea towel. I smack his arm away.

"For *Tessa*? For *Tessa* I'd be out of here tonight! I don't want her to grow up in a household where the only love she gets is from each of us individually—'cause that's what she'll have if we're separated." I bang my fist on the kitchen bench, catching the edge of my bowl with a knuckle. It tips upside down. "Fuck!"

"Look, I understand you're angry now. Can you just give it a bit of time?" Alex says, grabbing too much paper towel and wiping up my mess. I look at him as if his words went in one ear and out the other.

"I'll go pick up Tessa," he adds, throwing the yoghurt-filled paper towel in the bin and walking out of the kitchen.

"I thought you said you *couldn't*," I call out after him as his heavy footsteps head toward the front door.

"I'll reschedule." He jiggles his keys in his pocket.

"Well, I'm going to reschedule a few things myself. I need to get out of here. I'm going to take the job in London after all," I say to the ceiling, out of spite, with my arms folded under my breasts. I hear the front door open.

"Yeah, *well*," he calls back, his voice spiked with contempt. "I'd like to see you try getting Tessa out of the country. Legally."

"*What* did you say?" I run to the corridor where I can see him. I stunt my momentum by grabbing onto the sides of the archway. My body swings forward through the opening and back again as if it were barricaded by an elastic band.

"You heard me," he replies, looking at the door handle as he turns it. He gently closes the door behind him—as if noise might render his words inappropriate.

I stare at the front door, listening to the echo of Alex's footsteps as he walks down the stairs.

Clip. Clop. Clip. Clop. Clip. Clop.

I'm *alone*. I would *be* alone. Like this. Every night. Who would I talk to? Who would I cuddle up to on the couch when there's a good movie on TV? Who would … love me?

No! I can't crumple under this pressure!

I kick the wall—hurt my toe. I clutch at it. The throbbing ache that should be located in my heart is in a limb Ancient Chinese women used to break and bind beneath the soles of their feet. Well, my heart is broken. Can I bind it? Make it smaller to fit in with the Greek culture? With the ridiculously high statistics of anti-monogamous men?

I limp to the balcony and sit with Doggy on her dirty, hairy bed. I sob, gritting my teeth, hanging the need to scream on my tonsils.

Doggy licks away my tears, breathing heavily with affection. Her tongue hangs from the side of her mouth like a slab of meat—drools all over my crossed legs.

Get Tessa out of the country legally. Pft. Try and bloody stop me.

sixteen

Driving in Athens is mayhem. A flight schedule delayed from bad weather. A special occasion with a burnt roast chicken. A forgotten open tap in the bathtub. A burst sewage pipe in your lounge room. Salt in your coffee. Oil on your new dress. Aerosmith singing with Frank Sinatra. Planes on the ground, cars in the sky. Must I go on?

I've stopped at the first set of traffic lights on my way to work. I'm late. Very late. So late I think I might slip in through the back via the underground warehouse when I arrive.

I look at my phone, resting on the passenger seat—vibrationless. *Serena. Call me.* Give me something else to focus on while I'm stuck here, breathing in toxic urbanism, and the stink of deception, through the rear of a bus that's chugging like the motor's about to cark it.

When the traffic lights turn green, it rings. *Typical.* I shift the gear directly into third from first, revving the motor until the car starts to rattle. *I left my ear bud at home. Damn.* I drive past a squinting cop as I answer the phone and hook it between my ear and shoulder. I wink. He smiles. Ignores the fact that I'm breaking the law.

"Hey, Serena," I say with a puff.

"Hey. How's things?"

"Good. You? Beer on your lunch break?"

"Uh, yeah. Charlie and I were both in the same area and thought we'd meet at the pub for lunch. Cool, huh?"

"I guess." *Just tell her. But … you'll sound like a cold-hearted bitch. You're angry. Too angry to be upset. Right?*

"So. Melon! What's up? You thinking of finally following your dream? Wouldn't it be great? Me, Alex, and Tessa, watching you up there on stage. It'd be fab. I know you've got it in you."

"Um … I'd like to get back into it to some extent. Finally beginning to find a bit a free time."

"Oh, yeah? That'd be really good for you, I think."

"Yeah. It would." I screech on the brakes when I spot a child about to jump onto the road. Shift into first. Nod sympathetically at the mother mouthing some sort of apology for her child's sudden burst of energy, while I switch my mobile to speaker phone. I lodge the phone between my thighs, upside down so the mic faces upward. "Is Charlie still with you?"

"Yeah. Chat later, okay?"

"Okay, Luv ya," I answer in forged confidence, feeling my forehead and ears to see if I have a fever. I'm shivery. Nervous? *Breakdown?*

"Love you too, hon." Wind passes over the phone as she hands it to Charlie. She mutters something in the background that I can't quite catch.

"Hey, MD!" Charlie shouts, in the carefree tone I remember well.

"Hey! Charlie. It's been a while." I try to imitate the same cheer as I pick up a little speed and screech around the bend into the street that leads to my office. A lone ray of sunlight targets one eye through a gap in the clouds. I blink, and flick down the shade.

"Sure has. Listen up. When I got your message on FB, I had a light-bulb moment."

Wow, he still uses that phrase? "Oh yeah? And what would that light-bulb moment be?" I smile, amused and comforted by his guilelessness.

"You. *Gee*-tar. Band. Tour."

"What?" I stop the car in the middle of the road. Luckily it's not a residential area and the only traffic it sees is UTD Publications staff. "Ha. You get straight to the point, don't you? We haven't spoken for years."

Shouldn't expect any less from him, I suppose.

"Yeah, well, beatin' 'round the bush's over-ahhed. Whatcha think?" Charlie prods in his old-time grisly heavy-metal voice.

"Well ..." I find a park, turn off the ignition, grab my bag from the back seat, switch speaker phone off and put the phone to my ear. "I don't think I could just get up and leave everything, Charlie," I reply, knowing very well that I was willing to leave everything for London. *I'm not making any sense. Running away isn't going to solve anything. Is it?*

"The tour will only last a month. Com' on MD! You know ya wanna! Serena's spilled the beans 'bout your life."

"Has she now?" *Oh my God.*

"I know the go. Escape the daily routine. Yada yada." He

imitates the twang of a guitar. "And look. I know there was a lot of shit between us, but hey, it's all water under the amplifier ramp, right?"

"Ha. Of course. I'm not worried about any of that. It's just …"

"Just what, kitten?" *Kitten. Wow. Memories.*

"Charlie …"

"Look. Don't answer me now. I'll send ya an email. Tell ya all 'bout it. Decide when ya got all the nitty gritty. Deal?" he asks in an odd paternal voice I don't recall. *Has he had kids I don't know about?*

I sigh, remembering the day I broke up with him, changed my number, and never contacted him again. I was horrible.

Why is he being so kind? Surely he can't … still have feelings—

"What was that big sigh for? Sounds like a good deal to me."

"Yeah, okay, Charlie. I'll keep my eye out for your email. But I can't promise you anything. I'm er, a little—"

"MD, don't worry. I'm not gonna try 'n' get into ya pants."

"Charlie." I hang my head in my hands. Laugh under my breath. An image of Charlie and me, having sex on a plastic tavern table in the middle of the night, sends my knees into convulsion.

"I wasn't thinking that. I gotta go. Thanks so much for the offer. I'll think about it."

"Cheers. I'll be in touch."

I hang up. Throw the phone into my handbag and get out of the car.

Am I insane? I'd really love to do it. Escape for a month and pretend I'm a famous musician. Is it normal to think this at such a critical time in my life? In my marriage? What if I sleep with him? What if I become the woman I used to be? Do I really want that? Now, after all I've been through, and grown to become? Am I ... cut out for it?

Charlie and I used to attend each other's gigs like a Sunday church service. Charlie's gigs, however, were a lot different from mine, and I'm still not sure if we enjoyed each other's music as much as we enjoyed the fact that we were both musicians. His band wasn't the free-spirited, enlightening hippy-sort like mine. His band was the devil-worshipping, throat-hurting, head-throbbing, metal-cutting, and rage-enhancing type. I soon learnt that I had to wear black make-up, chains, and spiky jewellery in order to not draw attention to myself at his gigs, and he learnt to wear his rainbow-coloured trousers and tie-dye T-shirt to mine.

Although our relationship lasted for three years, we weren't in love. We just had great sex and a shit load of fun together. Music always came first. If love didn't need to be a major factor in a relationship, the two of us would have been the perfect bride and groom. Looking back, it makes me wonder whether it makes more sense to marry a great *friend*, rather than someone you love. Friendship does seem to last longer.

We met each other competing in a band competition. He approached me after my performance—drunk, slurring, "A chick on guitar is really cool, man."

Already editing at age eighteen, I snapped, "If you take a

better look you'll realize that I'm not male, nor am I a bird of any sort, the guitar is on *me*, I'm not on *it*, and in fact, it's not cool, it's pretty damn hot under those lights, so if you like, *man*, you can go and try that pickup line on my violinist. She's blonde."

"Ho, ho, ho, a chick with a dick! I *like* it!" he laughed, almost spilling his beer on my feet.

I bumped into him the next day when I was picking up some equipment from the pub. He was sober. Trying to speak as if he'd been raised in an upper-class environment—avoiding slang and whatnot. Although I could see through him, it amused me, and I ended up giving him my number. We hadn't even exchanged names at this point, so I wrote on top of the number: "chick with a dick."

He called the same night.

"Just one moment please," my mother said, swaying a little from her one too many vodkas. She put her hand over the receiver and whispered, "Melody, there's a guy on the phone saying that there should be a *woman* living here who gave him her number at the pub this afternoon. I thought it may have been for me—" She glanced around to see where Dad was, then whispered with gritted teeth, "I started speaking to him in my sexy voice, Melody! Then he said he thought he may have dialled the wrong number. So, I asked him if there was anything else written on the piece of paper."

She stared at me, hunched over as if in pain, clutching the receiver to her stomach. I held out my hand. Shrugged. Wiggled my fingers as a gesture to give me the phone.

She put the receiver back to her ear. "Er. You there? Sorry 'bout the mix-up. Can I have her call you back? Melody's not available to speak right now." She wrote down his name and number and hung up.

"What were you thinking, Melody?" Mum yelled.

"What were *you* thinking, Mum?" I snarled, crossing my arms and leaning my weight on one foot.

"Don't you *dare* speak to me like that." Mum pointed her finger at me as if a sharp weapon.

"You just spoke to *me* like that!"

"I'm your mother! I'm allowed!"

"What happened to the equal rights you were trying so desperately to preach yesterday when you got all ooh-la about sexual discrimination and decided you shouldn't be obligated to cook anymore?" I maintained a level tone, trying to pretend the conversation wasn't bordering on the aggressive.

"As long as you're living under *my* roof, you'll do as *I* say!" She moved her finger closer to my face. I can remember thinking, *Here we go again. Duck and run.* But I didn't duck and run. I kept testing my new boundaries. I had just turned eighteen—the legal independent age in Australia. I could do what I wanted. If my mother had decided to flip out again, I could have just left. And she wouldn't have been able to do a thing about it.

"When did you start becoming so conservative?" I screeched. "Living under my roof? What are you talking about, Mum? Don't give me that shite."

"Shite?" She snorted. "The character on the agenda today

is an unemployed Scottish bum. Let me introduce myself. I'm the Wicked Witch of the East. Nice to meet you," she narrated like a DJ accepting a radio caller, holding out her hand.

"Shut up, Mum. The problem here isn't me. It's you! And what do you mean *sexy voice?* I *knew* I should have taken your diary more seriously! But I—"

"*What?*"

"Yeah. I read your diary. Something about dreaming of kissing that 'lifelong' friend of yours in Greece! Wasn't he actually *Dad's* friend first?"

"How *dare* you—" Mum's jaw dropped. Her skin stretched so much her crying lines disappeared.

"Don't 'how dare you' me! I thought they were just fantasies. But it looks like you actually like to *bring them to life*!"

Our aggressive whispering mimicked a female Godfather duet. We were both irate and red in the face—my mother from holding her breath, and me from giving myself a tonsillectomy.

Dad walked into the corridor.

"What's going on?" he asked, his vocal cords doing a little dance as they do when there might be a threat of having his head bitten off. My mother was on the brink of telling him what I'd done, when I shot her an ambiguous glare. She responded with guilty calm—an invisible wink. So I took control.

"She took a message for me," I said. "From a guy I met at the pub and forgot to write down his number, so I got angry 'cause now I can't call him back and he's going to think I'm not interested." My mother moved the scribbled number behind her back with discretion.

"Ah," Dad nodded with a hesitant laugh. "Well, at least it wasn't me who answered the phone, 'cause then you'd *both* be having a go at me. I'll leave you two to it."

When Dad walked out, my mother pushed the number into my hand with the force of attempted crucifixion, walked into her bedroom and slammed the door behind her. I stared at the number for about ten minutes before I recollected myself and dialled it.

"Ye-ah?"

"Hi, it's me. Melody. You just called me."

"Hi MD! Charlie here. But you can call me whatever you like."

I chuckled. "Charlie's fine."

"Um, yeah, your roommate sounds a bit er … yoko."

From that day forward, we stuck together like 'cheese toast'. Charlie said that he was the toast, because he was hot and crusty, and I was the cheese because I was hot and squishy. It was fun being an ingredient of cheese toast. Until Greece ate me.

I walk into the office almost two hours late—worn out. I head straight for the coffee station for a double dose with my bag still hanging over my shoulder. I open the cupboard above the sink to pull out the jar of Nescafé. But there's only decaf.

Okay. Percolated.

No filters left.

Shit. I need coffee!

Just as I think things can't get any worse, I look down at my feet—and there it is—the *almost* reality of the turn-up-at-school-naked dream. I'm wearing two different shoes—one flip flop and one sandal. Not the *most* embarrassing combination in the world, but noticeable. If I didn't manage to coordinate shoes this morning, I dread to look at my face in the mirror. I didn't even wash off my make-up from last night.

I'm about to run back to my car to see if I have any shoes in my boot when my mobile rings. It's Heather.

"I'm in the coffee station," I say, leaning against the counter. I hit my head on the corner of the cupboard I left open. "Ouch!"

"What was that? What are you doing in the coffee station? How long have you been here? Why are you so late?" Heather speeds through the questions as if on *Who Wants To Be a Millionaire* and she's using the call-a-friend lifeline.

"Um …" I close the cupboard. "Hit my head. Trying to find some coffee. About two minutes. Long story," I answer in much the same fashion.

"There's no coffee," says Heather.

"Uh … duh!"

Duh? How old are you?

"What?" Heather asks, probably thinking the same thing. "Well, meet me on the lawn. I brought in a thermos of Jarrah's coffee."

"Really? Where did you get it? I thought they didn't sell it here."

"Long story. Come. Lawn. Now. Desperate." Heather hangs up.

I run back to my car to seek out a matching pair of shoes. Thankfully, I have an old pair of sandals in the boot from the island.

"Thank you thank you thank you, whoever is out there, thank you," I whisper.

I catch a glimpse of my wrinkly shirt in the rear view mirror. I freeze.

Don't do it. Don't look at your face.

I bend down toward the mirror—my eyes clenched shut.

Okay, do it like the Band-Aid trick. Open quickly and it'll all be over.

I open my eyes. *Oh. Mascara a bit runny. Nothing that a bit of saliva can't fix.* I lick my two forefingers and rub away the smudges. *Not too bad. I smile at myself. But then I remember.*

"There's nothing to be smiling about, Melody."

I look toward the tuft of trees at the end of the street. Anesthetized in this semi-humid, pre-summer atmosphere. Stagnant—numb—the way I should feel inside. But I don't even feel that. I'm beyond numbness. I've been through numbness, emptiness, nothingness. What I am, is detached.

You can't pretend everything is all right forever.

I cough away a swell in my throat as I push the side-view mirror in. The flick resonates through my fingers; the snap through my ears. I kick the car door. Dent it. Fuck you. The sound of reality making its mark.

Musician. Mother. Wife. Editor.

No.
Mother. Editor. Musician. Wife.
No, no, no.
     1: Mother / Musician
     2: Musician / Mother
     3: Editor
     4: Ex-wife.
Cheater. Liar. Bastard. Asshole.

As I reach my desk, the girls mumble "hi", as if programmed on a timer, all staring at their computer screens. A very temperamental bunch—on and off like bipolar emotions—switchless too. It's like the PMs have sprayed the office with a sedative gas. And it's so quiet that the most dominating sound in the office is my feet separating from the sweaty soles of my sandals as I crouch down to pick up a fly-away Post-it.

I catch a glimpse of Heather pacing back and forth on the lawn, swigging her thermos of Jarrah's as if a bottle of beer.

"Okay, Heather. Cough it up. What's up with you and the thermos?" I ask, scratching behind my ear.

"My daughter!" she wails, almost choking on her coffee. "She brought her boyfriend home last night and I let him stay over. I'm so irre*spon*sible; they were at it like flippin' seagulls at fish. All I could hear, *all* night, was her wardrobe rattling. She's too *young* for this. I thought he was just going to *in*nocently sleep over. Why am I such a sodding fool?" She takes another swig of coffee. Swallows it like whiskey—wincing at its potency.

"Um," I say, short and quick, uncertain whether it's my cue to speak. I wait for a signal. Heather throws up her arms and eyebrows in unison.

"Sorry if this is an insensitive question, but what's this got to do with the thermos of Jarrah's?" I step in front of her, halting her stride, and grab the thermos from her hand. I gulp down half a mug's worth. The warmth and smooth coffee aroma coats my mind with pseudo reprieve. "And *please* stop pacing up and down. You're making me dizzy." I sigh and hand her back the thermos.

"Well," Heather exhales, collapsing cross-legged on the grass. "She made it for me, my daughter, to stop me from asking her questions this morning. She was ever so helpful, making my lunch, brushing my hair, choosing clothes for me to wear—the whole shebang. Talking like a parrot in order to prevent me from talking about the wild sex I could hear last night. She talked right up until the moment she stepped out the door to go to school." Heather frowns—tears lingering in the corners of her eyes. "Want some more?" She holds the thermos above her head, like a wagging teen drinking a bottle of cheap champagne cross-legged on the train platform.

"Yeah, thanks." I take it and swig it—sit by Heather's side on the lawn. "So, what are you going to do?"

"To be frank, I have no sodding idea … can't bear to tell Chris. He'll ground her. I don't think a girl should be grounded for losing her virginity in her own *home*. I mean, that's pretty good, right? I mean, at least it wasn't in some dirty old public toilet in order to keep it a secret. Right?"

The corner of Heather's mouth turns up in a seeming effort to look on the bright side. But the lurking smile is instantly retracted when she clenches her fists and brings them to her chest, "Oh my God! What if that *wasn't* the first time?"

"Heather, don't worry." I try to sound as if I'm in the know. "She was all right when she got up this morning, right?"

Heather nods, sucking in her bottom lip. It reminds me of how Tessa slurps spaghetti.

"Don't worry. I'm sure it was her first time. As you said— be happy that she did it at home."

But what I *should* remind her is that if it was her first time, there's no way she'd be able to do it all night because she would have been in pain.

I remember the day I lost *my* virginity. I had just turned fourteen and had a crush on a young drummer called Seb, a couple of years older than me. Many girls left love letters in his locker, decorated with heart cut-outs and photos of themselves. But I couldn't even bring myself to utter "hello" every time I passed him in the corridor. Because I was the pretty, shy girl who looked the part of everything I was not and sung remarkably well in the daggy school choir, and he was the outgoing artistic version of a football star. A popular boy with a twist. Not twisted. Like me. I would dream though. Alone in bed at night. Pretend that my pillow was his face. But I didn't have to dream for long.

The day we met, I was putting books in my locker after class, and he appeared by my side with a huge grin on his face. His shoulder-length floppy blonde hair hung over his narrow brown eyes as he tilted his head forward and rested his dimpled chin on my open locker door.

"Hi," Seb said. He pushed my locker door shut and held out his calloused hand for me to shake, "You're Melody, right?"

"Um, yep. Melody." I shook his hand, nodding, trying to think of something cool to say. An entire corridor of students looked our way. Their scrutiny burnt holes in my stockings. I was sure they could see my knees shaking. Perhaps this is where it all began—the stage fright.

"I'm Seb."

"Uh, yeah, I know." I giggled stupidly, wondering why I was acting like the "other" girls.

"You have a free period now, don't you?"

"Yeah ... how'd you know that?" I was stunned by the possibility of Seb paying attention to my class schedule.

"Um, I just know." He smiled so wide I could see his full set of wonky, but very white teeth. "You wanna jam with me and my band?"

I couldn't believe it. Was this for real? I didn't want to risk being humiliated if someone was playing a prank on me, so I pulled myself together and said, "Well, I was just about to go to the canteen to buy some lunch. You can join me if you like. We can go and jam after I eat." I was so proud of myself for not letting him dictate the next move. If he wanted me to jam with him, he would have to wait.

"Oh." Seb sighed, sounding a little disappointed. "I don't really want to sit in there. There are too many ... you know, of those *girls* in there. I was hoping we could just skip lunch."

As much as I wanted to jam with him, I had learnt enough from watching American high-school sitcoms to act hard-to-get, so I said, "Um, no thanks, Seb. I'm starving. Maybe another time?"

I walked away, down the corridor, toward the canteen with wallet in hand. He just stood there, in front of my locker, watching me get away. But, just before I disappeared around the corner, he called out, "Party! My place! Saturday!"

I did go to the party that Saturday night, hearing my mother's recent act of parenting playing over and over in my head: *Here's a condom. Don't even* think *about using it.*

His house was located in one of the rich suburbs of Melbourne. It was a two-story mansion with about six hundred square meters of garden surrounding it. His parents were away for the weekend, hence the party. Of course. I silently gagged at the cliché. The entire first floor was full of grungy-looking pot smokers, gothic lesbian couples snogging each other in every possible corner and hardly coming up for air, and the blaring sound of Nirvana rattling the ornamental pebbles scattered all over the place like confetti.

Of course, I got a little drunk to shed myself of inhibition, and I can't remember doing much else than *snogging* and *snogging* and *snogging* until my lips stung. That, and taking intermittent sips of Smirnoff vodka straight from the bottle to top up my fuel.

Somehow I ended up in his en-suite watching him run a bath. I closed my eyes as he undressed me, and then himself, and we both lay in the bath together. The steam engulfed me like heavy fatigue. The heat of the water and weightlessness of his silky smooth body on top of me was like swimming in fog. That was until ... well, the whole bath turned red. Oblivious to the pain in my drunken state, Seb had already sprung out of the bath and wrapped a towel around himself, when I opened my eyes. Shivering, he wailed, "Freak!" and left me there to clean up.

"Heather? Shouldn't we get back to our desks? Where are the PMs?" I ask, hesitant to walk near the window where they might see me.

"Oh. Don't worry. They're at a conference. They won't be back till late afternoon. They won't even know you were so late." Heather stands and brushes dry grass off her bum.

"Oh-kay. Then why is everybody so quiet?"

"Because they're gullible. When the PMs left this morning, they said they'd activated the hidden video cameras." Heather laughs. "Jodie winked at me, knowing very well I know there aren't any. Poor sods—look at 'em working their bottoms off ... oh, and Dianne told me to tell you they won't be expecting you to write those kids songs anymore."

"Fine." *I couldn't care less.*

"Oh! *Damn!* Look at me going on and on about myself. What happened to you? What's *your* long story?"

"Oh, nothing really," I shrug. I brush away a strand of

Heather's hair caught in her eyelash. She blinks and smiles a thank you. "Just one obstacle after another this morning. Couldn't get myself together."

seventeen

Instead of heading straight home after work, I do something I wouldn't normally do. I send Alex a text message to say I won't be home for dinner—to take Tessa out for a kebab. No explanation, no mention of where I'll be at. I imagine, well hope, he makes an event out of it, by eating them in Lykabettus with the dog, for instance, instead of plonking Tessa on the couch to watch a movie while he messes around with emails. Wishful thinking?

I, however, drop my car off at home, and go to the only Irish pub in town—a place guaranteed to be brimming with raucous expatriates—a place where privacy is indeed given a new meaning. This place is always so crowded and noisy that it seems to reverse the effect—chaos turned silent white TV fuzz.

I drink *three* pints of Guinness, eat *two* plates of fish 'n' chips, and wander around the Plaka in the dark—a vibrant flea market by day, a seemingly abandoned crime district with hidden side-street gems by night.

The Plaka is situated below the Acropolis, which you can see from almost every angle of the city—especially at night, when it becomes a glowing dynastic beauty. Its cobblestoned streets are splashed with traditional taverns left, right, and centre, with loitering waiters trying to lure in passersby. On Sundays, these streets become even more alive when the flea market thrives with bargaining tourists and manipulative shop owners.

I buy myself a coconut ice cream cone, sit in the square by the metro station, kick my sandals off and watch. As. They. All. Glide. By. Me. Like over-exposed photography. A sea of kebab skewers and gyros wrappers, gypsies rummaging through the aftermath of tourist mayhem for leftover food.

My vision is. Spinning. Sleeping open-eyed in a river ... melting ... zesty sugar candy gloss falls on ground ... igniting thoughts ... chicken soup, curry green, milk ... drowns market stall full of vinyl and misplaced dreams ... my bare feet vibrate on chilly rough concrete ... queasy ... rumbling train ... stains white shirt ... thaws on skin ... sticky coconut syrup smells of tears, of years, of breast milk.

My eyes shut. The world turns black like a foggy wind-shield in the dark. I feel my head drop—whiplash—a tennis ball bounces behind my eyes. I wake to a stray dog licking melted ice cream off my toes ...

The apartment building is so quiet I can hear my stomach bubble. I burp up a thick bitter sweet mass of air as I unlock the door—it swims through my teeth like invisible dental floss.

I guzzle down a litre of water and a couple of aspirin, before checking on Tessa. I open her door, a touch—I refuse to go in and breathe my alcohol breath all over her precious pearl face. She's fine. Snoring. Gurgling yum yums. *Dreaming of candy? Ice cream ballet?*

Laptop propped on my knees, I lie, back against the wall, on the fold-up bed in my office. I switch it on—the device which holds my missing link, like a confidential dossier.

Charlie. Email. Please.

Yes!

```
To: Melody Hill Konstantinou
From: Charles Hughes
Subject: American Tour
Hey there, Kitten!

Just like I promised—an email with the
nitty gritty.

Right, a list of the facts:
Tour starts September 1, ends September
25

Rock band is called Muffin Lovin' (don't
ask!—I hate the name too, but they're
doing really well and selling fresh muffins
as merch)

They lost guitarist and backup vocalist
(they choked on muffins and died a slow
death in the corner of the rehearsal
studio while hugging their instruments—
the Mamas and the Papas all over again
lol)—joke Joice—if ya could do both,
you'd be a champ.
```

Need to know by weekend, to get things organized.

If ya accept, I'll send ya a CD of all the songs ya gotta learn, and I'll organize for ya to fly out to Melbs two weeks before tour to rehearse with the band—so it'd be six weeks away in total for preps.

Bring Tessa! We've great babysitting roadies—the bass player's a single ma and has two young rug rats tagging along too, so she won't be lonely.
Please think about it seriously. It's a great opportunity and we'd LURRRVE to have ya on board. Miss ya pretty face. And don't worry, I won't pull any funny business on ya. You can return to ya lovey when you're done without any battle scars.

Give us a call, or even an email to let me know.

Cheers,

Charlie
Charles Hughes
Tour Manager
Kit Ten Management
Email: chahug@kittenmanagement.com.au
Website: www.kittenmanagement.com.au

Is this for real? Have I just been given everything I've been craving? I stare at the email—the words swirl together like food dye in cake mix—dancing around my giddy head, drunk with buzz. I can bring Tessa!

There shouldn't be any reason I can't take the job in London and do this too, right? I will have been working for four months by the time I have to leave. If they want me so much, surely they'd make an exception. Wouldn't they? Well, I know they would here, but maybe the work ethic in London is a little stricter. *God, it probably is—they'd probably fire me.*

I've been living in organized chaos now for so long that I can't digest what's normal anymore. Maybe I can lie—say I have to return to Australia—someone in my family could be ill—they might need assistance. That would get me off the hook. *What a ridiculous thing to do—I might as well say my dog ate my homework.*

I need to talk to someone. I need to talk to Serena.

Please be online. Please be online. Please be online.

She's not online. I bite my nails—a habit I gave up when I stopped needing them short to play guitar. They're brittle between my teeth, but tear off with ease as if I've been soaking them in water. I stare at Serena's MSN icon, praying for it to turn blue. *What to do, what to do …*

I get up. Brush off my bum as if I were still sitting on the gravelly step in the Plaka. The realization that I'm not hits me like reverse amnesia. I go to the kitchen. Look in the fridge. I want something. I don't know what. I look at an open bottle of red wine. Wonder whether I should pour myself a glass.

You're too drunk already. You'll dirty dishes. Bugger it. I'll drink from the bottle.

I take the bottle out of the fridge—the cork out of the spout. Pop—like my mother's finger inside her cheek—or like the day she accidentally dislocated my shoulder spinning me around in the back yard. A happy moment turned bad. Shame.

Throw the cork away or keep it? How much wine left? I look through the opening like a telescope. Wine spills onto my cheek—cold, crisp, fruity—it cascades down my neck. *Damn.* I wipe it away with the collar of my shirt and hold the bottle up to the light. *Shoulda done that first. About a third left. Hmm. Throw cork away. I'll drink the lot.* I throw the cork against the wall. It ricochets and bounces down the hall. I shrug. *Meh.*

Back on the fold-up bed. Icon still not blue.

"Serena, Serena wherefore art thee? I pray for thee, but cannot see thine blue man be lit." I wriggle. Rub my hands together as if warming them by a fire.

It should be mid morning in Australia now. I could phone her, but then I'd wake up Alex and Tessa. I don't want anybody to wake up. I need to be alone. I need to speak to Serena alone.

Text message.

Pls log on msn. Need 2 talk. Desperatolita.

Staring at the icon. Staring at the icon. I'm staring at the icon like a moron. Staring at the icon. Staring at the icon ... icon blue!

Serena_Servais
What's going on?

MelodyHill(Billy?)
Big dilemma.
(Swig of mine wine)

Serena_Servais
What kind dilemma?

MelodyHill(Billy?)
Do you have time?
(My goodness this rhymes)

Serena_Servais
Yes, about five minutes. Are you OK?

MelodyHill(Billy?)
(Am I okay? No, in disarray.)
You're going to freak out.
(When you hear what this is all about.)

Serena_Servais
You not having affair are you?

MelodyHill(Billy?)
(Affair? Me? No way! Not true!)
What??? You kidding me?

Serena_Servais
Well, I don't know. Unusual behaviour
might lead to you unusually needing to
speak to me in middle of night.

MelodyHill(Billy?)
(Hmm. Okay. Rhyming over. Sentence too long.) Are you sitting down?

Serena_Servais
No, I'm typing standing up.

MelodyHill(Billy?)
Okay. To make a long story short. Got great job offer in UK, great salary, better country, good opportunity …

Serena_Servais
Congratulations!

MelodyHill(Billy?)
Thanks, but decided to turn down offer, because Alex didn't like idea. Didn't technically turn down job offer, just told Alex that I would …

Serena_Servais
That's naughty.

MelodyHill(Billy?)
Yeah, naughty … but minutes later I find out Alex had affair …

Serena_Servais
WHAT??? Are you serious? You not imagining this are you?

MelodyHill(Billy?)
NO! He admitted it.

Serena_Servais
When? With whom? I'll KILL HIM!

MelodyHill(Billy?)
Long story. Nuther time. Not before I do. Anyway, now what am I supposed to do? I've got great job offer and Charlie's offer to tour with band for month. Want both. Probably can't have both. If don't take either, stuck with Alex who is cheating bastard, and for what? Do I want cheating husband organizing my gigs? I don't think I do. At least not yet anyway. How do I know I'll get over it? And in the meantime, I'd be miserable and regret turning down two great opportunities. What am I supposed to do?

Serena_Servais
Melody, it would be huge shame to turn down opportunity with Charlie's band. If you need help with money, I can help you out. I got that inheritance from my grandfather remember? But you know, that still doesn't mean you can't resolve things with Alex.

MelodyHill(Billy?)
I know.

Serena_Servais
But on other hand, you should take job because it's the responsible thing to do and you've got Tessa to think about.

MelodyHill(Billy?)
Hey! That's not helping!

Serena_Servais
I know. LOL. No sorry. Bad time to laugh.

MelodyHill(Billy?)
Indeed :-(

Serena_Servais
Sorry. I'm being insensitive. I'm not myself today. :-(Regarding Alex. How? What happened???

MelodyHill(Billy?)
Can we talk about that another time? I need to know what to do about the job and tour!

Serena_Servais
Yeah, but if you can establish how you feel about Alex then maybe you can come to some sort of decision?

MelodyHill(Billy?)
Jesus.

Serena_Servais
Melody. Come on.

MelodyHill(Billy?)
I can't. Not now. I need to make a deci-
sion SO that I know what to do about
Alex.

Serena_Servais
Melody, I can't tell you what to do. Make
a decision and then talk to me about
it. That might work better. I have no
idea about running a family. I have no
idea about being married. If I were in
your situation I'd never want to see Alex
again, and I'd probably jump on that
plane to tour America in an instant,
but I don't have a kid to think about.
Just wait until the weekend and see what
happens. Go with your gut. Do what you
feel at the moment when you have to give
an answer. That's the best advice I can
offer. And remember what we talked about
when I visited for your birthday this
year? You need to get your confidence
back. Here is the perfect opportunity.
Don't ruin it. Fate is giving you signs.

MelodyHill(Billy?)
Fuck, Serena, you're a social worker!

Serena_Servais
And you're my best friend. It's different.
I'm not going to preach to you. I really
have to go. I'm late for an appointment
at UN. I'm so sorry Melody. Let's talk on
phone, when you can. MSN is too detached
and I'm sure I sound like bitch. If only
you could see my face and hear my voice.

MelodyHill(Billy?)
I know. Don't worry.

Serena_Servais
Luv you xoxo

My thirtieth birthday bash was on the eighteenth of March about four months ago. Unlike most women about to turn thirty, I had no problem with it. I wasn't depressed and making up ridiculous excuses to avoid celebrating. I just didn't want to turn what should be a memorable and joyous event into a night full of phony smiles and meaningless chit-chat with people I couldn't care less about. Thankfully, Alex understood. And he surprised me with the unexpected.

On the night of my birthday he put on Joni Mitchell's *Blue*, and set the dining room table with four large black square plates detailed with silver around the edges. He bought a brand-new crimson tablecloth and pewter cande-labra, and used my grandma's silver cutlery I'd hidden away in some difficult-to-reach place—how he found it is beyond me. The dining room radiated a red scent and shimmered with the warmth and glow of the fireplace.

Alex's eyes sparkled with satisfaction. I asked him who the fourth seat was for, but he just shook his head, smiled, kissed my cheek, and patted me on the head as if I were the dog.

Half an hour before the unidentified arrived, he locked me in our bedroom with my mobile phone. He said, "Just prepare yourself to see the one person on this planet who will make you whole again."

"But *you* make me whole. And *Tessa* makes me whole. Who else could possibly make me whole?" I replied, furrowing my brow.

"Okay. Then prepare yourself to see the one person on this planet who *used* to make you feel whole before you met me and had Tessa," he said trying to dislodge something between his two front teeth. "I'll call you when we're ready for you to come out."

I lay in bed wondering who he could be talking about. Who could possibly be here that used to make me feel *whole*? And what a big word to use. So many meanings—connotations. Whole? *How* whole? Can anyone ever *really* make you feel whole? Or is it just something we say. Like *I love you.* Words that become habits—you never really know if they've retained their original meaning, or if they are merely survival aids.

I could hear a lot of whispering, rattling, and feet to-ing and fro-ing. More than *one* person was visiting—I was convinced. Nerves prickled my ears like a sudden drop in temperature.

And then my phone rang. It was Tessa.

"Mummy, you can come out now," she whispered. I

could hear her standing outside the bedroom door. I peered through the keyhole—her eye stared back at me.

"Thanks, Blossom. Could you give me a clue about who is there without Daddy understanding, so I don't get a shock and faint when I come out?" I whispered through the door handle. I heard her shake her head against the receiver.

"I'm wearing the new beads you bought me, Mummy."

"That's not a clue." I opened the door to see her dressed in her favourite outfit—a short denim pinafore-type mini, with light blue and pink stitching, and sparkly purple tights.

"I know. I just wanted to tell you," she declared with a grin, turning the phone off with ease. She didn't even look to see where the button was.

As we walked out of the bedroom, she bolted down the corridor and disappeared from sight. There were two men dressed as caterers, with tea towels hanging over their left arms, waiting at the entrance of the living room.

"*Kali spera, Kiria. Chronia pola,*" (Good evening, madam. Happy birthday) they both recited as if rehearsed. They held the door open for me to enter. My pulse fluttered in my ears as if I were about to set foot on stage.

When I entered, no-one said "surprise" or got up to greet me. They just sat in silence awaiting a reaction—expectation adorning their features like a sharpie pen. One man standing to the left of the table, was another caterer holding a platter of food, waiting for me to be seated. Then there was Alex, Tessa, an empty seat for me … and on the right was … Serena!

We embraced and cried. And cried some more. It had been about eight years since we had seen each other face-to-face. Serena and I were speechless for a while. We just kept hugging, crying and stopping to get a good look at each other's faces at arm's length.

"If it wasn't for Alex, I wouldn't be here now," she said, kissing me firmly on the cheek.

"Why is that? You don't have to be invited to come and visit me. You know that." I grabbed a tea towel off a waiter's arm and wiped my eyes dry.

"No, it wasn't that. I've never been able to afford to travel this far away. I still can't afford to. I'm a sucker for volunteer work, you know that." She looked at Alex, then me, and at Alex again.

I turned towards Alex's smiling face, shiny from a few stray tears. "You didn't!"

"Yes, he did. He only informed me last week that he bought the ticket. I dropped everything in Nigeria to get here."

"Oh, Alex. I don't know what to say."

"Don't say anything. Just pull yourself away from Serena for thirty seconds so I can tell you how much I love you." He took my hand, seated me as if I were royalty, and placed my napkin in my lap with a little peck on the cheek.

After a brilliant meal, the caterers packed up their stuff and were off. Alex put Tessa to bed, and the three of us flaked out on the couch, stomachs full of food and heads full of booze.

Sipping on red wine, Serena spoke about her experiences

in Nigeria. I wondered why she hadn't said anything about them at the dinner table, but after she finished her story, I realized it wouldn't have been something I'd want Tessa to hear.

She'd spent a lot of time in a women's shelter and got to know the women in the HIV area. One girl had been seriously assaulted and left mentally disabled by the beatings, and it only took the girl a couple of minutes before hugging and kissing Serena in the most trusting way. Serena said that her reaction to the immediate physical contact, such as kissing her face, was *interesting* because those who are suffering from full-blown AIDS have odd mottled skin— not like the legions we have all seen in books. She said she was embarrassed by moving her mouth away, or making sure she didn't touch any broken skin, even though there was no blood in sight.

I can't imagine where she finds the stamina to put herself in these situations. I think Alex *finally* understood why I respect her so much. She was no longer that simple girl with the simple life I knew at university. She'd blossomed into a remarkable woman.

What I envy most is Serena's courage and desire to help the needy—something I could never do, mainly because I've spent my life trying to escape my own past. I don't think I could handle getting involved in someone else's. But when I hear stories like Serena's, it makes me wonder why Alex and I concern ourselves with such insignificant problems. That night, I promised myself I'd make an effort not to anymore. But when I found alone time with Serena, it all changed.

During Serena's two-week stay, I decided to take her out for a good old traditional Greek meal in the heart of Athens—the kind of meal I can't cook to save my life.

"Yourrr, eyeees, arrrre, killink, meeee," purred a lingering waiter, licking his lips at Serena as we approached the tavern I intended taking her to. Instead of entering the tavern, I nudged her forward and barked back in Greek, "If that's how you beckon customers, no wonder your restaurant is empty."

The man's jaw dropped, begged for our forgiveness, claiming to think we were *just* tourists, and offered a dish on the house if we sat down to eat there. So we did.

Despite having no qualms about turning thirty, my birthday surfaced something I hadn't expected—the awareness that my guitar had remained in the exact same place I put it when we moved in, untouched and lifeless.

"Is it too late, now? To bring it back to life?" I asked Serena as I stuffed my mouth full of calamari and washed it down with a swig of beer.

"What are you talking about, hon? Of course it's not too late. And since when have you ever questioned your ability to do something? Can't you remember? That day I met you outside the lecture hall at Uni?"

I cocked my head in question.

"I was complaining about lacking the time to write my essay and that I might as well just give up now because I thought it was impossible to write anything decent in two days? I was a mess. Remember?" Serena leaned back in her wood and wicker chair, flinging her long blonde hair behind her shoulders as if in a shampoo commercial.

"Yeah, I remember," I mumbled, poking my fork into three different salad ingredients at once, and almost poking my eye out with a lettuce stalk while shoving it in my mouth.

"And can you remember what you said?" She leaned forward again, grabbing my hand to stop me from eating, her intelligent grey-blue eyes turning me to stone.

"What did I say?"

"You said, 'If there's one thing my mum has done right, it's teaching me to never give up. If there's a will, there's a way, Serena. It's never too late to start anything.' "

Serena smiled with gratitude. I was speechless. Not only in regard to the positive attitude I'd forgotten I had, but because Serena had remembered every word I said that day.

"I never asked for another extension again. You know that?" Serena prodded as I wiped my mouth with my napkin.

"No. I didn't know that," I whispered, resting my knife and fork on the edge of my plate. I felt defeated, disappointed—I'd become a mother and a wife. *Just* a mother and a wife. It wasn't what I had planned.

"Well, it's true. I wouldn't be as confident or active as I am now without you. You gave that to me, Melody. You're the one who made me realize I could do anything in the world—anything at all. If it wasn't for you, I wouldn't have gone to Nigeria. If it wasn't for you, the two women I looked after would still be in abusive relationships. You know, I write those words on the first page of my diary, every year, as a reminder. Those words made me realize I wasn't taking control, and they made me *do* something about it. You have to start believing in yourself again, Melody. You used to be so confident. You used to do anything and everything you wanted—simply because you knew there was nothing stopping you. There's nothing in your life right now that should influence such negativity. Alex and Tessa should be a *part* of your life, not *be* your life. Play music again, Melody, and involve them. Make it a part of *their* lives too. There's no need to sacrifice anything. Have it all. Include your family in all your decisions, and encourage them to be as enthused about your music as you are."

I tried to respond. I wanted to say how afraid I was. I had gotten used to living in a cocoon. I knew where I stood; I knew what had to be done—I was safe from feeling. I'd created a comfort zone for myself, and I was terrified to break free.

I turn off my laptop and the night light—crawl under the covers. Moonlight pelts down on my face like a torch. I roll over and face the wall where darkness paints shadows I can sleep in. I close my eyes—try to imagine comfort—remember what it felt like to be cradled in my mother's arms, before she got sick.

Mum. I need you. I want to forget you—the other you that wasn't really you.

I want to forget your screams, your anger, how I used to hold my breath. I want to forget your pleading, your pain, smashing pots on your head. I want to forget your prayer to die, to pass out, sleep, to fail. I want to forget how you blamed me, pulled my hair, and twisted my neck. I want to forget the slapping, the sting, and the knives you thrust into Dad's back. I want to forget your punches, my sobbing, and my begging for you to stop. I want to forget the shrieks, the shrill, and the rage you'd blow into my face. I want to forget the carpet, the stains, your vomit and regret.

I want to remember your hugs—the one's that smelt like Estee Lauder. And I want to remember your kisses, painted red and warm with love. So why are the first thoughts that come to mind, the years of tears and torture? I wish I could render my memory blind, to the fear of remembering—to the fear of becoming a mother like you.

"Melody? Why are you calling so late? Is everything okay?"

"I just … needed to talk."

"You're feeling depressed again, aren't you?" My mother's calm oozes through the receiver like a sweet whisper.

"Mm-hm," I nod, holding my eyelids shut with my thumb and middle finger.

"Okay, look. You know that you go through these phases. You have since you were a teenager. And it's always either triggered by alcohol or painkillers or whatever other chemical you come in contact with. Remember all the headaches and aches and pains you got after you helped paint our house? And how you couldn't stop crying for days?"

"Yeah."

"We're both sensitive to these things, you and I, and no matter how much you try to deny it, Melody, it isn't going to change the fact. I know it's hard to believe, but if anyone would know, it's me. Please, just humour me and start cleaning your house with lemon and water. Get rid of all the toxic fluids. I'm so sorry you have to go through these things. I would never wish any of it upon anyone—especially you."

"I know, Mum."

"Sweetheart, please try not to get too worked up over the way you're feeling. It's chemical. It's *always* chemical. You don't have any real reason to be depressed, right?"

"Um … no," I can't tell her. I just want my mother's hugs. I need soothing maternal hugs without having to explain why. And even though the hugs are in the form of a gentle voice through a phone, I can still imagine these hugs—the reassuring scent of henna and coconut moisturizer—her smooth skin against my cheek as she kisses and breathes me in.

"Well, see? You'll feel better in the morning. Please just don't go and get stuck into the wine. It'll only make it worse."

I laugh under my breath. "Okay."

"I'll be up for a while yet if you want to call me back, okay?"

"Thanks."

"Love you."

"Love you too, Mum."

"Bye. Love you, bye."

For once in my life I wish my mum was right. I wish the solution was as easy as cleaning the house with lemon and water.

I could wipe my life clean.

I steal one of Alex's Camels and grab a box of matches. Sit on the floor in the living room, up against the wall. I strike a match, let it burn half way down, watching the blue base of the flame crawl along the stick as if lured by oil—kerosene candy. I light the cigarette, take a drag; breathe in a puff of liberation I haven't felt since I was nineteen.

What's the meaning of life, you ask? Wait, let me just check the dictionary ...

eighteen

It's Thursday morning. I stare at Alex while we eat breakfast. Tessa notices and ogles me, chewing open-mouthed, holding her toast in the air, hoisted by her right elbow, her fingers sticky with strawberry jam. She swings her legs backward and forward in unison. Each time they swing underneath the chair, it moves backward half an inch and scrapes the floor. She has a steady beat going. It creates a sense of power and confidence within me—an injection of courage. I don't look at her, but I can feel her looking at me—curious eyes—green, innocent, kittenish. I wonder if she finds this amusing or senses the disturbing air. She must know something's going on between Alex and me—but does she know it's not just a staring game?

Alex eats his cereal with his head down. His movements pick up speed—so do Tessa's. Tessa's scraping chair and Alex's chewing become louder and synchronize with my pulse. *Clang, drip, crunch, chew. Crunch, chew, clang, drip.* Oh, how much I'd love to squash someone's head between two trashcan lids. I could make music at the same time. Become a member of *Stomp*.

Tomorrow's the deadline to tell the PMs—to announce

my decision about the job in London. Has Alex forgotten? He hasn't even asked whether I've made any arrangements. Does he even care? I honestly think he would like me to go—to leave him here all alone, wifeless, childless, to do what he pleases at any time of day. Maybe that's why he hasn't said anything. Because he doesn't want to be accused of thinking exactly what he is thinking. Mustn't he feel ashamed? I hope so. Serves him right.

Tessa falls off her chair. Giggles. Holds her toast in the air as if she dived to the bottom of the ocean and retrieved a possession that was thrown overboard. Alex glances toward her. Sniffs. Continues to eat with his head bowed.

"Tessa. Wipe the jam off the floor. Get back in your seat. Sit still," he says as if reciting a newsreel. He dislodges something from his teeth with his tongue, drops his spoon into his bowl, scrapes his chair as he gets up to find the toothpicks, and sits back down probing his molars with one. I envision snatching it from him and inserting it into his eye.

I focus on the top of Alex's head while I unscrew the lid off the Vegemite jar, guided by touch.

Tessa gets back into her seat, pouting her bottom lip. The side of her mouth curls up on the verge of laughter. Her mouth twitches, trying to appear sad.

"I'm going to tell my supervisors today," I say, wide-eyed, scraping a burnt layer from my toast.

"Oh, really?" Alex mumbles with a mouthful of cereal, still maintaining the steady hand-to-mouth movements and downward gaze. If his eyes were lasers he'd have drilled a hole through the table via the bottom of his bowl.

"Yes." I pause. Alex's temples move up and down as he chews. The constant ebbing crunch and swallowing reverberate off every kitchen surface before making a full circle round the room. I turn to give Tessa a behave-yourself glare. But she gives Alex an I-hate-you look instead, ignoring me.

"Yes," I repeat a little louder.

"Yes, I heard you." Alex nods. "Glad you came to your senses."

"Hmm?" I squint at him sideways. He's still staring at his bowl. Can he not at least look at me during a conversation? A little respect after what he's done would suffice. "What do you mean? I thought you didn't like the idea."

"I don't." Alex shrugs. His jaw clenches. "That's why I said I was glad."

"What makes you think I'm going to say no?" I ask, confidence slipping like a weak grip on monkey bars.

"Oh? Er … Oh."

"Oh? That's all you have to say? Oh?"

"Er … no. Are you sure that's what you want to do?"

"Yes."

"Well, if that's what will make you happy. I'll, um … visit you as often as possible." Alex lifts his head, looking at me for the first time all morning. He stops chewing, his eyes as still as glass.

"Oh? Will you?" I ask.

"Of course I will. I'm your husband."

Tessa rocks her chair backward and forward again—licks escaping jam from the flat of her palm.

"Uh-huh." I've almost scraped a hole through the middle of my toast.

"What do you mean, 'uh-huh'?"

"Nothing. Just comprehending what you're saying." I spread Vegemite on my now very thin toast, wrap my mouth around it, consuming half in one go, and bite down so hard my teeth scrape against each other—fingernails on a blackboard. I try to hide the discomfort, continue to chew as if it doesn't hurt. I wipe the sides of my mouth with my right index finger, and raise my eyebrows.

"You don't believe me do you?" Alex asks, flashing a quick glance toward Tessa, who is feeding Doggy her breakfast.

"Not really." I smile, trying to maintain my calm in front of Tessa. "Blossom, can you please not feed the dog? She eats enough as it is."

"Not really or not at all?" Alex takes the toast out of Tessa's sticky hands and puts it back on her plate. "Tessa, don't pick that up again until you decide to eat it yourself. Doggy doesn't want toast."

"But, Papa, she does want toast." Tessa holds out her hand for Doggy to lick.

"No, she doesn't." Alex and I snap in unison.

"Well, whether I believe you or not really isn't the point, is it?" I half-whisper, gripping my butter knife so hard that my nails dig into my palm.

"I told you that—"

"No, I don't want to hear it." I get out of my seat and stack the plates in the centre of the table. "Tessa, eat your other piece of toast. We have to get you to preschool." She doesn't move. She is her porcelain doll twin. I take her hand—the one holding the toast—and insert it into her mouth as if operating a puppet.

"Bite. That's it. Now chew." I take intermittent bites myself to speed the process up until the toast is gone. Alex watches—mouth open, cereal spoon in hand. I yank Tessa out of her seat with a tight grip on her wrist, praying I don't dislocate her shoulder.

"Mummeee!"

"Get your school bag."

Tessa puts her hands on her hips and frowns.

"Go. Now!"

"Mel—"

"Oh, shut up, Alex."

The girls in the office are all standing in a circle surrounding Lucy—one of the assistants—when I arrive. Lucy is sick again. Lucy has taken fifty days of sick leave already and it's only midyear. Lucy is crying and everyone is being sympathetic. Lucy has a urinary tract infection. Lucy has to go in for knee surgery next week. Lucy will now get another three weeks off work and still get paid. Somebody please help Lucy!

As I walk to my desk, Sonia, another assistant, says as if broadcasting a rare occurrence, "Did you 'ear? Lucy's go' a go to 'ospi'al."

What I want to say is "again?" but instead force a polite "Really? What's wrong, Lucy?" and place my hand on her shoulder, hoping for the gesture to not resemble an *Absolutely Fabulous* Edina attempt at concern.

Melody, the bitch witch. I'm out with my claws. Present me with a minuscule of inconvenience and I'll attack.

Crack a whip. Watch out. I'll scratch your face. I've had enough. I want out. Because I know what's coming.

Not only is Lucy always sick, and as a result all her work is passed on to me, but I feel so *shit* about the decisions I have to make right now that it wouldn't take a genius to realize that everything is pissing me off. I feel sorry for the poor girl, but honestly, can't she just work from home? She wouldn't be the first to do so.

Of course, Heather is not in the crowd of partisans. She is sitting in her messy corner pretending to be busy with a slight smirk on her face—she's worse than me. She glances toward me and my false display of compassion and can't seem to tame her laugh any longer. Disguising it with a vicious cough, she races toward the exit holding her hand over her mouth.

"Whaz up wiv 'er?" Sonia asks. "Looks like she's 'bout to frow up."

"She's all right. She's just getting over a bad cough and doesn't want to spread the germs," I lie, organizing my desk a little, putting papers in piles, blowing dust off the computer screen, searching for missing pencils amidst the array of loose Post-its that have lost their stick.

"She waz fine yesterday," Sonia frowns, with a cartoonish air.

"Was she? Oh, well maybe it's coming back," I reply, hoping that Sonia is as gullible as she appears to be.

"Poor fing. We all gonna get sick bein' cooped up in 'ere like a flock've 'ens. Bloody air-conditionin'."

"Yeah." I nod, clicking my tongue.

I feel wicked—possessed by Medusa. Look me in the eye and I'll turn you to stone, then pitch a cannonball your way—crumble you like stale bread. What have these girls done to me? Nothing. But I hate them. I hate everything.

I bite the inside of my cheek. *Control yourself. You're turning into your mother!*

The PMs walk in and the girls cock-a-doodle-doo about, moving chairs, gathering notepads and pens for our Thursday morning meeting—a weekly tradition that doesn't achieve very much—bar the chance to give the big boss the impression we are all professional and dedicated to our jobs when he passes by—Thursday mornings at nine thirty like clockwork.

I neglect the ritual and sneak into Jodie's office to tell her my news.

What news? Do I actually want this? How did I reach this decision? When did I make it? A deviate force gagged it out of my mouth this morning without my prior consent. I haven't even decided against the tour yet. *Why do I want a cat? Why do I want to buy a pair of stilettos? What's that smell? Hmm ... mocha.*

I find myself standing in front of Jodie—mute—with my mouth open wide. All I need now is an insect to fly in and make my day. *Shit! Speak, damn it. Say something!*

"Jodie, I ... I have decided to accept the position in London." *Don't panic. Stay calm.*

"Oh that's ... congratulations, Melody. Oh, wonderful. Wait till I break the news to the girls. You'd better wear your evil eye for the rest of the week," Jodie winks. "Melody just accepted … did you hear that, Dianne? Melody just accepted the position in London."

I turn to my right and there is Dianne, as if she materialized out of thin air.

"Well done, Melody. Well done." Dianne nods, expressionless.

"Thanks, I hope," I laugh, bringing my hands to my hot cheeks. *Am I blushing? I hope I'm not getting the flu. This would be the most inappropriate time to get the flu. Vitamin C tablets. I'll purchase them as soon as I leave the office. No, actually, I wouldn't be surprised if Lucy had some in her handbag. I could ask her for one. Yes, that's what I'll do; I'll ask Lucy for a vit C.*

"Oh, of course *hope*. Good things to come. Good things to come. Shall we join the patiently waiting and curious editors out there and get this meeting on the go?" Jodie asks, tapping her pen on a pile of files on her lap, looking more excited about my decision than me.

I compose myself and nod my business-woman nod. "After you, Jodie." I nod again. "Dianne." *Don't forget to ask Lucy for a vit C.*

I roll my chair into the meeting circle and sit. Everyone turns to me, their lips glossy with jealous drool. The atmosphere in here is a mix between a gynaecologist's waiting room and a classroom full of teenagers praying that their upcoming test is open-book.

Heather mouths the words, "You accepted?" raising her eyebrows. I nod with my eyelids. She winks and gives me two thumbs up.

Sonia, who is sitting to Heather's left, whispers, "Waz goin' on?"

Heather returns the whisper with a triumphant smile and says, "Listen and weep."

Sonia huffs, turns to Lucy, who is on her right, and mouths, "Bitch."

I suspected Sonia had a cruel side, but not to the extent where she would verbalize it. Lucy rubs her lips together, pushes her glasses up her nose, and folds her hands in her lap, seemingly embarrassed to witness a fellow colleague use such bad language.

Dear me. Were they always like this? I can't ever remember seeing them like this.

"Right." Jodie wiggles chubby comfort into her seat—paper and pen in position. "Before we begin the proper meeting. I'd like to announce some wonderful news."

On hearing "wonderful news" everyone smiles, sighs, and shuffles in their seats. Heather's smile being the widest, most knowledgeable, and most *real*. At least there's someone in this world who is proud of me. The others don't really care about good news unless it has something to do with getting extra paid holidays, so their smiles are just preoperational.

"Melody has accepted a position in London," Jodie chirps, with a cheerful anticipation that seems to merge her nose with her forehead.

The room fills with a hum of multiple disappointed sighs, which makes Heather giggle.

"She'll still be working for us," Jodie lies. "She'll just be working from a different office in a different country." I wish she'd mention how much better my salary will be, but she doesn't—she's cautious, considerate. "Okay, enough of that. You can crack open a bottle of champagne when you get home, Melody. Let's get back to business for now."

I'm slightly disappointed she didn't rub it in a bit more. I feel a need for revenge and satisfaction. Revenge on what, I have no idea because these people have done nothing to me, and I'm being horribly awful, awful, *awful*. Why? Perhaps I want revenge on the world. Perhaps this office symbolizes my world at present—a drab, artificially lit, poorly ventilated box of ladder-climbing, order obeying, numb nuts who blindly fulfil the roles society has preordained.

Don't forget to get that vit C.

I watch a wave of pursed sour lips wash over each co-worker's face as they ready their paper and pens for rapid jotting. They look at me through invidious squints seeking information, while Heather wriggles her pastel blue, silver-glittered toes without a writing tool in sight.

After the meeting, I ask Jodie if I can take the work home and courier it to the printer's myself on Monday morning. She's hesitant but agrees. Is this the mark of freedom? Or have I trapped myself into a situation impossible to escape unharmed?

I clear my desk—you know, put papers in piles, blow dust off my computer screen, etc, when silence falls. Muffled, tense, unheard thoughts thicken the air with a smelly curiosity. My mind is absent, underwater.

"You leaving today, Melody?"

I look up, unable to locate the voice. "Hmm?"

"You're packing your things. Are you leaving today?" Heather says, a little louder for everybody to hear.

"Oh! Yeah. I'm going to finish the final touches of the book at home over the weekend."

They crowd around my desk, all trying to speak at once. Their voices unite like a tuning orchestra. Without faltering, I assume a front of importance and raise my hands, gesturing for them to hush.

"One at a time," I say. *Who are you? This is fake,* I think, but I continue anyway—anticipate being ridiculed, looked down upon, and laughed at, but to my surprise, their voices diminish and each wait patiently for me to indicate who may speak first. The back of my nose stings as if I've swallowed chlorinated pool water. *Definitely gotta get the vit C.*

"Yes, Sonia?" I ask, giving her permission to voice her question again. She moves to the front of the group like a gang leader.

"'Ow did vis 'appen? Why di'n't you say anyfing? 'Ow long 'ave you been 'iding all of vis behind our backs? Wha' kind of work will you be doing? When are you leaving?" She reels questions off, laced with contempt, arms folded, nose snubbed, with a rolled-up top lip. *Ok, forget it. You're not acting horribly at all. Look at these people. They're ready to attack!*

Lucy's timid and discomfited voice butts in, "Um ... how much are you going to get paid?"

Everyone nods—mumbles reinforce the question under heavy breaths as if that was the answer they've all really been waiting to hear.

I sigh, run my hands through my hair, "Um, Lucy ... you wouldn't happen to have any vitamin C on you, would you? I'm feeling a little fever—"

The office door swings open creating a gust of wind. "Good morning, ladies," booms Richard Viadro as if playing Mr Game Show Host.

I feel myself blush, and all the girls shuffle back to their seats. My body goes rigid—my smile wonky like the night I met Alex. I turn, attempt to head toward Jodie's office, afraid to look into button boy's eyes. But he approaches me. *Too late.*

"Where do you think you're going?"

"Um, er, nowhere, Mr Viadro, just clearing up my space. I ... uh ... accepted the job." I look my desk up and down; gather some useless papers into a clean pile.

"Melody. Please. Richard," button boy says in a purring semi-whisper, as he places his hand on my lower back and tilts his head to the side.

"Sorry. Richard." I laugh a laugh that sounds pre-recorded for a sitcom, move hair out of my face, scratch my neck, brush some invisible crumbs from my clothes, and put my hands on my hips. "Ahem, er ... I'm sorry, was there something you needed?"

"No, not really. I just dropped by to introduce myself to Jodie and Dianne. I'm to return to the London office this afternoon."

"Oh. Right. Well, have a safe trip, Mr ... er, Richard." I nod, moving backward an inch so he can't touch my lower back again, even though, guiltily, I'd love him to.

I imagine toplessness. Me. Him. Alone in the office. Silence. Twilight. Cicadas singing through the open window. His fingers brushing over my hips as he moves his hands toward the arch in my back. Our breaths hot. Skin on skin. He pulls me closer, his erection pushing against my pelvic bone as I bend backward—his firm hold balancing me like a dancer. He lifts me up onto my desk—I point my toes the moment my feet lift off the floor. He slips his hand up my thigh and unclips my garters—

SCRATCH!

I'm not wearing garters. I'm wearing my crappy white flowery panties that have been tinted grey after years of mixing them with blacks in the wash.

"It was a pleasure to meet you, Melody," Richard says, snatching me from reverie. He takes my hand. Shakes it. His skin is warm, soft, nails groomed. "I look forward to doing business with you." He bends forward. I stiffen. He kisses me on each cheek, Greek style.

I breathe in his aftershave. *Prada Pour Homme.* Woody, suede, bergamot, mandarin. The scent I bought for Alex.

The scent he never wore.

NiNeteeN

Leaving UTD for the last time feels like I've gotten away with faking a sickie—guilty, but dizzily satisfied. I leave earlier than usual, so decide to take the route along the ocean road to clear my head, shake thoughts of Richard from my skin, and mix them with the sand, out of reach—diluted with mother earth; a creature I fear to confront.

I find a convenient car park by the beach—the gods are working in my favour today—and slip on my blue and white chequered triangle bikini in the back seat. I throw off my shoes, lock my belongings in the car and march across the hot grainy sand and straight into the sea with blistering urgency. My head, being so full of contradictory feelings, needs to cool off.

Salty splashes sting my face with lament, as I push my body through a sea of sorrow and awe swimming alongside each other like water and oil. The saliva in my mouth is thick with disgust—toffee in teeth—at Alex, for making me want to break free from him, and at me, for feeling like it's the right thing to do, and for allowing my attraction to Richard to coax me like bait.

The cool sea caresses my body. I imagine the beginning of

life after death might feel like this. Like a baptism. Not of a new body or soul or mind, but of new skin; a little more flexible and impervious than the last. But I haven't finished living in *this* skin yet. So why do I feel like I need to shed it?

Because the love I hold for Alex is like water. It's needed to keep my body from cracking and peeling toxic waste into this sick universe. I know it's not irreplaceable. I can always coat my skin with moisturizer. It may not be the most natural hydration, but it's hydration nonetheless. But I'm not sure I'm ready to wipe my skin dry; to drown myself in a new ocean, where my desire for fleeing this emotional cage hides like a mermaid ambivalent about growing legs.

He's lucky. Alex. For if our love were like land—easy to burn—I'd risk throwing it in a fire, to see if it might grow back like torched eucalyptus trees do in the desert.

But we are floating now. Alex's love and I. Like we imagine angels might float on clouds—we want it to be real, but can't find the proof. I wish the earth would soak us up. Drench us in faith, make us soft and pliable, squash us, roll us into tiny little pearls, and place us together in the same clam. Under the sea. Where we are bound to return.

I hope fate has a say in us. Because tonight is the night I choose to make a better life for myself, and if it were only up to me, I think I'd run away forever.

The traffic this afternoon is worse than trying to drive a car over one hundred kilometres of speed bumps. Most afternoons I could probably walk home faster, but like the rest of the environmentally conscious who are all talk and no action I haven't attempted it yet.

I'm ashamed to say I've united with the majority after spending my whole life trying to be different, but I'm working on it. At least I have kicked the habit of leaving the tap running when I brush my teeth. But it's difficult to care for the environment when you're forced to wade through a river of litter in the streets every day. It seems so … pointless. Walking a kilometre to dispose of a lonely chocolate wrapper in a bin where there are mountains of other chocolate wrappers at your feet isn't worth the effort. At least that's something I don't do—walk all the way to a rubbish bin and throw the wrapper on the ground.

I'm stuck behind a truck and in front of a bus full of peak-hour people. Truck exhaust wafts through my air conditioning vents despite nothing being turned on, and the bus behind me inches further and further up my rear as if I've been inching forward. I haven't moved. Soon all the bus passengers will be getting comfortable in my backseat.

To my right is a bank. And I remember that I should have withdrawn money for rent and the apartment maintenance fee. I contemplate leaving the car to idle in the middle of the road, but decide against it when I visualize the bus driver suffering from impulsive road rage and squashing my olive green 1976 Mini Cooper like an empty soda can.

I pull up on the footpath leaving enough room for the bus to pass if the lights turn green before I've withdrawn cash. I step out of the car, and before both feet are off the road, it does, crushing my side-view mirror, and denting the truck's rear bumper-bar too.

I watch, jaw agape, rage bubbling like lava in the back of

my throat over the fact that I won't be able to do a *thing* about it. Well, not if I don't want to wait five years for the insurance claim to come through. I have learnt through trial and error that if I were to try to get the bus company to pay for my broken mirror, it would be a waste of time, not to mention more money.

As I grit my teeth and glare at the bus driver, a police officer taps me on the shoulder.

"*Kiria, einai afto to aftokinito sas?*" (Ma'am, is this your car?)

"I'm sorry, what did you say? I don't speak Greek," I say with a tight-lipped smile, playing dumb. The Greek police don't bother with foreigners—it's too much paperwork and they're too lazy to deal with it. The man smiles, swaying his head side to side with an I'm-cool-look-at-me-in-this-uniform-doesn't-it-turn-you-on attitude.

"I said, may you be, er ..." he winks and clicks his tongue through the back of his teeth, " ... owning this ve-hicle, miss?"

"Yes. I'm so glad you're here. Did you see what that bus driver just did to my side-view mirror? And to the back of that truck?"

He leans on one foot, tilts his head, and looks at me from above his shades, "Miss. Please be known that you are in discussion with an officer of the abiding law and that it is requirement that you speak in dignified manner."

"I *am* speaking politely—"

"No, it's good. You don't must feel the necessity to be apologetic."

I take a deep breath, resisting the urge to explain myself. It would only make this encounter longer than necessary.

"Thank you, sir. Will you please—"

"Miss. One moment. It is my duty to be you informed that you park illegally, miss, and I'm going to issue you paper ticket."

A ticket? For parking on the curb where there are already ten cars standing with emergency lights flicking away? He has got to be kidding me.

"What? *Me* a ticket?" I squawk, pointing to all the other cars. "Excuse me for being a bit blunt here, but where are you when people park in front of my driveway in the mornings and make me late for work?" I don't know what inspires me to blurt that out, especially since I don't have a driveway.

"Pardon, miss? I'm not understanding. Please do speak with correct diction so I can be to interpret your strange accent." His top lip moves like a wave as he runs his tongue along his teeth. He switches the weight to his other foot and wobbles his head.

I want to squash the arrogant little turd like a cigarette butt. Confidence mutates like bacteria. "Excuse me, but why do you spend all day giving useless tickets to considerate ladies like myself, but let men in suits double park in front of fire hydrants?"

"Pardon, miss. What is this 'fire hydrant' you describe of?"

I laugh, my voice on the brink of sarcastic mockery. I contemplate saying something that could put me in prison, but am saved by an old woman yelling like a wicked boarding-school teacher at the police officer through the bus window. He apologizes to her and refers to her as ... *his mother?*

"Please, miss, de-park your car and drive home in safeness," he says, in a hurry, blushing like a five-year-old boy who peed his pants in public.

"May I withdraw some money first?" I ask.

"No. You not need to give me money. I not issue you paper ticket. I let you disappear."

"Oh, I wasn't going to. I need some money from the bank. For me."

The police officer hangs his head, nods, defeated, scrunches up his nose and looks at his feet.

"Yes, miss. Do as you may be wishing."

He mounts his motorbike, hooks his arm through his helmet and takes off, navigating through the stagnant peak hour traffic like a dying bumble bee.

After half an hour of circling several blocks in my neighbourhood looking for a parking space, I find one in front of the guitar shop I have chosen to ignore all these years. I gaze at a gorgeous second-hand Gibson Les Paul 1957 gold top in the shop front window—just like the one stolen from Dad when I was a kid. He would be delighted if I bought it for him.

Bells jingle when a fifty-year-old-looking guy with a full head of greyish dreadlocks, ripped jeans and a red and black flannel shirt pokes his head through the shop door.

"Bee-ootiful, isn' it?" he sings in an authentic Australian accent.

I smile and nod toward the friendly, familiar voice, and ask if I can give it a play.

"Of course. Come on in."

The shop is packed to the brim with second-hand electric and acoustic guitars. The moment I enter the shop, the smell of musty wood and rubber amplifier leads reminds me of the rehearsal studios my parents often dragged me to—when I'd sit and draw, trying to mimic my mother's scrapbook fashion sketches from when she was a teenager.

The guy plugs me into a small practice Mesa Boogie Amplifier with a funky pink and white striped cable. He hands me a plectrum—resin-coloured—smiles with one corner of his mouth, turns off the stereo playing Jimi Hendrix, and slides into the back room. Only true guitarists know that a quiet moment between human and guitar is the key to developing a bond.

I pluck the crisp new strings, gaining no comfort from the tortured dirty rock sound of the original P90 pick-up. I don't feel a connection to the guitar at all. It's way too heavy and the friction too tough. But I'm glad I feel that way. This way I can buy it for Dad without the pang of loss rendering my generosity worthless when I give it to him.

I put the guitar down to look for the guy, but he is already standing behind the counter. *Hmm, intuitive.*

"So whadid ya think?" he asks, looking up and down with narrowed eyes and fiddling with something out of sight.

"Yeah. It's great, but not for me," I reply, scratching my

chin as if I have a beard. "How much is it going for?" I lift the guitar off my lap from the base of its neck, rest it face up on the ground, bend over with my legs spread like a bloke in dirty ripped jeans, and examine the almost unnoticeable scratches on the body as if a little short-sighted.

"Um, that one's going for two thou, but if it's too expensive for ya, we've got another gold top, but it's a 1975 DeLux with a mini-humbucker. Its neck is made from maple instead of mahogany, though. Not really the best quality if ya ask me." He stops whatever he's doing behind the counter and points behind him with his thumb toward the back room.

"Um, yeah, they didn't sell too well if I remember correctly." I click my tongue. "Look, I just live a couple of blocks down, can I think it over?" I ask, hoping not to sound as if I'm just being polite. I would really like to get it for Dad, but not sure if I can afford it. Maybe I'll ask Mum for some input. Make it a joint gift.

"Sure, no probs … um, you wanna take a card?" he asks, with a scrutinizing look in his eye. I'm positive he's trying to sum me up. Here I am, dressed in black tailored pants and a white shirt, with scraggly wet hair and a bikini strap sticking out of my collar, talking about guitars like an expert.

"Yeah, why not. Thanks," I say, smiling at the back of his head as he turns to find one. I wonder why he isn't he asking me which part of Australia I'm from. They all do—usually—expecting the world to have shrunk to the size of one city: *Oh, you're from Melbourne, hey? Well, maybe you've met my cousin, aunt, sister …*. Or they think because you're from the same country, you must have common interests: *Oh, my daughter lives there, maybe you two can go for coffee next time you're Down Under?*

The guy holds out the card like one would hold a cigarette. I take it and slip it into my trouser pocket.

"Ta." I open the shop door to leave, but the guy says, "Um, by the way, we've also got a really nice Gibson acoustic Hummingbird, out the back. I haven't displayed it because it's been really bashed around. There's no logo or markings left on it anywhere. It was one of the very first—a 1962 model. You wanna give it go?"

"Really? An original Hummingbird? I'd love to have a go."

I put my handbag down and have a seat on a leather footstool near the door. *A footstool near the door.* Weird. The guy goes to the back and comes out with what looks like a chunk of hollow wood with a hole in the middle and a few threads of metal stretched over the top—for all I know there could be a bird's nest inside. But I find myself strangely drawn to it.

The guy hands it to me—the neck warm from his grip— he must have been playing it himself. Before the first strum has even rung out, woe falls from me like loose autumn leaves in wind. I have fallen in love. I want to take this baby home. Replace my crisp, abandoned guitar—gifted with poise, passion, power—with something worn, used, loved for its purpose rather than its beauty. Perhaps this guitar will suit me better. Perhaps we'll understand each other.

I look up with an absent smile, hand the guy the guitar with a nod, and say, "I'll be back to buy them both next week," without even asking how much it's going to set me back.

Right here. Right now. I have to. It's now or never.

Outside, standing by my car, I sift through my handbag for my mobile phone, and search through my recent messages. I open one of Charlie's and press reply.

I type: ***I'm in.***

twenty

I stand at our front door, sea salt burning a small cut in my nose. I hold my shirt sleeve against it, with my wrist, trying to sooth the sting—my handbag falls down around my elbow. My hair partly dry, stuck together in clumps like dreadlocks, tickles the back of my neck. Like a birthmark, the scent of ocean owns me. Smells like … freedom? Salt grains exfoliating pollution from my skin.

Tessa and Doggy come charging for me like bulls. Tessa clutches Doggy's left ear. Doggy pants, her thick pink bouncy tongue hanging from the side of her mouth. I kneel down and hug them both at once. Warm wet drool splashes on my hand. I intend to scratch Doggy behind her ears, and stroke Tessa's hair, but my wires get crossed and I do the reverse. I wish the three of us could sit on the floor in the corridor all night—in a cocoon of unconditional love, freedom from the world, no responsibility, no ache, simple pleasure at its best.

Alex is sitting at his desk, blank-faced. I walk over to him, unsure of what to say, whether I want to say anything at all, or even if I want to be anywhere near him. I stand by his side. Don't utter a word. He doesn't look up. I bend down;

semi-consciously give him a peck on the forehead. I soar above images of my future on an imaginary flying carpet.

"What's up?" Alex asks, smirking as if I've given in.

Alex's voice snaps me back to reality.

"I missed you," I say, covering my bikini strap with my hair. "Doesn't mean I forgive you," I add, pulling back. But I didn't miss him. I missed the idea of him; the impression of how we used to be.

He looks at my breasts through my damp shirt exposing blurred blue checks below. Once upon a time he would have cupped his hands over them, squeezed them, and nudged me toward the bedroom. But now he looks at them as if I'm violating some cultural indecent exposure law.

"Mummy, what does 'forgive' mean?" Tessa tugs on my pants, looks up at me. Curiosity shines through her sad eyes. I never thought I'd witness melancholy from her so young. My airway constricts as she looks at the ground, picking at a fingernail the way I do when I'm upset and don't want to look Alex in the eye.

"Honey," Alex says, looking at me and then Tessa. "Someone has to forgive someone when they do something that hurts them."

"What did you do to hurt Mummy, Papa?" Tessa asks, pushing her fringe out of her eyes.

"I did something very bad. I did something that you won't understand right now, but I'll explain it to you when you're a bit older, Blossom." Alex shifts his eyes back and forth from Tessa to me. His seat creaks. His reassuring smile weakens—twitches to a frown, a result of guilt. He rubs his hands over his face as if attempting to wipe his feelings away.

Is he trying to make me pity him?

Out of pure concern for Tessa, I say, "Alex. Don't be silly. This isn't necessary."

He shakes his head and swallows. I can hear the saliva travel down his throat.

"Tell me what you did, Papa," Tessa says as if consoling one of her toys. "I'll forgive you. Did you break one of Mummy's dolls? Don't be scared, Papa. If you did, it doesn't matter, does it Mummy?" Tessa looks to me for affirmation, pulling her knickers out of her bottom. I laugh a little. "We can just go to Jumbo on the weekend and buy Mummy a new one, can't we Papa?"

I have no intention of letting Alex expand on his explanation, so when Alex opens his mouth, I interrupt. Shake my head. Stiff. Short and tight. Inconspicuous.

"Tessa, Daddy didn't break one of my dolls. He broke one of my plates." A pang of sympathy to match Alex's apparent appreciation stimulates a little nausea. Tears well up in Alex's eyes—prisms of blue crystal brimming with self-hatred. *I know what that feels like.* If I hadn't already doubted the success of our future together, I'd probably forgive him without a second thought. Despite the pain. Despite the little voice that would constantly tell me that men never change and he will do it again. Despite what Serena or Heather or anyone would advise. I would stay with him. Forgive him.

But at this stage in my life, I can't. I won't. I won't become my mother, who at fifty claimed she only ever loved my dad like a brother, but stayed with him because she was afraid to leave, and now regrets it; wonders whether she missed the chance to find a true soul mate. Is that what love is meant to be? Brotherly? Void of the deep hurt that twists your flesh at the mere thought of never being able to see or touch him again? Whatever happened to that? That ... that spasm ... of heartache ... that triggers a vicious thirst to hold on tight and never let go. Is that meant to disappear? And should I hang around to find out? I don't think I could forgive myself if I did. What if I realize that, "no," loving him like my own flesh and blood is not the way it's supposed to be?

"Was it your favourite plate, Mummy?" Tessa asks, flicking my knuckles to get my attention.

"Yes, darling it was," I nod, biting my bottom lip, swallowing diffident tears. "Daddy always liked to use it, but I'm not going to let him use my plates for a while until he learns how to take care of them."

Tessa mouths, "Ah," nodding as if she has just understood the meaning of life.

"Come on, Blossom," I pinch her cheek. "Go wash your hands for dinner." On her way she shoots Alex a squint, a finger shake, and says, "Naughty, Papa."

Alex forces a laugh and slaps himself on the hand.

It's the right thing to do, I say to myself. *Even if it's just temporary*.

I stand out on the balcony after putting Tessa to bed, in my dressing gown, inhaling the uncongested breeze we are lucky to have up here. Every now and then, if the wind is blowing in the right direction, I can smell the basil Alex and I planted together. I breathe a smile onto my face with the memory—our touching crouched bodies, cracking knees, dirt stuck below our nails—him nibbling on my ear as I'd pat down the soil, me drenching him with water after dropping mud down the back of my shorts. It was a time when we could be stupid and play pranks on each other without getting pissed off—inappropriately irritated at good intentions.

There's a false sense of security standing here, eight floors high. Away from chaos. Untouchable. Restful. Conscious. I ... *feel*. I move to the corner of the balcony and lift my arms into the air—trying to inhale what's left of the happy thought. But immediately bring them down when I realize I might appear to be re-enacting *The Titanic*.

I look toward the sky hoping to witness a shooting star— an omen for good luck?—but can't see any stars at all. The Sahara Desert is responsible for this night sky—the dark orange-brown sheath that hangs like fog illuminated by city light. I imagine watching sand encompass us like a violent hurricane from space, eventually suffocating our planet until all that remains is a dried-up prune. *Pop!* The Big Bang revisited.

When I look back down, Alex is standing in front of me. It seems he's been talking to me the whole time, but I only catch the last few words. " ... and the aliens will invade us."

"Sorry?"

"Was asking if you'd ever forgive me, but then realized you weren't paying attention, so made up an alien story. Funny, the things you learn from kids, eh?" Alex smiles, looking into my eyes as if searching for answers.

"Can you close the door? Mosquitoes will get into the house."

"Don't think mosquitoes can fly this high, Mel."

"Can you close it anyway?"

"Sure." He sighs, briefly pauses at the door before sliding it closed behind him.

He returns holding two glasses of vodka. Citrus vodka. My favourite.

"Thought you might need a drink," he says, handing me a whiskey glass filled to the brim with ice, garnished with lemon rind. It's cold in my warm hands. *Is that saying, "cold hands, warm heart" true? Is he trying to warm my heart?*

"Thanks," I say, hardly moving my lips.

"Well?"

"Well, what?"

"Will you forgive me?" Alex strokes my cheek.

"Oh. You were expecting an answer. Sorry, but I got distracted by the thought of you in bed with another woman," I reply, gently removing his hand from my face.

"Mel …" He swirls his drink, looks into his glass as if it might offer a solution, while holding himself steady on the iron barrier with one hand. He scratches the back of his left knee with his right foot. It reminds me of the time my prep teacher taught us how to pat our heads and rub our tummies at the same time. "Can you ... look, I'm so sorry. What do you want me to say? What do you want me to do? Get down on my knees and beg?"

I shake my head.

"Please, Mel. Please forgive me." Alex places his glass heavily on the barrier. It vibrates and hums end to end.

"Alex, I can't because—" I focus on his inert right hand gripping the hem of his *Kinks* T-shirt, willing myself to complete my sentence. *No cushions—just needles. Just say it.* I can't go through life tacking hems in the hope they don't unravel in the wash. I pull my dressing gown tight around my waist. "I want to separate for a while."

"What? Mel, it shouldn't have to come to this. We can work this—"

"No. No we can't. No matter what you say I'm still going to feel the same when you're finished. I don't know if I can *ever* forgive you. I—"

Scepticism mutes me like a button on a remote. I hang my head. Alex lifts it. Shakes his head in question.

"I ... I don't know if I can lie to myself anymore. Or try to convince myself that it never happened, or that you'll never do it again."

Alex turns. Looks toward the swaying trees in the square. It hurts to know this hurts him too, that he can't look me in the eye, and that from this moment forward, life will never be the same for us again. Does he feel like I do? Afraid of being alone?

"I don't want to wake up every morning looking at you, lying beside me in bed, and wonder whether you came home the previous night at four a.m. because you had to take a band out to *eat* after a gig or because a fan felt like fucking you, and you said, 'hey, what the hell.'"

Alex scoffs with acerbic scorn, leans his elbows on the barrier, and cups his drink in both hands. He looks down, spits, waits for it to land, then lets his glass go. Thoughts of being charged with manslaughter run through my head during the glass's short journey between leaving Alex's hands and the moment a stray cat shrieks when it shatters on the rubbish skip.

"What the fuck are you doing?" I screech, switching from feelings of hurt and betrayal to panic and relief. "You could have killed someone!"

"And? What does it matter?" Alex says flippantly, yet rubbing his face in angst. "I'll go to prison? I'm in prison now anyway."

"Excuse me? What do you mean you're in prison now anyway? If you feel like that, what makes you think you won't cheat on me again? You obviously still feel the same way, otherwise why would you say that?"

I glare at him—his solemn face drawing my stare like a magnet. My vision fluctuates—double, triple, half. I'm either over-stimulated with rage, or the vodka is swimming to my head, trying to break the world record. But I don't want to yell. I don't want to wake up Tessa. I blink, attempting to focus on Alex's stubble.

"Baby, I feel really guilty," Alex says, crunching a piece of ice he'd been holding in his mouth.

"Well, you should." *Baby? Now he calls me baby?*

"I mean really guilty. I almost thought about—" Alex pauses, levers himself onto the ground and rests his arms on his knees. A tear escapes and trickles down his left cheek—a drop of salty sadness I want to lick; to consume as a panacea—a symbolic gesture to mark the beginning of a pact to never hurt each other again.

"Almost what?" I kneel down beside him, willing to listen, but not give in, even though my instinct is pushing me toward taking him in my arms and comforting him like a child. I don't have to imagine what it's like to lose someone you love, but I certainly can't imagine losing two in a row. Am I being unreasonable? Am I making the wrong decision? Am I kidding myself thinking this is the best for all of us and not just me?

"Nothing," Alex replies, resting his head between his knees.

Nothing. Nothing? This is what is blatantly wrong with us. We don't communicate. Here I am trying to find out how he is feeling, instead of blabbering on about myself, and I still get nothing.

"Jesus, Alex," I snap, whacking him on the back of his furry, neglected head. "Can't you just tell me how you feel instead of hoping I work it out for myself? You constantly claim you can't read my thoughts, well, you know what? I can't read yours either. So spit it out. Please."

Alex's body shakes like he is laughing. But then he lifts is head. His face is completely wet. I want to share this ache, to help each other through. But I know as soon as I let myself fall into his arms I'll buckle and give him another chance. He may not know it, but I've already given him so many chances—silent chances—I've lost count.

"Oh, I'm sorry," I say, cringing at my own sarcasm. "Am I supposed to be compassionate toward you now?" I immediately regret being so cold.

Alex turns his head so I can't see his face. I reach for his chin and turn his head back around. I wipe away his tears with the back of my hand and lean my forehead against his. He closes his eyes and rubs my upper arm.

Our warm foreheads merge together like dough. I watch a couple of tears hit the ground and imagine a parade of crown splashes as if it were filmed and played back in slow motion.

"Did you fall in love with her?" I whisper.

"'Course not. But she reminded me of you, Mel. A lot. The you I knew when we first met. I miss that you, Melody. I want you back the way you used to be. I need you. I love you."

I can't help but wonder whether who he truly wants is his deceased wife. The thought makes me feel sick. I try to ignore it.

"Alex, I'm still me. I just ... became a mother ... and, okay, yes, you're right. I want to be the way I used to be too. But, Alex, you have to admit, you pushed me in this direction."

"What are you talking about?" Alex sits up, wipes tears from his nostrils.

"Alex, come on. Are you serious?"

He shrugs. Flings his hands in the air and lets them fall into his knees.

"You organize music events. I'm a musician. I stopped playing. Notice anything wrong with these sentences?"

"Melody, you can't blame me for that. You have a mouth. Why didn't you just ask?"

"Excuse me?"

"And besides, you looked happy. I knew you missed playing, but I had no idea you wanted to play gigs again until the other night when you told me."

"Alex, we're supposed to be in tune with each other."

"Mel, sorry, but if that applies to me, shouldn't it apply to you too?"

"What do you mean?" I cross my arms and slide away a couple of inches.

Alex huffs and leans his head backward. It impacts the barrier with a gentle thud. "When I come to bed after work in the middle of the night, you just turn your back to me to avoid being woken up. Never once have you opened your eyes to ask me how the event went—or whether I lost or made money—or even if I *feel* okay. When I'm stressed out about work and need to talk about it, your eyes glaze over and I feel like I'm talking to a brick wall. When I tell you I'm not feeling well, you respond, with, 'You're fine; you're just working too hard. Try to get some more sleep.' Have you ever stopped to wonder whether I really am sick instead of blowing me off? *And* when I'm in the mood to make love, *you're* always too tired. Yet, when you're in the mood I'm expected to jump at the idea despite how I'm feeling. And on that note—"

"Alex, stop. I get it. It looks like separating will do us

some good." I twist my tongue inside my closed mouth. I despise the fact that Alex is trying to make it sound like it's my fault he cheated on me, but … maybe … maybe he's right? I stand. Alex follows suit.

"Look, Mel. I'm really sorry for what I did, and you know what? I can handle the fact that you ignore me. It's not a big deal, and I'm sure now that you're aware of it you can work on it. And I'll work on being a better husband. And I won't cheat on you ever—"

"Alex, I'm going to go to London."

Alex retracts his attempt to stroke my cheek.

"Then … I'm going to go on tour in America with a rock band. And if you want us to work out our marriage, follow me to London after I've returned from the tour, and we can try to start again."

"You're kidding?"

"No. I'm not." I attempt a non-threatening smile, maintaining the strength of this everlasting wall I've been hiding behind since I was a kid. "It'll be good for us. We need the time apart."

"With whom?" Alex asks, his voice teetering on the edge of anger.

I will not hesitate. "Charlie."

"Charlie? Wasn't he …" Alex looks at the barrier, traces a crack of rust-stained paint with his middle finger, and clenches his jaw. His ears twitch. " …wasn't he the one … he was the one in the heavy metal band. Didn't you date this guy?" He taps the barrier, sending it into a fresh convulsion.

"That was a long time ago. And you just said that you

want me back the way I was, right? Well, this might help … don't you think?"

"You've got to be fucking kidding me, Melody. You're not going to fucking tour with your ex-boyfriend—full stop!" Alex pitches a punch mid-air.

"And why not?" I move closer, trying to make it clear that I'm no longer intimidated.

"That's just … wrong!"

"Wrong? I'm not going there to sleep with him, Alex. I'm going to play guitar. And if that's wrong, I think we need a whole new definition for you cheating on me."

"We're not talking about that now. Stop changing the subject all the time." Alex paces back and forth, shoving the plastic outdoor chairs into the table, creating a noise we are no doubt going to get complaints about from downstairs.

"Alex, this isn't changing the subject. I'm trying to tell you I need to get away. I need space. To get away from this. From this!" I hiss, gesturing back and forth between us. "I need to do something for me. Why can't you understand that?"

"Why should I fucking try to understand anything, Melody? You want to leave me and spend time with an ex-lover!"

"It's not about spending time with him. It's about music. It will be good for me, and it might be good for you too. The space. You know? Maybe I'll be a happier and more creatively fulfilled person if I have the opportunity to do this. Wouldn't you enjoy being with me more if I were happier? Alex, I miss playing music as much as I'd miss you and Tessa if you weren't in my life anymore. You have to try to understand, Alex. Please try to understand. I need to take this opportunity. I'll regret it otherwise. If I'm happy, it'll help *us*."

"No, I can't. I *can't* let you do it," Alex snaps without taking the slightest moment to think it through.

"Why not? What's so wrong with it? Give me a valid reason."

"The answer is *no*. Just no. Full *fucking* stop."

I swallow. Nod. Suck saliva to the back of my mouth so hard I hurt my tongue with my teeth. I want to scream. Break windows. Punch him in the face. Break his nose. *Just give me some fucking space! Let me live!*

"Well, what if I'm not *ask*ing you? What if I'm *tell*ing you?" I retort, grabbing his hand and digging my nails into his palm. His hands are as soft as Tessa's. I want to make him bleed. I push them in. Harder and harder. He holds my stare. Then realizes he's in pain and yanks his hand away. Looks at it. At me. His hand is shaking. I prepare for a slap.

Tessa runs out. Sliding the door with force.

"I can't sleep. There's a fairy in my mattress and she keeps poking me in the bum with her wand."

"We'll finish this later." Alex closes his eyes and slowly exhales. "You can count on it."

272

twenty-one

While Tessa is eating her snack—half a slice of whole meal bread spread with Nutella—and I'm watching she doesn't do anything that might compromise her well-being, she holds her new porcelain doll through the railings of the balcony barrier to introduce it to the view. Of course, in my absent-mindedness, the action doesn't register as anything to worry about, and it slips from her hands, falls, and shatters on the garbage skip.

"Oh no, Mummy! Oh no!" Tessa cries, jumping up and down on the spot, bottom heavy, face flushed, fists clenched, tears welling up in her eyes. Doggy joins in the dance, scratching Tessa's leg in the process, and then she screams even more, and kicks Doggy in her behind. Doggy yelps and scurries indoors to her blue furry bed to curl up into a sulking ball.

"What were you holding it through the barrier for? That was a silly thing to do."

"She's not an 'it', Mummy. She's a 'she'. Treat her with respect!" Tessa stops squealing and shakes her finger at me, lips pouting, saliva bubbling from the corners of her mouth. I rub an eye, wondering how she is such a sponge to my mother's banter.

I enter the apartment with every intention of going downstairs to see if I can salvage the doll, but I literally bump into Alex by the front door. He steps on my foot by accident, but instead of apologizing he says, "I told you so." He's holding my guitar. Why?

"Oh, piss off," I hiss, turning the door handle to exit, but he yanks my hand away and swings me around to face him.

"How about I do a little damage to this baby of yours, huh?" Alex raises the instrument horizontal to his head like a baseball bat.

"Whaddaya doing that for?" I gasp, the words flying from my mouth as one. I turn to my right, and Tessa is watching from the balcony door, hushed, hesitant to pass through, it seems, as her toes are placed exactly on the bronze hinge separating inside from outside.

"Blossom, I think it's time you go back to bed. I'll be there in just a minute." I wink, nudge my head in the direction of her room.

"If you go on tour with that shitty little pinhead," Alex sneers, "I'll make sure you don't get to take Tessa." He flicks his head toward her—she hasn't moved from the balcony door—and yells, "Tessa. Go to your room. Now!"

Tessa takes a deep breath, as if preparing to dip her head under water, and runs down the corridor—her hum bounces with each step. But instead of going into her room, she stops at the bathroom, and watches us from behind the door. I squint at her, shake my head, pray she gains some sort of telepathic gift to read my mind—*please, you mustn't watch. You mustn't see your Papa like this. It's not him, Blossom. This is not your Papa.*

"Can you please put my guitar down?" I whisper, trying hard for my pauses in between words to not sound patronizing. "Tessa shouldn't see you like this. Alex? Please?" I notice a tremble in my voice, and a little calm—the voice I used to adopt during my mother's irrational fits to tame the rage.

"Well, I'll make sure Tessa never has to see me like this again. As long as you're not around, I won't ever become like this. I'll file for divorce … and for custody!"

"Don't you *threaten* me," I scream. "I have a steady job and I've been *faithful*. There's no reason why you should get custody."

"Well, I know people you don't. I'll find a way," Alex retorts, lifting the guitar higher.

"What's wrong with you? Stop it! You're scaring Tessa! I didn't want it come to this. I've never even thought of divorcing you, let alone going through a custody battle. This is ridiculous. I don't want to divorce you. We just need a *break*."

"Well, you should have thought about that before." Alex inches closer and closer with the guitar, now hovering over his head.

"Thought about *what* before? I'm just trying give myself a little joy in this life. Can you please put the guitar down? *Please!*"

"I'm the man of this house," Alex roars, his face red, his voice becoming a deep growl. "*You* do as *I* say!"

"Excuse me? Who the *fuck* do you think you are? You don't own me!" I growl, throwing an aggressive finger at his face. There's no avoiding Tessa witnessing this now, and the least I can do is stand up for myself, give her a decent role model to look up to.

"In that case, get the fuck out of my house *now*!"

"*Your* house? *Your* house? Get a grip on yourself. Pull your head out of your arse for just one minute and think about what you are doing here. This is ridiculous! You want to smash my guitar into pieces because I want to play music? Alex!"

Alex moves the guitar backward, ready to swing, his eyes bloodshot, fingernails white from his firm grip around the neck—the strings crying out against his strength.

"Stop it!" I scream, bringing my hands to my ears.

The guitar splinters as he smashes it into the wall. A photo of my parents, in a silver metal frame, smashes on the floor. Splinters of wood and glass. Everywhere. *Can't let Tessa run in. Bare feet.* Calm overpowers me like steam in a sauna—hot with guilty relief, dripping with self-consciousness—I now have a *real* excuse to leave. I step over my guitar and walk down the corridor, take Tessa's silent hand, put her in her room. I stroke her cheek.

"Don't worry," I whisper, "Papa's just in a bad mood. It'll pass. Go to bed and I'll come in soon, after I calm him down." I wink. She lifts the collar of her night dress to her mouth, nods, and closes the door behind her.

Don't make this worse. Don't become equally to blame.

But I can't help myself. My mother is in me—somewhere—here—now—tearing at my inner wall—the cage of enmity. I go to the kitchen. Grab plates. Cheap. Useless.

Alex's face drops. Regret? Fear? Blank-out? *What? You wouldn't.*

I throw a plate at him. Like a Frisbee. Mind blank. He catches it. Confused. Arousing venom sears my tongue, my heart, my everything.

You fucking arsehole. I throw another plate. He ducks. It smashes. Small pieces. Very small. *Cheap shit. I knew it.*

Alex moves closer. I throw another plate. But it slips from my firm grip, detours towards the corridor. And this is when I see everything in slow motion.

Tessa flings her bedroom door open, comes running down the corridor, arms open wide, towards me—towards my legs. The very instant I see her, the plate leaves my hand, a flying saucer towards her head. *My baby! I just killed my baby!*

Alex kicks the demolished guitar out of my path as I bolt towards Tessa on the floor.

"Alex, get me a towel!"

All the blood rushes from my face at the sight of Tessa's blood gushing from her forehead. I'm going to faint. *I can't faint. I need to make sure Tessa is alive.* Alex brings me the towel, crying, breathing heavily, swearing under his breath, pacing, pacing—he punches the wall.

I pick Tessa up, despite the dizziness, the back pain, the nausea threatening to collapse me, holding the towel over her jagged gash. I bolt down eight flights of stairs with her in my arms, afraid to use the elevator. I pause mid-way, lean against the wall to catch my breath. I look down and she opens her eyes.

"Mummy?" she whispers.

"It's okay, Blossom. Mummy's here."

My legs wobble when Alex catches up to me—house keys jingling in his pocket. He takes Tessa. I follow him down the stairs, clutching tightly to the railing, trying to stay upright.

When we reach the car and I sit in the backseat, Alex places Tessa on my lap and looks into my eyes—his blink breathes an apology one can only fathom through silence. Regret. We *both* regret this. We both regret this.

We just failed as parents. We failed. We failed. We failed.

I failed as a mother.

I should have just bit my tongue and been the doormat.

The smell of the sterile hospital environment nauseates me; reminds me of all the times I spent waiting for the doctors to release my mother after one of her breakdowns. I'd sit in the nursery—waiting—stuffed toys bombarding me with sick voices, button noses, I thought them snobs, just staring at me like that.

"So how did this happen?" the doctor asks, removing a pen from behind his ear and jotting something down in Tessa's file.

"She fell face-first into her porcelain doll," I snap, before sound comes out of Alex's open mouth.

"It happened so fast," Alex adds.

"We, er, have the doll to prove it, Doctor," I say, regretting it instantly.

"That won't be necessary, Mrs. Konstantinou." The doctor

frowns. Tessa is right beside us and glaring at me, confused, with a thick white sticky gauze across her forehead. Her lips open and shut as if she wants to say something.

"Don't worry, Tessa, we'll buy you a new one," I add, before she speaks the truth. My mother did that once—lied to protect herself in front of doctors. My stomach turns at the thought. *What are you doing?*

I was fourteen. She slammed my hand in my bedroom door while I was trying to close it in her face to escape her violent rage. She broke my two little fingers. When the doctor asked her how it happened, my father froze, but my mother said, with a nervous laugh, "You know how clumsy kids are nowadays. The poor thing put her fingers in the hinge of the door just as I was closing it behind me."

I have sixteen missed calls displayed on my mobile phone when we get home. It's past midnight.

Mum. I call her.

"Melody! Thank God. Why weren't you picking up? I almost had a panic attack."

"Um, Tessa had a little accident. She, uh … fell over holding her porcelain doll, and it smashed and cut into her head."

"Oh, shit. Is she okay?"

"Yeah. I think she was in a bit of shock having to spend time in the hospital, but she's fine."

"You know, I dropped you down an escalator in a huge department store once. I got confused because you were hooked in my left arm, and in one hand I had shopping bags and in the other I was holding your pram. You began to slip and I intended on dropping the shopping bags to get a better hold of you, but I let go of you instead. Things like that happen. Don't beat yourself up about it."

"I'm not." *I am.* "It couldn't have been helped."
She knows I'm lying.

Tessa is lying on the couch, on her side, head on the arm rest, sucking her thumb. She's gazing outside, at blackness, blankness, silent leaves blowing in the wind; eyes glazed like marbles. I walk over to her, feel her head, ears, neck, for a fever. No fever.

"How are you feeling?"

She raises her eyebrows up and down in response—the Greek "no"—Tessa's recent adoption to let us know she's not listening, and doesn't intend to.

"Blossom. I'm sorry."

She turns, keeping her thumb in her mouth, faces the back of the couch, the wall. I deserve it. I lied to the doctor, and she's not going to forget it. I don't blame her. But what else was I supposed to do?

I sit at her feet—bare, dark grey with dirt and grime as if she's trodden on my horrid aura these past few weeks. I rub them, but she retracts her legs, curls into a foetal position, Barbie hooked under her arm. My heart sinks as if all sources of nourishment have been vacuumed out of it, leaving it shrivelled and wheezing and whistling with misery.

"I'm so sorry. So sorry." I swallow, my saliva hot in my

throat, and move to stroke her hair. "I love you so much," I whisper, my voice fluctuating like a pubescent boy. "Can you please forgive me?"

She raises her eyebrows again, flicks my hand off her head—rejected; spat out like fowl-tasting candy.

How do I fix this?

"Blossom, you have to understand that sometimes mums and dads make mistakes too. I made a *really* big mistake," I say, smiling and holding my arms as wide as they can go, trying to simmer the situation down to a jocular blunder, "and so did Papa. And we are both so so so so *so* sorry. Haven't you ever made a mistake before, Blossom? Surely you—"

"But I don't do them on *pur*pose. You ... you were naughty!" Tessa squeals into a cushion. "You said to the doctor that I did it my*self.*"

I fold my hands in my lap, scrutinizing my thumbnails; the way they grow slightly towards the left. "I had to make that story up to protect us. If they'd understood I injured you myself, they might have taken you away from us. I couldn't let that happen, Blossom. That's why I had to lie. I know it was wrong and bad and I ... promise it'll never happen again."

Tessa rolls onto her back and frowns—mumbles with her thumb still in her mouth, "Why would they take me away?"

"Because they would think we were bad parents and that you weren't safe."

Tessa looks at the ceiling, takes her thumb out of her

mouth, curls her tongue around, and holds it steady between her teeth. She sits up. Wipes her wet thumb on her thigh.

"You're not bad parents, Mummy. You're good parents."

"Thank you, Blossom, I'm very happy you think that." I hold my arms out for a hug, guilt-ridden, but relieved, and Tessa snuggles up to me, nuzzling her face into my neck. She takes a deep breath, and sighs—snot bubbles on my skin. I wipe it away with the collar of my shirt. "Are you okay to go to bed on your own, or would you like me to come with you?"

"I'm okay. I can go on my own. Can I still play with Barbie?"

"Sure. But don't stay up too much longer, okay? It's really late, and you need to get a good night's sleep."

Tessa nods, and hops off the couch, clutching Barbie from her hair—the only one she hasn't mutilated yet.

"Tessa?"

"Wha'?"

"Can you rinse your feet off a little before you get into bed?

Tessa rolls her eyes, "Yes, Mummy," spins around and stamps as loud as possible all the way to the bathroom.

Rattle, rattle ... slide ... crash!

There goes another frame.

In bed, Alex turns onto his side and wraps an arm around my waist. I stiffen as his fingers creep toward my crotch. I want to reciprocate the affection, but I don't want to give him the wrong idea. Is it okay to make love after this? After tonight?

I catch his wrist, move his hand away.

"Not sure if this is a good idea," I whisper, kissing his forehead. He smells like … *Prada Pour Homme? Oh no. He's wearing the cologne.* My pelvis trembles—a flash of Richard flits by like a laser beam on a skyscraper. Alex breathes into my neck and moves my hair to the side. I hear myself gulp. Alex pulls me closer, and runs his fingers up and down my stomach. I take deep breathes, trying to control my thoughts—trying to figure out if I can do this.

What happened to our marriage vows? Through sickness and in health. Right? Could infidelity be like a sickness? A psychological defect? Could sleeping with another woman just be a symptom of an unhealthy state of mind? If so, then shouldn't I be supportive and help him heal? Shouldn't I determine the cause of the problem and find a cure? That's what we do when we are physically ill, don't we? We go to a doctor. The doctor finds the cause of the symptoms and prescribes medicine to treat it. We don't feel upset and betrayed when our other half is physically ill, so why should we feel that way when they're psychologically ill? Why does society make us believe that infidelity is unforgivable and untreatable? After all, surely it only happens when one's self-esteem is low, and one is trying to find a sense of self worth again. Right?

Alex's hand moves to my crotch again. But this time he doesn't hover, and flicks his forefinger back and forth over my clitoris, bites my shoulder and breathes heavily into my ear. *I don't want this,* I think, but groan regardless—impulsively. I can't find the strength to stop him. I just can't. I need to escape the day's events. I need it like my mother needed her lithium.

I close my eyes, and let it happen.

I let my head spin …

Alex and I both lie on our backs, arms firmly at our sides. We stare into nothingness—indulge in silence—abeyance—a cloud of remorse code. Calm radiates from our bodies. I wish we could summon this calm when we temporarily forget we are parents who have responsibilities far beyond tending to our own selfish needs.

It could act like a natural sedative of anti-misdemeanour.

twenty-two

Kettle boils. Coffee in mug. Wipe sleep from eye. Lose balance. *Hm … bit dizzy. Weird.* Pour milk in coffee. *Gotta get that work done.* Vision a little hazy. *Oh … hot flush?* Fingers tingly. Shake hand. *Cut-off circulation?* Doesn't dissipate. Drop spoon in mug. Clang! Wipe splash off belly with sleeve of robe. *Gotta figure out what I'm gonna take to London. Gotta tell Tessa's preschool teacher.* Insects crawl up arm; ants nibble fingertips. *Um … Alex?* Hazy. Cloudy vision. I open my mouth, but no sound comes out. Intense wave of heat penetrates through bones—head to toe, like steam flushing through my veins. Heart beats faster. Breath quick. Short. Stilted. Sweat. Everywhere. Legs fleshless. Chest achy. Can't move! Stuck! Air hot—thick. Blocks the entrance to my lungs. Vacuum cleaner inserted into mouth—full speed, full suction. Heart palpitates in my ears—faster, harder, deeper, louder! I pull viciously at the collar of my night shirt.

"Somebody get this off! I can't … breath!" I shriek.

Alex and Tessa come running into the kitchen; they fade like TV fuzz, their footsteps gliding on a gymnasium echo. Next thing I know, I'm in bed. My throat's dry and my eyes are stuck together as if they'd been sealed with a soldering iron. I look up through one open eye and wonder if I've lost my mind. There's a man standing over me whom I don't recognize. Fuzzy, fat and furry. *Whoa. Now that's facial hair!*

"It seems you had a panic attack, Melody. Then you passed out," the man says, with a deep husky post middle-aged Greek grit. "It's a little odd, though. Panic attacks come on from too much adrenaline." He rolls his R so heavily I can feel my own tongue vibrate. "So you shouldn't really have passed out."

"Oh," I say, juicing saliva from the back of my tongue and hydrating the walls of my mouth. *What's he on about?*

"I've taken a blood sample. There's nothing to be alarmed about. Just for safe measure. Okay?"

I nod. So does Alex who is standing by my side, scratching his chin, it seems, with deep concern.

"How did I get here?" I ask, and then realize who the man is. It's Dr Leventis. He lives in our apartment building. *I had a panic attack? That's what my mother went through almost every single day of her adult life? Oh my God ... How could I be so cruel to her? How could I not show a little more compassion? I have to tell her. I have to tell her I understand!*

I make moves to get out of bed, but Alex and Dr Leventis shake their heads in unison.

"You get some rest," Dr Leventis says, as Alex pushes my shoulders back down muttering something I can't comprehend. "I hear you've had an exciting week. Congratulations on the promotion, by the way. It sounds as if your husband is very proud."

I glance at Alex. He winks, emitting a silent apology.

Dr Leventis smiles politely as he snaps closed his medi-kit, puts on his black pin-striped suit jacket and winks at Tessa, who is kneeling on the bottom of the bed, by my feet, balancing her chin on the foot rail, and staring at the doctor's every move with curious interest.

"I gave your daughter's wound a clean too. Looks like it will heal up very nicely. And quite fast too. It's not a very large cut at all."

"Thanks. That's very kind of you," I reply, with a crooked smile, wondering if Alex was put on the spot to explain how it happened.

"Take it easy. I've instructed your husband to take good care of you. I'll call ASAP with the results of the blood test."

Alex walks Dr Leventis to the door. I can hear them converse. "Thank you so much for coming on such short notice. Come visit us for dinner tomorrow night; I'd like to show some appreciation." *Dinner? What? He can't be serious.*

"Oh, I'm much obliged, but your wife should really spend tomorrow in bed. Tell her to get some rest." *Spend tomorrow in bed? But I have to finish my work off for Monday!*

"Tell her not to take any notice of her husband and child complaining about not having anything cooked for dinner." They both laugh. I imagine the doctor winking in jest and patting Alex on the back.

I look at Tessa, staring at the wall again, chin still hooked over the rail. Absent as if dreaming of rainbows. If only she were.

"Blossom, come here." I pat the bed beside me. "You're

going to choke yourself if you keep doing that." In silence, Tessa obeys, and cuddles into my side. I stroke her hair, without a word, knowing very well it's not words she needs for comfort. *Like mother, like daughter. This family is cursed.* I feel a little nauseated. *There can't be anything wrong with me can there? Not now. Definitely not now, please.*

Alex returns, sits by my side, and strokes my head the way I do Tessa's.

"So you're *proud*?" I ask, maintaining my gaze toward the foot of the bed.

Alex searches for my knee below the covers and gives it a little squeeze and pat. He sighs heavily, stands, and stretches his arms towards the ceiling. His tracksuit pants are halfway down his bum. I focus on the inch of crack that's visible and have an urge to stick my finger in it. *No. Stop it.*

"I'll go and make you some breakfa—er brunch," Alex says, and kisses the top of my head. Twice.

For the remainder of the day, I'm pampered with odd forehead kisses from Alex and uncharacteristic cuddles from Tessa. The kind of cuddles that seem like a plea for permanency; as if letting go will mean never coming back. I recognize it because I used to be like that—during my mother's fits of "normal".

By the evening, I'm feeling fine, and wonder whether my body was subconsciously reacting to stress. Well … *praying* my body was *just* reacting to stress. Because I can't stop thinking about my mother. She was my age when … it all started. Panic attacks. Then more and more, and more often; then medication, addiction, rage, depression, withdrawal, bipolar disorder diagnosis; gigs, festivals, more gigs, stress, tours, unhealthy lifestyle, alcohol on top of it all … then what? Habit. She was left with the bad habit of negative behaviour and ten records to show for it—each song a melodic cry for help to escape a life she was supposed to love; a dream she spent years aiming to reach.

If she had taken it easy in the very beginning would her bridge have remained woven, or would it still have frayed? Is today the day my bridge is beginning to fray? Should I *choose* to stop crossing it, burn the thread, seal the hole? Save myself, my family, before it gets out of control like it did with her? Before I realize it's not the life I really want, when the fact of the matter is, all I want is to be appreciated, loved, exist on this earth for a reason? Isn't Tessa a big enough reason to want to exist? *Yes. Yes, she is. But … Alex isn't.*

How do you keep a chemical imbalance like that under control and still do all the things you passionately crave in life? Is it even possible? I don't want to put my daughter through what my mother put me through because she was too stubborn to take a step back and see the bigger picture.

A couple of hours after I've put Tessa to bed, and pampered myself with a bubble bath, candle light, and Enigma, I poke my head through Tessa's bedroom door. She's still awake, examining a row of deformed Barbie dolls spread out in a line in front of her.

"Hey, honey, what are you still doing awake?" I ask,

wading through some stuffed toys on the floor and picking up odd dress-up items to return them to the basket.

"They were feeling sad because I chopped off all their hair," Tessa replies in a tone a little more adult than I have heard before.

"Oh, Blossom." I sit by her side and stroke her hair. "Are they feeling better now?"

"No. They are angry with me. They said that I'm a horrible person."

I'm stunned and angry and want to punch the living daylights outta these dolls. I envisage snatching them and pulling their heads off.

"Why? Why did they say you're a horrible person? That's a terrible thing to say!" I say a little too loudly, engrossed in my own imagination.

"No, Mummy, it's true. I *am* a horrible person." Tessa begins to cry, and crosses her arms in front of her chest.

"You are *not*! Don't believe a word they say."

Tessa falls face-first into my lap, sobbing and heaving a little louder than I think she would naturally.

"Oh, honey, what's wrong? Why so sad?"

She sits up, tears streaming down her cheeks. "Mummy? Are you going to die *again*?"

"Of course not! Why do you think I'm going to die? What do you mean again?"

"You died today, and maybe you'll die again and not wake up!"

"Oh Tessa, I didn't *die* today! I was just, sort of … well, sleeping."

"Sleeping? Oh. Were you having a siesta?"

I laugh, "Well, yes, you could call it that."

"Why?"

"Because I had a very hard day yesterday and didn't sleep well last night, and my body just couldn't keep me awake any longer. It needed a rest that I wasn't giving it on my own."

"Oh. But why did Papa look so scared?"

"He did?"

"Yeah."

"Well, he was probably worried because he didn't understand that I was just sleeping either. You see, my body didn't give me the chance to let you know beforehand. It happened by surprise."

"Oh. But he understands now?" Tessa scratches the corner of her mouth where a tear seems to be tickling her.

"Yes, he does. And so do you, right?"

"Yep." She wriggles her legs beneath the duvet to get comfortable again.

"But, you still haven't told me why you think you're a horrible person."

"I don't think I'm a horrible person, Mummy! My *Barbies* do!"

"Oh. Right. Why do your *Barbies* think you're a horrible person then?"

"I *told* you, Mummy! 'Cause I cut off their *hair*!"

"Right. Sorry. Silly me. I must still be sleeping," I say, laughing a little.

She looks at me as if I've lost the capacity to comprehend

the clear and simple. She's probably right. There always seems to be a hidden meaning I feel the need to interpret. But maybe there isn't. Maybe everything *is* just clear and simple. Maybe I take life too seriously and we are just material for mulch; on earth to merely keep the damn balls spinning.

"Mummy, I think it's time for you to go to bed," Tessa says with a stiff nod, attempting to imitate me. "It's eleven o'clock. At night!"

"Oh, is it? Goodness, we'd both better get some sleep then, hey?" I get up, tuck her in as she clutches onto her Barbie dolls again, and kiss away the remaining tears from her cheeks.

"Sweet dreams, say the jelly beans, it's time to sleep that means."

"Nighty-night says the little mite, then switches off the light." And with that, Tessa turns the light out herself, and says, with pure conviction, from within the darkness as I close the door behind me, "I don't think we need to sing that anymore, Mummy. Lullaby's are for babies. And I'm all grown up now."

twenty-three

Once I get to London, and Tessa and I are settled in, I'll pull myself together for this tour. Don't know what I'll say to Richard—*oh … Richard*—but I'll find a way for him to approve my leave. And then, once I've had my fun (because I could really do with a little leisure in my life) I'll work on my marriage; I'll make sure Tessa receives the upbringing she deserves, and most of all, I'll stop beating myself up over the choices I've made.

I have a beautiful daughter who needs me. She needs me to become the woman I am not. Strong. Stable. Able. I'll teach her to play guitar, piano, to sing, to appreciate art, whether it be music or some other avenue she has an interest in. I'll teach her to love herself as much as, if not more than, she loves her passion. I'll teach her to be confident, to never rely on a man to make her feel whole, to respect herself. I'll teach her that happiness does not come from others, or things, I'll teach her that it comes from self-worth; and if it is happiness she seeks, I'll make sure she knows she's not going to achieve it by *becoming something*—she's going to achieve it by allowing a passion *to become her*, void of pressure to tell the world why, or the expectation that she should have something to show for it in the end. I'll teach her that life *does* have meaning—life means *living*.

At the kitchen table on Friday morning, I sip freshly brewed coffee, Alex-style; reinvented, composed, considerate, and cautious to not ruin the air of calm settling on us all today. Tell me why I want to leave him again? Why is it, as soon as a man does something nice, you wonder whether all the disagreements between you were a result of your irrational temper and lack of patience?

And now I'm craving his attention—a stroke on the cheek, a kiss on the forehead, a smile that says more than words ever will. I want a guarantee he won't let our relationship die. I want him to tell me the date he'll arrive in London. I'm positive, that after a few months of separation we'll be able to wipe the slate clean. Start fresh. In fact, I'm looking forward to it already. Why so happy all of the sudden? Why do I feel like I'm dressed in silk, ready for a ball? *Bipolar? Exaggerated highs, exaggerated lows? Shit. Oh, who cares? I feel great!*

The atmosphere is so positive in the house today that I'm somewhat hesitant to bring London up. But I have to, and I will. Right now. If there's anything I've learnt over the past few weeks, it's to never wait for the right moment to speak up. There *never* is a right moment. Speak up before it's too late, or spin cycle in self-inflicted shit.

I walk to Alex's office—stand opposite his desk. With a sigh, I say in the kindest voice possible, "Let me know when you're ready to talk. Okay?"

He nods, with a melancholy smile, and rubs his hands over his face. A mannerism I've long associated with imminent anger. But I realize now, it's just his way to find a moment behind a closed curtain, to express emotion in private, without being judged. I kick myself for not noticing that before. Perhaps if I had, I wouldn't have been so afraid. Perhaps I would have found something in common—our way of coping: masking savage woes in the hope problems might disappear on their own.

"Sure," Alex says, looking me directly in the eyes. "Just finishing something up. Gimme five."

I nod, sick at my inability to express compassion towards him all this time.

I head back to the kitchen—stare at my empty mug. Should I clean up? Cook a meal? Bake a cake? No. Alex has already tidied everything up. *Now? Now that I'm leaving he decides to support my all-men-and-woman-are-equal rant?*

I don't know what to do with myself. I've spent so many years having something to do at all times, that I *need* something to do. I just want to be bored and enjoy it. I want to sit in front of the TV and relax, but I can't. Everything inside me is moving, muscles twitching. I pace the house, feeling a psychological magnetic pull toward the pile of press proofs on my desk. But I don't want to start them. I don't want to sit still.

I walk into my study—watch the wind toss the proofs off my desk—scatter them all over the floor. I ignore it—go to Alex's office, smile, he smiles back. I leave Alex's office, head into the kitchen, *still no mess*, leave the kitchen, sit on the couch in the living room, turn the TV on and off, get off the couch, stand on the balcony with the dog, throw the ball, leave the balcony, enter the bathroom, splash water on my face, leave the bathroom without even drying it, head down the corridor, see a Tessa fingerprint on the wall, spit on it, wipe it off with the hem of my night shirt. *Oops, Alex saw that.*

"What was that?"

"What do you mean?"

"What do you mean what do I mean? You spat on the wall."

"So?"

"So? That's disgusting."

"So?" I laugh, and Alex mumbles something in Greek and disappears. I follow him—stare at him again with an odd, half-possessed—half boredom induced pout.

"Don't you have work to do by Monday?" Alex asks, smirking.

"Yeah."

"So why don't you do it?"

"Don't want to sit still."

"*Don't* do it then."

"I'm not."

"Well, can you find something to do other than stare at me? Almost done. Just need a minute."

"Okay. I can be patient." *I think.*

The phone rings. I rush to the cordless in desperation for something to do even though Alex is only an arm's length away from the fixed line. My hands are sweaty, and I drop the receiver onto the black marble tiles in the entrance hall. It smashes to pieces. Batteries fly to one corner and the earpiece to another. I call out, "I'll get it! I'm coming! Don't pick it up!" I rush to his office to answer the phone in there. Sit on Alex's aristocratic black leather seat opposite his desk, and cross my legs like a young schoolgirl, feet hooked under my bum.

"Hello?" I gush, wiggling from side-to-side.

"Hello? Mrs. Hill-Konstantinou?"

"Yes, speaking." I freeze.

Alex looks up, squints and twitches his head in question.

"It's Dr Leventis here." *Am I sick? No. I feel fine. Of course, I'm not sick.*

"Oh, hello, Dr Leventis." My voice waivers. I cough, swallow a prickle of unease.

"I'm just calling to let you know the test result."

"Am I okay?"

Alex stands with a supportive smile. Crouches in front of me, rests his hands on my knees, when Dr Leventis tells me the result. Relief and shock merge to combine the perfect ingredients of nausea.

"Thank you, Dr. Leventis," I reply, trying to maintain a little joy in my voice.

The phone beeps when I hang up. My hand drops into my lap with a thud. *It's not bipolar making me happy. It's the hormones.*

"I'm not sick, Alex," I say, disappointment cutting through my effort to sound pleased. "I'm pregnant."

twenty-four

"You're going to have to tell your supervisors that you can't take the job," Alex says, massaging his brow, voice laced with a concerned mellow air.

"What? Why should I do that? My life doesn't have to stop just because I'm having a baby."

"*We're* having a baby, Melody. *We.*" Alex walks out onto the balcony. I follow him. He stares at his feet—smiling.

"What are you smiling about?" I half-whisper, leaning against the white prickly wall. "My life is finally going in the direction I want it to, and what, you're smiling now because you think you're going to get your way? Is that it?"

"Melody, you have *life* inside you," Alex says, holding his hands in the air, as if gesturing to some godly miracle about to rain down on us. "You should be happy about it."

"Well, Alex, I'm not. *We* haven't been happy about us for a long time. We need this break. If you want any chance of surviving as a couple, we need this break. Maybe I won't be able to go on tour anymore, but—"

"*Maybe*? Mel—"

"Let me finish." I rub my brow, taking a deep breath so as not to raise my voice. *No tour. Why? Why me?*

"Listening." Alex licks his lips—clicks his tongue with attitude and folds his arms.

"There's nothing stopping me from moving to London and continuing this job. I'm not going to sit around here all day cooking meals and washing dishes to the same dead-end tune. It's enough. I deserve more than this. And if I can't have music, I think I deserve the opportunity to have a proper career. At least that way, I can give Tessa the upbringing she deserves. And, see, now it's not only Tessa we have to think about, is it? We need the money. I mean, your events are great, when they work, but your job is like gambling! We can't rely on that anymore."

"Mel—"

"Alex, stop."

He puts his hands in his pockets and huffs like an impatient child.

"I do *not* want to divorce you. I want a *break*. That's all. A *break*. If you love me like you say you do, you'll understand how important this is. This can only help us. We. Need. This. Break."

Alex takes my head in his hands and looks at me as if he's about to say the most important thing I will ever hear. But he doesn't say a word. Instead he kisses me on the nose, leaves the balcony, and walks out the front door.

Two hours later, after sitting on the couch watching Greek-dubbed American cartoons with Tessa, biting my nails and trying to convince myself that Alex just needed some space, he comes back home with a guitar. The vivacious rattle of the door handle startles me, and I stand up in shock.

"I hope you'll play it for me once in a while," Alex says, standing by the open door. "You know. When I come to London." Alex puts the guitar down, protected in a case made with soft-toned brown and beige material, and gently shuts the door behind him.

I'm speechless. My gaze shifts from Alex to the guitar, to the front door, as if somehow the door is responsible for materializing this scene like a hologram. But a smile creeps up on me like drizzle turning to rain; a silent voice marking victory; a sense he has finally understood and accepted me for who and what I am. I walk to him, slide into his arms, and rest my head on his chest. His heart is beating fast, but the longer I stay wrapped in his embrace, the more it slows down. I balance myself on his feet—and we rock from side to side, to the same rhythm, as if we are silently singing the same tune.

Alex kisses me on the top of my head and says, "*Se'agapo, moro mou.*"

I look up. Nuzzle the tip of my nose into the dimple in his chin.

"I love you, too, baby," I reply. "I love you, too."

It's eleven thirty at night and my mother just called to tell me they've arrived at the hotel. I'm relieved to hear they'll visit around ten to ten thirty tomorrow morning.

The good thing about visiting on a Saturday morning is she doesn't expect us to be dressed or geared to go out anywhere. Visiting on a Saturday morning means she's prepared to laze around all day, enjoying everyone's company as if the primary resident of this household. Queen Bee-tty. I can deal with Saturday morning visits, because I know we'll simply chill out on the balcony and eat take-out *souvlakia*. Pressure low. Spirits high.

Tessa is finally asleep, and Alex has put his work to rest for the night. I pour us each a glass of red wine, take the glasses out onto the balcony, and light a few tea light candles. *Is this our goodbye, see you in the next life?* Melancholy soars through me like a hot flush. *Why do I feel so sad? It's not an end. It's a new beginning. And we're celebrating. Yes. We're celebrating.*

I sit in silence sipping my wine, looking into the brownish sky, imagining the stars I'd see if I were sitting on my parents' veranda on the island. Somewhere up there is us, a happy us, in some parallel universe, living the way we're supposed to be. I truly believe that the earth is our practice ground—the place where we are to test things out, to make mistakes, to discover what we believe in, what we are passionate about. Death is when we move on and go *up there*—to the real world; to start again, to rectify our mistakes and live a happy and fulfilling existence. There is no hell. Earth is hell. This is where we are allowed to sin. *Up there*, is where we no longer want to.

I can hear Alex fiddling with the old record player. The needle crackles as it lightly touches the vinyl before Elvis Costello's raw, defeated voice, murmuring synthesized strings, and solo guitar twang surrounds me like membrane. Alex comes out, downs his whole glass of wine and sings along to "*I Want You*", kneeling at my knees …

We listen to the song over and over again. Over. And over. And over. We make love to it. Over. And over. And over. On the couch, on Alex's desk, on the floor, drowning each other in defeat—in the dark—swimming in song, in lyrics that speak to us like hidden thoughts.

No poetry.

Just us.

"Hey, are you coming to bed?" I call out to Alex who is in the bathroom brushing his teeth, a little too loudly, forgetting that Tessa is asleep nearby.

"Yeah, just—getting something," Alex calls back, dropping volume halfway through his sentence.

Alex tiptoes back into our bedroom holding my new guitar. He hands it to me with a boyish grin on his face.

"Er, what are you doing?" I ask.

"Play for me."

"*Play* for you?"

"Yeah, play for me."

"Now? It's two o'clock in the morning. I'll wake Tessa up."

"No you won't, I'll close the door and you'll play softly." Alex hands me the guitar, smirking, I assume at my dropped jaw, and gets onto the bed, with a little bounce, the way he used to when we'd just met—when we'd spent twenty-four-hour blocks without getting dressed and made love like wind-up rock gods.

I take the guitar, identical to my last, cross my legs and rest it on my knees.

"Um … what would you like me to play?" I ask, swallowing an excess of saliva.

"I don't know. You choose."

"Er, okay. How about a bit of Joni?" *Can I remember any Joni?*

"Why not?"

"Actually, no, I know …"

I play the song I wrote the other night, when I stole one of Alex's cigarettes, at a volume so low any true rock artist would say was a crime. A steady and crisp drone of four/four rock chords act as a pillow for my soft, drawn out vocals:

> *so you want to live the life of a star*
> *and you want to be at peace with mankind*
> *really want to be a mother and father*
> *so you want to know the meaning of life*
> *want to be the ripple and wave*
> *really want to know yourself completely*
> *so you want to start your own revolution*
> *and you want to teach your daughter it all*
> *and you really want to fight this depression*
> *do you really want to hold emotions to ransom*
> *do you want to be cruel to be kind*
> *do you really want to lose precious intentions*
> *so you really want everyone to hear you*
> *and you want everyone to see*
> *but do you really want to be this famous?*

"Melody?" Alex asks, tears lingering in the corners of his eyes, when I finish playing.

"Hmm?"

"Do you think we are going to be okay?"

I put the guitar down and gesture for him to lie in my lap.

"Yes," I nod. "We'll get there. In time." I stroke his forehead and tears trickle onto my knee. Warm. Calm. And hopeful. A baptism of new life.

twenty-five

Our buzzer rings and Tessa jumps up and down squealing with erratic glee. My parents are here. I wonder if Mum will be happy to see me, or too distracted by one of Dad's mishaps to give me a long and meaningful hug—the daughter-turned-friend kind she always fantasized about and tried to discuss with me, odd smile breaching common aloofness, before I'd take off for school.

Her voice would muffle behind the crunch of corn-flakes—the swish of milk between my teeth. When I'd swallow, she'd be looking at me—head tilted—that smile on the brink of dwindling—corner of her mouth twitching in anticipation. Oh, how I wish I wasn't such a cold-hearted teen and listened in those moments when her voice was gentle and warm; when she needed to love me; when she needed me to love her despite the shit she put me through. Why didn't I see it then? Why didn't I stop chewing when I saw that smile? I wonder now if I had hugged her, given her what she seemed to be inadvertently asking for, whether we'd consider each other friends today. Perhaps if I'd hugged her—said, I *understand*—she wouldn't be so bitter and cold. But I understand now. Is it too late?

I open the door. Dad looks up from picking something off the hem of his blue and white plaid shirt, while Mum hisses some obscenity, I think, at him for not being careful about his appearance. Once they realize the door is open, Mum's face changes shape as fast as a portrait shot along a reel of negatives, to a beam of genuine pleasure. Dad stops picking and relaxes his shoulders—he often gets a break from Mum's nitpicking in the company of others—and shakes Alex's hand, doing the whole male Greek meet and greet—heavy pats on the back to masculinise the pecks on each cheek.

I fall into my mother's arms and breathe in her freshly hennaed hair—a pleasing scent of wet autumn leaves and mud. For a long time I denied that I ever did her wrong. I convinced myself that being a child I didn't know any better. But I do now. And now that I've had a taste of what she often went through, I feel a thumping need to let her know I'm sorry.

Mum doesn't try to pull away after the obligatory three seconds like I think she might. She instead pulls me in closer and tighter, scrunching my hair in her grasp behind my neck. She is gentle the way she used to be when I was too young to care.

She whispers, "It doesn't matter anymore."

I release her embrace and stammer a couple of unarticulated gurgles of surprise.

"Alex called. He told me. And anyway, no-one is to blame for anything. Stop feeling guilty. The past is the past!" She flings her arms in the air and reaches for Alex to give him a kiss hello. Alex winks at me over her shoulder, when Tessa pulls on Dad's jeans. Dad picks her up.

"G'day, Blossom. Oh, *my* have you grown since the last time I saw you! You're heavy!"

"Yeah, I'm all grown up now." She wriggles out of his arms, leans against the wall, puts her hand on top of her head to mark the spot, "See? Look how tall I am."

"Oh. Before I forget," Mum says, pulling me aside to talk over Dad and Tessa, "I've got something for you." She dips into her handbag and pulls out a framed, enlarged black-and-white photo of the five of us having dinner together on the island from last year. We all look so happy. We *were* happy. "Cool, huh? Anyway, I thought you might like to hang it on a wall somewhere." She looks around, already trying to pinpoint the perfect position, eyes shifting over the walls as if seeking out a mosquito.

"Thanks, Mum, it's really nice." I hold out my hand to take it.

"Where would you like me to put it?"

"Um, just leave it on the kitchen table for now. I'll find a home for it later."

"Oh, Mel? The hotel is really nice, by the way. Great choice, really great choice."

"I thought you'd like it there. Wholesome, I thought."

"You're right. They're kind." Mum nods with over-eager enthusiasm.

After making some coffee, we all drift into the lounge room. Alex and Dad sit on one side of the corner couch. Properly—legs crossed in the same direction. And do they realize they're holding their coffee cups in the same manner? With erect pinky fingers? *Since when does Alex ever do that?*

"So, you know how I was telling you about that crazy client the other day, right?" Mum asks, brushing non-existent crumbs off her slick, black satin pants. She's about to continue when she catches Dad looking at me questioningly.

"Mummy's going to get me a little brother or sister, Betty," Tessa blurts out, stretching her leg and pointing her toes to tap my mother's knee for attention. Alex laughs, briefly rubs has hands over his face and shakes his head. Dad's eyebrows raise and his nostrils flair as he grins. He opens his mouth to speak, but Mum jumps in first, "Of course she will, sweetheart," and takes a breath in preparation to continue, but pauses before exhaling. Her eyes widen like an owl. "Sister? Brother? What?" Mum squeaks, the bridge of her nose wrinkling like a pinch of skin.

"I'm pregnant," I say, stroking Tessa's arm in a semiconscious trance. Mum's eyes shift from my face to Alex's, to Tessa's, and back to my face again. Dad leans forward, balances his elbow on his knee, rests his chin in his palm and hides his huge smile with his thick folded fingers.

"You're kidding?" Mum cries. "Congratulations! This is cause for a celebration! Got any bright ideas, James?" She winks at him—infested with jovial cynicism. *Oh, don't. Please not now.*

"Let's go to the beach," Tessa squeals, jumping off the couch into a superman position.

I rub Tessa's back as if to console her zeal. "Blossom, I

don't think Grandma would really enjoy that. She doesn't like the beach."

"Then why does she live on an island?" Tessa screws her nose up in thought.

"Good point," Mum says. "How about you show me how to enjoy it then, Tess?"

"What, you'd really like to go?" I ask, astounded at her change of tune.

"Sure. Why not. I've got to stop being such a stick in the mud. Don't I Tess?" Mum pinches Tessa's belly. Tessa whinnies like a horse and playfully flicks Mum's hand away.

"I think it sounds fun. How about it, Mel?" *Alex is agreeing with Mum?* I hum in thought, not feeling quite up to the forty-minute drive. Of course, Tessa starts yelling and screaming with fruition, and before I can utter my opinion she runs into her bedroom and out again with her bathing suit, floaties, and goggles on, strutting her stuff in the living room like a model.

"I love the beach. Don't you love the beach, Mummy?" Tessa asks as she jumps onto the couch, treating it like a trampoline. I *tsk tsk* and gesture for her to stop and sit still, incoherently mumbling the request to avoid sounding too strict or grumpy.

"Look. I'm not feeling too hot, as you can imagine. I'm actually quite tired," I lie. "And I keep neglecting to finish off some work I'm supposed to have done by Monday. So, why don't you guys go without me? Tessa will love it, and it'll be a good opportunity for me to focus, and finish my work. Is that okay? Do you mind?"

Tessa protrudes her bottom lip in a forced whimper, and runs on the spot. Her bare feet pattering like she's running on dough.

Mum, Alex, and Dad shrug in hesitant agreement forming a trio of conquered sighs and grumbles.

"Why don't you take the car, Alex? It'll be a pretty tight squeeze with five anyway and it's better than the bus."

"You sure?" Mum asks, tilting her head with concern. I haven't told my parents about the move to London yet. Guilt pricks like an irate toothpick.

"Yeah. It's no problem. You all go and have fun. Tessa needs it anyway," I say, rubbing the back of my neck.

Everyone scurries around in preparation. I stand in the entrance hall, hoping to be of some help, but no-one needs me. I watch everyone scatter—leaving luminous trails of colour behind them—it floats around me like a sprinkler-induced rainbow as my vision goes a little hazy from fatigue. I can hear Alex emptying out the sheet cupboard, most likely looking for the beach towels we stuffed in the back, and our old bathing suits to lend my parents.

"Sorry, it's all I got," Alex says, as he hands my dad a pair of Speedos.

Dad shrugs with a curt wince and a brusque laugh. "Ta. No worries."

Within minutes everyone is standing in the doorway, holding so many bags I can hardly see their faces peering above them. Bags filled to the brim with snorkels, flippers, goggles, floaties, towels, beach mats, inflatable mattresses, picnic lunches, beach balls, cameras—*Where did Alex find all this stuff?*

"Right. We're off." Alex kisses me on the cheek.

"I wuv you, Mummy," Tessa says, in baby squeak as she hugs me around the legs.

"Okay. Have fun." I kneel down to give Tessa a kiss and she gives me a two-eyed wink, and then shoots out the front door, which Alex is holding open.

Mum and Dad kiss me goodbye in turn as we wait for Alex to load the elevator with the gear.

When I close the door behind them, I can hear Tessa giggling as she runs down the stairs, despite Alex inviting her into the elevator. She's always hated the elevator. She thinks it's boring.

I look around at the quiet empty house and smile with relief.

Peace. Finally.

The house implodes into a lull—a silent angst drunk with anticipation for the week ahead and a secretive intoxicating thrill. I dawdle down the corridor toward Tessa's bedroom to put her washing away, cracked plastic red bucket digging into my hip. My bare feet sink into the rough squishy carpet. I lie down on Tessa's bed—sinking like I do when drunk and passing out on the couch. Although this pregnancy has set me back music wise, life is finally feeling like my own. "*My* life," I say to myself in Tessa's Barbie handheld mirror. "I'll do it. It's just going to take a little longer than we expected. Right?" I touch my stomach. "Everything happens for a reason. The best thing Mum ever taught me."

About three hours later, I've completed two thirds of the

work I'm supposed to have done. Made and consumed three strawberry and honey smoothies, let the dog drink from my glass (something I never do), and written lyrics for two songs.

I should ring Charlie to say I can't go. No. Don't do that. What if I have a miscarria— Sheesh! What are you THINKING? Slap, slap, Melody. Slap, slap.

I turn on the radio—dial through all the cheesy Greek pop that modern Greek teens go *Beatles Frenzy* over, in search for Rock FM. When I find it, I raise the volume so high it makes the furniture rattle. I don't immediately recognize the band, but before I've had the chance to listen more carefully, I notice my mobile flashing, and turn the radio off.

I answer my phone and it's the guy from the air-conditioning repair centre—calling *three* weeks after us initiating a need for their services. I call Alex as soon as I hang up.

"*Parakalo?*"

"Hey, it's me."

"What's up? You all right?"

"Yep. Having fun at the beach?"

"The sea's a bit cold for me, but Tessa's loving it."

"Well, you're all going to have to come home as soon as you can."

"Why? What's wrong?"

"Nothing's wrong, it's just that the guy we called to fix the air-con is on his way, and the only key to the back balcony where the outdoor unit is secured is on your set."

"You're kidding? Can't you get him to come on Monday?"

"I already tried that. But he said he's making a special trip for us today because he's booked out for the next month."

"Jesus Christ."

"He said it's going to get really hot over the next few weeks."

"Where do these fucking handy people think they get off? Could have done with a bit more notice."

"I'm sorry. I tried."

"Fine. We'll be home as soon as possible. You sure you're okay?"

"Yeah."

"Okay. We're on our way. See you soon."

Two and a half hours later, I finish my work. They're still not home. The doorbell rings. It's the air-con guy—sweaty bald head shining under the muddy yellow hall light.

"I'm really sorry to have dragged you out here on a Saturday for no reason. But I'm afraid my husband still hasn't returned, and he has the key to the balcony."

The man grunts and re-enters the elevator—his thick white suit scratching between his legs as he moves. I close the door. The realization that Alex should be home by now flicks my consciousness like a Venus Flytrap. On the verge of panic, I pick up the phone and dial Alex's cell.

"The subscriber you have called is not available, and will be notified of your call via SMS."

My heart booms. *Try not to panic. You're overreacting. Just try again in a couple of minutes; maybe there's no signal where he is. Okay, breathe. Try Mum's phone.*

"The subscriber you have called is not available, and will be notified of your call via SMS."

Fuck. What were you thinking? If Alex's phone is out of range then why would Mum's be in range? Sit down. Stop being silly. Where's Doggy?

"Doggy? Ella tho … You wanna biscuit? Here you go. Good girl …" *Has it been a couple of minutes yet? Okay, try again.*

"The subscriber you have called is not available, and will be notified of y—"

Dial again …

"The subscriber you have called is not a—"

Again, Goddamn it …

"The subscrib—"

Christ. Okay. Let's calm down. I sit cross-legged on the floor. Maybe Tessa was having such a good time at the beach they didn't want to spoil her fun. Maybe they're on their way home right now, and I've happened to call while they're driving through the mountainous area, and that's why there's no signal. He could have called to let me know. Am I over-reacting? I think I'm overreacting. No, maybe I'm not over-reacting; because Mum would have been the first to tell Alex to call me so I don't get worried. So if they'd decided to stay on at the beach she would have told him to call me back … Or maybe Alex didn't say anything to my parents. Maybe they have no idea I called. Yes. That's probably what happened. Alex wouldn't think to call me if he was running late. He doesn't think like that. He doesn't know I worry. I've never told him I worry. I've never been worried before because I've always had too many other things on my mind. Okay. Melody. Stop it. Make yourself another smoothie and go back to the balcony. Play with the dog.

It's now three and a half hours since I called Alex. I try again.

"The subscriber you have called is not available, and will be notified of your call via SMS."

This is too much. This is too much ... Dad's phone! I never tried Dad's phone!

"6977 261 451 ... It's ringing! Oh, thank God!"

"Melody?"

"Dad! What's going on? Where are you? ... Hello? ... Hellooo?"

I've been cut off. Great. Where the fuck are they? Now I'm beyond worried—now I'm just pissed off. They could have at least let me know what the hell they're up to.

It's now *four* and a half hours since I called Alex. Twilight hangs like paper over a lampshade. I'm bloated and full and lethargic. Doggy is sitting in my lap, licking my face now and again. She jumps off my lap, runs inside towards the door, and barks at the handle. *Finally*, they're home. I walk to the door, surprised at the lack of noise behind it.

"Well, you really wanted the air conditioner fixed, didn't you?" I ask, looking down to nudge the dog away from the door as I open it. I'm about to lean forward to give Alex a kiss when I realize it's not Alex at all. It's a police officer raising his finger toward the doorbell.

"Ma'am? Are you Mrs. Melody Hill-Konstantinou?"

My head pounds as if lodging a flail. I swallow hot tears—tears that have been boiling on full for hours. They singe my throat on the way down and blister my mouth on the way up.

I vomit at the officer's feet.

part four

Please Take Me Back

Patience
silences snow on a grey woollen sweater,
and then drowns you.
Doubt
paints a black and white silent film
on your forehead.

Chorus:
Please don't tell me my baby's gone.
Please take me back to Saturday morn.
Please don't tell me my baby's gone.
Please take me back to Saturday morn.

Hope
chews toffee apples
and then breaks your teeth.
Desire
sprinkles sea salt in your wounds
in the desert.

Chorus

Oh why does reason
hide desire, hope, and doubt
in a patient box,
all for
fate to leave the box near the fire?

Chorus

twenty-six

The police officer escorts me to his car. A fist reaches inside my stomach and whisks my entrails like cake mix. This is nothing like heartbreak, nothing like betrayal, nothing like the lies I despised more than infidelity. My whole world has no more life to give. Plants have stopped growing and babies have stopped being born. And I don't even know what has happened yet.

The police officer drives me to the hospital. In a trance, I watch life—the living—rapidly pass by the window—night lights reflecting in the side-view mirror—epileptic reverie. I don't know if I should cry. Maybe they will be alive when I get there. All the officer said was that there'd been an accident. Alex's car toppled over a cliff trying to swerve out of the way of an oncoming truck speeding around a bend. The truck didn't even crash. I try to twist down the window, but I'm clutching the handle so hard I break it off. I stare at it—shaking. *It's a sign*, I think. *They're broken.*

Dad is sitting in the waiting room—waiting for me. I'm sure he shouldn't be there. He should be in his room, but a nurse seems to be supervising from behind the reception desk. I hug him tightly. So tightly he has to pull away. He has one arm in a sling and a big gash is weeping just above his left eyebrow. His arms and legs are already starting to bruise—pale lilac patches of pain. He dry retches when he opens his mouth to speak.

"Where are they? I have to see them," I say, fiddling with something in my handbag to distract myself from the abundance of possibilities swimming through my mind.

"Sweetheart, sit down … er … for a minute."

"No. Look, I'm sorry, I'm so relieved you are okay, Dad, but I really have to see them."

"I know you do, but plea—" Dad coughs and clutches at his side, grimacing until the brunt of the pain subsides. "Please," he heaves amidst tears streaming down his cheeks. "Please just … just sit down. You have to know—" He loses balance, and I drop my handbag to break his fall. He moans as a nurse runs out to aid us. She lowers him into a seat.

"Sir, we really ought to get you back to your room."

The nurse smiles a smile of low self-esteem—fighting to be classed as a smile, but insecure about whether it belongs here.

Dad has dry blood smeared from his cheek bone to his ear and down his neck.

"Shouldn't someone have cleaned him up?" I ask, directing my chin toward Dad's face.

The nurse nods and apologizes—claims Dad forced the doctors off him because he wanted to be in the waiting room when I arrived. I sit next to him and gently cup his cheeks in my hands. His tears trickle pink between my thumb and forefinger as I wipe them away.

"Dad. Listen to me."

Dad stares blankly into my eyes—his windows foggy with woe.

"What room are they in? I *need* to see them."

"Sweetheart—" Dad moves my hands away with his uninjured arm. He turns his head in the opposite direction where people are leisurely rolling in. "Alex ... Betty." He shakes his head. "They didn't ..." he breathes in sobs, hunches over, nursing his abdomen.

I take a deep breath in anticipation, but I can't exhale—it's stuck in limbo. I refuse to believe the connotations of what he neglected to voice.

"Tessa? What about Tessa?" My heart beats like a twig suck in bicycle spokes.

"She's alive, but she's ... in a coma, Melody."

Alive. He said "*alive*".

"Tell me where she is. I have to be there when she wakes up," I say, getting out of my seat so fast my handbag goes flying across the floor.

I didn't hear him. I didn't hear anything. He didn't say anything. No. Nothing. Alex and Mum are waiting for us—waiting for Dad and me to bring Tessa home. We were only all standing in the same room together this morning. It's impossible for them not to come back from the beach. Dad came back from the beach, Tessa came back from the beach, but it was such a tiring trip that she fell asleep in the backseat. Yes. She fell asleep. Now all I have to do is wait for her to wake up. When she wakes up, Dad and I will take her home to where Alex and Mum are waiting. Yes. They're waiting. They're waiting at home. And we'll all eat souvlakia on the balcony like we planned. Everything will be fine, you'll see. Everything will go back to the way it was. You'll see. You'll see, Mel. Everything will go back to the way it was.

I've been sitting at Tessa's bedside for two days listening to machines talk her through chokes and vacuumed air.

"I love you, Blossom," I whisper for the hundredth time, stroking her silky smooth cheek, and tracing her cracked lips with every single finger at least once over. "I'm sorry I didn't come to the beach with you. I should be the one in this bed, not you. I'm the one who has been a bad girl. I'm the one who should be punished. Not you. Not you, Blossom. … I'll never let anything bad happen to you again. I love you, Blossom. … Blossom? I've been such a bad mother. I'm sorry. … From now on, you come first. I promise. I promise, Tessa. Please forgive me, please … wake up."

I sing Joni Mitchell's "River." Her eyes flutter. I will them to open, but I guess I've been forbidden to grant miracles after receiving a decent share of my own. A great job *and* a tour. What was I complaining about? Was it a test? Was I supposed to turn them down, to discover that family was so much more important before it was too late? Did I miss the train? *I missed my train. You stupid, stupid woman!*

I don't want to leave her side until she wakes up. I have to be the first person she sees when she does. I've been waiting hours to go to the toilet just in case Tessa wakes up and I'm not here. I even pissed into a basin yesterday to avoid it—twice. Dad walks in, just released from hospital care, and sits beside me. His face hollow, body frail, legs like chopsticks.

"I was driving," he says, without even saying hello. "I killed your husband. I killed your mother. I put Tessa in this horrible state." Dad sobs, face embedded into his palms.

"No, no, no, don't say that. Don't say that, Dad. They're fine," I nod, licking my dry lips. "They'll be at home when we get there. Don't worry, you haven't killed *any*one," I smile out of need. "They'll be home when we get there. Everything will go back to the way it was. You'll see."

"*Listen* to me. Alex is *dead. Betty* is dead. Pretending isn't going to bring them back! It's my fault. It's *all* my fault! I'm too old to drive. I shouldn't have. And I'm sorry, Melody. Please … please forgive me."

He kneels down on the floor as if preparing to pray; his wrinkled brow beseeching me to love him. *I do love you.* I bend over and rest my forehead against his. Stunting this pain with imaginary reassurance thumps my temples like a migraine. I can't hold it in anymore. It hurts as it sweats from my glands—fills my mouth with rancid saliva—pain's placenta. It summons energy from my body—to thrive, to inject my soul with grief, with mourning, so it has strength to infect its next victim when I let it out. I open my mouth to scream, but I can't manage more than a silent wail as I drop to where Dad is kneeling at my feet. We hold our gaze until I see emptiness mirrored in his face. It is at that moment, that emptiness claims my soul—when pain runs rampant through a violent moan.

I'm gaunt and weak and Dad tells me to go home. I've forgotten about Doggy, but I refuse to leave until Tessa wakes up. He reminds me it could be days, weeks, months. I beg him to go and feed Doggy for me, but then realize he's still in a lot of physical pain and it's probably not a good idea for him to leave without assistance. We sit for a few more hours, hoping, imploring for Tessa to open her eyes and … she does.

"Tessa? Tessa! Blossom?" I touch her arm—give it a little shake. "Can you see me? Hear me? It's me, Mummy. It's Mummy, Blossom."

She stares. Blank. Lost.

"Tessa. Blink if you can hear me. Tessa?"

Tessa's lazy green eyes stare like embedded marbles—glazed—as if she's wearing foggy contact lenses. Desolate. Perhaps left behind.

I stand in my kitchen doorway—kick off my shoes. My feet face forward, knees locked, arms by my side. My fingers feel nail-less—yanked from their natural habitat. A wave of rheumatism washes through my body and a heavy pounding numbs my right eyebrow. I stare at the reflection of the coarse ceiling through the photo frame lying on the table. I pick it up—hands shaking. I watch a tear fall as if not my own, precisely upon Alex's face. Weightlessness creeps from my shoulders to my fingertips and the frame crashes to the ground. The sound depleted. Glass shatters everywhere. It wasn't long ago my mum put it there. "The hotel was great," she said. "Great choice, really great choice."

If Tessa were here she'd help me clean it up. I step on the

glass—invincible shavings of ice scorched on the fire—cut my naked foot. I take a banana from the fruit bowl. It's brown and mushy, but I peel it anyway. I eat the banana standing, staring at some blood trickling from beneath my little toe—the toe I've always hated; the toe that makes varnish look like dirt under the nail. The silence in this household hurts my head. I flatten the banana to the roof of my mouth with my tongue—the sound of gumboots in mud. I clear some space on the floor with my healthy foot and sit with my legs crossed. I move my right knee up and down—up and down—I can't stop it. It's like a twitch—I can't stop it. It swings so high that it flaps against my breast and my hip cracks. It hurts. I stop. I can't remember why I came home. The fridge starts to hum. I don't like it. It hums life. I pull the plug. I lean against the leg of the table—road vibrations on my skull. Can't understand how they travel eight storeys high.

The shutters are open in every room. Curtains blow about. Doors slam. Bills fly off the bulletin board. I haven't washed since the knock on my front door. I smell. Of salt and bad breath. My eyes are red, my nose split, and my mouth sticks together every time I close it. Time shrouds my head like a scarf. Still and protective until the convertible picks up some speed and blows it away.

I hear whimpering. I limp to the balcony spreading blood across the lounge room floor. I find Doggy curled up in the corner—her nose crusty, her eyes half closed. I bring her food and water. I sit by her side surrounded by urine and feces—ambivalent about the stench. There's a knock at my front door. I wonder if I should open it or just play dead.

Someone puts a key in the lock. *Alex!* I get up and run to the door. It opens before I get there.

It's Dad and Serena.

"Alex? Is Alex with you? Where's Alex?" I look out into the corridor and inside the elevator to see if he's hiding. But he isn't.

"He's sitting with Tessa in the hospital, isn't he?" I ask. Dad and Serena look at me— pity prettying their eyes. "Alex is a good father. He'll take good care of Tessa … Serena, would you like a coffee? Dad? Coffee?"

"No," they say in unison.

"So, Serena, when did you get here? What a surprise."

Serena looks down, her eyes focusing on the blood on the floor and my injured little toe. "Melody, I came as soon as I heard."

It's that voice. The voice I hate. The social worker's calm, soothing, phony escape from reality.

"Oh, don't worry. Tessa will be fine. She's opened her eyes now. Soon she'll be back to normal. Everything will be fine. Everything will go back to the way it was, you'll see," I say in confidence as I limp my way to the couch.

Dad shakes his head and leaves the room. My bedroom door opens and closes. Serena and I sit and listen. It sounds like he's closing the window and the shutters too. He must be sitting on my bed. In darkness. Serena wipes up smudges of blood from the floor, cleans my toe, and wraps a Band-Aid around it.

"There you go. We never liked those toes anyway, right?"

I nod. Serena looks up to me from her crouched position at my feet, rubs my knees, and smiles in sorrow. It seems as if she's trying to hold back tears.

"Do you want me to make you something to eat?" she asks, taking a deep breath and holding it with puffed cheeks.

"No, I think I'll wait till they get home, so we can eat all together."

"Melody. Stop it. Stop pretending for *one* minute and look at me. Look at me *now*. They're *not* coming home. Alex is gone. Your mum is gone. Tessa is in the hospital, and she just woke up from a coma. For God's sake! She hasn't even spoken yet! Nothing is fine! Stop pretending. I know you think I'm being cruel, but you have to see the truth. I'm the only one who's not going to play along with this silly game. You have to trust me. Let go. Let it out. Scream in my ear for all I care. Deafen me. The sooner you accept what has happened, the sooner you can get on with your life. … Goddamn it, stop *fucking* looking out of the *fucking* window and look me in the eye. Melody!"

I look at her. Cheeks hot with disbelief. But I don't see Serena's face. I see Alex's. Tears stream down my cheeks. I fall into her arms and nestle my head into her chest. I scream into her shirt, "Alex, I'm sorry. I'm *so* sorry. I should have come with you. I'm so sorry. Take me with you. Take me and Tessa with you. I'm sorry, Alex. I'm *so sorry.*"

Serena rocks me backward and forward in her arms. "Melody, it's okay. Just let it out. Let it all out."

"Oh for *fuck's* sake!" I scream, snapping out of my imaginary world, furious at Serena's social-worker tone. I stand and kick the couch.

Click.

Reality succeeds to gnaw through my brain. "I need to fucking *strangle* something!" I roar, feeling myself go red in the face. My throat constricts—I'm swallowing knives. I hold my hands out to reach of something solid to twist, to throw, to grip, squeeze to death. I go to the window—rip the curtains down and cradle the mass of fabric in my arms as if a human being.

"What the *fuck* have I done in this life to deserve this?" I heave, letting myself drop to the floor. "And Tessa! Her father is gone! Her grandmother gone! How do I explain that to her? How is she going to understand? Serena? Can you *fucking* tell me what I have done to *deserve* this? This is fucking insane! Is this for fucking real? Serena. Help me. *Help* me," I plead, banging my fists on my chest so hard I feel like I'm bulldozing myself to the ground.

"I don't know," I whisper, dropping my arms to my sides, "just … just hit me over the head with a frying pan or something. I can't take this. I want out of this body. I want out."

Serena doesn't move. She just stares with her bottom lip trembling.

"What? What are you staring at? You're here to help, aren't you?" I roar, levering myself up from the windowsill. Serena nods, holding her hands over her mouth. She cries. I feel nothing for her.

"So *help* me!" I scream even louder, but she doesn't move.

I run into the kitchen and grab a steak knife out of the drawer. I need to feel physical pain. I need to take the focus away from this twisted situation. But before I manage to touch it to my palm, Serena is behind me, sticking a fork into her bicep, and instead of feeling the need to cure my pain, I'm mesmerized by the amount of blood that is gushing out like a squirt gun.

"What are you doing?" I ask, frantically wiping away my tears.

"Well, it distracted you, didn't it?" Serena replies, opening a drawer and pulling out the first-aid kit.

"You're nuts."

"Yes. I am." Serena smiles and nods. Simple as that. Mission accomplished. "I'll help you through this," she says, not at all phased by her injury. "I'm here for you as long and for as many days as you need."

twenty-seven

Day One:

I get back from the hospital—sat with Tessa for eight hours—all I've eaten is a packet of dry water crackers. She still isn't speaking or moving her legs. They keep saying to give her time. What time? Next thing I know, we'll all be dead and it'll all be pointless. Fuck walking. I'll carry her. For the rest of my life, I'll do whatever she needs. I don't even care if I ever touch a guitar again. In fact, I don't want to. Screw music. Music makes me feel, and I don't want to feel. I want to be numb.

I stand in the hall. Stare at the floor—imagine carpet fibers expanding like thick slugs—a devil's accomplice—around my feet and legs like vines—they pull me into the ground where I belong. *I need to piss.*

"I'm making you a sandwich with feta and tomato. Is that okay?" Serena calls out as I head toward the bathroom.

"Fuck the feta and tomato," I mumble as I pull my pants down and sit on the cold flimsy toilet seat that sounds like two plastic plates knocking against each other in a sand pit.

"What? I didn't hear you."

I sit on the toilet, legs spread, surely exposing my naked unshaven crotch to Serena who is looking at me from the other end of the hall with impatience. Well, no, not impatience, I've never met a more patient person in my life, it's more like patience with a stern attitude. I begin to piss and slam the bathroom door closed with my feet.

I hang my head in my hands, elbows digging into my knees. My labia warms—burns slightly, as the last trickles of urine seep into my pubic hair.

I turn to face the mirror without wiping myself, without getting up. My face is pale, eyes bloodshot and murky green, as if they have been marinated in sewage.

I stare at myself. For too long.

The muscles in my thighs twitch—naked legs goose pimply—hairs standing on end like antennae. My vagina stinks. It's damp with discharge embedded into three-day old underwear. I need to wash.

Serena knocks on the bathroom door.

"What are you doing in there?"

"Huh?"

"You've been in there for almost an hour. Have you got diarrhoea or something? I wouldn't be surprised; you've hardly eaten anything substantial."

"Um. Yeah. Diarrhoea."

"You need anything?"

"No."

"Well, I'm waiting on the balcony with your sandwich. I sautéed some mushrooms for you too. And cut up some lettuce. It's all you had. I'll go shopping tomorrow."

I nod. Undress. Jump in the bath. I can hear Serena hovering by the door. I turn on the tap. Hot. Very hot. The bathroom steams up instantly.

"Okay. Have a bath and then come and eat. You need to eat."

I nod again, digging my teeth into my knuckle so hard I make it bleed.

Day Two:

Pasta. Twist fork. Lift to mouth. Insert into mouth. Chew. Pause. Stare at Alex's record collection. Tears. Breathe in heave. Breathe in pasta. Gets sucked into wrong hole. Cough and splutter like child. Spit out pasta. Serena cleans it up.

Day Three:

Serena walks me to the couch and turns on MTV. They're showing REM live in the centre square. I feel like I'm going to throw up. It's Alex's production. And it's going ahead without him. I frantically search for the remote, hot tears stunting my breath. *No, no, no, no!*

"Remote! Where's the fucking remote?" I cry, banging my fists on the coffee table like a misbehaving child. She turns around to leave. Ignoring me. The remote is sticking out of her back pocket.

"Give me the fucking remote!" I scream at the top of my lungs.

Dad races in.

"What's going on?" he asks, sleepy, weary, red around his eyes—he's been crying, alone, in Tessa's bedroom all day. "Serena? What are you doing?"

"She's got to face the truth. No better way than to look it straight in the face."

"It's too soon." He shakes his head. "It's too soon," he says again and leaves the room.

Serena glares at me with her arms crossed like a teacher disappointed in a student for not doing their homework.

I take a deep breath. Trying not to scream. But as soon as I will the anger to subside it's replaced with a grief so heavy I can't even hold myself upright. I can't decide whom to cry over—Alex, or my mother. *Oh, Mum. Just when I started to understand … Was my understanding the only other thing left that you needed in this life? Was it your cue to leave?* The room spins and I lower myself to the couch. Serena doesn't move.

"Please," I beg, putting two pillows over my ears. "Please!"

But instead of giving me the remote, she pulls the TV plug out of the wall and walks out onto the balcony, sliding the glass door closed behind her. She turns her back to me—looks out into the square.

I watch, stunned that she finally gave into my pleading. She buries her face in her hands, and her shoulders shake up and down.

Day Four:

The phone rings. I look at Serena and shake my head. I've ignored every single call since the accident.

"I'm answering it," says Serena, picking up the cordless and holding it in the air as if giving me an opportunity to take it myself. I flick my hand with dismissal.

Beep.

"Hello? … I'm sorry, Melody can't come to the phone right now, but maybe I can take a message? … Oh … Oh … well, I think she finished them before … yes, yes, indeed … I'll get them posted off tomorrow morning first thing … yes, okay, I'll tell her … Oh, thank you … yes, that's great … Mm-hmm … she'll appreciate that … Yes, thanks for understanding, Jodie. Bye."

"Fuck. I forgot about the proofs," I say when Serena hangs up.

"Don't worry, she was fine. I'll just post them off tomorrow. She also said you're welcome to take your old job back, as they're unable to wait for you to fill the position in London."

I smile, and give a half nod, feeling queasy over my disgusting infatuation with Richard Viadro. *Why couldn't I just appreciate what I had?*

"She did say, though, that Mr Viadro welcomes an application from you for any other position that might arise in the future."

"Okay ... let's talk about something else?"

But we're interrupted by Dad walking in the front door with two big bags from the local *Zacharoplasteio*. He holds them up with a big grin. The first I've seen since the day he arrived in Athens.

"I've got cake," he says with a half-possessed wink. "Let's make ourselves fat."

Day Five:

"I want to sell this apartment," I say to Serena while she washes some dishes. She nods as if she knows I won't do it. "And I need your help. I can't handle going through all the paperwork. I just want to move out and forget about ever living here. I'll give you power of attorney."

Serena pauses, scratches the side of her nose with sudsy fingers. "Are you sure?"

"Yes. And I need you to call ... you-know-who. I can't bear to speak to him."

"Who? Charlie?"

"Yeah."

"I already have."

"Oh?"

"Yeah. Don't worry about anything. Just, you know, let yourself heal."

"Let myself heal?" I scoff. "Let myself heal," I repeat sarcastically as I walk out of the kitchen. "Huh. That's a good one."

Day Six:

"Mummy!" squeals Tessa, from a wheelchair, as I enter her hospital room.

"Oh my God! You're speaking?" I bend down to give her a big squeeze and cup her face in my hands. "She's speaking," I exclaim to the orderly, who looks young enough to be my son, as he fiddles with the height of Tessa's chair.

"She's speaking," nods the boy with a wink. "When you have minute," he whispers, "Doctor wants speak you about your daughter's 'wheelchair situation'," he quotes with his fingers, and winks again.

Wheelchair situation?

"Your daughter and I, we did go for walk, just now. She like wheels, very much."

"Oh?"

"Yes." He winks again. "Will fetch Doctor. Will be just, one, two minute."

The orderly leaves, and I squat down to Tessa's level and take her hands.

"How are you feeling, Blossom?"

"Good. Look, Mummy, I've got my own personal car!"

I can't help but laugh at her enthusiasm. "Well, yes, I

suppose you do. But you'll have to learn how to drive. Have you got the patience?" I ask, trying to swallow the wretchedness of the situation and stay upbeat for Tessa's sake.

"*Yeah*-eah! Everyone's got more patience than you, Mummy."

I wince. "Yeah, I suppose you're right … um … Blossom, I have to speak to you about something." I sit on her bed and pull her chair close to me, so our knees touch. "Something that isn't very nice and you might get upset." I pretend I'm talking about going to the ice cream parlour to avoid an outbreak of tears.

"Mummy, don't worry. You've told me already."

"Pardon?" *Yeah, when you were in a coma.*

"It's okay. Papa and Betty are happy now. They told me so."

"What? They told you—"

In prances the doctor, stethoscope dangling around his neck like a gold medal.

"Good afternoon, ladies!" He puts his hands in his coat pockets, leans forward and swings his buttocks side to side as if preparing to role-play a dog.

"Hi. What's this *situation*, the orderly said you needed to speak to me about?"

The doctor puts his hand on my upper back and walks me to the door where he obviously thinks Tessa won't hear.

"Your daughter didn't suffer any spinal injuries. So her paralysis is temporary, initiated by psychological trauma."

"You mean she's … *pretending*?" I gasp, wondering why the hell Tessa would want to do something like that. The doctor laughs.

"No, no, no. She's not pretending. It's very real. But she is very likely to walk again, with rehabilitation. And she's young. Children always recover faster. She'll be fine. With the right support, and love from her parents. She'll be fine."

My throat tightens at the word "parents". Tears form behind my eyes. I look at the ground and take a deep breath. Smile a forced smile and thank the man.

I go over to Tessa and take the handles of her wheelchair. "Right. Let's go for a spin together then, huh?"

One Week Later:

Tessa is due home tomorrow. I want to jump with joy and celebrate, but I feel numb. I'm living the life of an empty shell. My body has been taken over by a person I don't know. And this person drags the real me along to watch. This person forces me to become reacquainted with daily routines I wish I could turn to glass and smash against a wall. I watch my limbs move—do all the things a human body is supposed to do when it's alive, but I'm not alive. Not really.

I can't imagine ever feeling alive again.

I lie in bed with the duvet puffed up beside me, pretending it's Alex. I can still smell him on our sheets—the sheets I refuse to change. I imagine listening to his rhythmic breaths and little interrupted wheezes like the ones puppies make when they're dreaming and flinching their paws. I used to lie awake at night wishing he would shut up. Now I lie awake at night wishing I could hear just one little wheeze.

I place myself a little farther away from his side of the bed than I would normally sleep so that, in a realistic situation, I wouldn't feel his body heat. Keeping my eyes closed,

I visualize an image of him next to me. I convince myself if I stretch my hand over, I'll be able to touch him. Then I stretch my hand over—but not all the way—I stretch it to *almost* where he would be, and then, with my eyes remaining closed, I picture him only millimetres away from my fingertips, and if I *really* wanted to, I could just reach a tiny bit farther and touch his precious skin.

And I fall asleep, with Alex just *millimetres* out of reach.

twenty-eight

Serena is in the kitchen with Tessa making dinner. She has propped Tessa up on five thick couch cushions in her wheelchair so she can reach the counter and help slice vegetables. I eavesdrop from the entrance of the living room while Dad sits on the couch flipping through my old photo albums.

"Serena, Papa was smart. He had a very important job. Did you know he had a very important job, Serena?"

"Um, no. Why was it so important?"

"Well, he was always writing emails to people. And you know where?"

"Where?"

"To *other countries*!"

"Really? Wow. That's sounds *very* important."

"Yeah. Papa was a *very* important man."

I'm picking at my fingernails when I realize I'm smiling.

I sit next to Dad on the couch. He's staring at a photo of me, him and Mum on the island when I was small. Mum, so beautiful, so young, so *healthy*, is holding me in her arms under the sun—her apricot-coloured dress flowing in the breeze, with huge Janis Joplin type orange-rimmed spectacles balancing on the tip of her nose as she eyes the camera from above the frames. She looks so free and happy—a few years before being diagnosed with bipolar.

"Tessa's got Mum's smile," I say, stroking my finger over her face.

Dad coughs up a little melancholic laugh while shedding a few stray tears salted with memories.

"Whatcha thinking about, Dad?" I ask, rubbing his upper back.

"Uh, nothing …" he replies, tilting his head to the side, wiping tears into his hair by his temples.

"Sure you are. Tell me. I can handle it." I nudge him gently with my elbow.

"Orh. Just how happy I was when I met your mum." He sniffs. "Can you remember much of when you were that young on the island?"

"Yeah, quite a bit," I nod, as I try to convince myself I do. Funnily enough, I get a flash of her laughing and throwing me up in the air—catching me just before hitting the ground.

"Your Papou and Yiayia always asked me when Betty and I would have a second kid."

"Oh, yeah? Why didn't you?"

"I didn't think Betty could have handled it. She started getting depressed, you know, and I didn't think it would have been good for her. Or for the kid … sweetheart …" Dad looks me in the eyes. "I'm sorry you had to go through so many horrible things with her. And I'm sorry I wasn't more supportive of you. But I was just … you know … trying to get a grip on everything myself too."

"I know, Dad. Don't worry."

Serena pops her head out from behind the kitchen door.

"Why don't you go and stay with James on the island for a while? It'd do you and Tessa good, I think. I could stay here and sort out a sale for this apartment, if it is, in fact, what you want to do."

"I'm not sure, anymore, though. Maybe I'll keep it."

Serena nods and disappears into the kitchen again.

She has asked us to go home with her, back to Australia—for the three of us to live in the house she inherited from her grandfather. I feel I'd be intruding, but she keeps insisting it's big enough for a family of ten, hates living in it alone, and had decided to put it up for rent before she came here because she hardly uses any of the rooms. But if we go with her, she said she'll remove the ad.

I don't know what I want. I don't know what would be the right thing to do. I've spent my life running away from pain. Would moving back to Australia be a repeat of the same thing? Maybe I should just keep living here, in this apartment—face-to-face with reality. I don't know if I can leave Dad either—living in that big house in the middle of a mountain all alone. Who would help him if he fell down the stairs, or locked himself in the garage?

Tessa rolls into the living room with a plate of chicken curry on her lap.

"Here, Grandpa. Here's your curry." Tessa hands Dad a steaming hot plate on a brown rubber-based tray.

"Thanks, cherry pie," Dad replies, kissing her on the forehead.

Reminded of Alex and the forehead kisses he used to

give Tessa, I swallow so hard, trying to inhibit tears, that everyone turns their heads.

"Don't worry, Mummy," Tessa says. "I'm going to bring your curry in too-*oo*."

Silently shaking myself from despair, I call out for Serena. "Can you help her bring them in? She has to do it one by one!"

Serena yells back, "Let her do it. It's good exercise. She wants to anyway."

Tessa rolls back into the kitchen and returns to the lounge with another plate of curry on her lap. But this time it's resting on a tea towel—the tea towel Alex incessantly kept by his plate when we ate dinner.

"Papa told me to tell you he loves you very much, Mummy," Tessa says as she hands me my curry. I freeze, plate mid-air. Dad's mouth is contorted mid-chew. I can even hear Serena holding the pot still above her plate, ready to fill her dish.

Silence.

"Tessa? Blossom? He *spoke* to you?" I whisper, bending down close to Tessa's face.

"Yeah," she shrugs as if it's completely normal, her eyes shifting left and right as if thinking she might have done something wrong.

"When?" I quickly stand and look around the house to see if I can catch a glimpse of him.

"Just now. He helped me make the curry with Serena." Tessa frowns. I hear Serena put the pot back on the stove. She pauses at the living room doorway, and eats standing up, unfazed. *Does she know about this?*

"Does he speak to you often?" I take hold of the wheel-chair and wheel her around the house in a frantic search for some physical evidence. I have to convince myself what Tessa is saying is true. Dad is about to get up and follow me, but he changes his mind after Serena flashes him a look.

"Yeah, all the time," Tessa says. "When you put me to bed, he comes and sings the sweet dreams song with us. Mummy, he sits right next to you. He puts his hand on your tummy."

At the thought of such a thing, I abandon Tessa in the corridor, run to our bedroom, and bury my head into Alex's pillow, still clothed in the same pillowcase it was in when he died. And I cry

And cry.

And cry.

Half an hour later Serena taps on my door. I don't say anything, but she comes in anyway and lies next to me. My breath must stink because after initially lying on her side to face me, she turns onto her back.

"Bad breath?" I ask, candidly, squinting with curiosity.

"Um … yeah," Serena chuckles. "I'm sorry. I'm sorry." She laughs even harder—so hard she brings her knees to her chest to accommodate it.

I don't manage a laugh, but I do summon a little smirk as I get up to brush my teeth. Serena turns onto her stomach, takes the duvet with her, and rolls up into a human-sized cocoon. When I get back from the bathroom, she's still lying there, hidden under a big pile of feather-down and soft pastel aqua linen.

"Did you eat your curry?" I ask. I hear a muffled "yep" before she exposes her teary face. I'm about to ask what's wrong, but notice mascara stains all over Alex's pillow. I panic, snatch it out from under her head and stare at it in my shaking hands. Serena sits up, opening and closing her mouth like a fish out of water. I rush the pillow to the bathroom and try to soak up Serena's tears with my bath towel in frantic desperation. Unable to control my anger, I yell, sitting on the bathroom floor, hugging Alex's pillow as if it were my own child and someone was threatening to take it away.

"You've ruined it! You fucking *bitch*! You've destroyed Alex's pillow!"

Serena kneels down to try and comfort me, but I push her out of the bathroom with my feet—she topples backwards and lands on her back with a thud. I slam the door closed, mortified, humiliated from my own aberration; my heartless ingratitude. Eyes wide with shock, I cover my mouth with rigid fingers, push my top lip into my teeth to stunt whatever other slander I might utter during this irrational tantrum. I couldn't expect anything less than verbal abuse in retaliation, but after all that, Serena still remains calm and *apologizes* to *me*.

"Melody?" she whispers through the keyhole. "I'm sorry."

I stand up and open the door. She's bawling—make-up running all the way down to her chin.

"No, Serena. *I'm* sorry. I'm so sorry."

twenty-nine

I had always dreamt of hiring an old beat-up Volkswagen van, with a mattress in the back, and taking a three-month road trip around Australia. So that's exactly what me and Alex did, before we had Tessa. We drove from Melbourne to Darwin and flew back to Athens from there. I had always wanted to see Alice Springs with my own eyes—the TV never did it justice.

After reconciling with Serena, I have a nap and I dream of the night me and Alex camped, in the middle of nowhere, probably illegally. Surrounded by vast nothingness—a fierce silent roar—more powerful than any sound this earth is capable of spawning.

Imagine standing in the middle of a field. Imagine red dirt. Distance and more beyond it. Imagine searching for the end of this distance, where the stars join to it like pins to a tent in loam. Imagine looking up to a cluster of approving eyes. Lying naked beneath them with the man you want to spend the rest of your life with. Imagine a silence that echoes the touch of your hand to his cheek. Imagine existence being loud and small, the way the Sun lights up the Earth. Imagine you are the Earth and he is the

Sun, that silence is tangible, and the stars are the souls of your previous lives. Imagine distance is the place you'll find life and death, where soil is your skin, and the dry fields your bones. Imagine love is the desert.

———

I wake up when it's dark, still clutching onto Alex's pillow. Serena is lying next to me, examining my face with remorse.

"G'day stranger." She strokes my hair.

I sit up and look at the stained pillowcase and suddenly remember.

"I'm so—" I croak, attempting to apologize again for my behaviour.

"Don't worry, I understand. *I'm* sorry. I wasn't thinking straight."

We lie there, for too long, on our sides, like fresh lovers wondering who is going to make the first move.

Serena breaks the ice. "I made an appointment for you at the gyno. Tomorrow, ten a.m."

"Thanks. Where's—"

"James is watching TV with the photo album still open on his lap, and I just put Tessa to bed."

I jump out of bed and bolt towards Tessa's room, hoping I haven't missed Alex. Maybe he's singing to her without me. But when I get there, Tessa has already fallen asleep. I turn around and Serena is standing right behind me.

"Honey, he'll come to you when the time is right. He may have been a bit of an idiot to cheat on you, but he loved you. I know that for certain. Believe me. I'd have been able to see it in his eyes on your birthday if he didn't."

I nod and sigh and run my fingers through my hair.

"Are you hungry?" Serena asks. "Do you want me to heat you up some curry?"

"No thanks."

"You *have* to eat something. You haven't eaten *all* day."

I shake my head.

"You're eating. And that's my final word."

Serena goes into the kitchen and I make my way into the living room to sit with Dad. He's entranced by the TV. Watching, but not really *seeing*.

How is he coping with this? How does one mourn their wife and support their mourning daughter at the same time?

"Dad?"

"Hmm?" Dad hums through tight lips.

"Do you want me to take you back to the island?"

"If I'm getting in your way." He nods, still staring at the TV.

"You're not getting in my way at all. I just want to know how you feel."

"Whatever's best for you, sweetheart," he replies without a flinch.

Submissive. Always damn submissive!

"Dad, for once in your life can you speak up? I'm not Mum; I'm not going to dictate how to live your life." I raise my voice a little too much, bordering on loss of control. His frown creates an air of irritation I've never sensed before.

"I'm sorry. I'm sorry." I shake my head. "That was a terrible thing for me to say. I'm sorry."

"That's okay. I understand." He faces the TV again.

Bite your tongue. Melody. Don't. "I'm really sorry," I say again, hoping it will tame the urge to voice an opinion that is surely not sought after.

"I said, it's okay," Dad replies, his tone increasing a tad, but still refusing to show any sign of life.

"Do you want something more to eat?" I ask, hoping to make things right.

He grunts an affirmative response, so I get up to help Serena in the kitchen, but before I have the chance to walk out the door, he stops me.

"Mel."

"Hmm?"

"You know what? It's *not* fucking okay. I *loved* your mum. I don't give a shit if she ordered me around, or told me when to comb my hair, or ... or anything! I *let* her tell me what to do because that's what made her *happy*. That's how our relationship *worked*. You have no right to judge me." Dad pokes himself in the chest with a thump. "You have no right to judge *her*. I loved her. I *loved* her, Melody. And I will *always, always* love her!"

I can't help but smile. He spoke. And he said something real.

"Okay. I said I was sorry, Dad."

"I know," he replies in a calmer tone. "It's okay ... and I *would* like you to take me home. But don't even think about asking me to live with my sister. I don't want to stay with her. I want to go back home. I want to go back to where I'll remember Betty. And don't tell me I need to move on. I'm too old to move on. I want to stay right where I am, and

I don't care if every single day is filled with grief, because that grief is the only thing that is going to keep me alive. If I don't have that grief, Betty will stop living in my heart and if that happens, I'll stop living. *I'll* stop living … so, Melody don't even *think* about calling my sister. I'll be fine on my own. I *want* to be on my own."

"Okay, Dad." *How did he know I was thinking of calling his sister?* "I'll take you home. I'll take you home tomorrow if you like."

"Yes. That would be nice. I would like that. Thank you."

I have another dream about Alex. At the Patti Smith concert. Tessa was on stage, head-banging to rev up the stagnant Greek crowd. Alex took me in his arms, kissed me and whispered, "Teach Tessa." And that was it. He disappeared and left me staring at a teenage Tessa playing air guitar to silence. *Everything* was silent. Except for Patti's voice: *not to die, but to be reborn, away from the land so battered and torn.* And then I woke up.

Those lyrics, being a Jimi Hendrix cover, reminds me of Dad's obsession with him when I was young. It also reminds me of the gold Gibson guitar I wanted to buy him. So, while Dad is packing away his things, preparing for his journey back home, I call the guy at the music shop to tell him I'm coming to buy the electric guitar I had looked at a couple of months ago. I give him my credit card number so we don't have to worry about money when we arrive.

"Dad, I've got a surprise for you."

"Oh?"

"Yeah, come with me."

"Okay, when I've finished packing."

"No, you can do that in twenty minutes. Just come with me."

Dad stares at me and Serena grinning from ear to ear in the doorway.

"Now. Come on!"

I take the clothes out of his hands and throw them on the bed. I grab a scarf and blindfold him. And the three of us accompany Dad to the music shop.

"Can I get an ice cream, Mummy?" Tessa asks as I roll her onto the footpath.

"Sure, but on the way home, okay? We have to do something else first."

"Where are we going?" Dad asks as he trips over a crack in the pavement and Serena takes the weight of his fall.

"Whoops! You all right?" she asks, straightening his blindfold.

"Is this thing necessary? I could just close my eyes, you know."

"It's necessary!" me and Serena exclaim and then laugh at the synchronicity.

"Jinx!" Tessa squeals, jiggling left to right in her chair.

When we arrive at the shop the guy is standing in the entrance, still dressed in his flannel shirt and ripped jeans.

"G'day, how's things?" he asks. I put my finger to my mouth—signal him to hush. He mouths "Sorry," recedes his neck into his shoulders and tiptoes backward a couple of feet.

"Who was that?" Dad snaps. "Where are we?"

"We're right … here." I pull the blindfold from his head as if revealing a rabbit in a top hat.

Dad's expression turns from annoyed to stunned when the guy opens the case to reveal the famous gold Gibson Les Paul. Speechless, Dad bends down and strokes it like a cat. He looks up, chuckles like a school boy, lifts the guitar out of its case and hangs it over his body, then jiggles it up and down.

"Wow. I forgot how heavy these were," Dad grins, showing his crooked stained teeth.

"It's a present … from Mum," I lie. "She never got the chance to …, you know, have it wrapped."

Without a word, he lifts the guitar to his mouth and kisses the strings right by the bridge, then lays it in its case.

"Thank you, Betty," he whispers, as if in prayer. "I couldn't have asked for anything more precious."

Before setting off to take Dad to the port to catch the ferry, I go to see the gynecologist. The baby is in good shape, and the doctor said it wouldn't be a problem if I wanted to move back to Australia before it was born. So, today I decide it's what I'm going to do. I have to stop thinking about the possibility of leaving Alex's spirit behind. Surely he can follow us?

I won't sell the apartment either. I can't bear to think of someone else living amongst our history. It's Tessa's home. I won't take it away from her. If I never return to Greece myself, maybe she will, so I want her to always have a place to stay.

Serena and Tessa stay while I drive Dad and Doggy to the port. I'm worried about him, but he insists he's going to be okay. I suppose I'll just have to take his word for it. At least he's taking Doggy with him. I'm going to miss the sweet little soul, but she'll be much happier running around with the goats than being shipped off to the Land of Oz.

People are already boarding the ship when we arrive. And it occurs to me only now that this is goodbye. *Will I ever see him again?*

"Dad, you know you are always welcome to come back to Australia with us," I say, focusing on the flurry of feet scurrying past us for fear of looking him in the eye and breaking down.

"I know." He smiles, with a glint of hope shining in his eyes for the first time since the accident. "But Greece is my home. I can't imagine living anywhere else anymore." Tears trickle down his cheeks and onto mine as we embrace.

Oh my God. He's leaving. He's really leaving. Stop it. Don't make him sadder. Keep it together, Melody.

"Have you got Mum's ashes?"

Dad nods and looks out to sea.

"What are you going to do with them?" I ask, not really sure if I want to know.

"Well, remember that chest your mum and I found on the shore near our home last year? You know—the one that sits next to her piano?"

"Oh. Yeah?"

"Well, I'm going to put her ashes inside that—loose, without the urn—along with the lock of hair and baby teeth she kept of yours."

She kept my baby teeth?

"I also wrote her a song I was planning to play for her when we got back from Athens. I'll write up the lyrics and the sheet music for it and put that in too. Then I'll go back to the place we found the chest together and throw it back in the sea."

"You wrote her a song? And she never heard it?" The thought makes my heart ache.

"Yeah, it's okay. I don't feel bad about it, sweetheart," Dad says, wiping away a tear hanging from the end of my nose with his knuckle. I hadn't even realized I was crying.

"I sing it to her in my head every night. I'm sure she can hear me from somewhere. Don't you think?"

I nod and give him one last hug. "I love you, Dad."

"I love you too, Melody … *aw*, don't cry. You and Tessa will be a lot happier in Australia. And I promise I'll come and visit once you're settled in."

"Okay, go." I flick my hands in the direction of the boarding ramp. "You'll miss the boat." I bend down to give Doggy a quick hug and a pat. "Give … Mum a kiss … for me … before you … throw her into the … um … sea." The words escape my mouth in bursts as I try to swallow thick lumps of grief, sorrow, relief, and looming happiness wrapped all into one, as they walk to the ferry.

"I will, sweetheart. I love you."

Dad waves and blows me a final kiss goodbye. Then he and Doggy disappear. Behind a humming motorized door.

thirty

When I tell Heather I'm moving back to Australia she bawls her eyes out like a drama queen and insists on coming over to help me clear out the house. I had intended on going through Alex's belongings on my own, but with both Serena and Heather adamant as to why I shouldn't do it on my own, I seem to have no choice in the matter. But they're cramping my style. Every time I try to sneak an item of Alex's clothing into my baggage, they catch me out. They won't let me take anything.

"But I have to take something," I cry.

"Why? What's the point? Who's going to wear them?" Serena retorts, as she folds my underwear into perfect little squares and fills all the small pockets of my suitcase with them.

"Exactly," Heather says, nodding with her eyebrows so high I wouldn't be surprised if she pushed her scalp off her skull. "Who's going to wear them? I can't imagine you letting your second husband wear Alex's clothes."

"I'll never have another husband." I look down at the long-sleeved shirt I was trying to hoard—a deep, yet faded navy blue, with dark brown stitching around the hems and high square collar. It's the shirt he was wearing the day we met.

"Well, don't go cutting yourself off from the world," Heather says. "That won't do you any good either."

"Since when do either of you know what's best for me?" I ask, bringing the shirt to my nose to smell. I hope to breathe in remnants of cologne, but all I get is the standard laundry powder aroma.

Heather tries to answer, but Serena interrupts.

"What *Heather* is trying to get at here ..." Serena gives Heather *the stare*—her social-worker stare that seems to mean, *I'd stop while you're ahead if I were you,* " ...is that keeping Alex's clothes locked away isn't going to bring him back. It's better to be rid of them, so you don't keep going to them for comfort. If you keep them, every time you feel sad you'll just wallow in his clothes. It won't do you any good."

"Don't you think it's a bit early to be forcing me to do this?" I ask, snatching another shirt from Heather's hands. "It's only been a few months."

"When do you think it *is* a good time to do this? After we get back to Australia?" Serena asks, flinging a shirt over her shoulder and letting her arms drop sluggishly by her side.

"Yeah, but what if Tessa is right? What if he *does* come and visit us at night?"

"Even if he does, Melody, having his clothes is pointless. It's just more weight."

"I don't know. I just feel having some of his things around might lead him in the right direction once we leave."

"What are you talking about?" Heather asks, glancing at me, at Serena then back at *me*. "Has Tessa said that Alex visits her?"

"Yeah, not only that, but she says he speaks to her too. He never comes to visit *me*. I don't get it."

"Maybe she's just pretending. Maybe that's just her way of dealing with the loss," Heather replies, emptying my sock drawer onto the bed.

"But maybe not. She's always been quite logical with her inventions. She even tells me I'm silly for thinking dolls can talk. Anyway, I've always believed that spirits linger around in some form or another, whether they are reincarnated, or simply let to roam free, if for some reason they didn't finish what they were put on earth to do. What if that's what it is? What if he's going to linger as a free spirit for the rest of eternity because we never had the chance to reconcile our differences?"

"God, that'd make me miserable." Heather rummages through Alex's shirts.

"I thought you didn't believe in God," Serena asks as she investigates the top cupboard for a soft piece of baggage.

"I don't."

Heather frowns.

"I just believe … oh, I dunno … I suppose, in notions true believers might like to debate about. Anyway, I—"

"Oh, this'd look nice on my husband," Heather interrupts, holding one of Alex shirts against her torso and looking at herself in the mirror. "Can I—"

I glare at her.

She drops it back onto the bed as if it stinks and continues to sort through my socks for ones without holes.

"Do you think it's possible to feel miserable when you're a spirit?" I ask, hoping for dear life that it's not.

"Of course not," Serena says jumping up and down, trying to hook the handle of my sports bag with a coat hanger. "Don't be ridiculous." She catches it and it drops to the ground. "Heather, get your bloody head out of those shirts. Jesus … Melody just pick one. You can have *one*. I wasn't going to let you because I'm still letting you sleep in the same bloody bed sheets you slept in together and that's probably worse, and not to mention unhygienic, and in my opinion, just *gross*. But I give in. I can't possibly be the person responsible for not letting you keep one of your husband's shirts. It's your right—I just couldn't live with myself. Go on. Pick one."

She waves her right hand in the direction of Alex's shirts on the bed, and nurses her forehead with the back of her left wrist.

"Hey," Heather squeals. "I thought you said not to give in no matter what."

"Yeah, well, I made the rule. I can break the rule," Serena huffs, laying out the shirts she seems to think I should choose from.

"So you two have been discussing it behind my back, have you?" I ask. "Great. They are *my* husband's shirts, if either of you can remember correctly."

"Well, I'm giving you a say now. Go on. One shirt," Serena repeats, slapping Heather's hand away from the one she wants to take for Chris.

I look at all the shirts, each one bound with the memory of a specific event, specific date, specific time of year, holiday, season, celebration, and I can't choose. How can I pick just *one* shirt, when I long so much to take them all?

"Can't. Can't take any," I cringe and turn to look out the window.

"You want me to choose for you?" Heather asks.

"No. Forget it. You're both right. It's probably better if I don't."

Heather empties Alex's part of the wardrobe into two massive cardboard boxes. I want to ask what she's going to do with them, but I bite my tongue. If she tells me where she's going to put them, I'll probably end up traipsing all the way to wherever they are in the middle of the night to retrieve them.

I look down at my dresser drawer and remember the family photo my mother gave me the day they arrived in Athens is in there. I open the drawer and pull out the photo. I stare at it. Mesmerized by our smiles. *Were we really that happy?*

I wish I could have Alex here for just five more minutes. Five more minutes to see his amazing smile; to let him know that no matter what happened between us I will always love him. Five more minutes to feel the warmth of his skin against my lips. I would do anything for five more minutes. Of Alex. To tell him all is forgiven; to feel him close—just one more time—One. Last. Time.

"Mummy, what's this?" Tessa asks, putting the brake on her chair as soon as she approaches the doorway. She's holding onto a 2mm resin-coloured guitar plectrum. Serena and Heather look at me in dread and stop folding the clothes. I can smell their anticipation like a dog. I ignore it.

"It's called a plectrum, Blossom. You use it to play guitar," I reply, managing a brief smile.

"Orh! Cool! Can I play the guitar, Mummy?"

"Um ..." I hum, glancing toward the guitar Alex bought me sitting in the corner by the window. I remember my dream: *Teach Tessa.*

"I guess," I say, pursing my lips in thought. "Do you want to have lessons?"

"No, Mummy. I mean, can I play with it na-*ow*!"

"Oh. Why not. Wait, just let me get it out of the case for you."

Serena and Heather exchange surprised glances as I reach for the guitar. I lie it down on the ground, open the case, trying not to breathe in the scent of fresh wood and hand it to Serena to hold. I wheel Tessa into the living room, sit her on the couch and place the guitar in her lap. Tessa is still clutching onto the plectrum as if her first ever coin. Without any further instruction from me, she places her whole hand over the first fret and plucks the bottom string. She plays an F. She shrieks in excitement and grins from ear to ear looking at the three of us for approval.

"Yay!" We applaud.

"What's this called, Mummy?" Tessa points to the neck of the guitar.

"It's called the neck."

"Um ... what are these?"

"They're called keys."

"Like what you lock the front door with?"

"Um, yeah, sort of, except the keys on the guitar lock a certain note into a string."

"Oh!" She looks up and down the guitar as if searching for something else to inquire about. "How about this?"

"That is called the bridge."

"What's it for?"

"Well, that is one of the most important parts, Blossom. If the bridge isn't straight, or built properly, then the strings won't sing very well—the guitar will be out of tune."

"Out of tune?"

"Well, I guess that just means, not quite right—when strings are out of tune, they sound a bit sad."

"Are you out of tune, Mummy? Because you sound a bit sad."

I squat and squeeze Tessa's knees.

"Blossom," I nod. "I *am* a little bit out of tune. But I'll find myself a better bridge very soon. And then I'll be in tune again. Okay?"

Tessa nods and smiles and plucks the E string with fervor, banging her head up and down to the erratic beat.

"Rock 'n' roll," Tessa says with a cheeky grin, and licks her lips.

And we all break out into laughter.

thirty-one

In the evening, Serena, Tessa, and I watch a movie and order pizza. When Tessa finishes eating, we transfer her to the couch and sit her between Serena and me. I stroke her hair while Serena massages her legs to keep her muscles warm—doctor's orders. She falls asleep—ear to my stomach, and breathes a smirk onto her face as if the corner of her mouth is being hitched up by a peg.

"Do you want me to put her to bed?" Serena whispers, removing Tessa's legs from her lap like fragile explosives.

I shake my head. "Thanks, but I'll do it. I might lie in bed with her for a while. Do you mind sitting on your own for a bit?"

"No worries, I'll just do the dishes," Serena winks.

"Ha, yeah, you do that," I titter.

I lift Tessa off the couch. The warmth and weight of her petite legs fall limp in my embrace; her small tired body sinks into my arms like dough, over-exposed to heat.

I lay her in bed, admiring the rosy innocence flushed through her cheeks, her emotional strength, and will to keep on keeping on. I haven't even seen her cry. Perhaps she doesn't need to. Perhaps Alex and Mum really do talk to her during the night. If so, she probably sees more of them than she did when they were alive.

I lie next to her, without touching, being careful not to press down on the mattress too fast. Her body heat radiates through my clothes like a hot water bottle even without physical contact; a feeling I have been deprived of for way too long. I listen to the purr of silence surround her soothing elfin wheeze, when fleeting warmth caresses my cold fingertips and toes—and I *know* we are not alone.

I imagine it's Alex—I *hope* it's Alex, watching; somehow granting Tessa the life I never had. A thick curl of hair falls over Tessa's face as she wriggles onto her side. I delicately remove it from her face, and I have a sudden urge to sing. I sing Joni Mitchell's, *"Both Sides, Now"*—the song my mother used to sing.

As I reach the end of the song, my unborn baby moves for the first time. I lay flat on my back, and focus on a drip of paint, frozen in time, in the corner of the ceiling. I listen; crackling stillness; feathery buzz—the room fills with an overwhelming sense of love and I smile; I let it infuse me like a drug.

"Alex," I whisper, tracing my fingers around in a circle on my stomach. "I'll call you Alex."

thirty-two

I've prepared everything for our departure early so Tessa and I can spend our last day in Athens at the Acropolis—490 feet above sea level among the ruins of an ancient city built during the fifth century BC. You can see Athens in its entirety from up there, when you spin full-circle; where the air seems to blow in from another world.

Fresh, clear, and flavoured with fragments of history, the wind dashes across my face, marinated with late Cretaceous limestone dust that once accommodated the feet of countless ancient civilians. The grounds are bristled with tufts of dry and newly sprouting grass, and scattered with rock shavings, large and small and just plain humungous. A thick film of beige dust has settled over the entire area, and I can't help but wonder, when I rub it between my fingers, whether I am touching the remains of a Greek God or Goddess.

I have never taken Tessa up there before, but I'm not going to drag her to Australia without seeing it at least once. What would I tell her when she grows up? Sorry, darling, but you lived in Greece for the first four years of your life, but never saw its most significant monument?

Climbing to the top along the slippery cobblestone path proves to be difficult with Tessa's wheelchair, but I manage to get her as far as the entrance, where the wide but bumpy road ends and the stairway to heaven begins—a stairway I now wish Tessa could walk up herself.

Shading my face with my right hand from the scorching early September sun, I look around scanning for women tourists.

Perhaps someone has a child carrier Tessa could fit in.

To my surprise, a short, plump old lady wearing white sneakers and black widower's attire taps me on the shoulder and says in English, with an exquisite and gentle Greek accent, "You want take child, I take wheelchair. I wait here, yes?" She removes her long, thick, black scarf from around her head and ties it around my neck and shoulder like a handbag. "This will help, *agapi mou*. She can sit, like chair. See?" She pushes her hands into the scarf to open it up.

Stunned at her kindness, all I can immediately manage is an ebullient nod and smile.

"Thank you. Thank you, so much," I say, brainstorming how to demonstrate my appreciation. "Um, wait. One moment."

I dash to the kiosk and I buy the lady a cheese pie and a bottle of water. The lady takes a seat in the wheelchair, and a hearty bite out of her pie, then holds it in the air as if toasting a glass of wine. Nodding and smacking her lips together, she says, "I wait here. You no worry. You *no* worry, *agapi mou*. Go. Go see brilliant structure." A flake of pastry drops off the pie and onto her chin as she takes another bite. A protruding skin-coloured mole secures it in position as she nods again in thanks.

"Thanks so much. We won't be long," I say, nodding and smiling in gratitude as we begin the daunting climb.

"Darling, this is called the Parthenon," I puff, pausing at the grand entrance and shifting Tessa's weight to my opposite side. "It used to be the temple of the Greek goddess, Athena."

"What's a temple, Mummy?"

"This is a temple, Blossom, this big building. It's sort of like the castles you see in your fairy tale books."

"What's a goddess?"

"It's a girl deity, sweetheart."

"What's a deity?"

I laugh, twisting my hair with one hand and shoving it down the back of my T-shirt to stop it blowing in my face before moving on. "A deity is someone who isn't human, and who has special magical qualities. It's also someone that the everyday man worships, just like people worship God, or, you know, the Pope, or Queen of England."

"But if Athena wasn't human, why did she need a temple?"

"Um, *she* didn't use it. The people who lived in the city, here, used it."

"But that doesn't make sense, Mummy."

Almost out of breath, and wondering how I am supposed to explain such a complicated story to a four-year-old, I remove Tessa from the sling and sit her on a stray column block. I bend over forward, stretch and shake my legs and arms to loosen myself up.

"Blossom, because that's what the history books say. Anyway, it doesn't really matter now, does it? Just think— you're standing on something that was built *thoooousands* of years ago." I swing an arm backward, with a heavy, out-of-breath sigh, to signify the amount of time that's passed. "Isn't it amazing up here?"

"Mummy, *you're* standing on it, not me," Tessa says with a giggle.

"Ha! Aren't you clever to make a joke like that?" I put my hands on my hips and take a breath of fuel. "Okay then," I chirp, lifting her off the column block and hovering her above the ground so her feet are touching it, "Now *you* are standing on it." I wobble with her weight and summon one last morsel of strength to lift her up to my waist. "Come on. Let's go sit on that bench over there. I need a rest."

On a wooden park bench in the middle of the Parthenon, while we're sharing a bottle of water, a thin white kitten with one blue eye and one brown, jumps up and sits next to Tessa.

"Oh, Mummy, look," Tessa squeals, bringing her fists to her mouth. "Can I pat her? Please?"

I take a quick look to make sure her eyes aren't weeping. They're not.

"Sure, but we'll have to remember to wash your hands afterward, okay?"

Tessa chuckles and wriggles her fingers in excitement.

"Slowly, Blossom, don't scare the little thing away."

And as she pats the kitten, with her gentle and dainty little fingers ... her right leg swings below the bench.

thirty-three

Six months later:

Serena, still being the most selfless person I know, is now living off the very large and unexpected inheritance from her grandfather (and probably will be able to for the rest of her life) and volunteers full-time for United Nations in Melbourne.

The apartment in Athens is empty. Well, not all the time. Dad says he likes to go there on occasion to get away from whatever it is he wishes to get away from—I don't dare ask what that something is, but at least he sounds well enough. It's ideal for me, too, because at least I know the apartment isn't going to disintegrate, and he can make sure Alex's record collection stays safe.

On my dresser in my bedroom, in Serena's house, sits the black-and-white photograph that Mum gave me the day of the accident. Every night before I sleep, I say a little prayer to it—my own personalized religion—three members and going strong with only one of them actually alive.

The day I gave birth, I got my five minutes. Whether it was real or my imagination, I don't care to know. But there was Alex, standing by his son's crib, kissing life into his tiny little face.

"You came to me. You finally came to me," I whispered, as I sat up in bed, nursing my cesarean stitches.

"Shh." He put his finger to his lips. "Don't say anything. I hear you. Every night, I listen." He stroked my cheek; it tingled as if he was transferring energy into my soul.

"Melody, I'm sorry I hurt you," he said.

Then he faded away.

"Heya, kitten, how's the bub?" Charlie asks, when I answer the phone. It's the first time we've communicated, one-on-one, without Serena acting as my safety blanket.

"He's great, thanks, Charlie. How are you?" I ask, trying to be polite, but I don't want to speak to him. His voice makes me feel sick about accepting the proposal to tour. Realistically, I could have just accepted Alex's help, despite his affair. It was still in the cards for him to get me a gig. Did I say yes to Charlie out of spite? To piss Alex off? What was I running from? My own insecurity?

"Er, ya know, same old same old," Charlie replies, clicking his tongue. "Um, I was just thinkin' … wanna join Serena and me for a beer later this arvo?"

He was "just thinking" my arse. Charlie's been pestering me to come out for a beer for months. Well, not pestering me directly—pestering me through Serena. I suppose I'd better just get it out of the way. I'm tired of finding excuses.

"Um … look … Charlie, I'll come, but I can't stay for long 'cause I'll have the kids with me."

"No probs. The more the merrier. See ya there."

Is there really any need to go for a drink with Charlie?

What are we going to talk about? Babies? How pleased I am that Alex's poo isn't as runny as it was yesterday, or that it looks slightly green and "Do you think I should take him to the doctor?" Should I show him what it looks like in the nappy to get a more educated opinion? This should be interesting …

Afternoons at the local pub are rampant with screaming kids and tipsy parents trying to escape life by living it. There's a sign on the front door that says:

```
Dear Mums and Dads,
Our furniture has been trained to sit
quietly and not run around and jump on
your children, so we would appreciate if
your children would sit quietly and not
run around and jump on our furniture.
Thank you.
```

Serena and I decide to drink chardonnay before Charlie shows up. Tessa silently reads a library book about fairy gestation, sips on a Mars bar milkshake and hums along to background music. Talk about multitasking—I think I may have a genius child on my hands (or is that just me being a proud parent?)

Baby Alex, thank God, is asleep for now in his baby carrier. He reminds me so much of his father I sometimes have to look away when I'm in public in fear of sending myself into a trance.

"Hey, hey, hey!" Charlie sings, as he leaps and bounces into the beer garden, full of cheer.

"It's Saturday," I reply, with sarcastic joy, as he pecks me on the cheek as if it were only yesterday we'd hung out.

"Is it?" Charlie frowns at his watch. "Oh, ha! Right, gotcha," he chuckles pointing a finger at me and wobbling his head in jest. "So! Good to see ya, Melody. Finally. I suppose this is *thee lurvely* Tessa? What's up, chickie-dee?" He bends down and holds his hand out for her to shake.

Tessa, being in the middle of slurping her milkshake, forgets to take the straw out of her mouth before sitting upright, and the opposite end of the straw regurgitates shake into Charlie's hand. Without comprehending what has happened, she lets the straw drop from her mouth and into her lap. She says hi, with timid apprehension, and then puts her hand into Charlie's milk-filled hand to shake. Gives a whole new meaning to *handshake* really.

Charlie, not really giving a shit—exactly the way I remember him—wipes his hand on his jeans. I silently gag as I witness him lick the stickiness from between his fingers—consuming not only smeared milkshake, but the little denim fibers that are stuck to his hand too.

How could I have ever been attracted to this? Ugh!

"And this must be your little stud muffin, huh?"

I nod, keeping my pasted smile in full motion. Serena crosses her legs and leans her head against the red brick wall with a teetering grin.

"Hey, Alex! How's it hangin' little fella?" Charlie tickles Alex on the belly, waking him up. Alex screams, the way babies do only when in public, and heads turn our way.

"Oh shit, matey, I'm sorry," Charlie says, biting his thumbnail like a schoolboy about to be scolded.

"Don't worry about it," I console, lifting Alex from the crib. "It would have happened at some point during the afternoon. You just … you know, sped the process up a little." In my attempt to sound reassuring, I realize I sound bitter and sarcastic. "Um, Charlie, I didn't mean to sound—"

"Nah. Nah. It's cool." He reaches into his back pocket. "I'll be back, just gonna get a Stubby. You ladies right for drinks?"

Serena and I nod in unison. Once he's out of sight, I raise my eyebrows at Serena while trying to nurse Alex back to sleep.

"He's nervous," she says, downing half her chardonnay in one go. "He's not usually so … jittery. It's been a big buildup to you two meeting again, you know. You put it off for so long it's become this big … THING." Serena flicks her eyes into the back of her head and her fingers out like a jazz dancer.

"Yeah, I suppose." I bend over and pretend to vomit.

"Yeah, that was pretty gross, I have to admit." Serena laughs. "Here, give Alex to me. I'll calm him down."

As I hand Alex over, I realize my breast milk has leaked. "Um, maybe I should just feed him. That'll calm him down. I think I need a bit of, um … relief," I say pointing my chin toward the wet patch on my left breast.

Just as I pull my breast out, Charlie returns. He glances at me briefly, but then turns to Serena.

"Hey, Serena," Charlie blushes, folding up the cuff of his right jean leg. "Check out my new boobs— I mean, boots!"

I burst into uncontrollable laughter and in my gusto, squeeze my breast a little too hard and squirt Charlie in the eye. Then Serena bursts into laughter too. Charlie wipes it away with his milkshake hand, which sends me into hysterics, cackling like a hen in heat.

"I bet you don't want to lick *that* off your fingers!" I squeal, struggling to catch my breath.

Charlie looks at his hand, as if a foreign object. Tessa giggles, straw clenched between her teeth. She reaches into Alex's supply bag and pulls him out a baby wipe. I'm so proud. She's known the man for two minutes and is already offering him a helping hand.

"Oh, thanks, chickie-dee!" Charlie exclaims, taking the wipe and bouncing on the spot like a pogo stick.

Tessa pulls the straw out of her mouth and says, "Charlie, my name's not chickie-dee. My name's Tessa."

I'm instantly reminded of the day Charlie and I met at the band competition.

That's my girl … you tell him.

Following in my footsteps? Or just plain cheeky?

thirty-four

I'm sitting in Serena's red-tiled kitchen in my chunky white dressing gown, drinking decaf espresso at her large perfectly-square chocolate brown table. Serena is making me and Tessa French toast and squeezing some fresh orange juice. She serves us our breakfast and then goes to fetch *The Age* from the letter box before joining us at the table. As I reach for the Real Estate section to look for a place to rent, Serena slaps my hand away.

"If you so desperately want to be independent, look for a job, and when you finally have some money, then I'll let you spend it. I'll babysit for free." She winks and sits down opposite me.

"I have the money. I told you. I have the twenty grand Mum gave me."

"No! That's for you to make a record. Your mum wouldn't have wanted you to spend it on anything else." She passes me the business section. I flip to the Classifieds, and right there in front of me, in bold capital letters, is the all-too-familiar UTD Publications logo. *Since when did they have a department in Australia?*

"Serena. Shit!" I thump my finger on the ad and spin the newspaper around.

"Well, that's fate for you. Call 'em up."

"You reckon?"

"Of course. Why not?" With one look at my face, I know she knows what I'm thinking. She shakes her finger at me. "No, no, no, no, Mel. Don't start thinking like that. It's moving *for*ward. It's a new beginning."

"You sure?"

"Of course I'm sure. Call them."

I jump up and approach the collector's spin dial phone in the hall. All it takes is two minutes explaining my history with the company to the receptionist and she puts me through to the Human Resources department.

"They want me to come in for an interview!" I scream down the hall when I hang up.

"Great! When?" Serena yells back, poking her head above the newspaper.

"Now. Shit." I run down the eight-meter long hall and lose a slipper in my haste. "Can you—?"

"Yes." Serena nods, waving her hand for me to go and get ready.

"Alex needs—"

"Yes, I know. Don't worry about it. I got it. Get dressed!"

"—a nappy change!"

"I'll deal with it. Go."

"It's a bit runny, honey." I contort my face, trying to make her laugh.

"I'll. Deal. With. It. Get dressed," she growls wide-eyed.

I'm about to run back down the hall to my bedroom when I'm struck by a daunting thought.

"Um … Serena, *in what*?"

"What do you mean? You're being a drama queen."

"What am I going to wear?" I whisper, as if speaking more quietly might make me seem less insane.

"Oh, right. Come on, Tess. Let's help Mummy choose some clothes."

———

While seated in the waiting room, I check my face for squashed bugs in my compact mirror. Comfortable in a soft jade Indian silk skirt and sleek black body-fitted blouse with a low neckline, I silently congratulate myself for not slipping into my comfort clothes. No more floppy male shirts and black trousers for me.

I can't believe I'm about to have a job interview at UTD. I can't believe I have this second chance. Am I dreaming? Did I imagine the whole newspaper ad and phone conversation with the receptionist, and find my way here while experiencing some kind of alien possession? What if I'm waiting here like an idiot without an appointment?

"Mr Viadro will see you now," the receptionist says, tapping the counter. *Mr Viadro?* I stare at her. Jaw open.

"Um, Ms Hill? I said you can go in now," the receptionist repeats, pointing towards a door with her pen. On the door is a plaque that reads, *Publisher*.

I walk into Mr Viadro's office, hoping it's not him; hoping I can escape the humiliation only I can understand. But no, there, sitting behind a grey stained-glass art-deco desk, with a pale orange backdrop, is button boy.

"I had a feeling it was you, Melody," he says, holding

his hand out to greet me. "When HR told me you were coming in for an interview this morning, I took the liberty to cancel all my appointments and interview you myself."

I try to speak, to thank him, but I stammer something incomprehensible.

"I'm sorry, I've shocked you. Can I get you a cup of tea? Coffee? A glass of water perhaps?"

"Er … water … please … thanks," I stutter. *Either I've completely lost it, or Serena is playing a practical joke on me.*

"Sure, take a seat and I'll tell Helen to fetch you some."

I sit down and Richard pokes his head out of the office door and mutters to the receptionist.

"So, Melody, it's great to see you again." He sits back down behind his desk. "Before you say anything, I'd first like to apologize for having to re-employ your position in London. And I'm terribly sorry for your loss. It can't have been easy and I want you to know if there's anything at all I can do, just let me know."

"Thank you, Richard." I fold my hands in my lap and try to inconspicuously smell the air for remnants of cologne. *If it's Prada, I'm bolting. I can't live every day with that scent rubbing unwanted memories into my face.*

Richard scans the floor for something, gets up, comes around to my side, bends down next to me and picks up a black pen.

"I wondered where that got to," he winks, returning to his seat.

Nope. Nope. Don't recognize the smell at all. Okay. Relax. First sign is peachy.

"Second, I'm not going to interview you because I know very well how qualified you are, and I'd like to offer you a position here at UTD Australia."

"Oh?"

"Yes. Now——" Richard leans back in his seat and scratches under his arm. "It's not the position that has been advertised because I believe you are far too talented to simply be a commissioning editor. In fact, I'm going to offer you a position I have just today, decided we need—a position I have not yet had the opportunity to advertise. Now, I'd just like to make it clear that this is in no way favouritism." Richard pauses, seeming to expect an emotional response. But I keep a straight face, and nod to let him know I'm following.

"I've created this position due to the fact that UTD Publications is in great need of some innovative talent and improvement. Some of the books being made these days are just atrocious and so utterly old-fashioned. Sales are dropping worldwide, and I believe we need someone, like you," he points his pen at me, "for us to bounce back in the market. I'd——"

The receptionist enters with my glass of water.

"Yes, thanks, Helen. Hold all calls until further notice, hmm?" he says, gesturing for her to close the door behind her, again with his pen. *They seem to like pointing pens around here. What, do they double as magic wands?*

"Right. Where was I?"

"Bouncing back in the market?" I prompt, feeling unusually like I belong in here and at a desk like this. This whole corporate concision is tempting. I can smell fresh crisp stationery and paper; hear the photocopier upstairs running on overdrive through the ceiling; women chatting at the coffee station next door in friendly Australian accents. *Perhaps I'll meet someone like Heather. I could probably find myself millions of Heathers here*—in an *English-speaking* country. The thought makes me buzz.

"Yes. Yes! Melody, I'd like to offer you the position of Creative Director. You'd have your very own office, much like this one, on the floor below, and the flexibility to work from home twenty hours a week until your son qualifies for preschool. Now, those are very unusual benefits, Melody, but I like you. I like what you represent and I like what you are capable of. Therefore, I am more than happy to offer you this incentive to join our team. So, what do you say?'

"I—" *want this. I want this* bad.

"Of course, excuse me for pushing you straight into the ballgame, you'll need time to think this over, discuss it with your—"

"No. Er, Richard, your offer sounds wonderful. I …"

I look out the window and see a band lugging their sound equipment into the pub across the road, but without a second thought I draw my attention back to Richard's kind and charming hopeful smile.

"Richard, thank you so much," I say, holding my hand out to shake. "When would you like me to start?"

epilogue

I had Dad bring over a few things from Athens when he visited, after I'd finally saved enough money to buy an inner-city Victorian townhouse big enough to fit it all in.

Tessa is going through some pre-teen blues, and has all of her father's records sprawled across the lounge room floor, feeding her need to wallow in adolescent angst. Little Alex is picking out all the ones with psychedelic-coloured covers, not really knowing what's what.

"How about this one?" he squeals, holding up Jimi Hendrix's *Axis: Bold as Love* album over his head and prancing from foot to foot. "This looks awesome!"

"No, Pinhead! I don't want to listen to that one! That's old people's music. Get it out of my face. Jeez, you don't know *any*thing about music. Why are you pissing me off?" Tessa retorts, getting to her feet to move away.

"Hey!" I call from the kitchen counter, labouring over my first homemade *mousaka*. "Don't speak to your brother like that. Let him have some fun, for crying out loud."

I close my eyes and hear a big grunt and a shove and a thud as I assume she pushes Alex onto the couch and out of her way. I open my eyes, hoping the catastrophe is over and Alex comes running towards me, still holding the Jimi Hendrix album above his head.

"Mum, can we listen to this?" Alex moves his silky black hair out of his face, stares at me with his sparkling blue eyes and displays a ridiculous fake smile, while wobbling his bum side to side like a happy dog.

"Sure, honey, but not just now. We're about to eat dinner."

"Orh!" Alex contorts his face and jumps up and down, making an effort to land as hard as possible on each impact.

"Orh, nothing. Go and tell Tessa to put all the records away 'cause we're going to *eat*, okay?" I remove the *mousaka* from the oven. It smells delish. Baked eggplant, ground lamb, smothered in tomato and *kefalotiri* (a hard Greek cheese), seasoned with onion, garlic, bay leaves, cinnamon, and dry red wine. The aromatic steam fills my nose with pride and makes my mouth water. I did it. Yes!

As Alex is about to tell Tessa what to do, she joins us holding a limited edition single of Joni Mitchell's "*Blue*".

"Mu-*um*," she cajoles, in her typical I-want-something way.

"Ye-*es*," I reply, mimicking her tone.

"Can you teach me how to play this for the end-of-year concert on Grandma's piano?" Dad also got Mum's piano shipped over for me. It's got an entire room of its own, and the walls are decorated with my parents' album covers and band photos.

"Um, you might have to get your piano teacher to help you with that, but I can play the general chords on guitar for you and teach you how to sing it properly. Does that sound okay?"

"Cool." Tessa does a little dance on the spot and gives me a peck on the cheek.

"What was that for?" I ask. "An hour ago you said you hated me."

"Well, I love you now," she replies with a wonky grin.

"Okay, then, if you love me now, do you think you could set the table?"

She nods, screwing her face up to the side, grabs plates out of the cupboard and the cutlery out of the drawer. When she's finished, I bring the *mousaka* and a jug of water to the table. I pour myself a glass of wine. But Alex has disappeared with the Jimi Hendrix record.

"Alex, Dinner!"

He comes running down the corridor and sits at the table and hangs his head in his hands.

"What's the matter?"

"I want to listen to that record," he whines.

"You will, when we finish dinner. Now eat. … Um, Tessa?"

"What?" she snaps, exposing a full mouth of mushy *mousaka*.

"Why have you set the table for four?"

"Oh. Whoops! I forgot Grandpa left this morning … um, Mu-um?"

"Hmm?" I hum, trying not to sound annoyed that I haven't yet had the chance to taste my very first traditional Greek meal.

"When can I come and see you play at the pub?"

"I told you, when you're eighteen and old enough to get

in the pub at night," I reply monotonously, due to repeating it for the millionth time.

"But you used to take me there when I was a kid."

"That was different." *Can't I buy any more time?* "That was during the day. And there are different laws for after dark."

"But you said that Grandma used to take you to her gigs when you were a kid."

"I know, but she wasn't supposed to."

"Why not?"

"Because."

"Because why?"

"Tessa. I said no. Full stop." I sigh, dreading the feeling this might actually be the night I give in.

"Please." She drops her knife and fork, folds her hands under her chin, and bats her eyelids.

"Okay, how about I make you a deal?" *I hope I don't regret this.*

"What kind of deal?" Tessa wriggles in her seat, a habit she hasn't yet grown out of.

"When you turn thirteen, you can come along with Serena." *That's it. There's no going back now.*

"But that's a whole month away," she squeals, almost deafening me.

"A month will fly by, hon." I keep my cool.

"Why don't you ever become famous, Mum?" she asks in a breezy, relaxed tone as if her previous outburst hadn't even occurred.

"I can't just snap my fingers and become famous, Tessa."

"But Serena said you got offered a contract and you turned it down."

What? How could she? She knows how impressionable Tessa is. Christ.

"Tessa, I don't need to be famous. I have you and Alex and enough stuff to do at work. I don't have the time."

"But you wouldn't have to work if you were famous."

"Of course I would. I'd have to work harder, and I'd have to be away from you guys all the time. I don't want that. I'm not interested."

"Orh ... well, I thought it would be cool to have a famous Mum." Tessa bats her eyelids. Again. *Who taught her that?* "Anyway, nice *mousaka*."

"Really? Thanks."

"That's cool. I didn't know you could cook stuff like this. You should do it more often."

"Yeah, I know. It did turn out pretty cool, didn't it?"

"Orh, Mum, stop trying to sound ... *young*," Tessa groans, flinging her head backward.

"What do you mean?"

"You keep saying cool."

"That's 'cause it is cool."

Tessa rolls her eyes and shoves her mouth with too much food. Unable to chew it properly, she spits some out onto her plate.

"That's disgusting!" Alex cries.

"Yes, it is," I say. "Can you watch your manners, please?"

Tessa rolls her eyes again, picks up a small amount of food on her fork, makes a huge display of how much is on her fork, by presenting it to us like jewellery on a TV Shopping channel, delicately places it in her mouth and chews in slow motion with her eyes closed.

"Mu-um?"

"What, Alex?" I huff, dropping my cutlery in my plate.

"Was Jimi Hendrix Dad's favourite musician?"

"No, Pinhead!" Tessa barks. "You asked me that before and I said no!"

"Tessa, calm down." I take a sip of wine. "Alex, Jimi Hendrix is Grandpa's favourite musician. Dad's favourite was Elvis Costello."

"Orh. Well, can we listen to Elvis Costello then?"

"Honey, please, can you wait till *after* we've had dinner? Dinnertime is conversation time. You know that." I touch Alex's hand.

But he doesn't give up. Alex gets out of his seat, runs down the corridor towards the music room.

"Where you going? What about dinner?"

I look at Tessa for answers. She shrugs.

"Why is he in such a mood?" I ask.

Tessa shrugs again.

Alex returns holding my guitar. He sits on the couch, with it on his knees, and slowly plucks the bottom string with his tongue sticking out of his mouth.

"Alex, what are you doing?" I smile. In shock, in awe, in admiration.

"Well," Alex replies, "If you're not gonna to let me *listen* to Dad's music, I'm gonna have to make it myself, aren't I?"

During sound check I only have to tune my guitar once now that it's accustomed to my regular bashing. The sound engineer wishes me luck with her reassuring wink from behind the mixing desk. Sensitive about my lighting needs, she reminds the lighting guy not to use red. He nods, laughs and gives a thumbs up.

When the venue is full, I step back onto the stage, breathing freely; knowing that my engineer is going to make me sound like an angel despite still being a bit croaky from the flu. My footsteps vibrate through my body, as laughter turns to talking, talking turns to mumbling and mumbling turns to absolute silence.

I look down at my bare feet, making sure they're inside the lucky circle I stuck to the stage with gaffer tape for security. I convinced myself that as long as I stand inside it, everything will work out the way it's supposed to. I look up and out into the small crowd of about two hundred. I spot Serena, Tessa, and Alex drinking lemon squash at a table closest to the stage. I wink at them before letting out a hot steady note that thrusts the crowd into whistles and applause. Each hair on my bare arms rises, one by one, as each succeeding note escapes me like a precious secret wrapped in their individual unique gift boxes.

I continue my all-original set, and each song receives a bigger applause than the last. Relief flushes through me like divine déjà vu, immersing me in a warm bath of velvety freedom. *I did it. I did it again and I'm alive.*

"Thank you!" I say as I put my guitar down. "I'd just like to let you all know I've finally released that album I've been going on about for the last six months. It'll be in stores next week and it's called *On the Other Side*. Keep an eye out for it. Have a great evening everyone, and thanks again for coming."

Amidst uniting applause and cheering and whistling and static amplifier fuzz, the background music begins to play. Serena gestures with her own unique sign language that she's going to take the kids to the burger joint over the road. I nod and sign back that'll I'll be right behind them. But just as I'm stepping off the stage, guitar in hand and leads hanging around my neck, I spot Richard entering the pub. He waves and puts his hands in his pockets.

"What are you doing here?" I ask, resting my gear on the ground. "I'm just about to leave, Serena's got the kids and they're—"

He puts his fingers to my lips. "I just came here to tell you something," he says with a cheeky grin on his face. "After having a very serious discussion with my daughter, and discovering that she would like it just as much as I, having grown to love Tessa and Alex like brother and sister, I have come to let you know that we would very much like to accept your offer."

"Really?" I ask trying to compose the potent thrill buzzing through my limbs. "You've finally decided to move in with us?"

"Yes," he says, pulling me in for a warm hug. "Let's cross that bridge, shall we?"

acknowledgements

First I'd like to thank my parents, Erika Bach and Demetri Vlass for being the most supporting and loving parents I could ever ask for. You have always been there for me through every choice I've made, and encouraged me to reach for my dreams no matter how unrealistic they seemed. And again, to my mother, for relinquishing one of her cherished songs, "Famous", for me to rerecord and make my own for the book trailer. The song also helped me mould Melody into the character I had long been striving to create through numerous drafts of this book.

I'd also like to thank my partner, Spilios Tzemos, for supporting me through every single joyful and agonizing moment I went through to get this book published.

To my sister, Allison Bell, who read through, with speedy critical eyes, every single imperfect draft (and there were a lot!). This book would not be what it is today without you, Allison.

And to Dawn Ius, for being one of the most thoughtful, insightful and encouraging writing partners I could ask for. She kept my chin up during the rewriting of the very last draft and did wonders for boosting my self-esteem.

Of course, I can't forget to thank George Priniotakis and

Alex Bolpasis from Artracks Studios for their expertise and creativity in giving the novel's soundtrack life.

I'd also like to thank this long list of people for their continuous support, encouragement and/or feedback on my very early drafts when I had no idea what I was doing: Angela Bandis, Angelique Geitenbeek, Anthony Bell, Caitlin Griffith, Danielle Whitman, Dione Davids, Eleni Yiannoulidou, Erika Stiles, Fleur Waters, Henri Richardson, Ivana Kohut, Jenny Heath, Karen Fisher, Katrina Cayzer, Leigh T. Moore, Margaret Bell, Matthew McNish, Nicole Ducleroir, Paula Berinstein, Rachel Finnie, Rachelle Koeppler, Sally Reiffel, Shannon McMahon, Susanne Lakin, Talli Roland and Vivian Clark.

To receive the all-original soundtrack, *Melody Hill: On the Other Side*, go to *jessicabellauthor.com/contact* and send Jessica your book purchase receipt.

The soundtrack is also available to purchase at iTunes and other online music retailers.

Enjoyed this book?
Go to *vineleavespress.com/books* to find
more from *The Bell Collection*.

To sign up to Jessica's newsletter
and/or connect with her on social media
go to *jessicabellauthor.com/contact*.

Are you a writer?
You might be interested in Jessica's
Writing in a Nutshell series.